Tyrant

Book 3

Voyage to Oblivion

Published in Great Britain by Open Circle Publishing in 2022

ISBN 978-1-909607-24-8

Open Circle Publishing
49-51 St Thomas's Road
Chorley
Lancashire
PR7 1JE

For Henrik, Maggie, Ida, and Alfred

1

Ant watched the thin tendrils of light as they intertwined and poured upwards towards the heavens. The pattern he'd made had adopted a life of its own and had ceased to be earthbound. The wind that blew cold and harsh across the hillside was having no effect on the delicate wisps of energy as they poured out of the ground.

He sat for a very long time, joining in the gentle flow with his mind, allowing himself to be swept skywards through the mists to bask in a warm cloudless place before being drawn even higher towards the cold blackness that was the infinite void. A cacophony of voices began to assail his ears, telling him things he had no wish to hear. Withdrawing his attention, he retreated gently until he was back sitting cross-legged in the forest, feeling the wind in his hair.

Reaching down, he took a double handful of soft earth and held it up to his face. The energy patterns flickered and changed. Tiny vortices began to form as the upward flow became less coherent and more hesitant. Questing strands of light played around the handful of soil, and Ant felt the beginnings of change.

In response to the light from the vedhana, the earth in his hands took on a new lightness, as if it was able to contribute to its own support. The pile increased in size even as it became lighter. There was a faint popping sensation as little eruptions appeared on the surface of the soil. Slowly and very carefully, he released the earth into the centre of the vedhana, then drew a small knife from his belt.

Ant took a deep breath, then pricked the second finger of his left hand with the point of the knife. He encouraged the blood flow by squeezing until he'd deposited six full drops onto the pile of dirt. The blood sat on top of the soil as a single globule for a few seconds before it was absorbed into the brown mass.

He sat perfectly still, closed his eyes, and kept his attention on the pile. The cool energy began to concentrate around the mound of soil. A mixture of excitement and dread coursed through his body as the inanimate muck woke up and became aware of his attention.

He breathed and counted. One in, one out. Gentle and full. Body relaxed. Mind anchored in the present despite the clamours of the past and future. When he reached one thousand, he opened his eyes. The sun was suspended barely higher than the surrounding hills and the wind had a harsher feel to it as twilight approached. In the fading light, Ant watched the pile of dirt take on form. First, a rough ovoid sitting on a bigger one. Then thinner protuberances formed makeshift arms and legs. It became a human figure seemingly fashioned from misshapen potatoes. When it stood up, Ant might have thought it comical if it hadn't been for the dire memories that the apparition evoked.

He held out his arms towards it, his heart beating nervously hard. It staggered towards him and put its sausage-shaped appendages into his hands as a child might seek support from a parent. Ant felt a shudder as they touched, but it lasted only for an instant, to be replaced by a calmer feeling of connection. A flow of energy passed between them, accompanied by a surprising sensation of joy. The tiny figure that stood barely ankle high to Ant let out a squeak from the hole it had made in itself to serve as a mouth.

Almost imperceptibly, the rough-hewn figure began to transform into recognisable human form. As he held them, Ant felt the blunt ends of its arms become minute fingers. Its tiny face gazed up at Ant and he stared back into small reflections of his own eyes. 'Hello and welcome,' Ant said.

The small man began to laugh. 'Is that all you can say after the miracle you've just witnessed?' Its voice was high-pitched, but clear and confident.

Ant laughed. Whether it was in triumph or in joy, he couldn't decide. Nor did he care. It still felt glorious either way. This marvellous creation was the culmination of years of work and practise and its appearance had exceeded his wildest expectations.

'Now what?' Ant asked.

'That's an interesting thing to ask me. I thought you would know that. You must have a purpose for me or you wouldn't have gone to all this trouble. Or am I some plaything that you've made for your own entertainment? Perhaps you want to take to the road, displaying me in every town and village? I'm sure that there's a good living to be made from a fairground doll like me.'

'I made you because I need a companion,' Ant said. 'Someone I can trust.'

'Wouldn't it have been much easier to find a human to carry out that role?'

'I don't want to put my friends at risk. Although they would readily volunteer themselves, they have their own path to follow. Mine is a dangerous one, as experience has shown. Anyone around me is placed in peril.'

'Then you've not been having very good experiences, have you?'

'I suppose not. But that's the nature of this world, isn't it? We're here to be tested and sometimes it can be more than we can bear,' Ant said.

'Then a spirit guide might be a better option. Something a little more ephemeral, but just as helpful.'

'Hah!' Ant let out a sharp breath. 'I once had a spirit guide who I trusted with my innermost thoughts and desires. He let me down terribly just when I needed him most. I'll never forget that betrayal, though I do blame myself for being so naïve.'

'Maybe I'm the worst option of the lot. Have you thought about that? How can you be so sure that I'm any more reliable than your own wayward spirit?'

'Because you're of my making. You owe your very existence to me. That should count for something, shouldn't it?'

The tiny figure gave a laugh, like the tinkle of coins falling into a metal beaker. 'You have no idea what you've done, have you?'

'I've made a golem,' Ant said. 'I've animated the earth using the power of the vedhana. That's what you are, or do you think differently?'

'You and I can't think differently because we're the same being. I'm you, you're me. We're made from the same stuff and imbued with the same spirit. My soul is your soul. We share everything. I'm not what you call a golem. That would make me a crude lump of muck staggering around without sense or purpose. What I am is an avatar. A representation of you in an alternate form.'

Ant sank back onto his haunches, feeling very weary. An ankle-high version of himself that his life depended on keeping unharmed wasn't what he'd intended, not by a long chalk. He took a leather pouch from his pocket and held it out. 'Can you climb in here or will it be too uncomfortable?'

'I can do anything you want me to. Watch.' The avatar dissolved into black earth that spiralled upwards to form a dark cloud level with Ant's head. Then it grew wings and transformed into a beautiful bird with iridescent plumage. The bird alighted gently onto the lip of the pouch, turned back to soil, then poured itself into the bag. Ant tied the pouch to his belt.

When he tried to stand, Ant found his legs too weak to support him. He rested for several minutes before trying again, with the same result. The wind blasting the hillside had become colder as the sun was setting. If he was trapped here for the night, he'd probably freeze to death before morning.

Using what little remained of his strength, Ant rolled himself into the centre of the vedhana, the fiery wisps of the energy field coiling around his stricken body. He felt a tight constriction in his chest, then a sudden jolt as he was transported off the hillside and into the warmth of his father's house.

Ambrose helped him from the vedhana and onto the couch in front of the fire. 'What on earth have you been up to, son?'

'In the hills,' Ant replied. 'I got tired and cold, that's all.'

'You look terrible, as if you've not eaten for a month. How can being in the hills exact such a toll on your health in only one day?'

Ant sighed. His father had once created a huge golem that almost killed them all and he'd warned Ant of dire consequences if he ever attempted to do the same. 'Maybe I'm sickening for something,' Ant said.

'Well, you'd better get better very quickly because the King has sent word that you're to go to the palace tomorrow.'

'I don't think I'll be doing that,' Ant said. 'Even though Cuthbert is the new King, I get the feeling that he's becoming more like the old King every day. Whatever he wants, he can get it from someone else. I'm staying here.'

Ambrose threw a large log onto the fire and Ant watched as the flames began to splash and flicker around it. 'The summons was very clear,' he said. 'It's a matter of grave urgency involving Queen Cassie and her sister. If you won't go for Cuthbert's sake, it seems he's counting on you being more than willing to help the girls.'

2

Tyrant felt irritated and alarmed, despite the warmth of the sun on his outside and the glow of the licker inside. 'I'm not going, and there's an end to the matter,' he said.

Petra stood in the middle of the tater patch and wiped her face on her sleeve. 'Of course you are.' She shook her head as if she'd been confronted by a recalcitrant child who was refusing to eat his gruel. 'The King has summoned you. There's no choice in the matter.'

'Everyone knows I don't do summonses, especially Cuthbert. If the lad wants to talk to me, he knows where he can find me.'

'Obviously,' Petra said with a laugh. 'His messengers had no trouble in finding us. So much for your idea that we were living somewhere so remote and so completely hidden that nobody would ever bother us.'

'They never have,' Tyrant said.

'Oh, really? What about the men who came here and buried me in a hole? Cassie and Bee didn't feel very safe or hidden, did they? All sorts of horrible things could have happened to them. Nowhere is safe or hidden these days.'

'But I came along in the nick of time and saved you all, didn't I?' Tyrant said.

'More by luck than judgement if you ask me. And don't remind me who it was that gave them the map of how to get here.'

'I didn't give it to them; they stole it.'

'They took it while you were drunk.'

'Asleep. You can't expect me to stay awake every minute of every day.'

'Where were you sleeping?'

'It was the only building there with a roof of sorts. I thought it looked like rain.'

'It was the tavern, wasn't it?'

'I suppose so.'

'And you'd been drinking, hadn't you?'

'It would have been rude not to. You can't occupy a seat in a tavern without at least sampling their ale. Anyway, I don't see what this has to do with the King's summons. We're far too busy to go in any case. There's licker to brew, taters to grow, not to mention the chickens and the vegetables. What are we having for lunch, by the way? I'm getting a bit hungry.'

Tyrant watched Petra's face contort into an expression he knew from experience was nothing to do with deciding what to serve him for lunch. For some unknown reason, he was in trouble again. Perhaps it was something he'd said? He considered this thought carefully and analysed the conversation for instances where she might have taken umbrage, but without success.

'Get off your fat arse if you want something to eat. And put down that licker jar; you've had too much of it already. How many times do I have to tell you that it's dangerous to drink so much of it? It's an addiction, and it's going to kill you if you keep on as you are.'

That old chestnut again, thought Tyrant. A man was entitled to taste a drop or two of his own licker from time to time. Call it quality control if you like. Anyway, it relaxed him. He'd had a hard life and was surely entitled to a bit of relaxation after all he'd been through.

'You're right about one thing,' Petra said. 'I'm far too busy to go with you to Gort. You will have to go on your own, but I'll expect you straight back here as soon as you've seen the King. No loitering about in taverns, understand?'

'If I did make the trip, I'd be wise to check in with a few of our customers, wouldn't I?' Tyrant was beginning to warm to the prospect of a few days away from Petra.

Her response to his question was a severe shake of her head. 'You can go straight to the palace through the vedhana in the tower. That way, you won't be tempted. Then back here the same way. You'll be gone less than a day. I reckon I'll manage that long without your assistance.'

'The King has banned the use of the devices. I thought you knew that. It seems he considers them to be unnatural and dangerous. The vedhana in the tower may not be there much longer if he ever finds stonemasons brave enough to erase it.'

'Then you'll have to go to Malachi's house. I can't see that old wizard abandoning his means of flitting around the place, whatever the King might feel about it.'

Tyrant felt uneasy at the prospect of becoming reacquainted with Malachi and his insidious wife. 'I'd rather walk,' he said. 'The exercise will do me good.'

'If it's exercise you're in need of, you can get to work digging these taters in. You can't make licker from green taters and that's what we'll have if they're left as they are. Now, get off to the palace, see what the King wants, then get back here.'

'I don't care what he wants,' Tyrant said. 'I've done enough for that lad already. Anyway, he's changed now that he's been made King. If you ask me, he's more like the old King than the Cuthbert I knew.'

'Being King changes people,' Petra said. 'It's the responsibility. Now, be off with you right now and take your sword.'

'Why would I do that?' Tyrant asked. 'I don't need a sword. I've got my reputation, haven't I?'

'You should be more grateful that Ant took it away from Gilgamesh before he buried him with the golem. Anyway, it's a mark of respect to your King. You have to go as if you're ready to defend him if required. It's what he'd expect.'

'Then he'd be expecting too much. My days of fighting on anyone's behalf are long gone.' Tyrant weighed up Petra's changed expression and came to the conclusion that he'd better qualify his latest remark. 'Obviously, I'd fight for you, my love. That goes without saying.'

Petra stooped and picked up her shovel. 'You'd be fat use to anyone even if you did have a mind for it. Now be off with you and make sure you're back before sundown or it'll be the end of the easy life for you.'

3

Lone watched as Cat prowled amongst the vines, causing the grape pickers to freeze in alarm. The morning sun was steaming the dew from the vegetation and the temperature was set to rise to unbearable levels before much longer.

'Get on with it,' she shouted. 'The cat won't harm you if you work hard. I can't promise anything if you stop, though.'

From the slopes of the grassy hill created by earthy remains of the Golem that had buried the palace, Lone had a view of the whole city, the river, and much of the surrounding desert. In the distance, she could see the green smear of the dense jungle that was populated by her beloved chickens and the dark roofs of her winery. A large sailing ship, an unusual sight, was moored close to the bridge, and she resolved to investigate its origins as soon as she'd finished supervising the morning's harvest.

She felt a sudden disturbance at the extremity of the vineyard. At that distance, and with her line of sight interrupted by the rows of vines, Lone couldn't clearly make out what was going on and had to rely more on her emotional reaction than her other senses. She took a long breath and felt into the earth beneath her bare feet, connecting with the mass of roots in the sandy soil. Her questing energy surged through the ground and encountered the source of the distress.

A young woman had been pinned to the ground by a much older man. One arm was across her throat, preventing her from crying out, while the other was savagely spreading her legs. Lone's anger burst out of the ground and into the body of the huge male. She breathed out slowly and squeezed, her fists clenched and her muscles taught. The man rolled off the girl and clutched at his own throat.

Lone felt the girl slide away to safety, knew that the man was incapable of any further molestation, yet continued to squeeze hard. Her mind kept telling her that she could let go now, that there was no more danger, that the man could be punished in a more appropriate manner, that he might be persuaded to see the error of his ways. Despite this, she continued to increase the pressure until, quite suddenly, she could feel no further resistance. Then, she withdrew, pulled her awareness back into her own body and acknowledged her weariness by sitting down.

After a few minutes, Lone felt well enough to walk down the rows of vines to where the man lay. His face was purple and contorted, blood trickled from his nose and ears. The object of his attack, a teenager called Ayesha, stood a few strides away, her face awash with tears. 'He was my uncle,' she sobbed.

'Then all the more reason for him to show some respect,' Lone said.

'My father told me he meant no harm.'

'Your father should have protected you from men like him. Perhaps he needs to be reminded of his duty towards you?'

Ayesha's eyes widened. 'Is he dead?'

'Looks that way from here, but I'm not a doctor,' Lone said.

'I'll be blamed for it,' she said.

'I don't see how. The man dropped dead of his own accord. It must have been his time. We all have our time for dying; there can be no suggestion that you were in any way responsible for this. Now leave him, take your basket and his to the cart, then go home. Hurry, I don't want that fruit drying out in the sun. I can't make wine with raisins.'

'Your handiwork, I presume?' A familiar voice spoke from behind her.

'What makes you think that?' Lone laughed. 'I can't be held responsible for some fat old man being overcome by lust and giving himself a heart attack. Anyway, I'm more concerned with what my husband is doing so far away from Gort. Aren't you scared that events might occur without you having a chance to influence them? Can the King really be trusted to rule without your assistance for a whole day?'

'You overestimate my involvement, dear. These days, I'm rarely at the court or go there uninvited. It seems that the young King has a very low opinion of my counsel.'

'And why do you think that is?' Lone smiled.

'I really can't think of a valid reason. I've always served the monarchy faithfully and well.'

'Don't make me laugh,' Lone said.

'It's true that the new King hasn't had much use for me, but the old King held me in very high regard.'

'The old King that you tempted down here into the desert so that he could get himself killed? You call that good advice?'

'It was his choice entirely.'

'I very much doubt that.' Lone laughed once again. 'But tell me your purpose in honouring me with your presence. Have you run short of wine, perhaps?'

'I have to admit that the quality of your produce is nothing short of miraculous, and I'm always happy to return with a few extra cases for my cellar. However, I'm here to deliver a message. It's actually from the King himself. You are summoned to Gort. Immediately.'

'Then you can tell your King that I'll think about it. Oh, wait a minute, I just thought about it and the answer is no. If he wants to talk to me, he can come here to do it. Not that I'm expecting that he will, not after the fate his predecessor met. I'm much too busy to be bothered with the northern King.'

'He's not just King of the North, may I remind you. His domain stretches down here and beyond. Or do you openly dispute that? Have you declared yourself Queen of the South at long last?'

'If that's the kind of nonsense you've been feeding Cuthbert, it's no wonder he wants to talk to me. Go back and tell him that his loyal and faithful servant Lone sends her greetings and a few cases of wine as a tribute to his glorious majesty. Now, piss off. I've got grapes to carry back to my winery. If you like, I can get Cat to escort you back to the vedhana.'

4

'Your majesty.' Malachi bowed deeply at the reclining King who was stuffing his face with pastries he had an obvious pressing need to avoid. The once youthful figure had been transformed into what looked more like a fat old man with jowls of flesh hanging from his throat and a paunch that threatened the integrity of his ample trousers. 'May I present your champion, Tyrant, and my previous apprentice and your very good friend, Ant.'

'Where's that wayward wife of yours? Didn't I make it clear that she was to be here?'

'Alas, your majesty, she has been unavoidably delayed. It's a very long way from the City on the River. She begs your pardon and requests that I serve as her representative at this gathering. I will speak on her behalf as well as my own.'

The King shifted slightly and his belly wobbled. 'It's completely unacceptable. I make a simple request and this is what I'm faced with. That woman will rue the day she ignored my summons. I'll not have that kind of insubordinate behaviour. My authority is being directly challenged and I'll not permit that to happen. Do I make myself clear?'

'Perfectly,' Malachi said.

'Come on, Cuthbert. Stop stuffing your face and tell us what we're here for,' Tyrant said.

'You need to show more respect for your King,' Cuthbert said.

'You'll get all the respect you deserve from me; you don't need to worry about that,' Tyrant said. 'I would also remind you that we're the ones that saved your hide on more than one occasion and you wouldn't be lounging around eating pies if it weren't for us.'

Malachi winced as he anticipated the King's response. He waited for the angry outburst, but none came. Either the King hadn't heard Tyrant's impertinent rejoinder or he was choosing to ignore it. 'We're all at your service, sire. As always,' Malachi said.

'Even your wife?' The King was wrinkling his nose as if he'd detected a bad smell. If he had, there was every chance it had been emitted from his own person.

'Especially my wife,' Malachi said.

'This is no trivial matter,' the King said. 'The whole kingdom is at risk. My beloved Queen and her sister have been taken. Kidnapped. Held to ransom. They are demanding that I cede to them the southern half of my domain. The City on the River and all the lands that surround it. If I don't comply, it is promised that the Queen and the Princess will suffer terribly before they are killed.'

Malachi held his breath. Why had he not had wind of these momentous events? Surely the King would have confided in him as soon as the discovery had been made? 'When did this happen?' he asked.

'They've been gone nearly a week,' the King answered.

'Then why leave it until now to do something about it?' Tyrant said.

'Delicate negotiations have been taking place in secret. Any word of them would have jeopardised the Queen's safety. I had hoped to bring the matter to a swift and satisfactory conclusion, but that hasn't been possible. That's why I need you.'

'Where are the girls now?' Ant asked.

'I believe that they are on a ship that is taking them to an island in the southern sea. I need you to find them and bring them back.'

'The southern sea is uncharted,' Tyrant said. 'Even I know that. We'd have no idea where we were going even if we did have a ship to follow in, which we don't.'

'That's where Malachi can help. You have charts, don't you?'

Malachi felt the glare of attention switch to him. He didn't like the idea that his secret charts might become common knowledge. The power in them resided in keeping them hidden and only using them for his own purposes. 'I have compiled a little information about the area surrounding your majesty's domain,' he said.

'You have comprehensive maps of the whole region, including the southern sea, do you not?' the King said.

Malachi squirmed, felt heat rising in his chest, then answered by merely nodding his head.

'So Malachi can plot a course to intercept them. You, Ant, can make one of those infernal devices to bring them swiftly back here as soon as you find them. Tyrant will, with the help of Malachi's powerful wife, provide all the protection you will need without involving the mobilisation of an army. There's a ship in the City by the River waiting for you. I suggest that you make haste down there and get on with the mission. Any questions?'

The King slumped back into his couch as if he considered that his work was done.

'Who has committed this foul act?' Ant said.

The King stared blankly at him. 'I don't know. Some over-ambitious lot from over the sea, I suppose. Whoever they are, they will get their comeuppance in good time. Once I get my Queen and her sister back, I'll show them what happens to anyone who tries it on with me. Until then, though, I have to act cautiously, which is why I can't despatch a fleet of warships and a vast army.'

'Do we have a fleet of warships?' Tyrant asked. 'Or even one warship?'

'We can build them. Until then, you will have to manage with the merchant ship I've hired for you,' the King said. 'As it's a national emergency, I'm granting you a special dispensation to use vedhanas. Now be on your way.'

5

Lone strode across the springy gangplank and onto the deck of the ship. A bearded man put down the rope he had been busy coiling and picked up a short, curved sword. 'Take it easy,' Lone said, more to Cat than the sailor. Neither seemed to take any notice. 'I've not seen a vessel as large as this on the river before,' she said. 'Where are you from?'

The sailor kept his eyes on Cat as he answered. 'Kish.'

'Never heard of the place.' Lone watched Cat grow tired of menacing the man and curl up on the deck in a pool of sunlight. The scimitar lowered in response and the sailor stood more upright.

'Then you're an ignorant savage like the rest of them.'

Lone laughed. 'Then enlighten me, I pray. Tell me about Kish. Where is it? How long is the journey? How many people live there? Do they value good wine?'

'Wine?'

'Yes, wine. I'm a winemaker and I'm always happy to discover new customers that appreciate a superior product.'

'We have our own wine in Kish. We have everything else, too. We live well, in a green and productive land. Not a scorching dry desert like this infernal place.'

'Then what are you doing here if you don't wish to trade?' Lone looked up at the great mast from which huge triangular sails hung slackly in the still desert air.

'That's our business and not yours.' He flashed a broken landscape of yellow and black teeth at her.

'I think you'll find that it is,' Malachi's voice boomed from behind her. Cat didn't even open a single eye to mark his approach, and Lone felt a twinge of disappointment that her husband could surprise her so easily. The intensity of the feeling doubled when she realised that he must be here for a purpose and that would inevitably involve her.

She turned to face him and saw the bloated figure of Tyrant swaying unsteadily as he tried to negotiate the gangplank. He looked as happy to see her as she felt to see him. There were still major scores to be settled between them despite a fleeting moment of enforced cooperation that had culminated in Cat dragging the big idiot from beneath a collapsing palace. Had she been given the choice, she'd have been happy to see him crushed to death and buried beneath the rubble, but she was duty bound to protect him because of her agreement with Patch. Ant, Malachi's cunning and resourceful assistant, was bringing up the rear. He looked to have aged much more than he should have in the couple of years since he'd tackled the golem.

'Good to see you've come to your senses, my dear,' Malachi said.

'That's not an assumption you should make without better information,' she replied. 'What are these two doing following you around? Haven't they got better things to do?'

'We are all here on an errand of mercy. The King himself has requested our help, and that includes you. It's a request that cannot be ignored.'

'Maybe not by you fools,' Lone said, 'but I can manage that simple task quite easily. The King has no hold over me. I don't like him and certainly don't need him to tell me what to do. Here in my city, I decide what goes on and how things are done. If he wants to take his chances and come down here to discuss it with me, I'm afraid he'll get the same welcome as his predecessor did. He might even suffer a similar fate.'

'So you say,' Malachi said as the other two men stood on the relatively stable sanctuary of the deck gratefully. 'However, there are changes afoot that even you cannot withstand. Forces from the south are poised to take your city and destroy everything you've built. Your vines and your chickens will be things of the past.'

'Let them try,' Lone said, but her heart felt sadness even at the imagined loss. She'd fought hard for a way of life that brought her comfort and satisfaction. She'd fight again to protect it, of course she would, but peace was such a fragile feeling that it could be shattered irrevocably by exactly the actions she would take to preserve it. She sighed deeply, expelling the foul air of hopelessness and greedily trying to inhale fresh hope.

'We are going to prevent matters getting out of hand, but we need you to help us,' Malachi said. 'Remember that a pinch of prevention is worth a whole cartful of cure.'

'Save your platitudes for the weak and impressionable,' she said. 'Tell me honestly, if you're capable of such a thing, what you're really up to.'

Tyrant stepped forward. 'The bastards have taken Cassie and Bee. They'll kill them if we don't stop them. You have to help us to save them.'

'I'm sorry to disappoint you, Tyrant, but I'm still the same woman that you abandoned in the desert. What makes you think I would give a single grape for your little girlfriends?' Lone's stomach gave a tiny heave as she recalled the price she'd had to pay for her release from being marooned. 'Or any of you, for that matter. I'll take my chances here. I don't believe a word of what you're telling me in any case. The city will defend itself against any hostile force, have no fear about that. The river god will protect us.'

'The river god will always do what's best for the river,' Malachi said. 'That's not necessarily what you might imagine or wish for. All this uncertainty and conflict can be averted by one simple act. All we have to do is to bring the Queen and her sister safely back to our King. Then you can go back to your chickens in the knowledge that you have the goodwill of your monarch. If you really value your way of life, you'll be well advised to invest a little of your time in recovering the ones that the King holds most dear from the hands of desperate savages. If we fail because you've rejected his heartfelt plea for help, there's going to be no end to his animosity. Your position here will be under far more threat than a bunch of marauding savages could ever pose.'

Lone felt the sense in what Malachi was telling her but also understood the danger of heeding his words. He was a master of manipulation, an architect of plausible half-truths, a weaver of delicate tendrils of possibility on which he dangled your heart's desires. 'How long will we have to extend this fool's errand in order to satisfy the King?'

'A few days, ten at the most,' Malachi said. 'That's a small investment for such a great return. This ship will take us to the mouth of the river where we will intercept the vessel coming from the north, which is carrying the ladies. Because we were able to travel here instantly by means of the vedhana, our journey is much shorter than theirs and we should arrive well before our quarry.'

'The King doesn't need any of us to do that,' Lone said. 'He could just send a few soldiers instead, if what you say is true.'

'It's a little more involved than that, my dear. I alone have the charts and the expertise to plot our position, a skill that will be essential if we are to wait at the mouth of the correct river. There are many branches and tributaries that form the river mouth; we have to identify the one that carries the ship from the north,' Malachi said.

'Then he could send you and a few soldiers,' Lone said.

'Tyrant is more than a match for a hundred soldiers, as you well know. As for Ant, he will create a portal for our swift return. There's a great deal of good sense behind the King's plan.'

Lone looked at Tyrant's portly figure and doubted he'd be a match for even a single swordsman of reasonable ability. He'd put on a lot of weight since she'd last seen him, and looked like a man who would fall over exhausted after even the slightest exertion. He was still puffing after the short walk onto the ship. 'Then you don't need me,' she said. 'You seem to have everything covered between the three of you.'

'I think you know why we need you, my dear. When it comes down to it, there's nobody that can protect those ladies like you can. Tyrant may be able to fight, but we will be relying on you to keep us safe in the melee of battle. The King has made it very clear that he considers your involvement to be crucial.'

Lone had that familiar hollow feeling that arose when Malachi's words became compelling. She couldn't bring herself to resist, despite her misgivings born from years of his lies and trickery. A few days, two weeks at the most, were scant reason to offend the King. Whatever she might think of him, he was certainly capable of making her life extremely difficult should he choose. 'I'll need some time to organise the grape harvest,' she said.

'There is none,' Malachi said. 'We have to set sail immediately if we are to have the best chance of success.'

Lone caught sight of Ayesha's enquiring face gazing up at her from the quayside. The girl had taken to following her around after the incident with her uncle, and this now gave Lone an opportunity to send a message back to her businesses. She ran down the gangplank and confronted the girl. 'I have to go away for a few days,' she said. 'You will be my representative while I'm gone. Make sure that the crop is harvested and that the wine is kept safe.'

Ayesha's eyes widened. 'I can't do that. Nobody will listen to me.'

'They will not only listen to you, but they will obey.' Lone motioned with her hand, and Cat came bounding obediently to her side. 'Cat will protect you and punish anyone who tries to stand against you. I'll be back very soon. Remember that men are weak and powerless in the face of female strength.' Lone turned her back on the girl and boarded the ship. It wasn't going to be easy for Ayesha, but she hoped that somewhere in the girl's heart there was enough courage to stand proud in the face of the inevitable opposition she would face. As for Cat, there was no telling what she would do. There was an equal chance that she'd turn on the girl as help her. Lone's only hope was to get this thing done quickly. Even then, there was the distinct possibility that there would be nothing left of her businesses when she returned.

6

Ant found himself sleeping a lot. The gentle slopping of the water under the boat and the complete lack of any need for him to do anything had a welcome soporific effect. After three days or so of nodding off, eating a little, then sleeping some more, the bone weariness that had afflicted him recently had begun to recede. His mind felt sharp for the first time since he'd conjured up the avatar on the windy hillside.

The ship's progress had become slower as the river widened. They were relying on the sluggish current to propel them as the winds were generally in the wrong direction to be of any assistance and the two large triangular sails remained for the most part tightly furled.

It was the largest vessel Ant had ever seen and required three men to sail it. The captain of sorts was an uncommunicative and sullen man who had to be cajoled before he'd issue a single word. Even then, his thick accent was difficult to decipher. The other two sailors hardly ever spoke within Ant's earshot, and when they did, it was in a language that he couldn't understand.

Ant watched as Malachi pored over the charts he'd brought, occasionally taking out the strange instrument that they'd liberated from the ruins of the palace and pointing it at the sky. From time to time, he'd summon the captain and complain about the slow progress they were making.

Tyrant seemed to be spending half his time eating and the other half spewing his half-digested meals into the river. Ant was fascinated by the shoals of hungry fish that gathered in response to the yellow streaks with which Tyrant was decorating the water.

Lone, mercifully, was keeping as far away from him and Tyrant as the confines of the boat allowed. Ant's guts churned with repressed longing at the thought of her. Nights of swollen imaginings crowded his thoughts. Here she was, in all her glory, when he'd been desperately trying to conjure a picture of her in his mind for so long. She'd turned an even darker shade of brown now, but her body remained as lithe and tantalising as ever. When he met her eyes, they forced him into welcome surrender. All his determination to keep away from her had been in vain.

One look from her and his equilibrium was upset. The old longings came flooding back and threatened to catapult him into being a love-sick teenager.

'Here is where we are.' Malachi stabbed a bony finger at a thin blue line on his chart. 'This is the river we're on and this'—his finger moved position—'is the river that the kidnappers are using. You can see that both rivers run into the same sea. Our plan is to sail down to the sea and then westwards to the mouth of the other river. There, we will intercept the other boat and rescue the young ladies.'

'Will we be in time to do that?' Ant asked. 'They've had a long start on us.'

'Yes, that's true, but they began their journey much further north than we did. Using the vedhana for the first part of our journey should have given us the advantage, though it may be a close-run thing.'

'What if we're too late and miss them?'

'That would be a problem,' Malachi said. 'We have no way of knowing their ultimate destination. Once they get out into the vast expanse of the sea, I fear that they will be lost to us.'

'But this boat is hardly moving. Are you sure we're going to arrive ahead of time?'

'That may be our problem. Both vessels rely on the current to carry them to the sea. Our river is very wide and consequently flows very slowly. The current in the other river may be stronger for all I know. The chart can't tell me if that's true or not. I've told the captain to make all haste, but he's not willing to use the sails because that would involve having to track from one side of the river to the other to use what little wind there is. He says that the occupants of the riverbanks are too dangerous to risk even a fleeting visual contact.'

Ant sighed. If the captain was impervious to Malachi's expert urgings, then the denizens of the forest that lined the river must be fearsome indeed. The plan sounded plausible to him without the benefit of being able to read the chart, but he wondered what was really going on and whether anything being said was even approaching the truth. Malachi was a master at messing with people's heads, of painting a false picture that seduced them into doing whatever it was that he wanted. Some of his lies had been so outrageous that only his devious mind could

25

have been capable of inventing them. Ant's experience reminded him to beware of the silver-tongued wizard, but he was powerless to change anything. While they remained on this ship, they were all sailing under Malachi's command.

7

Tyrant clung desperately to the thick wooden rail that was the only thing preventing him from plunging to his death. Swimming wasn't a skill he'd ever acquired, and he doubted any of his companions on board would have either the ability or the will to save him if he lost his hold and fell into the water. The river looked calm enough, but it still made the boat sway and lurch in a very unsettling manner. His stomach was having trouble adjusting to the strange feelings of insecurity and had decided to exercise itself by throwing up anything it contained. Even though it had now thoroughly emptied itself, it continued to subject him to violent dry heaving as it practised for the next time.

Ant looked in even worse shape. When they'd met in the King's chamber, Tyrant had noticed an unhealthy paleness in the boy's face, as if someone had been draining blood from his body. All he'd done since was to sleep in seeming obliviousness to the bobbing motion of the vessel. Something that Tyrant would dearly love to emulate.

'Look at the little fishes,' Ant said, pointing at the thin trail of vomit that Tyrant had managed to dribble into the river.

'It's those big dark shapes in the depths that are worrying me,' Tyrant said between heaves.

'They can't get us while we're on a big ship like this,' Ant said.

Tyrant took a deep breath and washed his mouth out with water from a cup on a string that he dangled into the river. He took care not to let anything down his gullet in the forlorn hope that this might be the final act of expectoration and everything would calm down from now on. He didn't want to give his stomach anything to work with. 'Best not fall in, then. I reckon those monsters are just waiting to get their teeth into us. Mind you, it might be a better way to go than having your guts turned inside out.'

'Do you reckon you could swim all the way to the shore, then?'

Tyrant shook his head, then regretted it as another wave of nausea engulfed him. This time, his heaving yielded nothing of interest to the fish, large or small. 'It's got too far away now. At first, I thought I'd be able to hold my breath long enough to walk over to the bank while underwater. Now, there's no prospect of that, I suppose. I don't see why we don't sail closer to the shore, though, just in case something happens to the boat.'

'Malachi says that there are dangerous things hidden along the banks of the river. The captain has told him of horrible creatures that nobody has ever seen and lived to tell the tale.'

Tyrant felt like laughing for the first time since he'd walked over the flimsy piece of wood that had connected the ship to the shore. He resisted the impulse, though, in case it provoked another bout of sickness. 'How can people be so stupid as to repeat madness like that? If nobody ever lived to tell the tale, how come the captain knows about these terrible apparitions? It's all gossip and speculation, I'll wager. Tales to keep bored sailors amused.'

'Malachi was trying to get him to put on some sail to speed up our progress, but he refused because the manoeuvres he'd have to make to catch the wind would bring him closer to the riverbank. He seemed to be terrified enough to withstand Malachi in full flow, if that counts for anything,' Ant said.

Tyrant knew that Malachi wasn't easy to resist and that might mean there was more to the captain's fears than he'd thought. He was considering a reply along those lines when his guts began to churn, as if he'd recently gobbled a dozen rancid squirrels. The very thought of squirrels intensified his nausea to the point where he did manage to expel a small quantity of bile and make the fish excited. 'I wouldn't trust the word of a man who carries a silver flask tucked into his belt,' Tyrant said. He'd watched the captain take a substantial swig of whatever potent licker it contained almost as often as he drew breath.

'You should be getting your sea legs by now,' Ant said. 'Maybe you should try to eat something.'

'I'm perfectly well up here on my own, dealing with my stomach in my own way, thank you.'

'Here,' Ant said as he proffered what looked like a shrivelled turd that he'd extracted from his monkish robe, 'chew on this root. It will help calm your nausea.'

'I already tried it; didn't work; didn't like it. Tastes horrible,' Tyrant gasped between retches.

'Try it again,' Ant said.

Tyrant nibbled the end of the woody nub and was rewarded with a bitter sting on his tongue and a bad taste in his mouth. It was better than the first time he'd tried it, so he reasoned it may be having some positive effect after all. 'I should never have come,' he said. 'I'm no use to anyone in this state. They'll all be laughing at me; my reputation's suffering and I'll have none left by the time we return. If we ever do, that is.'

'Tell them you're looking out for sea monsters and frightening them away with your mighty powers.'

Tyrant looked carefully at Ant, trying to detect any hint of sarcasm, but the boy stared unashamedly back into his eyes. Since Ant had returned from his time living in the monastery, Tyrant had noticed that there was less of the manic Malachi influence detectable in the way he acted. Ant was a much calmer soul and Tyrant was grateful for it. He was also happy to have him along on what could turn out to be a long quest.

'I don't understand why Bee and Cassie were taken in the first place. Who would do such a thing? And why?' Tyrant said, the root having at least temporarily stilled his heaving guts.

'Cassie is the Queen after all. By taking her and her sister, they seek to influence the King, force him to do their will,' Ant replied.

'So the King says, I'd no more trust him than I would Malachi.'

'I thought you had more regard for Cuthbert than that,' Ant said.

'He's changed since he became King. It's not the Cuthbert that you and I hiked up hill and down dale to rescue from hanging. He's the King now and it's changed him for the worse. I can hardly believe he's not the old King returned the way he's been carrying on. Put a tax on licker for a start. How's a man to make a living if half the proceeds are supposed to go to the King? That's not the action of a friend, that's for sure.'

'Then why bother trying to help him?'

'You know how much those girls mean to me.' Tyrant bit a more substantial piece off the root and chewed carefully. 'I'm not even sure that I'll be able to help when we get there. I may have established a mighty reputation, but we both know that's more story than substance and any opposition we meet won't give a fig for it.'

'I'm sure you'll do what's necessary when the time comes. You underestimate yourself, Tyrant. I've witnessed your heroism first hand

and I can honestly say that there's nobody I'd rather stand beside in a crisis situation.'

'I'm beginning to feel mighty hungry all of a sudden; I think it must be that magic root. Maybe I should have something to eat?'

'There's some gruel if you want it. I recommend a small bowlful to begin with. I'll fetch you some.'

Tyrant carried on watching the mysterious dark shapes in the river; his nausea was slowly being replaced by a new feeling of foreboding. There was something wrong that was even worse than having to share a boat ride with Malachi and that witch. Even the comforting taste of the gruel did nothing to dispel his feeling that this expedition would end badly.

8

'Here, guard this with your life. There are only two of these instruments in the world,' Malachi said.

'What is it?' Ant asked.

'Hold it out on the palm of your hand. Now, see the little pointer in the middle of the dial? One end is coloured red. Got it? It's pointing towards the river bank. Now, turn yourself right around, keeping your hand flat. See what's happened?'

Ant looked at the small circular amulet in his hand. No matter which way he turned, the red marking was indicating the exact same direction. If he turned, it adjusted itself until it was pointing to the very same spot on the river bank as before. 'It's some kind of magic, isn't it?' Ant asked. 'It has imbued the device with a will of its own.'

'The red needle always points north. That's all the magic there is to it. The casing allows it to move freely and keep itself aligned. You're going to need it to navigate your way to the mouth of the other river. See where we are? It doesn't look like a long way on this plan, but there may be difficult terrain that stops you from travelling in a straight line. That's where this device will keep you on the right track. All you have to do is to line up the dial with the pointer and keep on walking in a westerly direction. Understood?'

Ant nodded and placed the device in his deepest pocket. 'What about the inhabitants of the forest that the captain is so afraid of?'

Malachi smiled and Ant's heart jolted in alarm. 'Between you and Tyrant, I'd say that anything you encounter should be more afraid of you two than you need to be of them. Go carefully, by all means. Leave nothing to chance and remain vigilant and I'm sure that you will be safe. There's a good chance that the talk is just that, in any case, tales that sailors tell each other to keep themselves from dying of boredom.'

'How do we get on to the shore?' Tyrant asked. 'I'm not taking to the water, if that's what you're suggesting. I'm not a swimmer and there are things in that river that have had their eye on me for a long time.'

'Wait!' Lone's head appeared through the hatch and she climbed gracefully onto the deck. 'You go with Tyrant. Leave the boy with me,' Lone said.

Ant stood still, frozen into inaction by the sound of her voice. She affected him so powerfully that his much-practised awareness was swept aside to leave him dangling at her command.

'I hardly think that's wise, my dear. Better that we two stay on this vessel so that our powers can be combined when we meet the other ship. Ant and Tyrant will be covering the small possibility that our quarry has taken a different channel, that's all. Once we have made the interception and rescued the Queen, we can pick them up again before we sail home.'

Lone laughed. 'That's a nice plan, Malachi, but it lacks imagination. How do you think these two might manage to capture a ship sailing down the wrong channel? The big one is scared of the water and the young one is good only for making devices to get us home. If, as you say, your powers are needed to save the girls, then you go. Take Tyrant, though I don't see the use of him myself. Ant and I will remain on board. I'll protect him so that we might be spared a long and arduous journey back upstream.'

Malachi's face darkened and his eyes flashed defiance, but he stayed silent. Ant returned the direction finder, hands shaking at the prospect of being left with Lone. Terror and excitement fought for precedence, but it was a close battle and there was no clear winner. His legs buckled and threatened to give way as his head filled with clouds of imagination that drew his energy out of his body.

'Don't worry about me.' Lone's lips drew aside to show the whiteness of her perfect teeth. 'I'll not need your assistance to overcome a few men on a boat.'

9

The tussling between Lone and Malachi left Tyrant wondering what they were really up to. It was likely that Malachi had planned to rescue Bee and Cassie himself. Once done, Tyrant doubted he'd bother trying to recover the landing party. He'd sail back to the King, present him with his Queen, and take his place once again as the King's trusted advisor.

The only surprise was Lone's insistence on an alternative strategy. Either way didn't matter. As long as he was allowed off this lurching platform and onto solid land, it made no difference. Ant would have been a more conducive companion with which to traverse the jungle, but having Malachi with him felt like a guarantee that he wouldn't be dumped here and left to rot.

Malachi's presence at least meant that they were to be carefully deposited on the shore, despite the protestations from the crew that this would endanger the ship. They were reluctantly lowering the small rowing boat that was lashed to the stern while complaining loudly about the trouble and the risk. The wizard made it abundantly clear that he wasn't prepared to get wet, despite having been content for Ant and Tyrant to leap into the river and take their chances.

Ant pressed a leather purse into his palm. 'Take this with you. Keep it safe.'

'What is it?' Tyrant asked.

Ant's eyes darted over to the witch, who had her hands on her hips and was giving them her unwelcome attention.

'Move your arse and get into the boat,' she said. There were other words muttered under her breath that Tyrant couldn't decipher. It didn't matter, he doubted they were complimentary. Quickly securing the heavy purse to his belt, he heaved himself over the side and lowered himself into the dinghy, where Malachi was already seated in the prow.

They were rowed across by a crewman who had lost a lengthy and vehement argument with his shipmates, culminating in the captain putting a sword to his throat. When they reached the shore, Tyrant struggled to stand up. The boat bumped against the riverbank and he took his chance to leap ashore. One foot landed in the soft vegetation, the other slid backwards in the mud and he teetered on the edge of falling into the river. A black figure materialised by his side and grabbed his arm.

The two men scrambled onto firm ground. Tyrant turned to see the boat was already detached from the shore and heading back to the ship. Ant's face stared wide-eyed from the stern with Lone standing with one hand on his shoulder as if to prevent his escape. The boy had every right to look worried, having been left alone on the ship with her. Tyrant had spent enough time in her company to know her as ruthless and manipulative. Nobody had a chance of withstanding her will, not even her husband. The poor boy would be soft clay in her hands.

As he watched the boat sail away from them, he was grateful that nothing had leapt out of the trees to attack them, despite the dire warnings of the crew. Nothing unless he counted the swarm of black flies that adopted him as their very own source of nutrition and amusement.

While on board, the pace of progress had seemed frustratingly slow, but once on shore, the boat quickly disappeared downstream. Malachi looked at him, then down at the heavy pack that Lone had provided. Tyrant stared back. Neither man moved despite the hot sun and the proximity of shade. A shadow passed across the wizard's face and Tyrant felt his throat tighten for an instant.

'We'll take turns with the bag,' Malachi said. 'You first.'

Tyrant bent and hefted it onto his shoulders. By the time he'd staggered the twenty paces into the trees, he was ready for a rest.

It was hard going. The trees were close together, with prickly bushes growing beneath their canopy. Tyrant had to push his way through tangled vegetation that grabbed at his clothes and snagged his heavy pack. Becoming hopelessly enmeshed and unable to continue, he resorted to using his sword to hack his way through. All the time, Malachi followed closely behind, complaining constantly about his lack of progress without volunteering to have a go himself.

The pack dragged and chafed, the flies clogged his mouth and nostrils, and the plants were becoming sharper and more clinging. His noisy progress sent all manner of creatures scurrying and slithering for safety. There were mice and rats, some with long pig-like snouts, and numerous snakes of many different sizes. Fortunately, nothing challenged his right to blunder through their habitat, though some of the huge spiders whose webs festooned the trees might have easily sent him running back to the river had they tried.

Amongst the heady fragrance of warm vegetation, there were frequent undertones of musky scents and the occasional eye-wateringly pungent stink that he thought might be cat piss. It could be a small, very smelly sort of cat, but he doubted it. There were other signs, like tremors in the foliage ahead, to indicate that there were bigger things than spiders and rats being disturbed by their passage.

Eyes unable to focus because of flies and sweat, hand too slippery to wield his sword, and too exhausted to continue, Tyrant sat down and watched a stream of ants run over his legs.

'Come on,' Malachi said. 'We have to keep going if we're to intercept the boat that has the Queen on board.'

With insufficient breath left to reply, Tyrant took a restorative swig from the jar of licker he'd brought, then dragged the pack from his back and began to rummage inside it, looking for food. There were heavy cooking pots, some spices and a bag of salt, a thick black cloak, presumably a spare for Malachi in case his became soiled or torn, a couple of blankets, but no food. Lone must have packed this because every item had been chosen for maximum weight, largest volume, and least value.

'Your turn with the pack.' He pushed the useless, heavy thing towards the wizard.

'I'll carry it tomorrow, you finish the day,' Malachi said. 'There's no time for sitting around; we can rest when we get to the other shore.'

'It's alright for you to say,' Tyrant replied, 'but I'm not used to hacking my way through a jungle. It makes me tired. Why don't you take the pack and the sword? Hack away to your heart's content. I'll follow on when I'm ready.'

'We have to stick together,' Malachi said. 'That's the plan.'

'This plan of yours makes no sense to me. Don't get me wrong, I'm happy enough to get off that horrible boat. My stomach still thinks I'm on it the way it keeps rolling around and trying to come up my throat. We should have all got off if this is the way to find the girls.'

Malachi sighed, opened the bag, and withdrew a large piece of parchment, which he unfolded carefully and smoothed out onto the ground. 'This is where we are,' he said, a bony finger prodding at the paper. 'This is the river we sailed down and here is the channel we are heading for. It's very narrow at this point and we should have no trouble spotting the kidnappers' vessel if it takes this route.'

No matter how hard Tyrant squinted at the map, it made little sense. 'What's this?' His finger left a dark smudge as a permanent guide to where he meant.

'That's an island on the other side of the channel. The fugitives could pass either side of it. Our ship will sail past it to the main channel where it's more likely to emerge. Our job is to keep watch in case it comes our way.'

'If that's the case, we should be walking in this direction and waiting there.'

'That's the sea,' Malachi replied. 'We can't walk on water.'

'Oh,' Tyrant said. There was an awful lot of sea then. Most of the map was sea. Getting off the boat suddenly seemed to have been a crazy idea. As if he was excess baggage and someone had decided to get rid of him. These were perilous parts, according to the sailors who were afraid to get close to the shore, let alone set foot on it. Yet here he was, blundering through the undergrowth on the orders of a witch. Malachi was just as much in thrall of the woman as the rest of them.

The memory of Ant's face as the boat sailed off made him think that being abandoned wasn't the worst thing that could have happened. His hand picked up the leather pouch that Ant had given him and he thought about having a peek inside. It felt as if it were a bag of sand, but that would make no sense given the urgency with which it had been passed to him. There had been an air of reluctance involved, which concerned him. It was as if Ant had been in two minds and the decision hadn't been an easy one.

'We really must get going,' Malachi said.

'Then leave the pack here if you like. I'm not lugging it any further. It's full of useless junk anyway. We don't need it.'

'Pick it up. Every item in there has a purpose and may be the difference between life and death.' Malachi's voice deepened to almost a growl and Tyrant found himself heaving the bag onto his shoulders.

Better not to make a fuss. Though how some pots and pans and a blanket could be described as essential was quite beyond his imagination.

'What do you think it was that scared the sailors?' Tyrant asked.

'Superstition most likely. Perhaps born out of someone dying from snakebite and blown up out of all proportion. Snakes are prone to slither onto ships by means of the ropes that tie them to the shore. There's usually a rational explanation for even the wildest story.'

'So you don't think that we're in danger from some mysterious invisible predator that might swoop down on us when we least expect it?'

Malachi made no answer other than to wave Tyrant ahead so that he could resume hacking his way through the forest, keeping a wary eye out for snakes as he went. His passage provoked plenty of scurrying sounds, a lot of disturbed vegetation, but only the occasional glimpse of a fleeing rodent. Still, if there were rats, there would be snakes, he supposed.

Tyrant had spent most of his life sharing his bed with whatever creatures happened to be occupying the same piece of ground. It was unusual for these visitors to cause him anything more than minor irritation. His sleep had been routinely disturbed by cockroaches trying to crawl up his nose, rats crawling on his face, ants nesting in his undergarments, and beetles exploring his crevices, but none of these things caused him any harm.

Malachi's suggestion about some form of deadly snake that liked to creep onto ships was a worry because it was outside his experience. Being stung, bitten, clawed, gnawed, and tickled was part of being alive in a world teeming with life. As long as the normal order of things applied, he found nothing to be afraid of. Wary, perhaps. Wary was a good state to adopt. It offered respect to the other lives he might affect. They all had a right to exist even if he was keen to prioritise his own. Something different had to be a worry, though. Part of him hoped that Malachi was right and it was a snake. Better that than a spider. Spiders would be harder to deal with because they weren't confined to the ground and much more mobile. Watching his feet was an effective precaution against being surprised by a snake, but spiders could be dangling anywhere.

Whatever it was, if it were anything at all, he hoped it would be big. Not huge, not a giant monster like the demon he'd once been confronted by. Something large enough to see, but small enough to defend against. Something his sword or his fists might prevail against. His nervousness grew with every step. Malachi was keeping a few paces behind and having an easy passage cleared for him. 'Maybe you would like to take the lead for a while?' Tyrant stopped and turned to the wizard.

'No, you're the one with the sword. You're doing a fine job. Keep going.'

Tyrant held out his weapon hilt first. 'Here, you can have the sword.'

Malachi's answer was a shake of the head and an imperious wave of his arm. Tyrant turned back to his jungle-chopping duties, keeping a weather eye out for snakes. His vigilance was rewarded when he avoided stepping on one as thick as his arm that had curled up under a bush that his sword had demolished. The serpent reacted by rearing up and facing him. He backed off a couple of paces, then stood perfectly still. Maybe this was the dreaded beast that had so alarmed the sailors. His hand gripped his sword tightly as he weighed up the prospects of striking more quickly than the snake.

A blue forked tongue flickered in and out of the scaly mouth as if tasting the air. Black pinpoint eyes stared impassively at him. His anxiety rose to breaking point, and he prepared to take a pre-emptive swing at its head.

'Why have you stopped?' Malachi said, pushing past him.

'Wait,' Tyrant shouted, his sword arm now blocked by the wizard standing next to him. 'It's a snake. Ready to strike.'

'Is that all?' Malachi waved his hand, and the snake slithered away and disappeared. 'If we stop to admire every little animal, we'll take forever to reach the other coast. Remember that the lives of the Queen and her sister are depending on us. I'd appreciate it if you would show a little more fortitude. After all, you are reputed to be the bravest and mightiest warrior in the kingdom.'

'I thought it might be one of them,' Tyrant said.

'One of them what?'

'One of those sneaky scary snakes that crawl onto boats and kill everyone that you told me about.'

'I really have no idea what you're blabbering about, Tyrant. Now, get on with it.' Malachi prodded him in the back with a bony finger to propel him forward. Considering that he was much bigger, possessed of a fearsome reputation, and wielding a sharp-edged sword, Tyrant thought about making all this pushing and prodding into an issue. Clear the air, so to speak. Make it absolutely plain that he wasn't the kind of man to put up with this sort of treatment. One glance at Malachi's hawkish face convinced him to let the matter rest for a while and resume chopping his way through the jungle.

Progress was halted when Malachi tugged on his shirt. 'Listen. Can you hear that sound?'

Tyrant stopped swishing his sword about. There was a noise ahead and to the right. Squealing. Agonised screams that grew in volume and frequency.

10

Ant watched the shoreline recede and Tyrant turn away. The impulse to part with the precious purse containing his avatar had been rash and foolish. There was no means of knowing what would happen when the two of them were separated by a long distance. There was also the inadequate instruction he'd given Tyrant, as if he'd handed him a bag of flour and not his life.

Lone's hand felt hot on his shoulder. It was the nearest the two of them had been. The most intimate contact he'd had with the witch since he'd become besotted with her years ago. Without conscious permission, his body reacted with neediness and desire. Trying to remain dispassionate, Ant teetered on the bank of the emotional river that beckoned him into its rushing waters. Turning to face her, an almost irresistible impulse to take her in his arms and swear his undying devotion left him trembling with the effort to hold himself back.

Lone's lips parted, drew back slightly in a half smile, half pout. Her tongue flickered lizard-like into view for an instant before withdrawing. 'What did you give to Tyrant?' she asked.

'Oh,' Ant stumbled for a response. 'A bag with something he might find useful.'

'Look at me,' Lone said, putting both hands to his face and staring into his eyes. Even if he'd wanted to, there was nothing he could do to resist. 'Now tell me honestly. Do you think about me when you're pleasuring yourself?'

Breath caught in his throat, and heat blossomed all over his head. He tried to avert his eyes, but she held him firmly with her hands and her gaze.

'Don't be shy. Everyone pleasures themselves, though few would ever admit it. It's such a natural act, yet it has been made shameful by a narrow-minded society. Relax, Ant. You're not doing anything wrong when you touch yourself like that.'

Now he was panting, mind and body in turmoil at her words. The images of her hand down there, rubbing herself and thinking about him, were too much to bear. His hands came up from where they had been hanging loosely at his side and rested tentatively on her hips. There was a warm shock on connection, but no resistance. He was touching her. For the first time. Energy flowed up through his feet and warmth poured from his hands, heating up her skin to sweating point. Her hands dropped to his shoulders, but her touch remained firm.

'I often envy your ability to achieve almost instant gratification,' she said. 'For us women, it is a much longer and gentler process. Men are built like they are so that they can mate quickly. You should practise a much gentler form of pleasure, Ant. Learn to take your time. Savour the pleasure. Feel it. Enjoy it. Cast aside any thoughts of shame and unworthiness. Do you know what it is that women most need in order to indulge fully in lovemaking?'

Ant shook his head slowly.

'Trust. That's the essential ingredient for us women. We have to feel safe enough to surrender ourselves completely. Without trust, that's impossible, and the act of love becomes a male exercise that leaves the woman completely unsatisfied. Couplings like this are not only common, Ant, they are universal. Women are dominated and forced into them as an expression of male power. I will not tolerate that kind of behaviour. There has to be absolute trust between us if I am to take you as a lover.'

The word 'lover' caused a deep involuntary intake of breath. What was she saying? The implications were so serious that any exultation he might have felt was overwhelmed by fear. Unworthiness dug a hole in his guts. Self-loathing placed a shield around his heart. While she was a distant object of desire, while she remained completely unattainable, he could objectify her with prurient thoughts without fear of sanction. Now that this connection had been made, now that the unattainable was dangling within reach, he'd never be able to think of her in the same way. He owed her a duty of care and respect.

His hands gripped her more tightly around the pinch in her waist. He wanted to move them, to caress her, perhaps to touch her buttocks or the top of her thigh, but prudence dictated he bided his time. And savoured the feel of her delicious warmth under his fingers.

The entire crew, three sailors and the captain, were on deck and staring at them in an obvious and off-putting manner. Lone must have detected his discomfort, for the momentary connection between them was broken and she took her hands off his shoulders and stepped away from his feeble embrace. 'Get on with your work,' she addressed the onlookers, who made no move to comply.

The grizzled captain staggered over and stood uncomfortably close, his acid breath and body stench overwhelming Lone's sweet fragrance. 'We've been having a discussion, the crew and me. Seems there's a renegotiation to conduct. Room for discussion, so to speak.' A silver flask appeared in his hand, which he put to his lips and sucked noisily from. The heady smell of licker added to the stench assailing Ant's nostrils.

Lone dismissed him with a wave of her hand. 'There's nothing I want to say to you.'

The crew members shuffled closer, effectively blocking them and preventing him and Lone from moving out of range of the noisome captain. 'We was thinking,' he said, scratching his groin with his left hand while his right one hovered next to the pommel of the short sword stuck in his belt. The weapon was new; Ant hadn't seen him armed before and wondered about the significance of this. The crew were empty-handed, but each of them had a knife tucked away yet readily accessible. 'Now that there's no men on board, we have decided to offer our services, haven't we, lads?' The crew noisily agreed with their leader.

The sting of being slighted and dismissed as a mere boy ran the length of Ant's body and caused him to momentarily bunch his fists. Before he could respond, Lone placed a hand on his shoulder and he took this as a sign to remain quiet.

'That's very thoughtful of you,' Lone said, 'but there's nothing we need from you apart from the sailing of the ship. Please get on with that task and be assured that if the situation changes, we'll let you know.'

'But it has changed,' the captain said. 'There's responsibilities been heaped on our heads, what with having to care for a woman and a boy left all alone in dangerous waters. Extra responsibilities warrant extra benefits, if you get my drift.'

'You're being well paid for your work already,' Lone said. 'Providing the mission has a successful outcome, I'm sure there will be some extra money available for you all to share.'

'That's nice to know, but money isn't everything. Especially money promised and not yet received. That sort of money ain't worth much any roads. We're talking proper looking after, the sort that the boy can't possibly manage.'

Ant watched in horror as the captain winked while grabbing hold of his crotch. 'We know what you want, lady, and we're all going to give it to you. Now stand out of the way, lad. You can join the queue at the back if you fancy a bit of sport.'

The man's intentions were crystal clear, but Ant couldn't believe anyone could be so gross and so stupid. The anticipation of Lone's response had him shuddering. 'Leave her alone,' he shouted in the captain's face. A calloused hand came up to slap him, but he moved his head backwards and the blow missed. As the captain's right arm swung across him, Ant helped it on its way by grabbing the elbow and pushing sideways and upwards.

It became the pushing hands exercise he had learned from Malachi. His feet were firmly planted, shoulder-width apart and knees relaxed. Automatically settling into the familiar posture gave him perfect poise and a deep root from which all movement could begin and end. In contrast, the captain had responded in anger and thrown himself off balance. All Ant had to do was to move the flailing arm a little further to force the captain's body to twist, one foot leaving the deck and the other struggling to keep him upright. Thanks to his daily routine, Ant stayed perfectly calm, ignoring pricking thoughts of fear and anger.

The captain staggered, weight all on his left foot. Ant calmly kicked his standing leg just below the knee and, as he fell, plucked the sword from his belt.

Holding the tip of the sword a few inches from the captain's face to deter his next move, Ant allowed his attention to shift to the crew. 'Let's put this misunderstanding aside,' Ant said, 'and get on with the voyage.' The sword clattered to the deck beside the fallen captain, who grabbed it and rose to his feet.

The two men stared at each other, one in anger and hatred, the other in calm readiness. Taking a measured breath, Ant allowed himself some congratulatory thoughts. He'd bested the captain in combat with one flick of his wrist, defended his woman, and demonstrated his mastery of the situation. They could all get back to the job in hand now, with the captain's wounded pride as the only casualty.

The man was staring at him as if letting things rest was the furthest thing from his mind. Standing in perfect poise, Ant was ready for anything, though. Another attack, even using the sword, could be just as easily defended as the first. No matter how hard he tried, the captain's incoherent energy and lack of equilibrium would prove his undoing.

Lone's vulnerability was his main concern. Malachi had once described her as the most dangerous person he would ever meet, but without the big cat to defend her, she would have been at the mercy of these disgusting rapists. He shuddered as a picture of what might have taken place without his intervention flashed through his thoughts. After this, she might be grateful. View him in a new light. Realise that he was a man, not a boy. Trust him. Perhaps trust him enough to—

His thoughts were scrambled by a blow to the side of his head that his reactions were too sluggish to block. A crew member had come up behind him, dealt a heavy blow, then grabbed him so that his arms were pinned by his side. Another slapping, stinging smack to his face, this time from the captain. Ant's eyes blurred as a punch hit him hard in the stomach, making his legs buckle and unable to provide any further support. He collapsed and lay breathless on the hard planking.

The captain stood over him, foot crushing his windpipe, and spat on his face. The slimy mucus slithered from the bridge of Ant's nose and dribbled off his cheek. The sword hovered a fraction from his right eye.

'Chop him up small,' the captain said. 'Let the little fishes have a chance of a feed. You two, get the woman and hold her down for me. Quickly, boys, my pecker won't wait any longer and the sooner I deliver my present to her, the faster you'll get your turns.'

Ant was powerless. Unable to compose any form of coherent thought or energy. The sword withdrew into focus in preparation for the final thrust that would skewer his head. The words *his woman* pricked painfully at his heart. How could he have been so presumptuous? She deserved more respect than that derisive label, yet, in his imagined triumph, his male pride had surfaced and he'd reverted to the unconscious stereotype that he shared with the captain and his crew.

'Enough!' Lone's voice carried no hint of pleading. The sword wavered uncertainly, but its proximity kept Ant nailed to the deck. Losing his life here and now was what he deserved after the wave of vanity that had distracted him, upended him, brought about his downfall, both physically and energetically. Then the sword withdrew completely, and he was able to raise himself to a sitting position. The captain dropped his sword, clutched his midriff, then sat down heavily on the deck. He began to moan, a deep guttural noise terrifying in its intensity. The crew froze and stared at their leader. The hands that were reaching out to Lone were withdrawn, the men standing next to Ant made no move to prevent him scrambling to his feet.

'Come here,' Lone instructed him. She grabbed his arm and pushed him behind her. 'Hold on to me. That's right. Now press your body against mine.'

His legs pressed against her thighs, his chest felt the warmth of her back as he dutifully put his arms around her waist and clung on tight. Her body accepted his touch without resistance.

The captain sat hunched forward, staring at his stomach. His screams increased in intensity. Something seemed to be moving inside his clothing. Ant watched with horror as a black tendril appeared from his waistband, followed by an insect face that gnawed its way through the cloth. The thing that emerged was a wasp as big as Ant's thumb.

The captain's trousers were ripped apart by the force of several more insects bursting out of them. A bloody, gaping mess was all that remained of the captain's lower body. His screams stopped suddenly as blood and guts showered onto the deck. He fell backwards, his head hit the floor with a thud, and he lay still apart from the commotion in his guts. Dozens of maggots, sickly pale amongst the bloody insides, writhed and feasted. Ant could hear their voracious feeding noises and watched them bloat as they consumed the captain's entrails.

One maggot burst, then another. Wasps crawled out, flexing their newly formed wings. As if in response to a silent command, they began to fly. A macabre buzz filled the air. The crew began to flap their hands wildly at the approaching swarm.

One by one, the men were overwhelmed, screaming in pain as they were stung again and again. More insects came out of the captain's hollow bleeding husk and headed towards Ant. He felt Lone tense, then his own insides threatened to burst as if he too had maggots inside him.

The buzzing grew in intensity, then changed to a popping sound as the wasps burst open, spilling gobs of yellow pus before spattering the deck. Each time an insect came within an arm's length of him and Lone, it met the same fate.

The crew weren't so fortunate. One of them ran screaming, face covered with wasps, and flung himself over the side of the ship. The other two lay writhing in agony, feebly clawing at their myriad attackers. Lone tensed again. This time Ant's whole body began to vibrate, inside and out. There was nothing he could do to resist the painful waves of energy as they robbed him of all bodily control. Despite his best efforts, his bladder released its contents and his bowels opened into his trousers.

There was a loud hissing in his ears, and his eyes oscillated in their sockets so that his vision became blurred. The deck seemed to heave as if it had turned to water and he was standing on a wave. The incessant popping suddenly became a loud bang, then everything was quiet. His eyes cleared. The deck stopped moving. His insides settled down.

The ship was covered in blood. The crew had been ripped asunder and the contents of their bodies spread far and wide. Nothing moved or crawled. Wasp husks lay scattered like yellow and black blossoms. Lone relaxed and peeled Ant's reluctant arms away from her body.

She turned and supported him by putting her hands under his armpits. It was difficult for him to draw breath, let alone stand unaided. The stink of his voided bowels was a shameful reminder of his inadequacy.

'Oh dear,' Lone said, 'that didn't turn out very well, did it?'

'What happened? How did you—'

'Never mind about that now; you need to get yourself cleaned up. Meanwhile, I'll see what I can do about this mess.'

Ant opened his mouth to protest, but closed it again. He was in no condition to talk rationally, especially to Lone. The suddenness and brutality of events had gone far beyond anything he was able to come to terms with. She was right. Best to get a bucket, have a wash, find some clean clothes, and wait for his senses to settle down.

The cool quiet and privacy of below decks soothed his raging spirit. His mind continually replayed his confrontation with the captain and the bloody chaos that followed, and each time, his emotions flared out of control. Ambrose had been right when he'd warned him about Lone. She was dangerous. Scarily powerful. How could he even have thought for an instant that she was in danger from those nasty men? Why had he assumed he should act the role of her protector? What must she have thought about the botched attempt that left him in a heap and at the mercy of those thugs?

The ritual of washing and dressing salved his turmoil. What was done was done. The past was gone and all that remained was the present. She was unscathed. He was alive and the only thing hurt was his pride. Breathe in the good, breathe out the negative thoughts. In. Out.

When he emerged into the harsh light, Lone was sloshing water from a bucket to chase lumps of bloody detritus into the river. The bodies were gone, presumably heaved overboard. The same place he'd been destined for before Lone took a hand. Hands dripping with blood, she turned towards him and put down the bucket.

'What a mess,' she said, wiping a red streak across her sweaty brow.

His heart froze at the sight of her. His pulse raced, not with customary desire, but with fear. He'd seen what she was capable of and would never look at her in the same way again. This was no soft object of desire, someone to protect against a harsh world. Lone was every bit as dangerous as Malachi had said. Even more so. The carnage he'd witnessed was seared indelibly into his memory.

'What did you do?' Ant asked.

'I defended us the only way I could. Unfortunately, the crew couldn't be saved.'

'Then you shouldn't have conjured those insects,' Ant said, but immediately regretted the defiant tone in his words and braced himself for retaliation.

Her face fell for an instant, then her eyes widened and she began to laugh. 'Oh, now I understand why you're looking so worried. Those weren't my insects, they had nothing to do with me. Come over here. Don't worry, I won't bite.'

The deck was slippery, especially where it was streaked with dark stains and it was hard to keep his footing. Nevertheless, he obeyed her command and presented himself an arm's length from where she stood.

'You look so nervous. I can understand why you're shocked, but there's no need for you to be afraid of me. Quite the contrary, I'm impressed with the way you protected me from those disgusting men.' She plunged her hands into the bucket, pulled them out dripping pink, and stepped towards him. It took all the willpower he could muster to stand his ground when she drew him to her and kissed him gently on the lips.

'There you are,' she said, stepped back, and shook the water from her hands. 'A reward for being so brave.'

An hour earlier, the kiss would have had him dancing for joy in raptures of triumphant excitement. Instead, he was confused. His mind told him to be afraid, but his body remembered the years of devotion and longing. He wanted to run away, but there was nowhere to run to. He needed to take her in his arms and claim her, but she was already out of reach. All he could do was stand, arms dangling, in stunned silence, being a disappointment to himself and to her.

'Do you know how to sail this thing?' Lone stood behind the big wheel and began spinning it around. The boat lurched and veered off to the right. She spun it in the opposite direction and they resumed their course down the middle of the river that was widening as they went.

'I've watched the crew at work, but have no real idea what they were doing or why.'

'It can't be too difficult if a bunch of morons like them could do it. While we're on the river, the thing more or less steers itself, but we'll soon reach the sea where we will have to raise the sails and take a more active interest in proceedings. Take the wheel while I finish scrubbing the decks. There are enough flies already, no sense in attracting even more.'

Steering was a simple enough job. He learned to make small movements of the wheel and wait patiently for the boat to respond, which it did in a very sluggish manner. Lone worked hard to remove the grisly detritus and blossoms of dark crimson that spattered the deck. Watching her made him wonder whether he should have let her steer while he did the heavy work. These were her instructions, though, and his instinct was to obey. There was insufficient energy left in his system for him to do anything else.

When she'd sloshed the final bucket and transformed the last dark stain into a minor blemish, she came and sat at his feet. Her hair was matted, her dress bloodstained and soaked in sweat. The scent of her was gloriously enticing and he found all his usual thoughts and desires re-establishing themselves at the forefront of his mind, pushing the fear back down inside.

'If those insects weren't your doing, what were they? How did they get inside the captain?'

'Seems to be that they were hatching inside him. Some creatures like to lay their eggs inside hosts so that they have something to feed on when they hatch. That's what they appeared to be doing. It's a pity it happened; now we have no crew and that might be a big problem for us.'

'But he was going to chop me up in pieces, then they were going to rape you. He got what he deserved and so did they.'

'Everything was under control until the wasps appeared. You were doing an amazing job. So brave. The way you knocked the captain on his backside was very impressive.'

'But he got up again and then they all ganged up on me and I couldn't do anything about it.'

'Let that be a lesson then, Ant. Next time you put someone on the floor and take their sword, don't give it back to them. I know what you were trying to do, and it was doubly brave and very sensible. Seeking to repair relations and declare a truce was undoubtedly the very best option. What you failed to take into account was male vanity. That man was never going to take being bested lying down. Next time, remember that people don't think rationally like you do. They can't remain calm; only you can do that.'

'So what should I have done differently?'

'Kept hold of the sword, at least. Given him a prod with it, perhaps. Something to grab his attention and keep him occupied trying to staunch the blood from a decently large wound. Doesn't have to be fatal, at least not immediately, just something to incapacitate him and make him realise that things aren't going his way. You'd be surprised how a big hole in a man's guts alters his perception and reduces his ambition.'

'But I didn't do that and I put you in danger by being so merciful.'

49

'Men are always a danger to me. I've learned to fend for myself, unlike most women who have to put up with the degrading and disgusting things that men do to them. You men are a product of society. Taught that females are inferior and have no rights to their own lives. That girls are possessions and no better than animals. Every minute of every day, women suffer from that terrible injustice.'

'Not me,' Ant said. 'I'm different. I respect women, especially you.'

'You do try.' Lone smiled up at him. 'I'll grant you that. However, the prejudice is ingrained in you. You can't help it. Boys become their fathers whether they like it or not. That's the way of things.'

'I'll never be like my father; you're wrong.'

'Then there's hope for us all in men like you. Stay awake, though. The lessons of early childhood make deep ruts in our behaviour patterns.'

The sun became a red glow behind the trees and stars began to appear. A cool breeze made him shiver. Lone disappeared below decks and reappeared with a blanket over her shoulders and one in her hands, which she gently placed around Ant. His longing to wrap her in his arms intensified. Trepidation churned itself into excitement. Danger transmuted into exhilaration. She curled up at his feet like a cat and closed her eyes.

There was a difficult period when the light had faded too much for him to see anything ahead. Ant closed his eyes and became perfectly balanced and completely still. His breathing became gentle and regular. The ship became part of him. The creaking of the hull, the bow slicing gently through the water, the gentle clatter of ropes in the breeze. The more he settled, the better his connection. The wheel seemed to turn itself, making tiny and precise corrections that compensated for wind and current.

When he opened his eyes, the sun was gone, and the stars were glistening on the water. The banks were shadows that grew more distant as they sailed.

The proximity of Lone's sleeping figure exaggerated his fatigue and turned the slight chill into biting cold. Wrapping his blanket tightly, he clung onto the wheel, determined to steer them to whatever it was that represented safety and success. The responsibility hung heavier than his weariness.

When his legs gave way, he managed to hang on to the wheel and prevent himself from collapsing. Had he fallen asleep? The river banks were both comfortably distant, so it hadn't mattered if he had. It was hard to remain upright, though he resisted the urge to wake Lone and ask to be relieved. Let her sleep. This was the least he could do to help her. Tomorrow she'd need all her considerable abilities at the peak of their powers if they were to manage a rendezvous with the kidnappers' vessel.

Hanging on grimly, he breathed himself a second wind, flexed his legs, planted his feet on the deck, and drew strength from the ground.

'Come here.' Lone had pulled back her covers to reveal her recumbent body.

'I have to steer.'

'Let it steer itself for a while. The worst that can happen is that we might bump into the riverbank. Leave it and lie here with me.'

As he lay down next to her, she drew him into her arms and wrapped them both in the blanket. Her warmth was intense. His head was cradled in the crook of her arm and his cheek pressed against the softness of her breast. Something stirred deep inside. A tiny baby, mouth open, seeking a nipple to latch on to. With it came sorrow that was beyond endurance. He began to cry. A mournful expression of grief that had been stored in his body but inaccessible to his mind. All the mothers he'd lost as a baby. His birth mother followed by a succession of mothers who held him, fed him, loved him, then abandoned him. Mona was the last of these, but he'd been able to understand the terrible pain and know that it wasn't his fault that she was gone. Baby Ant had been indelibly wounded by every loss. His tiny soul had been ripped apart again and again.

Tears soaked Lone's thin dress as he buried his sobs in her chest. Her fingers left a tingling caress on his soaking cheek. He cried for past hurts, for undeserved sorrows, and in joy at being returned to the safety of loving arms. His pent-up emotions curdled together and vented through his face. She held him gently, soft soothing hands stroking his face and body. He stopped trying to resist what was happening and surrendered to every emotion that welled up inside.

When he awoke, he found his head was resting on a folded blanket. The sun was warming his face. The deck was empty. Neither riverbank was visible.

11

It was a pig that had been screaming, but now it lay silent with its guts ripped open and insects buzzing around the wound. A large wasp flew at Tyrant's head. He flapped at it with his hand and was rewarded by solid contact that made it fall to the ground where a carefully placed boot finished it off.

'Nasty,' Tyrant said. 'I wonder what sliced it open.'

'Whatever it was, I suggest we give it a wide berth,' Malachi said. 'I don't like the look of those wasps, though I doubt they were capable of killing the pig. There's something bigger inhabiting this place. We'd do well to remain vigilant.'

Tyrant changed course and slashed his way through some thick bushes until he encountered a clearing with a definite track leading away from it. 'That's better,' he said. 'I can give my sword arm a welcome rest.'

'Until we meet whatever it is that made the path,' Malachi said. 'Better be on your guard.'

Having been constantly on the lookout for snakes, beset by spiders, and threatened by all manner of prickly plants, Tyrant wondered how he was expected to increase his already prodigious level of vigilance, but wasn't in the mood to start a discussion about it. At least progress became quicker and easier, even if the heat had become even more oppressive.

'Can you hear that?' Tyrant asked as he sat exhausted, wiping the sweat from his face with his shirt.

'I can hear many things. Wind in the tops of the trees, small animals rustling the undergrowth, birds calling, the occasional screech of a distant monkey. You'll have to be more specific,' Malachi said.

'I was referring to the buzzing. It's getting louder. I think those wasps we saw are following us.'

'Now you mention it, I agree that the intensity of insect noise has been increasing. Whether it's the wasps or not, some kind of swarm does appear to be heading our way.'

12

Lone appeared, carrying a bowl. 'Porridge,' she said. 'It will do you good.'

It was impossible to look her in the eye after his display of childish weakness. After last night, she'd forever see him as a bawling child. The gruel was thick and tasteless, but he wolfed it down dutifully. 'Where are we?'

'This is the end of the river and the beginning of the sea. We need to be sailing in that direction.' Her finger pointed amidships. 'I need you to help me hoist the sails before we get too far off course.'

The crew had made the process look easy, but the big triangular sail was heavy. Their combined efforts were only just enough, and he was left panting with exhaustion by the time the sheet bellied, whereupon the boat lurched alarmingly and threatened to capsize. Lone took the wheel and spun it rapidly. The boat slowly righted and began to run sideways to the waves. The new course involved a lot of pitching and rolling, which threatened to expel his recent breakfast.

'Tell me about your mother,' Lone said.

Ant's ears and face burned. 'She died.'

'And what about your foster mother; what was her name?'

'Mona. She left when I was ten. Father told me she'd died, but I think he was lying to stop me from looking for her, but I still did. I saw her once in the marketplace, but couldn't bring myself to disobey my father's threats in time to approach her.'

'Don't be ashamed to feel bad about what happened to you as a child, Ant.'

'But I'm a man now and I have to get over it.'

'Nonsense, that's not what makes you a man. Quite the opposite. A real man can face up to his childhood suffering. Feel it. Comfort his inner child when he shows up.'

'I'm sorry, I was overwhelmed by yesterday's events. It won't happen again.'

'Oh, but it should. That's if you want to grow into a man. It's the only way. Let those experiences surface and accept them as part of your life. Malachi will have taught you to recognise the real you from the one you pretend to be. Becoming that authentic being is hard. It involves terrible suffering and at the end of it, there is nothing. Hasn't he told you that?'

'Yes. Being in the monastery with Col and Pepper has also taught me many things. Like how I live my life asleep with only brief flashes of awakening.'

'Last night was part of that awakening. The business with the parasitic wasps and the crew jolted you back to an early age so that you could process your pain. You did well. There's nothing at all to be embarrassed about. You have my admiration, for what it's worth.'

The boat rolled alarmingly, pitching him across the deck. Crashing into the rail on the side, he hung on desperately to prevent himself being thrown overboard. Below, the waves had developed white foaming crests and were getting bigger. The deck remained tilted at an alarming angle.

'We need to steer into the waves. If they continue to hit us broadside, they will sink us,' Ant shouted.

'That's not the way we need to go,' Lone replied.

'We have to stay afloat. I can't swim.'

As Lone spun the wheel, the sail slackened, then began to flap. The boat turned sluggishly to meet the swell and the deck resumed a more comfortable angle. A sudden crack split the air as a gust filled the sails. The boom swung violently across the deck, catching Lone on the side of her head. As he bent to assist her, the boom flew back over his head, the sail snapped as it filled with wind, and the boat canted to one side.

Spinning the wheel in either direction seemed to have no effect. The boat had a mind of its own as it reacted to the wind and the waves.

Lone sat up, holding the side of her head. 'It's getting worse,' she said.

Remembering the lesson he'd learned on the quiet river, Ant stopped his frantic attempts to pilot the boat and waited. The prow slowly came around so that it began slicing through the swell. He slackened off the rudder gradually and the ship stabilised. They were heading out to sea.

13

Tyrant stopped and stared back down the track. 'It's getting louder. It could be there's an awful lot of them, or perhaps they're huge. Either way, I have a bad feeling about this.'

'Get on with it,' Malachi said. 'A few insects are to be expected. They'll probably pass by harmlessly unless you do something to enrage them.'

'Haven't you got some way of stopping them? Some magic to make them disappear, maybe?'

'I do have the power to constrict your throat and prevent you from uttering any more useless comments. Swatting insects isn't a form of magic that I'm familiar with or one that interests me. We need to get moving, otherwise we might as well have remained on the boat.'

Although he'd been grateful for getting his feet on dry land again, those feet were blistered and the rest of him was weary. Better to be enduring slight nausea while resting than this frantic dash through impenetrable jungle.

'Ouch!' Malachi was flapping at a wasp the size of his hand. The jungle reverberated to the sound of many more. The knowledge that he'd been right and Malachi wrong gave him no pleasure. It would have been better the other way around. Being stung to death was scant reward for an accurate diagnosis of their situation.

His sword was next to useless for pest control, so he uprooted a leafy plant and began swishing it about. The first sting was on his neck. A hard slap dislodged his attacker and his boot heel ground it into the forest floor. Dozens more flew all around his head, undeterred by the death of their comrade. Waving the branch around was having little deterrent effect.

Malachi was five paces to his side and busily extracting items from his voluminous cloak and throwing them to the ground. A pall of white smoke began to billow from the fire he'd started and this soon enveloped the two men in a ghostly fog.

The humming reached a new pitch. Tyrant's whole body was vibrating with the intensity of the noise. Another sting on his cheek had him jumping with pain. With every moment, more wasps were arriving to join in the concerted attack. Already, he could feel the weakening effects of the insects' venom.

The pouch on his belt began to writhe about as if there were wasps inside it. He unfastened it and threw it to the ground, where it burst open. A stream of grey powder erupted from the bag and shot into the air. The fine mist coalesced into tiny particles that ripped through the cloud of wasps closest to Tyrant. A shower of shattered insects spattered gently at his feet.

The grey matter formed itself into a cone, wider at the top, and began to rotate. Faster and faster it spun, letting out a ghastly hum of its own to rival the higher pitched buzzing from the wasps. As it spun, wasps were sucked into the top of the whirlwind and were spat out of the bottom. They went in whole and alive but came out separated into black legs, translucent wings, and yellow and black decapitated bodies. The ground became littered with thousands of dismembered insects.

The buzzing stopped and left an eerie silence. It was as if the jungle was holding its breath against the outcome. There was a pause before the usual sounds of scraping, humming, tweeting, and rustling returned. The grey cloud returned to its pouch and Tyrant bent down, picked it up suspiciously, felt its quiescence, and carefully tied it to his belt again.

Malachi emerged from his thick white cloud. 'That seems to have done the trick.'

At first, Tyrant thought that Malachi was referring to the awesome power of Ant's gift, then the wizard's smug face told him different. Did Malachi know about the pouch and what it contained? After all, Ant was his pupil; he should know what he was capable of. On the other hand, Ant had entrusted the pouch to Tyrant and done it surreptitiously. Malachi might be his travelling companion, but he'd never liked the man. Not since they'd first met in prison. His opinion hadn't been improved by the way Malachi had left him to bleed to death when he was struck down by an arrow after bravely fighting his way out of jail. It was true that Malachi had been obeying orders from his witchy wife, and that woman's will was impossible to resist, but that was no excuse. They were both as bad as each other.

'What did you do?' Tyrant asked as innocently as possible.

'Oh, it was a combination of an old purging spell and some alchemical ingredients of my own. Seems that I got it exactly right; the damned wasps couldn't survive the miasma I created. That was lucky for you, Tyrant. Without it, I fear you would have been overwhelmed.'

The man was insufferable. Almost to the extent that Tyrant nearly succumbed to the temptation to disabuse him of his triumph by explaining what had really caused the wasps to die. If he did that, though, Malachi would surely take the pouch from him. There might be more encounters with wasps and the like where having a magical whirlwind would come in handy. Better to bite his tongue and let Malachi have his misguided triumph.

They reached the coast as the sun was setting. Across the water, there were vague shadows of a distant shore, but nothing else was visible as they settled down for the night. Tyrant fell into a troubled sleep where Ant appeared to be drowning.

14

'We have a choice. Stay afloat and let the boat take us where it wants, or go in the direction we need to and risk capsizing,' Ant shouted above the noise of the slapping sails, the wind, and the crashing waves. The ship was groaning as if in pain.

'There is no choice,' Lone said. 'We have to try to sail back to shore. We might stay afloat, but we'll die of thirst out there in the vast ocean. I'd rather take my chances on drowning.'

'The wind is in the wrong direction. We're at its mercy.'

'Then we should take down the sail,' Lone said.

'We tried without the sail and were at the mercy of the waves. We need it so that we can steer.'

Lone was already untying the rope that held the sail aloft. As she released it, the sheet crumpled and fell to the deck. 'Help me raise the little one at the front of the mast,' Lone shouted.

The tiny sail was easily deployed. The wind caught it and provided enough propulsion for the helm to feel responsive. Gradually, he managed to turn the ship towards the setting sun. Everything steadied. They sailed majestically for several hours. Ant had adopted a relaxed mood of self-congratulation and was beginning to wonder what there might be to eat for supper when a big wave swept over the deck.

The cascade of seawater prised his hands from the tiller and carried him across the deck until his head hit the gunwale and he found himself trying to breathe underwater. A paroxysm of coughing gripped him unmercifully. As he tried to expel water, uncontrollable gasping for air filled his lungs with liquid again. He grabbed the side of the boat and pulled himself upright. His lungs were burning, convulsions racked his body as it tried to vomit out the fluid.

The next big wave caught him standing and threw him over the rail and into the sea. Completely submerged, he had no option but to keep his mouth shut and resist the insistent urge to gasp for air that wasn't available. As he sank beneath the waves, a peaceful feeling suffused him. This was drowning. There was nothing he could do about it. He couldn't swim. This meant he would continue to sink to the bottom.

Once he managed to stop the panic and accept the inevitable, his body relaxed. A miracle happened. His head came out of the water long enough for him to sip a tiny amount of air before it was covered again. Flapping his arms like a great underwater bird, he managed to poke his head upwards and gain another reward of life-giving breath. Bobbing up and down, judging the moment to breathe and to stop, he began to attune to the rhythm of the sea. It was a process that left no room for mistakes. One more gulp of water would undo all the good work and finish him off.

He closed his eyes. Allowed the sea to carry him. Took conservative breaths. Spread his arms and legs into a star shape. Water swept over his nose and mouth, then receded for an instant, and that's when he took his chance to get a bit of air. Not enough, though. His body screamed out for more. Wanted to be greedy. Being greedy made him take in water. Then he'd miss his next opportunity to breathe.

There was a rhythm to the process. A wave washed over his head. Then he was clear of the water and could take in air. When he bobbed to the surface he breathed in, as he went under, he breathed out. Calm, gentle breaths were the answer. If he sipped air gently, it allowed him to stop before too much water slopped into his mouth. When he panicked, his intake was mostly water, and he choked.

The stars were out, but there was no moon. No sign of the ship, or anything else. He was a tiny speck in an ocean of nothingness. The slivers of light blurred as water filled his eyes, then slowly resolved to pinpricks as it drained away. Learning when to breathe was only going to bring him a brief respite. His extremities were becoming numb with cold. The rest of his body was chilled, and his mind was becoming sluggish. A great desire to abandon his struggle to survive and allow himself to sink gently into a watery sleep was beginning to take possession of his will.

Moment by moment, he concentrated on living. As his energy seeped away, movement became more difficult. It was hard to get his head far enough above the water to clear his mouth. One breath at a time. One thought only. Breathe.

It wasn't enough. Weariness overcame him. Salt water clogged his mouth. Blocked his airways. Coughing only brought in more water. Then more paroxysms. Out of control. Involuntary gasping in the wrong medium. His body no longer responded to his mind. He was no longer part of it and it was no longer his. Withdrawing from the pain and the panic, his spirit soared above the waves. The tether to his body was becoming more tenuous by the second. When it gasped its last, made its final heartbeat, stopped fighting the fear and discomfort, then he would be free. Thought what that freedom might bring was unknown. Maybe nothing. Perhaps oblivion. Most likely a diffusion of spent life force into the welcoming void. No matter. What would be, would be.

15

There was searing pain where none should exist. Hadn't he obtained his freedom? Wasn't he detached from bodily sensations?

His dream came back. Half-remembered, vaguely felt arms that held him up. Propelled him through the water. Squeezed the water from his lungs and sucked in the air. Soft voices in his ear. Comforting, whispering encouragement. Supporting body and soul.

The warmth. Clammy wetness replaced by life-giving heat. Body wrapped in soft comfort. Eyes still in blackness. His groin, inflamed by heat and movement, suddenly being enveloped. His energy, his attention, concentrating on pleasure only imagined. Wished for. Longed for.

Convulsions. Uncontrollable paroxysms of release. The most exquisite feeling he'd ever experienced.

Another cascade of vomited sea brought his mind back to the present. Everything hurt. The agony of throwing up was unbearable, but he wasn't being given a choice. His body had taken over and was intent on saving itself.

Warm hands pressed his back, pumping the sea from his lungs. Breath came, ragged, agonising, head clearing.

Opening his eyes found him no longer in the sea but lying in the small boat. Lone was pressing hard on his chest and muttering indecipherably. Remembering his climax brought excitement, fear, and doubt in equal measure. What had she done? Had all his desires come to fruition during his rescue from a watery grave?

Sitting up, spluttering, watching her face transform into mirth. 'I see you're back. Amazing. I thought you were dead and gone. Long dead, in fact.'

'What?'

'It's a big sea. Look around you. What are the chances of finding someone in all this water?'

The surface of the sea was empty. No ship, no sight of land. Only waves heaving their tiny craft up and down. Small waves, thankfully. More coughing yielded a little more fluid for him to spit out. 'Thanks for trying.'

Her face twisted slightly, but her eyes lost none of their amusement. 'I didn't. As soon as I realised you were gone, I knew that there was nothing I could do to retrieve you. Anyway, I was too busy trying to save myself. Launching this boat during the storm was hard enough. I was lucky to survive the night without being tipped upside down and drowned.'

It was morning. The wave had washed him overboard as the sun had been setting. His entire night had been spent in the sea. 'But you found me anyway. For that, I'm very grateful. And brought me back to life with your…' Ant struggled for words. She must have employed some magical technique to revive him, and having sex was part of the ritual.

'My what?' she prompted.

'It felt as if we were making love,' Ant said.

'Really? All I did was crush your chest to rid your lungs of water. You have a strange notion of what sexual congress entails if you mistook it for the application of a little pressure to your abdomen. All I can say is that you're even more easily pleased than the rest of your gender.'

'No, you don't understand. It felt real. Closeness, warmth, I was inside you, everything happened. I can't have been mistaken. The expulsion of water was long after it was over.'

'If you had sex, then it wasn't with me. You can count on that.' Her eyes blazed and the twisted grin had broadened. 'Unless you dreamt it, you must have been intimate with your rescuer. The one who brought you to me.'

'What was she like and where is she now?' Ant's discomfiture changed rapidly to relief that it hadn't been Lone. The ramifications would have been too problematic, especially when he had to face Malachi again.

'She swam away.'

'Didn't she say anything? Where was her boat?'

'I doubt she was ever in a boat and wouldn't want to be. As for speaking, I was unable to decide whether the clicking sounds she made were a form of communication. There was nothing I could understand in any event. All I know is that she, if it were a female, helped me get you on board and then left with a flick of her tail and a smile on her snout.'

62

Ant's mind raced through the possibilities. Lone's description was alarming, yet could be the only explanation for his experience. This was a sea creature, warm-blooded and able to mate with humans. With him. 'Why?' he gasped.

'Why did she save you or why did she mate with you?' Lone's grin had developed a chuckle in her voice.

'Both.'

'I can't think what possessed her to take the trouble to rescue you, especially when she'd got what she wanted. As for the mating, there are plenty of species who can interbreed and I see no reason why a sea creature like her couldn't be one of them. It's possible that sailors' tales of exotic beauties beckoning them from the waves are true after all and these are the products of breeding with humans. Maybe you have created a mermaid daughter, Ant. Don't be hard on yourself. I doubt you had any say in the matter. You males are merely mobile packages of sperm willing to donate with the minimum encouragement from any female. The animal kingdom thrives because males know their place and their function. Unfortunately, human males have delusions of grandeur that force them to subjugate women and rob them of their rights and position. That's what I'm all about, Ant. Restoring the natural balance. Don't worry. You were only behaving naturally if you did impregnate her.'

'Malachi has taught me that I have a higher self that doesn't have to get lost in urges and emotions. I'm able to decide what's best for me without being swept away by uncontrollable forces.'

'He's right, of course. I'm certain that you have practised diligently to arrive at a state where this is true for you. However, the urge to reproduce is such a strong one that overriding it is nigh-on impossible for a man. That's why women are so much stronger and more reliable. We need a moment of a man's attention on very few occasions in our lifetime in order to fulfil our needs to reproduce. Whereas men are programmed to be in constant turmoil, desperate to release the pressure inside their genitals on a daily basis. It clouds your thinking, Ant. No matter how wise you become, that constant urge remains.' She was staring through his eyes and deep into his soul, which was nodding vigorously in agreement.

16

The wind had remained mercifully quiet, allowing the sun to evaporate the dampness from Ant's chilled body. Working the oars in any meaningful way was beyond his reserves of strength. All he could manage, despite the benign conditions, was to keep the boat pointed in the direction of the smudge on the horizon while Lone rested. What little progress they made was entirely due to her efforts.

There was no food on board to sustain them, but the crew had left a small barrel of smelly but drinkable water, presumably in anticipation of having to abandon ship at some time. Without it, they would have little chance of reaching the distant shore.

As he watched her sleeping, curled up like a cat, Ant relived his memories of dying and being brought back to life. The more he thought about it, the less he believed Lone's version. It was unthinkable that he could have had sexual intercourse with some sea creature. It had to be Lone. Or a dream. Yes, a dream. Anything other than a dream was impossible to bear. Recalling his experience made him shudder with fear. Looking at Lone brought him to a state of panic. Fishy eyes seemed to peer at him from the crest of every wave.

Reaching land did nothing to dispel his insecurity, but it did mean some nourishment that his body was desperate for. Lone brought him strange fruit with yellow flesh that was sweet and delicious. He ate until his stomach cried out in protest, then he slept on the warm sand in the shade of the looming canopy that fringed the shore.

Standing precariously on shaky legs, wafting away the flies with his hand, he watched Lone emerge from the forest carrying firewood. Tiny jumping things rose out of the sand and nibbled at his ankles, leaving pinpricks of red where they gorged their minute bodies with his blood. A cool wind blew in from the sea as twilight approached and the shadows beneath the trees became dark and menacing.

'We'll be glad of a fire tonight,' she said. 'It should deter the larger beasts from approaching.'

The warmth from the blazing wood made him shiver as it soaked into his body. The bright flames drew his gaze so completely that he became aware that the rest of the world was now shrouded in darkness. The pool of light created by the fire served only to make the surrounding blackness more oppressive. Fear took over from temperature to make him tremble.

Lone was already lying on the opposite side of the fire curled up protectively, her eyes closed and her face relaxed. When he tried to copy her, sleep failed to overcome his turbulent thoughts. He found himself staring at her and wondering what was going on inside her head. One thing he could be sure of was that she had saved him from a watery grave. It was very likely that he'd been drowned and she'd retrieved his lifeless body, which she'd then contrived to reanimate. Whether the process had actually involved intimacy of the most extreme sort or had merely evoked a physical reaction from a dream-like state didn't matter. Either way, he was lost. She had hold of him even more tightly than his previous starry-eyed lust.

A spider as big as his outstretched palm made its way slowly into the ring of brightness. Another shudder, this time in revulsion at the ugly creature. Heart racing, he cast about for a weapon, but found only a short stick that had escaped the fire. The black hairy thing crawled towards Lone. Small spiders could deliver dangerous bites. A spider that big might kill her. Blood thumped in his ears. Raising the pathetically inadequate twig, he waited for his hand to steady before attacking. If he missed, or failed to incapacitate the monster, there was no doubt that it would react. Spiders could be very fast when they wanted to be. Even jump large distances. Land on their prey and bite it to death. Run up the stick and bite his wrist.

As if detecting a threat, the spider paused. Its front legs quivered and tested the air around its head. It moved forward. To within an arm's length of Lone's face. Ant felt a surge of excitement energise his body. He would be saving her. Repaying his debt, or at least making a start.

The spider stopped moving. Something flipped the creature onto its back. Its legs waved frantically for a few moments, then became deathly still. In the flickering light, Ant could make out a crust of smaller insects lying dead beneath the spider. There was a tidemark formed by hundreds of dead creatures that outlined Lone's recumbent form. The spider was the largest and latest to wander into the killing zone that she had created to protect her. He wondered what would happen to him if he were to invade her space, and decided his curiosity wasn't great enough for him to risk testing it. The memory of the crew lying splattered and bloody was too fresh.

The sea creature returned in his dreams. Warm, kind, friendly, unthreatening, honest. Pure goodness that was easy to love in every way possible. Emotionally, physically, mentally. He awoke feeling a deep, natural connection that was strong and permanent. Their hearts remained tightly connected, beating together as one. Their bodies unable to exist in the same medium.

***

The fire had burned to cold ashes in the morning light. Lone was sitting in the middle of her killing circle and looking at him. Her gaze provoked an instant hot embarrassment, as if his dreams had been played out in full view. A turmoil of confusion gripped him.

She smiled and picked up the enormous spider that he'd watched die in the night. 'Here, have this morsel for breakfast.'

The black-legged horror spiralled through the air and he had to jump aside to avoid it hitting him. When it landed close to his scrabbling feet, he fully expected it to reanimate and hurl itself at him in violent retribution for the ignominy it had suffered. Mercifully, it remained inert. All the life had long been sucked out of it. 'I can't eat that.' Ant tried to speak with a normal voice but failed. It sounded like a whining squeak.

'Then you can't be that hungry. Insects are very nutritious. There are enough of them scattered about here to feed us both.'

'What killed them?' Ant asked. 'I watched this spider die when it crawled towards you in the night.'

'I killed them, or rather my ward did. It's my way of protecting myself while sleeping. Rather than be kept awake by all that crawling and biting, I prefer to be left alone. Anything that has other ideas is made to expire quietly.'

'What about me?'

'What about you?'

'Would I expire quietly if I approached you while you were asleep?'

'Why would you do that? You're a polite man who respects my privacy and need for space.'

'Maybe I needed to rouse you. You know, in case of emergency.'

'You could achieve that without having to lay hands on me, couldn't you?'

'Yes, of course.'

'Then you'd be in no danger. When I say no danger, I really mean little danger. We're none of us ever completely safe, are we?'

'I think you might have warned me that I could be killed if I touched you while you were asleep.'

Lone laughed. 'You stand a good chance of that if you touch me under any circumstances. Asleep or awake, makes no difference. Unless I want you to touch me, of course. That would be very different.' It was as if she were playing him like a stringed instrument, twanging one string after another to see what might happen.

'How does it work? The spell, I mean.'

'Why do you ask? Would you like to learn how to do it?'

'Yes, why not?'

'There are many reasons why not. You may not be capable for a start. You may not give the process sufficient time and energy for another. It might never work properly or in the way that you desire. Spells are fickle things that become very personal.'

'I'd like to try.' Ant imagined the massive improvement in his peace of mind if he could protect himself as she did.

'Then I'll teach you on one condition.'

'Name it.'

'First you show me how to make those travelling devices you're so adept at.'

'Vedhanas are tricky things to create. I've tried teaching Malachi, but he's never been able to make one successfully.'

'But the monks make them and your father once famously created one for the King that brought disaster to Gort. Like you, I'm willing to learn.'

'I'll show you how to draw the pattern, but I can't guarantee that it will work for you.'

'At least that will be a start. Apart from the time I was stranded in the desert, I've never had the need for such a device. The City on the River is my home now, and I have managed to fulfil all my needs and desires while living there. Now, however, my husband tells me that the new King has expressed interest in becoming more involved in my city. You know what that means, don't you? He wants to grab all the good stuff for himself and most of it belongs to me. That's why we were sent on this foolhardy, dangerous, and probably futile expedition.'

'If that's what you think, why did you agree to come along?'

'I was persuaded to do so. As you're well aware, Malachi can be very convincing when he puts his energy into it. At the time, it seemed reasonable to obey the King, as the alternative would have been outright opposition that would have quickly led to armed conflict. A war for which I'm not ready. There was, however, another, more compelling reason. I wanted to spend time with you, Ant.'

Ant's blood filled with thrilling energy at the recognition he'd been granted. His worship from afar and his longing to be noticed by her had at last been fruitful. There was something between them, after all. It didn't only go one way. She'd been thinking about him. Meanwhile, he'd been learning and growing. Becoming a man who could stand straight in front of her power and hold his ground.

Savage doubt doused his excitement as if he'd been drenched in tepid water. How had he been behaving in front of her? More like a needy child than a man. She'd had to rescue him from the crew and the wasps and then from the sea. Without her protection, he'd be dead three times over. Not the best claim for equality.

But she wanted to learn from him now. If she mastered the vedhanas, she would be able to travel instantly to any part of the kingdom. Even the King and all his forces would be hard-pressed to intercept her if she wanted to evade them. The notion that his knowledge might serve to keep her safe heartened him. Where could the harm be in that?

It should be an exchange, though. One powerful magic for another. Her spell for his. Being able to secure his body against harm while his attention was elsewhere would allow him to explore his full potential. Then, he'd be a force to be reckoned with and most importantly, a man she could consider an equal. 'Tell me more about your protection spell. How does it work?'

'In simple terms, I isolate myself from this world. Anything that attempts to get close finds that it has entered a realm in which life cannot be sustained. I think of it as a void, an absence of all and everything. It tears living things to pieces, sucks the life out of them.'

'But where does it come from? How do you conjure it?'

'It doesn't come from anywhere. It's always present. All I do is acknowledge it. Enable it to, well, unravel, I suppose. Take the wind as an example. How do you experience it, Ant?'

'I can hear it in the trees and feel it on my face.'

'So you know it's there, but you can't see it?'

'Nobody can see the wind.'

'Exactly. Now imagine if you had no feeling, no hearing, and no sight. How would you experience the wind then?'

Ant thought for a moment. Closed his eyes. Felt into the breeze that came in from the sea. Sucked the salt air into his nostrils. 'I would smell it.'

'So you would. Now, you know that the wind is there, but how does its nature change with the way that you perceive it?'

'I suppose it changes from a movement in the air that I can see and feel to something very different. The phenomenon of fragrances that come and go. Is that right?'

'It doesn't matter. I'm only using it as an illustration that we are limited by our senses. Malachi will have taught you that there is more to the world than we can detect with our human bodies. The void is always present. So are many different versions of existence that we cannot experience directly. We are like blind, deaf, unfeeling creatures that slither around on our bellies unaware of the sun and the sky. Because we can't see them, doesn't mean they don't exist. Can you understand what I'm saying?'

'Yes, I believe it as well. But I don't see how knowing that there are other worlds out there makes any difference.'

'Knowing is one thing, interacting is another. It's like sniffing the wind, Ant. Noticing what's there and how it changes. Once you can do that with a completely open mind that's free of the constraints imposed by your body, then you have a chance to unfurl the potential that's all around. Take Cat, for example. She lives in between worlds. That's how she can be here one second and gone the next. Your vedhanas must be something similar, offering portals not only between places in our world but also between worlds. That's what interests me. I no longer want to be limited to one form of existence.'

'What about demons? Where do they sit amongst all this nothingness and chaos?'

'Demons have a different set of senses, that's all. I believe them to be as much in the dark as we are, but they perceive it differently. Cat is a form of demon. Maybe all cats for that matter. At least their behaviour suggests as much. We could sit on this beach for days debating the nature of reality, Ant, but there are more pressing matters to attend to.'

'Like the rescue of the Queen and Princess Bee?'

Lone shook her head. 'I very much doubt they need our help; wherever they are.'

17

'How much longer do we have to sit staring at the water?' Tyrant had been glad of a rest from plodding through the relentless jungle, but even his considerable capacity for idleness was beginning to wear thin.

'As long as it takes for a ship to appear.' Malachi sat motionless, head retracted inside his voluminous hood.

'It's been two days.' Tyrant realised he was pointing out the obvious, but he had little else to say. Truth was he missed Petra's busy energy. She was always on the go and mithering him to be the same. Obviously, he needed his rest more than she did and his major responsibility of making sure that every batch of licker they made was of merchantable quality limited his availability for menial chores, a situation that made for frequent discussions and even some shouting. Still, it was the life he'd chosen for himself and a good one taken as a whole. His taste buds flared and filled his mouth with saliva at the thought of licker. A plentiful supply would have made the wait bearable, but he'd used up all that he'd brought with him while trying to counter the effects of sea-sickness. The last swallow had been taken for medicinal purposes to steady his frayed nerves after the wasp attack.

'What if no ship comes? Are we going to sit here being gradually devoured by flies until there's nothing left of us but dried up husks of skin for the rats to gnaw at?'

'One or the other will appear. If the kidnappers have used the other channel, then Lone will intercept them. Then she'll come here to pick us up. Be patient.'

While Malachi was a taciturn and unreliable travelling companion, his wife was worse. He'd been grateful that she'd insisted he leave the ship to go ashore. The nausea was one thing he'd avoid, but getting out of her way was the greater relief. Had Ant been sent with him, it would have been perfect. Instead, he was beginning to realise that getting out of here relied on the witch bothering to come and rescue them. Judging from the disdain with which she habitually treated her husband, she was just as likely to leave him to fend for himself. As for Tyrant, her opinion of his worth had been obvious from the start of their acquaintance. She'd left him to die once and there was no reason why she wouldn't do it again.

'I don't think either ship is coming,' Tyrant said, realising the unhelpfulness of his remark as he spoke.

'I'd examine the rational basis for that belief if I hadn't better things to occupy myself with. The air is warm enough without you trying to heat it up with empty words spoken for the sake of speaking.'

'I'm going for a walk to look for food.' He struggled to his feet and swished away through the soft sand. Some tiny creatures followed him, jumping and dancing around his ankles.

Malachi was right about one thing. It was hot. The relative cool of the jungle was inviting despite the lurking presence of just about anything he could imagine and one or two things besides. Not only that, but it would keep him hidden from Malachi and what he intended was not for the wizard's eyes.

Wading through clinging vegetation for a while brought him to an area of sparser growth beneath a tree with low-hanging green fruit. Some of it was hard, but most of it yielded soft and succulent yellow flesh to his bite. Regardless, he ate until he felt satiated, then had half a dozen more as a precaution against future deprivation.

Wiping his lips with the back of his hand, he sat on the grassy floor and undid Ant's pouch from his belt. When he opened it and peered inside, all he could see was fine grey dust. Shaking it about provoked no response. Poking it only caked his sticky fingers with dirt. Maybe if he poured it out onto the ground, it might jump back into the bag. What if it didn't? Then he'd be scraping it up himself together with all kinds of rubbish.

It was very disappointing. Since the wasp attack, he'd been wondering what else it could do. There wasn't much point to it as a defensive weapon if he had no certainty of its capabilities. 'Come on, you little bag of tricks,' he whispered, conscious that he was talking to a pile of earth in a bag. 'Give me a sign that you're still alive.'

The thought occurred that this might have been a one-off spell. Something that Ant had created to cope with a single emergency, which was now past. It was doubly disappointing. The jungle around here undoubtedly held worse dangers than wasps, and it would have been nice to have protection. Just as satisfying would be the possession of some magic that Malachi was blissfully unaware of. His performance in claiming responsibility for killing the wasps was testament to the man's overblown ego. Anything that might prick that pompous bubble was worth having.

The air was fresh and wholesome here, away from Malachi's looming presence. Come to think of it, he felt better now than he had in a very long time. The heavy-headed befuddlement that was the result of constant and copious licker intake had lifted. His belly had shrunk to what might be considered a reasonable size, even to Petra's critical eye. She would be incandescent at his absence, convinced that he was lying inebriate in some tavern. She couldn't be blamed for that assumption; in truth, it had been his intention to engage in a few days of serious social drinking once he'd answered the King's invitation. Instead, he'd been whisked off on the ship and subjected to ridiculous deprivation.

It had to be Malachi's doing. Manipulation was his trademark, after all. His words burrowed deep into your head like a worm into an apple. That wife of his was even worse, though. It would have been so much better if Malachi's suggestion had been adopted, and Ant accompanied him on this fruitless trek, leaving the two sorcerers to each other's company. Come to think of it, Malachi usually got his way, so perhaps it had been decided like this in the first place and a little pretence enacted to keep him and Ant guessing until it was too late.

Apart from the worry he was causing Petra, being in a forest on his own was familiar and comforting. Whatever Malachi might think, there wasn't any useful purpose in having him tag along on this quest. His fighting days were long behind him. Even when he was at his peak, it was his speed off the mark that was his most useful weapon in getting him away from trouble. Nowadays, his legs could carry him only a few paces before they had to pause to allow his breath to catch up. It would be best to leave Malachi to it while he headed north, back to where they'd started from.

His quiet contemplation was interrupted by a flash of bright green caused by the semi-visible snake curled around a branch uncomfortably close to his eyes, pulling back its head into a position ready to strike.

18

Ant pinned the strand of vine into the sand with a stick then began to inscribe a circle, keeping it taught.

'Wait.' Lone held out her hands. 'Give it to me. I need to do it. You stand back and issue instructions.'

'It only seems to work if I do it.' He allowed the improvised string and stick arrangement to be taken from him, but something inside him made him reluctant to give it up. Teaching Malachi had felt very different and, anyway, all of the many vedhanas he'd constructed had remained only patterns on the ground. None of them had shown any signs of life.

She was precise, deft, and quick to follow his orders. It was as if she'd been creating this complex pattern all her life. He helped her to find and place stones at the points of intersection to complete the design. She stood back, eyes on her handiwork. 'Now what happens?' she asked.

'It lights up. Sometimes it's hard to see in full sunlight.'

'How long does it take?'

'No time at all, usually. For me, that is. Malachi hasn't managed to get one to work yet.'

'So he tells me. Is there anything else you have to do or is it only the pattern? Any incantations? Spells? Energies that have to be released? What do you feel inside when you activate a vedhana?'

'There's a constriction here.' Ant placed his hands on his chest. 'I let it squash my heart a little and then breathe it away slowly. That's the best I can describe it.'

Lone sat cross-legged next to the pattern, eyes closed, one hand between her breasts and the other on her thigh. She was completely still for several moments, then Ant detected the rise and fall of her chest had deepened. Several breaths later, she was gasping in mouthfuls of air and expelling them with a whooshing sound. The first tendrils of flickering light began to play around the edge of the circle she had inscribed in the sand. The ghostly flames quickly spread until the whole pattern was covered.

'I see what you mean.' Lone opened her eyes. 'It needs some fire to get it going. No wonder Malachi couldn't manage it. He has plenty of knowledge, but I fear he'll never have enough fire. There, my very first vedhana. I have to thank you, Ant, for showing me how. Now it's only right for you to receive my gift in return. What is your heart's desire?'

You. Your attention. Your praise. Your respect. Your love. Your body next to mine. My body intimate with yours. Our bodies rocking gently in a passionate embrace. He took a deep breath. 'My mother. I want to see my mother again.'

'I thought your mother was dead.'

'My birth mother is, but my actual mother, the one who nurtured me, was sent away by my father. It's her that I miss.'

'Didn't you try to find her?'

'My father forbade it. I once saw her in Gort, but my fear of what my father would do to me prevented me from speaking to her. By the time I gained enough courage, she was gone.'

'You were young. You couldn't have done any more.'

'But I'm not young anymore and I could have tried to find her. Instead, I spent my time learning so that I could take revenge on the old King.'

'Things have a habit of getting in the way of what we really want and need. Clarity is a valuable resource. Being able to see through the self-imposed veils of confusion is a difficult skill. Now that you truly know what you want, life will be easier. Keep your goals uppermost in your mind at all times and don't be distracted by trivia.'

Ant found his eyes staring down at the sand. 'I will,' he said. 'But first, we have to rescue Cassie and Bee.'

He looked up to see Lone standing uncomfortably close to him. 'See what I mean? You've already lost focus and are back to serving the will of others instead of doing what's right for you.'

'But we have to find Tyrant and Malachi and the girls.'

'If that's now your true heart's desire, then I say go for it. I'd be concerned that you're changing your mind a bit too often and that might be a sign that none of the things is what you really want deep down.' Her eyes widened. 'If I'd had to guess what you really wanted based on what I've seen, then I would have said that it was me that you desired.'

Ant's head flared and his mouth froze.

'You're a big boy now. Have the courage to choose what you really want from now on.' She brushed his lips with hers, then stepped back, turned, and walked into the vedhana. The lights intensified and when they dimmed, she was gone.

19

A gust of gritty wind stung Tyrant's face, and the snake was swept to the ground and slithered away. The shimmering stream of particles returned to hover around the pouch, gradually forming into a knee-high human figure. One that looked familiar.

'Ant?'

The head nodded, and the mouth began to form soundless words.

'I can't hear you.'

The tiny figure beckoned and set off towards the sea. Tyrant followed.

When they cleared the trees and reached the sand, Little Ant pointed down the coast, shaking his dust-formed arm in a gesture of urgency.

'Go this way?'

Little Ant nodded vigorously.

'And hurry?'

Another nod, then the tiny man disappeared.

'What's going on?' Malachi's voice boomed in his ear.

Tyrant flinched and swung around to face the wizard.

'What's in the pouch?'

'Some things I've been collecting for Petra. You know, seashells and decorative twigs. That sort of thing.'

'Decorative twigs?' Malachi laughed.

Tyrant took the bag from his belt. The weight of it felt as if Ant had managed to change to dust and return before Malachi had seen him. He held out the pouch. 'Have a look. There's lots of good stuff in here. Petra will be very happy when I bring it home.'

Malachi looked at the bag as if were something that Tyrant had squeezed out of his backside. His eyes moved to the sand beneath his feet, where an arrow had been clearly marked with the head pointing in the direction that Ant had indicated.

'What do you make of this?' Malachi pointed at the drawing in the sand.

'I was going to ask you,' Tyrant replied. 'Maybe it's a message. We should follow it.'

'Unlikely,' Malachi said. 'But it does beg the question of who drew it and why. Seems we're not alone here.'

'It suddenly appeared,' Tyrant blurted. 'Before my very eyes. Had to be magic. I think it was Ant trying to guide us.'

'Magic, you say? More likely to be witchcraft. I know Ant and this isn't something he could do. On the other hand, Lone is perfectly capable of moving things at a distance. If it appeared before your very eyes, then it must be Lone.'

'And we should follow?'

'Without delay. I wouldn't want to keep her waiting. Perhaps she has already retrieved the young ladies and is waiting to take us home.'

Tyrant set off down the beach at a determined pace. From the look on the face of miniature Ant, he was certain that Malachi's optimism was unfounded.

'She's a remarkable woman,' Malachi said. 'Amazingly resourceful.'

Tyrant would have used other words like cunning, conniving, dangerous, frightening, implacable, and remorseless to create a better description, but didn't feel that sharing these with Malachi would be productive. At least they were heading in what he hoped was the right direction. 'She is very special,' he replied. 'How did you come to marry her?'

Malachi gave him a look that made him wish he'd minded his own business, but it softened slightly as he spoke. 'Now that is a story,' Malachi said. 'It began a long time ago in a small village south of Gort.'

20

'I had taken up residence in Spelt, a sizeable habitation of several hundred which lay a day's ride south of Gort. Over time, I gained a reputation for wise counsel and arbitration, assisting with disputes mainly over the ownership of land and livestock.'

Malachi's story began in a way that told Tyrant it would not be short. He'd asked the question, though, and Malachi was entitled to take whatever time he needed to answer. They were plodding down the shoreline together, and he had nothing better to occupy his time than to listen to the wizard drone on. As long as he wasn't going to be asked to recall any details, he could let the noise buzz around his ears, like the swishing of the ocean and the rustling of the forest. 'Why there? I thought you would have lived close to the seat of power in Gort,' he asked by way of encouragement.

'I spent all my life in Gort right up until the time my master was taken and I had to flee. That's why I lived in Spelt.'

'You were learning wizardry and witchcraft in Gort? Right under the King's nose? Wasn't that bound to end badly?'

'My master taught us awareness. Awareness of self and awareness that we are part of a single consciousness. There were twelve of us; I was, by many years, the youngest. When the soldiers came, they took Master and the others, but ignored me. I'm ashamed to say that I made myself invisible to save my own skin.'

'So you did learn magic.' Tyrant was finding the account more interesting than he'd been expecting. 'Why didn't your master use it on the soldiers?'

'He forbade any act of resistance, seeking to persuade the King that we posed no threat to him. It was the right strategy. The strategy of a sane and wise man.'

'It didn't work, did it?'

'No, we were not dealing with the sane or the wise, but a crazed and vindictive ruler who had them cut to pieces as soon as they were inside the castle walls. To my eternal regret, I watched from a safe distance but did nothing.'

'I don't get it,' Tyrant said. 'I've seen what you can do to people. Twelve more like you would surely be able to defend themselves.'

'Master accepted his fate and urged the rest of us to do the same. All obeyed except for me. I neither obeyed nor resisted. I fled.'

Avoiding being brutally murdered seemed the sensible option to take, if available. The look on Malachi's face seemed to indicate that the wizard was less sure that it was. Though it could be the result of the gathering gloom casting deeper shadows into the lines on his face.

The stars were beginning to appear. Smudges of powdery light were establishing themselves as the primary source of illumination now that the sun had fallen into the sea and been extinguished. 'OK, I get it,' Tyrant said. 'You ran off to Spelt and there you met Lone, fell in love, and married her.' Tyrant stopped walking and sank down into the rapidly cooling sand whose insect denizens were performing a celebratory dance to welcome the onset of night and the prospect of sucking Tyrant's blood for supper.

'We should keep going,' Malachi said. 'The message may be urgent. In fact, I'm sure that time is of the essence, otherwise she wouldn't have expended such a large amount of her energy to deliver it.'

Tyrant rose to his feet. The dancing changed to desperate jumping as the fleas realised their disappointment. 'Am I right?'

'Almost never.' Malachi chuckled. 'Right about what?'

'Lone. You met her in Spelt.'

'That is true, though only a very small part of the story. However, we can leave it at that if you don't want to hear anything further. There are weighty issues involved here which, with respect, I doubt your capacity to assimilate even if you were willing to try.'

Tyrant had smacked more than one head because of the use of the words *with respect,* coupled with that same tone of voice. His hand twitched and his fists bunched momentarily, but that was all. Hitting Malachi, however satisfying it might feel at the time, was almost certainly the prelude to painful unpleasantness that he could do well to avoid. 'If you're referring to the way your master accepted a horrible death as a weighty issue, then you're correct. It sounds ridiculous and stupid to me. How long did you spend in the service of such an—' Tyrant was about to finish off his sentence with the word idiot. A perfectly

80

reasonable observation based on the information provided by Malachi himself. A very obvious conclusion to be drawn from the circumstances described. There was a faint glint in Malachi's eye, perhaps the result of a new star awakening in the heavens, but more likely caused by a spike of anger at the way his master was being described. '—interesting person?'

'Ten years. Master wasn't at all concerned with his own physical death because he knew it was irrelevant in the grand scheme of things. His true self, his beingness if you like, would endure, no matter what.'

'Then you've got me there. In my experience, when you're dead, you're dead. I've never seen anyone come back. Don't you think there's a possibility that your master was mistaken?'

'Not at all. The others had been studying much longer than I had and they had all embodied his teaching and were strong enough to follow his example. I wasn't.'

'There still seems little sense to it. Especially if they had the power to resist,' Tyrant said.

'Imagine that you are a leaf. A tiny leaf, one of countless numbers on a huge tree.'

'I can try,' Tyrant said, 'but I don't see the point.'

'Answer me this; what happens to a leaf?'

'It grows?'

'And then?'

'It turns brown and falls off?'

'Correct. Exactly as humans do. Grow, die, go back into the ground.'

'So there's no point at all to being alive?'

'On the contrary.' Malachi grinned. 'Tell me, what would a tree do without its leaves?'

'That's easy,' Tyrant said. 'It would surely die. Trees need leaves, even I know that.'

'So it is with humans. Individually, we are nothing. Together, we allow the tree of consciousness to exist. When a leaf falls to the ground, it is absorbed back into the soil, which feeds the roots of the tree. Don't you see what happens then? The leaf remains part of the tree. So it is with humans. Our spark of consciousness never disappears. It re-joins the wholeness, just like the leaf.'

81

Tyrant concluded he would rather remain a leaf as long as possible and what happened after he rotted away was unlikely to interest him. 'I understand what you're saying, but I don't see what it has to do with magic.'

'Understanding isn't enough, knowing is the only true state. All else is illusion. As for magic, that word covers any action that taxes the comprehension of the onlooker.'

'How can knowing you're a leaf, or a tree for that matter, allow you to strangle people without even touching them?'

'It doesn't. That particular technique is something I learned from my wife. She has a unique capacity for accessing realms of reality that are excluded from the rest of us. Lone can see invisible connections and use them to transfer energy. Compared to her, we are stumbling around with our eyes closed, thinking that it's dark while her eyes are wide open.'

'What about Ant?'

Malachi stopped walking. 'What about him?'

'I was wondering where he fitted in to all this magic business. After all, he can create vedhanas and they have to be very powerful magic if you ask me. Then there was that big thing made out of earth that buried the palace of the southern king. The way he dealt with that had to be magic. Did you teach him or is he more like Lone?'

'I taught him everything.' Malachi's voice rose in pitch. 'Everything. When I took him under my wing, he was a normal boy. By practising the things I have shown him, he has begun to access his core being. That's what has enabled him to do what he has. My teaching. My pupil.'

Malachi took a breath, then resumed the starlit walk.

Tyrant waited until he felt another question might be better received, then asked, 'That golem thing, could he or anyone else make a little one?'

'It was his father who created the golem. I doubt that Ant would either be capable or interested in repeating that folly. Those things are abominations with no feelings or intelligence and once released, there's no knowing what dreadful harm they might cause. We were fortunate that Ant managed to deactivate it so that it became a hillside of rich northern soil for Lone to grow vines in.'

Tyrant patted the pouch on his belt. Whatever was inside couldn't be a golem, then. Little Ant was something different. The realisation made him relax. It could be trusted. He was doing the right thing by following the arrow and not telling Malachi about it. 'You still haven't told me the story of how you and Lone got together.' Better to change the subject in case the wily old wizard got wind of the reason for his question about the golem.

'Over the years I lived in Spelt, the residents learned to respect my privacy and mostly left me to my work. There were occasions, however, when they sought my counsel. Lone was the subject of one such enquiry.

'Her family had arranged for her to marry a much older man, as is the custom. The ceremony took place, and all seemed well with the couple until the wedding night when the unfortunate husband died. Examination of the corpse revealed no signs that would indicate foul play. He'd apparently died of natural causes.'

'Sounds reasonable enough; why would they need to involve you in something like that?'

Malachi took a deep breath. 'Because this wasn't the first time this had happened. A year earlier, the exact same circumstances had occurred. Lone was married and her husband expired the very same day. The coincidence was deemed to be too great and the Elders of the village decided that witchcraft had to be involved.

'I was asked my opinion regarding the likelihood of her innocence and whether I could devise some form of test to determine it. They wanted confirmation that their decision was the correct one so that any recriminations from her family could be quelled.'

'I've heard that if you throw a witch into water, she will float,' Tyrant said.

'Most women, witches or not, would not only float, they would swim away.' Malachi laughed. 'Lone was brought to my house and I questioned her privately. When I asked her what had happened to her husbands, she told me she had been defending herself. Marriage was one thing, she said, but molestation was another. Anyone that tried to take her against her will was going to die in a similar manner.

'I suggested to her she'd admitted to witchcraft and that she was liable to be hanged for it. Her eyes narrowed and the intensity of the look she gave me left me in no doubt that she was immensely powerful, even at such a tender age. I knew that she'd destroy the whole village, me included, if they tried to do away with her. I'll tell you, Tyrant, that was the most terrifying moment in my life. Being confronted by such raw power was also the most exciting experience I'd ever had. That meeting changed my life. Everything I'd learned from my master was brought into a clearer perspective. She was living proof that we are more than we can ever know. My excitement overcame my fear.

'I went back to the Elders and told them that she was not to be hanged merely because of an unhappy coincidence. The deaths, I said, had been brought about by an excessive surge of lust overloading the hearts of both her bridegrooms. A diagnosis that was very nearly true. The remedy, I said, was to allow her to marry again.

'They listened to what I had to say, then pointed out that no eligible man would be willing to take the risk and that, in the absence of one, they would be best to have done with her just to be on the safe side.

'I told them that I would marry her. If I survived, they would have their confirmation. If I died, then they could carry out the hanging. After much discussion and shaking of heads, it was agreed. Lone and I were married. As you can see, I survived.'

'What happened on your wedding night?' Tyrant asked.

'Nothing. That's why I survived.'

'And since?'

'We have enjoyed a mutually beneficial arrangement. Lone gets the protection of a husband and I have had the company of a truly remarkable woman who has the ability to perceive dimensions of existence that are hidden from the rest of us.'

'And who can kill you at a distance without any weapon but her witchcraft.'

'We'll rest here for the remainder of the night. I'm getting weary. Not from the walking, but from your questions. I'm relying on them stopping when you go to sleep so that I might enjoy a brief respite, at least.

'Witchcraft is merely a way of describing something that isn't understood. Or explaining why women are intellectually superior despite all the disadvantages they suffer.'

Tyrant stretched out on the soft sand and allowed the tingle of tiny bites to lull him to sleep. In his dreams, Petra turned him to stone, stood him in the garden like a statue and spent every day berating him for abandoning her. There was nothing he could say in his defence, even if he'd been capable of speaking. His mouth was solid stone, but there were holes in his ears that meant he had to bear the full brunt of her anger.

21

Lone's words swirled around his head as he hesitated in front of the vedhana. *If the step you are about to take doesn't take you one step closer to where you want to be, then you should ask yourself why you are taking it.* Why was he hesitating? She'd gone through the portal. He had to follow.

Pepper and Col once disappeared in exactly the same manner, and then his hesitation had cost him dearly. Now he was wavering again. Tottering on the brink. Peering down into the depths. Thinking too much instead of following his instincts.

Surely, wherever Lone went was where he needed to be?

Another thought replaced this one. *Let your first action be inward.* Malachi's teaching. Throwing himself headlong in pursuit was hardly an inward move.

Recognise those moments when you give yourself away.

He forced himself to quieten, sit in the sand, and close his eyes. That felt more peaceful. Lone's absence was less of a loss and more of a relief. Clouds were lifting from his mind. The longer he sat, the greater the clarity.

She had him mesmerised. Every time she spoke, he jumped to obey. Pleasing her was his only purpose. Only in her absence could he come to this realisation. Now that she was gone, he could seek some relief.

The vedhana still beckoned, its seductive fire promising relief from the gritty sand and bright sun. She could have transported herself to a dozen locations that he knew or even to one that he was unfamiliar with. Had she wanted him with her, it was necessary for them to travel together. Perhaps he should have made that clear. Maybe she was already aware.

Then there was the reason they were here in the first place. The girls. Tyrant would do anything to protect Cassie and Bee. Malachi and Lone would remain involved only as long as they could derive some advantage. She had already seemingly abandoned the quest. Tyrant would need all the help he could get now that they had no ship, no crew, and no means of finding the girls. Lone's disappearance seemed a reasonable response to a hopeless situation.

Postponing any decision until the others arrived, he sat in the sand and closed his eyes. The redness behind his eyes changed abruptly to black. Fighting for breath, he pushed against his surroundings, no longer the soft sea air but the dark confines of burial. Chest heaving with panic, he returned to his body and forced his eyes open to the glare of the sun.

A whirlwind of sand whipped around his feet, then coalesced into a tiny likeness. 'I'm on my way,' the avatar said.

'I tried to connect,' Ant gasped.

'I know. That's why I came ahead.'

'I couldn't breathe,' Ant replied. 'It was as if I'd been buried deep underground.'

'You should remember that I'm essentially a lump of earth. I don't breathe except when I have to make sounds. Better that I come to you in future.'

'Have they found the girls?'

'No. Have you?'

'No. What happened to Malachi and Tyrant? Where have they been and what have they been doing?'

'They're here now. Ask them.' His effigy dissolved into a pile of sand.

The familiar figures of Tyrant and Malachi plodded around the edge of the jungle. Their pace quickened as they spied Ant.

'Where's the ship?' Malachi asked.

'Gone,' Ant replied.

'And the crew?'

'Dead.'

Malachi sighed. 'How did that happen?'

'Don't you want news of your wife?' Ant asked.

'Yes, of course. Where is she?' He looked around as if expecting her to materialise at the mention of her name.

'Also gone,' Ant said.

'With the ship?'

'No, through the vedhana.'

Malachi gathered his cloak around his waist and lowered himself onto the sand beside Ant. 'I would appreciate a full account rather than having to rely on your less than helpful answers. What happened?'

'First tell me what happened to you two.'

Tyrant slumped in an untidy heap close by. 'We walked a long way for nothing. Some wasps came to attack us. Not much else, really.'

'Big wasps?' Ant asked.

'Enormous scary nasty wasps,' Tyrant said.

'I produced a miasma that killed them all by combining certain chemical items about my possession. Were it not for my speed, presence of mind, and expertise, we might both have been killed,' Malachi said.

Tyrant let out a long sigh, which could have been a result of him having to relive the horrifying onslaught of the wasps.

'We encountered wasps on board the ship a day or two after we left you. They were growing in the stomach of the captain. Lone killed them all, but was unable to save the crew.'

'So who was sailing the ship?' Tyrant asked.

'Lone and I tried, but when we got out to sea, the wind and the waves made it impossible. I was swept overboard and Lone took to the small boat so that she could rescue me. That's how we arrived here.'

'So you made a vedhana and Lone used it to leave,' Malachi said.

Ant nodded. Because he'd spent so long teaching Malachi without success, he was reluctant to tell him that his wife had managed it first time. The thought of Lone being able to create portals wherever she wanted was a disturbing one. In truth, he'd been confident that her attempts would fail.

'Did she say where she was going?' Malachi asked.

Ant shook his head.

'It's going to be dark soon,' Tyrant said. 'We'll need wood for a fire. Ant and I will collect some while you light it.'

Malachi glowered suspiciously at Tyrant, then began to gather kindling from the shoreline.

As soon as they were out of sight, Tyrant took the pouch from his belt and handed it back to Ant. 'If you hadn't given me this, I'd be dead. Take no notice of Malachi. He doesn't know what saved us and I didn't think you would want me to tell him.'

'Keep it.' Ant pushed the bag back into Tyrant's hands. 'I'm not sure if I want it anymore. I think it was a mistake.'

'Not to me it isn't,' Tyrant said. 'If it weren't for your little friend here, I'd be wasp food. What is it exactly?'

'That's the problem, I'm not sure. It says that it's an avatar; that it's me. But it's not. I made it so that I'd have something to help me I could trust. I also thought that I'd be able to see and feel everything it does, but I can't. No matter how hard I try.'

'If you'd seen what it can do, then you'd try harder. Whatever is inside this pouch has wonderful capabilities.'

Ant shuddered at the prospect of having to confront his avatar. Something about it made him very nervous. On reflection, he realised that it was because he couldn't control it. That had been the one thing he'd counted on. Making something, animating some dull earth, should have put him in charge. It ought to be awaiting his commands. But it wasn't.

The fire was a crackling beacon when they returned to the darkened shore with armfuls of firewood. As the night intensified, they squatted close together in the bubble of light that separated them from the surrounding blackness. The hissing of the waves was too gentle to compete with the intensity of the insect noise from the forest. Ant occasionally detected larger shadows moving in the periphery of his vision, but neither of the others seemed to be aware of them.

'Tomorrow we take the boat across the bay to the other side. There, we can patrol the other channel and hope to intercept the kidnapper's vessel,' Malachi said.

'I can't see the point,' Ant said. 'We've lost the ship. Lone's already given up and gone home. We should do the same.'

'We're here to save the girls,' Tyrant said. 'While we still have a chance to do that we must carry on.'

'Then we're agreed,' Malachi said. 'Tomorrow at first light, we row ourselves across to the other side. We may still be in time.'

'I'll guard this channel,' Tyrant said. 'That little boat's too small for the three of us.'

'Nonsense,' Malachi said, 'it's plenty big enough.'

'Let me put it another way,' Tyrant replied. 'I'm not getting in that tiny boat and that's final. The big ship was bad enough, but going to sea in a thing like that isn't for me. Leave me here.'

Malachi looked as if he was about to launch into a threatening tirade but seemed to think better of it. After several deep breaths, he got to his feet, walked off towards the shoreline, and was lost in the darkness.

The atmosphere around the campfire lifted. It was good to have Tyrant back.

'So, what happened with the witch?' Tyrant asked.

'She killed them all. Though I can't really blame her. The crew were being very threatening and I'd got into a fight with the captain. At first, I thought the wasps were her doing because they appeared as he was about to kill me, but they weren't. There were so many of them and they attacked so quickly. It was awful.'

'Why didn't she kill the wasps and leave the crew?'

'I think she was angry. I had to stand very close to her, otherwise I'd have been ripped apart like they were. She has this defensive spell that she can employ to stop anything getting near her, and I think she could have used that to protect us. What she did was extremely violent. The worst thing I have ever witnessed. The crew was torn apart. It was as if their insides had been made to burst through their skin. Horrible.'

'It sounds as if she is growing in power,' Tyrant said. 'A grim prospect for the rest of us, if that's true.'

'There's something else.' Ant lowered his voice. 'I taught her how to construct a vedhana. She made this one and then used it herself. Apart from myself, only my father and certain monks have been able to do that. Malachi has tried and tried, as have many others. The pattern is not complex, but the activation process seems to depend on the person creating it.'

'Then she is even more powerful than I thought. She could be laying waste to my home as we speak. Petra could be in deadly danger. That witch has always had it in for me, but for some reason, hasn't been able to harm me directly. Now her revenge could have no limits.'

'I understand your concern about Petra, but my impression is that she has more pressing matters to attend to. Maybe the King is the one who should be worried?'

'No matter.' Tyrant stood up. 'I'm going to check that things are well at home. I can use the vedhana and be back before first light.'

Ant was suddenly aware that the vague shadows he'd been seeing had solidified into hulking solidity. The creatures were taller and bulkier than Tyrant, ape-like and covered with long grey hair. Tyrant struck out at the nearest one, but his punch had no visible effect. As he bent to retrieve his sword, another grey ape swung a large club and felled him with a savage blow to the head.

Arms grabbed Ant. He wriggled and fought, but every movement brought a mind-numbing slap to his head. It was impossible to resist being picked up and slung over a brawny shoulder. The fire erupted in a brilliant flash and several greys were enveloped in flames. Ant's captor crashed through the jungle, smashing down trees and bushes as he went. Behind them, angry bellows were mixed with screams of pain.

22

Tyrant's head hurt. It was a dull residual pain reminiscent of over-indulgence, but lacking the mind-numbing qualities of Petra's best licker. Rolling on to his back gave him a view of a lattice of bamboo between him and the mercifully dull grey sky.

Ant was sitting with his back resting on the wall of the cage, his face ashen and his eyes staring out of sunken hollows. At first glance, Tyrant feared he was dead.

Outside, there were a dozen of the great grey beasts busying themselves while holding an uncanny silence. One of them met Tyrant's gaze with a chilling implacability.

'I thought you'd never wake up,' Ant said.

'Well, I have, and it's time to make these apes suffer for what they did to us. Where's Malachi?'

'I don't know. When the greys attacked, there was a flash of light and he disappeared. I hope he followed us here and is planning a rescue.'

'That wouldn't be the Malachi I know, then. Don't get your hopes up. I doubt the possibility even entered his mind. He'll be keeping well away from anything that might put his precious skin in danger. We don't need him, anyway. We've got Little Ant.'

'Don't call it that; I don't like it.'

Tyrant felt the pouch tied to his belt. It was empty. 'Where is he?'

'I thought you had it.'

'I did, but now he's out of his bag, he could be anywhere.'

Ant frowned. 'Don't keep calling it a he. It's not a person, it's not me.'

'Then what is it?'

'It's a monster that leeches off my energy but gives nothing back. Like now. Where was it when we needed it? Why didn't it warn us of the greys? Why didn't it help us when we were attacked?' Ant sighed. 'I only wanted something I could rely on. Something I could trust. It was a big mistake.'

'You don't know that for sure. Give him a chance. Come on, Ant, what's bothering you? I know you've been tired all along and it might well be that the avatar thing is doing that, but there's something else, isn't there?'

'You'd be tired if you'd fallen into the sea and nearly drowned.'

'But you didn't. Lone saved you. That doesn't sound like something she would do unless she wanted something in return.'

Tyrant watched Ant's face regain some colour and his breathing become ragged. 'I don't know what happened. That's what's so terrible. I was in the water for a very long time. All night, perhaps. It felt as if I drowned. Something awful happened to me. I only remember it as if it were a dream, but it felt as if she and I made love. That's what revived me.' Ant's face was suffused with red now and his eyes were as wide as if he were staring down a snake. Tyrant's stomach churned in response to the boy's distress.

'I doubt that happened. From what I know of that witch, I don't believe that any man who got that close would survive the experience. She almost certainly tricked you into believing it to make you more susceptible to her wishes.'

'On the contrary, she denied that it ever happened. She said that some sea creature saved me and brought me to the boat.'

'Then forget it, Ant. Or put it down to wishful thinking. Our minds can play tricks at the best of times. If you were in the sea all that time, it's no wonder you experienced hallucinations. I've seen the way you look at her.'

'It doesn't matter, anyway. I've been watching these greys and they're making a long fire pit.'

'Then they must be expecting colder weather.' Tyrant smiled in an attempt to raise Ant's flagging spirits.

'You know that's not true. They're going to cook us and eat us and that will be the end of us.'

'They might think they are, but they're going to get a nasty shock. I was taken unawares last night, but I'm ready for them now. The next one to open that door will find out what it means to mess with Tyrant. I can see where they left my sword. Once I get hold of that and start chopping off limbs, they'll soon learn not to bother us again. I might even have one of them for breakfast; I'm feeling very hungry.'

He was rewarded with a faint smile that played around Ant's features and a corresponding brightening of his eyes.

As if in response, one of the greys began to untangle the web of bindings that secured the door to the cage. It wasn't the largest of them, nor was it the smallest. No matter, it was as good a start as any. Rising slowly to his feet, he braced himself in readiness. The key to success was going to be speed and determination. He knew what to do. Aim beyond the actual point of impact. Act as if he was going to run right through the target. Smash it out of the way, then continue running out of the cage and grab his sword. His hand curled with the anticipation of wielding his weapon and dealing deadly retribution for his treatment. Another opportunity to enhance his already formidable reputation. He licked his lips in anticipation.

The grey took an age to pick at the knots and all the while Tyrant's rage was being allowed to simmer nicely. When the door was finally flung open, he was good and ready. Digging his toes into the dirt, he sprinted forward, covering the few paces to his assailant in no time at all, but thrusting every jot of power he had into every stride. His shoulder smashed into the grey's chest with the full force of his weight behind it. The grey stood firm. It was like hitting a column of rock. Tyrant's shoulder blossomed into pain and his legs buckled beneath him. He found himself sliding down his opponent's body much as a cow pat might after being flung at a wall.

Despite all the pain he was feeling, it was disappointment that hurt the most.

23

Bee bounded up the steps and burst onto the sunlit deck. One crewman was on the tiller, and two others were tidying up. There was no sign of Jake, the youngest one, who had smiled and winked at her. Cassie was already up, standing by the rail, observing the scene with that face of hers that looked as if she was being assaulted by a very bad smell.

'You've pulled that face so often I'm afraid it's stuck,' Bee said.

'What face? I have no idea what you're babbling on about.'

'Your *everything's too awful for words* face. The look of distaste that you've been wearing ever since Cuthbert became king. The *I'm so superior to everyone else* expression—'

'Shut up. I'm so tired of your whining, Bee. I wish you'd not come on this trip at all. It was stupid of me to invite you, thinking that I was being kind. Instead, all you ever do is whinge and moan about how I behave. I'm the Queen. I can behave how I want and don't you forget it.'

'There's nothing stopping you being my sister for a change. What happened to your sense of adventure? Have you forgotten all the fun we used to have?'

'If you mean traipsing around with Tyrant, then that wasn't anyone's idea of fun. We were cold, tired, hungry, and in deadly danger most of the time. How can you prefer that to the nice, comfortable surroundings of the palace? Don't you like being well fed and kept safe?'

'That's another thing.' Bee laughed. 'We're a bit too well fed, if you ask me. Have you looked at yourself lately? You've put on a lot of weight.'

'Nonsense, I was too scrawny before, everyone said so. Now I'm more normal. Cuthbert likes me with a bit of meat on my bones.'

'He just wants you to be as fat as he is, so he doesn't look quite so gross.'

'Are you criticising the King? You'd better not be 'cos that's treason and you can be hanged for it.'

'Hang me then. It'll at least save me from watching my sister turn into a pig.'

Cassie reached out, grabbed Bee's hair, and tugged hard. The sudden pain made her lash out with her fist. Cassie staggered backwards clutching her nose, almost toppling into the river. Blood began to drip off her chin, diluted by the tears streaming down her face.

'Sorry,' Bee said, 'I didn't mean it. You shouldn't have pulled my hair, though.'

'You deserved it.' Cassie paused her sobbing to allow a few words to come out. 'You're a horrible mean girl and I hate you.'

'I've said I'm sorry and I am. You can hate me all you like, but you can't stop me being your sister and worrying about you.'

'You only care about yourself. You're jealous 'cos I'm Queen and you're only a Princess.'

'You're wrong. I'd hate to be a queen, especially if it made me as miserable as you are.'

Cassie smeared blood across her face with the back of her hand. 'I've told you, I'm not miserable. Being Queen is a serious business. There are standards to uphold and protocol to follow.'

'It's stopped bleeding,' Bee said.

'You've probably ruined my good looks forever. I bet it's broken and will never grow straight again.'

'Then you'll be famous as the queen with the wonky nose.'

'If I am, I'll make sure that you're known as the Princess with no hair.'

'Then you'll be the queen with the bitten-off ear.'

'At least I'll not be the Princess with teeny tiny tits.' Cassie laughed.

Bee felt her eyes filling up and the knot in her stomach tighten. That wasn't fair. She couldn't help having small breasts. Just because Cassie had big melons, didn't give her the right to make hurtful comments. She took a deep breath. At least Cassie had finally found something to laugh about at long last. It might be painful, but it felt as if she had her sister back, at least for a few moments. 'Some men prefer small bosoms,' she countered.

'Only the desperate ones.' Cassie was still smiling; the venom had gone from the conversation.

'They're the best sort.' Bee grabbed her sister and held on tight. The ice melted and Bee was transported to a windswept mountain where they clung together for warmth.

After the long, glorious, joyful hug, Bee stared into her sister's eyes. The old Cassie was in there, of course she was. It had needed a smack on the nose to entice her out, though. 'I'm glad we came,' she said, and meant it.

'I'm not,' Cassie said. 'It's horribly smelly and uncomfortable on this boat. The crew is vile and the scenery is so boring. Trees and bushes day after day. Then there's the sleeping arrangements. I hate that cramped dark hole they put us in. And not even a proper bed.'

'I like my hammock,' Bee said. 'I'm thinking of having one instead of my bed when I get home. It's so swingy and comfortable.'

'Until you fall out,' Cassie said.

'Even falling out isn't so bad. Anyway, how would you know? You never fall out.'

'That's because I cling on tight instead of sleeping.'

'You should share mine, Cassie. It'll be even more comfortable with two of us and we can stop each other from falling out.'

'Then we'd both fall out. I know you too well. You only want me so you have something soft to land on when you do.'

Bee's heart felt lighter than it had in months. Maybe this silly trip was a good thing after all.

The youngest member of the crew poked his head out of a hatch, then clambered onto the deck. 'Oh look,' Bee said, 'there's Finn. Don't you think he's cute?'

'He's got no teeth,' Cassie said.

'Yes, he has. He's got lots of teeth.'

'Most of his teeth are missing and what's left are black and mouldy. When he smiles at me it makes me shudder.'

'Then don't look. Anyway, he's not smiling at you. It's me he likes.'

'You're more than welcome.' Cassie laughed. 'Don't forget you're a Princess, though. You can't marry a deckhand unless he's a prince.'

'I wasn't thinking of marrying him,' Bee whispered, and her remark brought whoops of laughter from her sister.

'I should hope not with teeth like that,' Cassie giggled in reply. 'It's not his teeth I'm interested in.'

24

It was always the same with boys. Things would be progressing gently and pleasurably when they'd suddenly grit their teeth, pull a face, and that would be that. Finn had been no exception. Still, Bee thought, it had been better than nothing and perhaps he'd have a bit more stamina next time.

'They'll be wondering where I am,' Finn said.

'Let them. I'm in charge of this boat 'cos I'm the Princess. You all have to do my bidding.'

'I might get into trouble, though.'

'You'll be in big trouble if you try to get out of this hammock.' She gave his balls a gentle squeeze to emphasise her point. 'A gentleman always engages in conversation with his lady afterwards. You do want to be a gentleman, don't you, Finn?'

'Yes.'

'Then tell me all about yourself.'

'There's nothing much to tell. I've been mostly sailing ships all my life.'

'Then you must have been to some interesting places,' Bee said.

'Not really; this is the first long voyage I've been on. Nobody bothers with this river; it's too dangerous. I'll be glad when we get back to Kish.'

'Is that where we're going?'

'Yes, of course it is.'

'Why would the King want to send us there?'

'I'm not allowed to say anything,' Finn said. 'Not even where we're going.'

'Yes, you are. I command you to. Don't forget I'm the Princess and my sister is the Queen. Apart from the King himself, we're the most important people in the world. You have to tell me everything or the King will have you punished.'

'I don't answer to your King,' Finn said. 'He's not my King and has no power over me or anyone else on Kish.'

'I beg your pardon, but the King is in charge of the whole world, including Kish. You could get in a lot of trouble if you say anything different.'

'He might think he is, but he's not.' Finn's eyes were wide and staring, as if he were worried that someone else might be sharing the cramped space of Bee's tiny quarters. 'I shouldn't have said that. We were told not to speak to you at all. Maybe we should stop doing this; I might get into awful trouble if they find out.'

'You'll be in even bigger trouble if you disobey the commands of a Princess.' Bee laughed.

'Even so, I should really keep my head down for a while at least,' Finn replied.

'That's the least you can do,' Bee said. 'And this time, don't be in so much of a hurry. Soft and slow and gentle. I don't like to be rushed.'

25

The atmosphere on deck changed abruptly. Amiable conversations between crew members suddenly stopped. Work was carried out more vigorously. Bee felt it as a sudden icy blast that cut off her account of Finn's ministrations in mid-flow. Cassie could obviously feel it, too. She looked apprehensively over Bee's shoulder.

Bee turned to see the head and shoulders of the man they knew as Gil appear through a hatchway. He was in charge and everyone was scared of him. From a distance, he looked like a young man. His body was lithe and well-muscled, his skin taut and darkly tanned, his hair lustrous, long and black.

On close inspection, though, there was something very odd about his face. Bee likened it to a porcelain doll because no part of it moved. There were no lines or wrinkles; it was as if it had been cast in marble.

Gil strode over to greet the girls. He was dressed in a remarkable tunic, and trousers coloured various shades of brown and green randomly distributed in no discernible pattern. At his side, he wore a thin sword with a golden pommel carved into the shape of a bull. Bee suppressed a shudder as he approached.

'I trust you have spent a comfortable night,' he said.

'Yes, thank you,' Cassie replied. 'How much further do we have to travel?'

'Not too far, be patient. As I told you both, this journey is for your own good. To keep you both safe.'

'Where exactly are we going?' Bee asked.

'That's not something you need to concern yourselves with, my dears. Leave all the arrangements to me and enjoy the voyage.'

'Why are we going to Kish?' Cassie asked. Bee felt her face glowing red. That wasn't something to be asking Gil. Silly Cassie, she shouldn't have been told. Bee thought of Finn and what Gil might do if he suspected the source of their information.

'What makes you think we're going there?' Gil's face remained impassive, but his eyes had taken on a new intensity.

'It's a guess,' Bee said. 'We were having a wager about where we were heading and Cassie made up this place called Kish. It's not real, is it?'

'Where did you hear about it?' Gil asked.

'Like she said, I made it up. I called it Fish at first, but Kish sounded better,' Cassie said.

'There's loads of fish in the sea,' Bee said. 'I think it's a stupid name. I bet we're going to Pumpkin Land. Are we?'

Gil ignored her prattling attempts to distract and stared hard at her sister. 'You must have heard the name from someone. Tell me who.'

Cassie met Bee's warning glance and her cheeks bloomed red. 'Maybe it was something one of the crew said,' she replied.

Bee wished she could have clamped her hands over Cassie's mouth before she'd opened it. Thrown her into the river, even. It was alright for her; she didn't particularly care for Finn. For Bee, though, he was the only thing that made this boring journey even remotely bearable.

'Which one?' Gil's voice was deep and coercive.

'She can't remember, can you, Cassie?'

Cassie looked confused for an instant, then seemed to pick up on Bee's intent.

'No, that's right. Could have been any of them. Or maybe even something you said, Gil.'

Gil leaned over the gunwale and looked down into the water. 'Come over here. Tell me what you see.'

'Water,' Cassie replied.

'Look harder,' Gil said.

Bee caught a fleeting glimpse of something dark below the surface. Something large and ominous. 'I saw it. A big long shape. Is it a big fish? Can we catch it for dinner?'

'It's not a fish and it's more likely to have you for dinner. The ancients called them saltwater crocodiles. They're bigger than you are and very fierce. If you went into the water now, you'd be gobbled up. Eaten alive. No question.' He grabbed Cassie by her waist and dangled her over the side of the boat.

'Let her go,' Bee shouted. 'She's the Queen. The King will have you hanged when he hears what you've done.'

'Who told you about Kish?' Gil asked. 'Tell me or I'll throw her overboard.'

Cassie was screaming for help, but none of the crew so much as looked up from their tasks. Bee began to beat at Gil with her fists, but he didn't flinch. His skin felt like rock beneath her flailing hands.

'It wasn't anybody,' Bee shouted. 'We just heard it generally. They was just talking about home, I suppose. Can't be any harm in that, can there?'

He deposited the kicking and screaming Cassie onto the deck and stood over her, hands on hips. 'It was always going to come to this at some point,' he said. 'Look over there, both of you. Stop shouting and tell me what you can see.'

'Trees and bushes,' Bee answered, relieved at being able to give an answer that wasn't going to result in her sister's immediate death.

'Jungle,' Cassie said as she sobbed.

'What do you imagine lives in that jungle?' Gil asked.

'Snakes?' Bee suggested.

'Creepy crawlies,' Cassie replied in a soft voice and remained sitting on the deck.

'Both sides of this river are inhabited by the most fearsome savages. Nobody who goes into that jungle ever comes out alive. The Grey Ghosts are everywhere. They creep up behind you, bash your head in, and eat you. But don't worry; they cook you first. They might be savages, but they at least know how to prepare meat.' Gil laughed as if he found the prospect of being eaten a humorous one. 'So, if you jump in the water, the crocodiles will get you. If for some reason they don't, you'll be eaten by the Grey Ghosts. Do you know why I'm telling you this?'

'To scare us?' Cassie whispered.

'I'm telling you because I need you both to understand that there is no escape. You will stay on board this ship and cause no trouble, otherwise I'll kill you myself.'

'But you said that we had to come with you so that we'd be safe. That Cuthbert had asked you to look after us,' Bee said.

Gil shrugged his shoulders. 'I lied,' he said.

'What are you going to do with us?' Cassie asked.

'Nothing,' Gil answered. 'At least not for the present.'

'The King will find out what you've done and then you'll be in trouble,' Bee said. 'He'll send an army after you. He won't rest until you're dead and we're both safe.'

'I hope he does. My only worry is that he cares little for either of you. I'm hoping he'll at least take your abduction as a personal insult and retaliate with everything he's got.'

'He'll send Tyrant,' Bee said. 'Then you'd better watch out. Tyrant is the greatest warrior that ever lived.'

'If Tyrant is the best he can do, then I pity him. I'd prefer it if your King mobilises his whole army and sets off in pursuit. I'm going to kill him, and it will be easier to do that if I can entice him away from his palace. Yes, my dears, we're going to the wonderful island of Kish and I've made sure that your King knows exactly where you are going so he can come and get you. As for Tyrant, I have a very old score to settle with him and would relish the opportunity to meet him again.'

26

Cassie was too frightened to sleep alone, so they crammed head to tail in Bee's hammock. Bee had her arms around her sister's legs, which were still trembling. 'Don't be scared,' Bee whispered. 'We've been in worse situations. Cuthbert will see to it that we're rescued unharmed.'

'I can't think of one,' Cassie hissed in the darkness.

'There was the time that the big crazy man had hold of me and was smashing everyone's head in with a mace,' Bee replied.

'Tyrant shot him in the eye with my bow,' Cassie said, 'but he's not here now to save our hides.'

'Then there was the time those horrible men came to Petra's house, and you made them that poison stew.'

'Tyrant came back and killed them both. What's the chance of that happening this time?'

Bee rested her head on Cassie's feet. 'Every chance, if you ask me. As soon as he hears we're in trouble, he'll be after us like a shot.'

'He's got a bit fat for rescuing, don't you think?'

'Never,' Bee said. 'What he's lost in speed, he makes up for with guile and experience. At least that's what he told me the last time he was in Gort.'

'I'm worried about Gil. There's something not right about him.'

'You mean his face? He's what people call a Money. Looks alright at a distance, but close up, he's really horrible.'

'You are funny,' Cassie said. 'Why would you say he looked like money? That's silly.'

'It's an expression; Mona uses it all the time. Someone who looks attractive until they get close. Like money, I suppose. Or things that look like money until you examine them more closely.'

'And they turn out to be stones rather than coins?'

'Exactly,' Bee said. 'Like Gil's face. Made out of stone rather than flesh and blood. How do you think he got like that?'

'I have no idea, but it stops anyone from reading his expression and being able to tell when he's lying.'

'I can tell when he's lying,' Bee said.

'How do you do that? His face is totally expressionless.'

'Watch his lips.'

'How does that help?'

'If they're moving, then he's lying.'

Cassie's tremors intensified for a few moments as they transformed from fear to suppressed laughter. 'You're such a laugh, Bee. I'm glad I've got you.'

***

Bee managed to survive the night without the pair of them falling out of the hammock, though there were a few close runs. Cassie, for her part, seemed to sleep well judging from the snores that made Bee grateful their heads were at opposite ends. Cracks of sunlight were making the dust motes dance, and she could smell cooking and hear things being dragged about the deck above.

Before she could ease herself out of the hammock, the door of the cabin flew open and a gruff voice told them they were wanted on deck. Cassie sat up suddenly and Bee was ejected by the sudden shift in weight. Her sister joined her on the deck with a thud. They threw some clothes on and stumbled up the ladder into the harsh light. Gil was standing, arms folded, as if he was waiting for them.

'Good morning, or should I say good afternoon? You royals sure know how to lie in bed while the rest of us have to work.'

'What do you want?' Bee asked, rubbing her eyes and wondering if there was any breakfast going. Even gruel would be better than nothing.

'I have a little demonstration for you both. Something that will, I hope, convince you of the need to behave yourselves and obey my every command as if your lives depend on it. Which, of course, they do.' Gil strode over to the bow and dragged a large piece of sackcloth aside to reveal a strange device mounted on the deck. The thing was made of grey metal and had a long tube that protruded from the front.

'What's that?' Bee asked.

'That, my dear, is an ancient and magical device known as a cannon. I thought it might be instructional for you both to witness its capabilities.' He turned to a crew member. 'Launch the boat,' he commanded.

Bee watched with her heart beating uncomfortably fast as Finn clambered over the side, sat in the little rowing boat, and began to move

106

downstream, away from the ship. What was going to happen? Was Finn in danger? She looked hard at the contraption on the deck that Gil was now attending. He was looking intently in the direction the tube was pointing and suddenly Bee realised what was going to happen. This had to be some kind of catapult designed to launch the grey tube. Finn had been sent to retrieve the projectile after it had been fired.

The tiny boat was dwindling from sight, almost lost round the bend in the river. Bee became anxious that they were going to leave Finn behind.

Three hard bangs sounded. So close together that they almost merged into one horrendous sound that slapped at her chest so hard she almost fell backwards. The tube stayed where it was. This was a surprise and a relief until she switched her attention to Finn and his boat. A column of water was obscuring her view of her friend. When it fell back into the river, the boat, and Finn, were gone. All that remained to signify their presence were some shards of floating debris.

Gil let out a series of exultant whoops. 'There you go!' he screamed. 'What a great shot. Right on the money. Perfect.'

Bee's ears were ringing. Her brain had frozen, and she stood unable to move or speak. Finn was dead; that much she understood, though how and why, there was no reasoning. She grabbed hold of Cassie and the two of them sobbed out their fear in unison.

'Did you see that?'

Bee realised that Gil was speaking to them. 'Yes,' she replied. 'What have you done?'

'Shown you my power,' Gil leered. 'It was worth sacrificing a boat to demonstrate to you both what will happen to anyone who comes to rescue you. I can kill an entire army with my cannon. Nobody can withstand my power.'

'What about Finn?' Bee said.

'A lesson for this bunch of idiots. It's what will happen to any of them if they so much as say a single word to either of you in future.'

'So you killed him?' Bee said.

'Let that be a lesson to you as well. No more fraternising. I won't allow it.'

'I'll get you for that,' Bee said. 'I'll not forget what you've done. You'll regret it. I'll make you sorry you ever set eyes on me, you alabaster-faced freak.'

'Oh dear, you've really got me worried.' Gil bared his teeth, but the attempted grin failed to spread anywhere else on his features. Then his face changed back to normal and his eyes widened. 'There are worse things I can do to you than shoot you with a cannon. That death is a quick and easy one. Watch your tongue or you'll soon wish you had been on the boat with your friend. When your King arrives with his puny forces, I'll give you a chance to persuade him to submit and save countless lives. But only if you improve your behaviour. I demand the respect that I deserve, and I mean to have it.'

'You'll get what you deserve alright,' Bee muttered under her breath.

27

'He's dead 'cos of me,' Bee moaned into the darkness.

'He's dead 'cos of Gil. He likes killing people, you can tell by his eyes. He's a nasty man and Tyrant will make him sorry when he gets here.'

'Is he coming, though? I'm not sure he will. Maybe no one knows we're here or worse, nobody cares.'

'Course they do. It's his plan, isn't it? Entice everyone down here, then shoot that cannon thing and kill them all.'

Cassie's breath wafted softly across her cheek. After today, she needed to be at the same end as her sister, and to hell with a few bruises if they kept falling out of the hammock. 'If they come after us, he'll kill them and then us. If they don't, he'll kill us and think of another plan. Either way, we're for the chop. We're going to have to kill him before he does anything else,' Bee whispered.

'How do we do that? You've seen him; he's as quick as a bull and as strong as a snake.'

'Very funny. None of that matters if we poison him. Like you did the stew at Petra's house.'

'I'd need those special plants to do that, and I bet there aren't any on this ship,' Cassie replied.

'Then we have to nip off the boat and gather some when he's not looking.'

'Now you're talking daft. It's a long way to the shore and there's lots of river monsters waiting to gobble us up.'

Bee let out a long breath. 'And you believe that, do you? Are you telling me that everything Gil says is a lie apart from that? He's making it all up just to frighten us. I bet those big shapes are very friendly fish that like to help people.'

'Even if we got to the shore, there's those ghosty things that cook you and eat you,' Cassie said.

'More lies. What Gil said was so stupid, I nearly laughed in his face when he said it. Nobody ever gets out alive, he said. Then how does he know about it, eh? Who told him if they're all dead? It's obvious it's a lie. He must think we're stupid.'

'Neither of us can swim, though,' Cassie said.

'Good point. Though it can't be that hard, can it?'

'Bit too late to find out it is when you're under the water and can't breathe.'

'Pity Finn took the little boat or we could have used that,' Bee said. 'What do you think happened to him?'

'There was a big splash where he was and then he was gone. And so was the boat.'

'Maybe he dived overboard in the nick of time and swam to the shore. Underwater. He's a sailor and I bet he's a good swimmer. He was good at holding his breath too.' Bee felt another tear emerge. Her eyes knew that Finn was dead even if she didn't want to think it.

Cassie went silent and held her tight. The hammock swayed menacingly, but they managed to lie perfectly still until it regained some sort of equilibrium.

'We need to think of something,' Bee whispered, then allowed herself to fall asleep.

28

Tyrant hit the Grey with the speed and power of an angry bull. Ant was on his feet, ready to run out of the cage and follow him to freedom. When Tyrant slumped to the ground and lay prone at the Grey's feet, Ant considered his own attack, but dismissed this notion and bent down to attend to his stricken friend.

'Must have been a bit off balance,' Tyrant said as he gasped. 'Give me a moment; I'll have him next time.'

The Grey reached down, hauled Ant to his feet by the scruff of his neck, then dragged him out of the cage. He was deposited roughly next to the now-blazing fire pit. Another Grey approached, carrying a cleaver. Ant tried to make contact. No matter how hard he tried, there was nothing for his mind to grab hold of. 'Let me go,' he screamed. His voice sounded eerie and childlike.

The nearest Grey took hold of his arms and hauled him upright, while his clothes were roughly stripped from his body. All through the process, Ant shouted at his assailants, but they completely ignored his pleas. It was as if they weren't even listening.

Rope was tied around his wrists, he was picked up, and hooked over the branch of a tree. His legs thrashed and kicked against the trunk in protest, but he had to stop moving to reduce the excruciating pain in his shoulders. It felt as if they were being wrenched from their sockets.

As a Grey approached with a knife, Ant realised what they were doing. All sensation ceased. His whole body became numb with fear. He was about to be gutted. They would slit him from chest to crotch and allow his intestines to fall to the ground. He'd seen it done with pigs, and the brutality of it had turned his stomach. Now it was his stomach that was about to be ripped from his body.

Over the shoulder of the advancing Grey, Ant saw Tyrant get to his feet. The door of the cage had been left open, and he staggered towards Ant, looking in no fit state to take anything and certainly no match for even a single one of these invincible apes. They'd do the same to Tyrant. Hang him, gut him, cook him, and eat him. What a terribly disappointing end to the both of them.

Ant thought of Lone. She'd sort these bastards out. But she was long gone. Malachi had fled, presumably unable to stand up to the Greys, but possibly deciding that the risk of trying was too great. He couldn't be blamed. The scrawny old wizard would inevitably have ended up in the same position as Ant.

Mona came into his head. Her voice was soft and reassuring. She was telling him that he was loved, that he was forgiven, that he'd done everything he could in his life, and could be proud of his little self. Ant felt comforted but unconvinced. Maybe if he'd worked harder, he might have learned something that could be used in his defence. If only Lone had passed on the secrets of her powers, he might have used them to rip these savages apart.

Tyrant was roaring now, stumbling towards him. A Grey stood in his path, holding the cleaver aloft. Tyrant ground to an unsteady halt. He was looking at Ant as if he'd seen a ghost. As if he realised that the situation was completely hopeless. As if he'd given up completely.

Then the Grey turned. Its jaw dropped open as if in astonishment. Ant tried to twist his neck to get a view of what had grabbed everyone's attention. For an instant, he imagined Lone striding into the clearing with that huge cat at her side. What he saw dashed every hope. It was another Grey. This one was huge, two or three times the size of the others. It stomped silently towards the fire. From the reaction of the Greys, this wasn't a welcome intrusion. On the contrary, they all seemed surprised and worried at the appearance of such a large version of themselves. It was as if they hadn't seen such a creature before.

Ant found no consolation in their discomfiture. Being eaten was the same, regardless of who or what consumed him. From the looks of things, this monster was intent on stealing the Grey's dinner and they were preparing to put up a fight.

The Grey with the knife turned away from Ant to confront the interloper. For a moment or two they locked stares, bodies tensing for attack. Then the giant raised his arms, beat his fists soundlessly on his chest, and opened his immense mouth to reveal massive teeth. This proved too much for the Grey; he turned and ran. Every one of his comrades followed suit, leaving Ant tied to the tree and Tyrant standing in shocked stillness to face the terrible giant.

Tyrant recovered from his thrall and ran to retrieve his sword. Swishing the blade from side to side, Tyrant approached the giant who had stood passively, arms dangling as if contemptuous of the prospect of being attacked by someone so much smaller. There was justification in that apparent lack of concern, judging by the way that Tyrant had bounced off his much smaller kin.

The first sword thrust went clean through the monster and most of Tyrant's arm went with it. He recovered his balance and began to slash at his opponent. It was as if he were fencing with thin air. The monster was as insubstantial as a wraith risen from a swamp.

The thing spoke, its voice ridiculously soft and polite for such a massive beast. 'You'd be better using that to cut down Ant,' it said. 'It can't be very comfortable hanging naked from a tree.'

Tyrant's arms dropped to his side. 'Little Ant? Is that you?'

The beast reduced in size until the knee-high version of Ant stood revealed. 'We should make our escape while we can,' he said. 'Those big apes won't stay scared for long.'

The drop to the ground was painful, but welcome. While he tried to massage some of the pain out of his shoulders and some utility back in, Tyrant gathered up a handful of things, including his clothes. 'No time for that now,' Tyrant said. 'We need to make ourselves scarce.'

'I'm not running naked through the jungle, so don't even try to persuade me to. Give me those clothes and keep guard. If the Greys come back, you have my permission to teach them a lesson they'll never forget.'

Tyrant reluctantly dropped the bundle at his feet. 'Hurry,' he said.

'Don't worry,' Ant said. 'My avatar will see them off even if you can't.'

'I wouldn't be so sure of that,' Tyrant said. 'All they have to do is throw something at him to discover there's nothing substantial about him. Then you'll be strung up again, ready for the spit.'

Ant pulled up his pants and threw his aching arms into his shirt. 'Isn't that Malachi's bag?'

'Leave it, there's no food in it and it's heavy,' Tyrant replied.

Ant picked up the bag. Tyrant was right, it was almost too heavy for him to lift. 'We should take it to him.'

'This way.' Tyrant led him into the jungle in the opposite direction that the Greys had fled.

'Hadn't we better head back to the beach?' Ant asked.

'We need to get away first. Put as much distance between them and us.'

'What about Little Ant, as you call him?'

'He's back in his pouch now. I think he needs to rest.'

'He should have killed them all.' A surge of anger swept through Ant's body.

'I don't think he could have done any more than he did,' Tyrant said. 'He's only a pile of dust, even if he can make himself appear differently. Anyway, you should know what he can do. It was you that made him.'

'You've more experience with his capabilities than I have. All I know is that he's not turned out like I hoped he would.'

As they made their way through the forest, Ant's feet began to hurt. 'Hold on,' he said, sitting down to prise off his boots and replace them on the correct feet. Tyrant hovered over him, eyes anxiously staring in the direction they'd come from.

Ant listened. There was no obvious sound of pursuit amongst the cacophony of humming and screeching. Tyrant bent down and handed him the pouch. 'Here, you need to have this back.'

'I'm not sure I want it,' Ant said.

Tyrant's face clouded over. 'Now you're acting like a disappointed child. How do you think Little Ant feels about all this? He's new to the world and all he gets from his father is negativity.'

'I'm not his father,' Ant said.

'Then you're the nearest thing he's got, poor thing. Stop wishing for the impossible, Ant. Face up to reality. Little Ant might not be what you intended, but from my point of view, he couldn't be better. He's already saved me from the wasps, stopped me from being bitten by a snake, guided me back to you, and sent the Greys packing when they were about to eat us both. What more could you want, eh? Yet all you can do is moan about the things he's not.'

'I expected to be able to keep in contact with him. Experience what he does, see what he sees. I wanted a friend that I could trust implicitly.'

'Wake up and understand that you've got something much better than a puppet that dances to your tune. Treat him as a friend and trusted ally. Stop judging him against unrealistic aspirations.' Tyrant hauled him to his feet and gave him a long, hard stare.

'What if he lets me down?' Ant said.

'What if you let him down? Until you think of him as an equal and treat him with respect, all you're going to have is a plaything that has no notion of how to behave towards you. Come to an understanding. Be adult and mature about this, Ant, otherwise you're inviting the disappointment that you're so frightened of.'

They resumed their trek through the forest. 'You sound like Malachi,' Ant said.

'That's not good.' Tyrant laughed. 'Some of his pomposity must have rubbed off while I've been forced to spend so much time with him. Has he ever told you the story about his master and how he died?'

'No,' Ant said.

'He told me. He also told me how he met his wife and came to marry her.'

'Why would he tell you those things?'

'I asked him the questions, and he answered them. Maybe that's how it works with Malachi. If you don't ask, you don't get.'

'Tell me about Lone,' Ant said, his insides beginning to churn.

29

Malachi struck out with all his psychic power, but failed to connect with the ghostly shapes. His attempts to twist, strangle, probe, and damage failed. There was nothing he could grab or influence. It was as if the shapes were inanimate.

They were, however, all too physically real. One grabbed at him, but caught only the hem of his cloak, and Malachi's desperate tug had him free for the moment. It was a grey ape but more man-like than monkey. For an instant, their eyes met and Malachi was able to detect something more than savagery behind the eyes.

The firelight provided sufficient illumination for him to watch Tyrant being struck down and Ant carried aloft. He did the only thing he could, threw a pouch into the fire and turned away quickly before the incandescence bloomed. Even the sky lit up under the fierce brightness.

Malachi stumbled against the boat, barking his shins painfully. Grabbing it with both hands, he began to push. For a tiny craft, it proved hard to shift. His feet sank deep into the soft sand, robbing him of purchase. Once the boat did begin to slide, the process became easier. All the time, Malachi anticipated the ape's hands catching hold of him and preventing his escape. A glance over his shoulder gave him a glimpse of his pursuer seemingly staring transfixed at the pyrotechnical display emanating from the fire.

He redoubled his efforts and was rewarded with the initial resistance of water, followed quickly by the boat becoming lighter as it began to float. He scrambled over the side, lay down in the bottom, and pulled his cloak over his head.

The boat bobbed gently in the waves. Either it would be deposited back onto the shore, or carried out to sea. There was only one way of knowing, but he was reluctant to expose his face over the side of the boat. His best chance lay in becoming invisible to the brightness-affected eyes of his pursuers.

Every moment brought fresh opportunities for his discovery. The apes would be recovering some night vision, but he could hear only the lapping of the waves on the bow and no splashing footsteps heading towards him. He kept his head down.

When he could no longer hear the hissing of the sea as it hit the shore, Malachi gingerly raised his head. The fire was a distant red glow. The sea had swept his small craft away from the mayhem and into the relative security of the depths. Taking a deep breath, he felt around for the oars and positioned them. By making an occasional stroke, he tried to keep station and waited for his chance to return to the shore.

By the time he decided it might be safe to do so, the fire had died completely and it was impossible to mark exactly the point from which he'd embarked. Rowing as quietly as possible, he pulled himself nearer until the faint glow of the vedhana provided a welcoming point to aim for. The shoreline was empty. Ant and Tyrant were gone, as was the precious bag containing his equipment.

It was hard to drag the boat from the clutches of the sea, but he managed with a good deal of grunting, sweating, and the occasional curse. Then he sat by the vedhana and contemplated his next move.

Tyrant was no great loss. Ant was, however, a different matter. The years of instruction were beginning to bear rich fruit. It wasn't only his remarkable ability to build and operate the magical portals; there was an underlying strength to the lad that was beginning to emerge from the chaos of childhood conditioning and reactive habits. Then there was the bag. Tyrant had complained about it often enough and even sifted through the contents while objecting to carrying it. There were items in it that were precious and unique. Items that Tyrant's eyes had no means of recognising. The loss of the bag, if permanent, would be a hard blow to take.

Lone had taken the opportunity to escape using the vedhana, and this seemed the more sensible option. If he remained here, the apes would come back while he was sleeping and take him. If he tried to follow them to retrieve the bag, his fate would almost certainly be the same. This was their habitat, not his. Also, they seemed immune to his influence, which left him almost defenceless.

Ant had even less chance of survival, though. Losing him would be difficult to bear. Leaving him to his fate might be a decision that he'd live to regret. On the other hand, even if he did locate the boy and the bag,

117

what chance of retrieving either did he have against what seemed a powerful and implacable foe?

Lone might stand a chance against the apes. Her powers were formidable. If they were made of flesh, she would tear them to pieces. If not, she could sweep them aside and consign them to oblivion. Perhaps he should search for her. Follow her lead through the portal and enlist her urgent assistance.

But where had she gone? The only portal she'd ever been through had transported her into the desert where she'd been left stranded for a long time. If she'd ended up there again, it might be as impossible to find her as it had been after it had first happened.

The bag and the boy had to be retrieved. Not necessarily in that order of priority. But how to do it without sacrificing himself?

30

The blackness underfoot stung the soles of her feet with heat and sharpness. Lone could hardly breathe in the acrid fumes that watered her eyes and caught in her throat. Molten rock spattered the ground, thrown high into the air by eruptions of red fire.

Small things skittered beneath her feet. Crab-like creatures with oversized eyes borne aloft on long stalks. Black slugs slithered towards her as if curious. She shuddered as one sucked at her ankle. It slid away, presumably unimpressed with the encounter.

Three moons hung overhead. Giant spheres that dominated the night sky. It was as if this place weren't strange enough and they had been installed as a stark reminder that she was far away from anywhere she might call home. No matter, this was where she had decided to come. She had work to do. Dangerous work that was as likely as not to end her life. Work that she had to perform if she was to get what she wanted and avoid that life being in vain.

The vedhana had disappeared the moment she'd stepped from it. It didn't matter if it were gone completely or only invisible; once she stepped away from this location, her way back was lost. Quelling a momentary surge of panic, she told herself that success would mean that she had no need of the device and if she failed, there would be no way back.

Shaking with loathing, she bent down and grabbed the nearest slug. It writhed, hissed, and bared tiny teeth. She held on tightly to its hot slimy body until it quietened down. 'Take me to him,' she said. 'Tell him I'm here with a proposition. One that will interest him.'

Underneath the fear caused by uncertainty, Lone's body was boiling in exultation. She recognised this place, not by sight or smell, but by feeling. There were resonances here that were reminiscent of the long meditative search for a demon ally. Her essence had touched this place before. That experience had allowed her to direct the vedhana and project her body to the place that her mind had only caught glimpses of.

A grotesque figure the size of a large dog toddled into view across a pool of fire. It looked like a maggot with chicken legs. When it stood close to her, she realised its face had human features. 'Go away.' It spoke in calm, measured tones reminiscent of Malachi. 'That's if you value your life. Humans can't survive here.'

'I've come to speak with him,' Lone said, stifling a cough.

'Then you've come to the wrong place.'

'I think not. This is where I first encountered him.'

'That may be so, but he's not here.'

'I don't believe you,' Lone said, the fumes beginning to eat their way through the lining of her lungs.

'Please yourself.' The maggot turned away.

'Tell him I'm not leaving until I've given him my offer. It's an offer he will want to take advantage of.'

'Tell who?' The maggot paused and turned back to face her; its features changed to a disturbing effigy of her own.

'Too late,' Lone said. 'You should have asked me that right at the start. You know exactly who I'm referring to and you also know what he'll do to you when he finds out that you've failed to inform him of something he needs to know about.'

'Even if I did know who you're talking about, and I don't, what would interest him about a human wandering into his realm?'

'An opportunity, that's what. A once in a lifetime chance to change the whole pattern of existence.'

'Big words, lady, but meaningless coming from you. Humans have nothing to offer the likes of us.'

'Let him be the judge of that or you might find yourself on the receiving end of torment you could do well to avoid.'

'I could equally argue that bothering him with trivia invites similar, possibly worse, retribution.' More pairs of chicken legs sprouted from the underside of the maggot's body as it ran over a rocky outcrop and disappeared from view. Lone watched the scurrying crabs beat a similarly hasty retreat. Something must be happening. Either he was being summoned, or there was another reason for the local denizens to keep well clear of her.

Breathing was becoming difficult. The acid gases were catching in her throat. Every time she inhaled, she felt weaker. If he didn't appear soon, she would die before she had the chance to bring her plan to fruition.

When her legs would no longer bear her weight and her lungs were too full of fumes to function, she felt herself collapsing. Her head was dizzy, her eyes couldn't focus, and the control of her body was lost. She fell to the ground, hit her head a jarring, painful blow, and everything went black.

It was still hot. Even hotter, perhaps. But when she opened her eyes, she was dazzled by bright sunlight. She was lying on soft sand. The alien volcanic landscape had been replaced by a familiar but disturbing one. The desert. Not just any part of the desert, but the place where she'd been abandoned by Tyrant and spent so long trying and failing to escape from. Her determination evaporated, replaced by despair. If this was his response, then she had failed.

The greenery was as she had left it. The cool shelter of the trees was as welcome as ever. Sitting motionless, stilling her mind, allowing her thoughts to evaporate brought a new perspective. If this was his doing, and it had to be, then he knew she had visited his lair. Was he keeping her here so that he could find out what she had in mind? Or was it only a sardonic reaction involving the most amusing death he could devise for her?

Either way, she was trapped. Until he decided otherwise, she would remain here. Her newfound ability to build a portal might provide a means of escape, but she doubted it. He had the power to nullify anything she tried, but there was always the chance he'd overlooked the possibility.

Casting around for the means, she found a rope tied to a pointed stick neatly stashed away in the makeshift shelter she'd lived in for all that time. Smoothing out the sand, she carefully inscribed the pattern, resisting the urge to rush the process in her desperation for it to work.

When the vedhana was complete, she sat beside it and closed her eyes. Feeling deep into the earth, she sought the energy needed to activate the device. Slowly, painfully, the ground yielded its bounty, and tendrils of power began to course through her body. She was energised like never before. It was as if she could soar into the air and instantly transport herself to any place she chose. This was what she'd hoped for. The desert could no longer hold her hostage.

Even in the harsh sunlight, the vedhana began to glow brightly. It was spectacular. The whirling fire danced high into the sky, forming a burning tunnel up to the heavens. Gently, slowly, imbued with vibrant energy, Lone rose to her feet and prepared herself for the journey.

As she was about to step into the vedhana, a figure appeared amongst the dancing flames.

31

'Which way?' Ant surveyed the welcome sight of the shore for familiar signs but was undecided whether they had emerged to the east or west of the vedhana. The portal wasn't their objective, though. It was the boat.

They chose the right way, and it took only a short walk before the vedhana's wispy presence could be detected. The little boat was pulled high up on the sand, out of reach of the gently lapping sea.

Tyrant had remained adamant that, regardless of the risk, their priority had to be Bee and Cassie. Using the vedhana to escape the Greys wasn't an option. Despite Ant's doubts about the wisdom of continuing what might prove to be a fruitless and deadly quest, he couldn't bring himself to abandon Tyrant. The big man's intentions were undoubtedly good, even if they might be impossible to fulfil.

The strap attached to the heavy bag had chafed a tender groove across his shoulder, which spiked with pain as he allowed it to slip to the sand.

'I told you it was heavy,' Tyrant said.

'If Malachi dragged it all this way, it must contain important things,' Ant said.

'It doesn't; I've looked. There's no food, just heavy things wrapped up in leather. No use for any of it. Anyway, it was me that dragged it around. Malachi never lifted it once, despite making many promises to take it from me. Somehow, he always convinced me that a few more steps and I could leave it to him. That never happened, though why I didn't realise I was being taken for a fool, I don't know. Seems so obvious now.'

'That's Malachi's power. You find yourself doing what he says even if you don't want to.'

'Take a look inside. See what you make of the contents.'

Ant overcame his reluctance to interfere with anything belonging to Malachi and opened the bag. His hands encountered a tubular parcel half the length of his arm. Laying it gently on the sand, he carefully unwrapped the leather bindings and extracted the item contained inside. 'What's that?' Tyrant asked. Ant didn't have an answer.

The tube was bright scarlet and made of a strange substance that was smooth and pliable. It was neither wood nor metal nor any cloth he'd ever seen, smooth to the touch and bearing an indecipherable series of inscriptions in yellow letters. Tyrant grabbed it, sniffed at it noisily, and began to shake it next to his ear.

'There's something inside,' he said. 'Maybe I can poke a knife down and see if I can extract it. The covering seems quite soft.'

'No, that might be dangerous.' Ant was uncomfortable at the way Tyrant was roughly handling what must be a magical item. The thought of him slitting it open and releasing whatever was hidden inside gave him shivers. 'If Malachi dragged this all through the jungle, it must be important.'

'He dragged nothing,' Tyrant said, holding the red tube aloft. 'It was me did all the carrying. Anyway, he's not here, so everything belongs to us now. There might be food inside it. Have you thought of that?'

'What do you think might be edible inside that strange covering? A sausage perhaps? If it were something to eat, I'm sure it could have been wrapped more simply. Be careful with it. Malachi's things can be very dangerous. It's undoubtedly an ancient and magical device and not something to be messed about with.'

Tyrant stood with the tube in his left hand and peered intently at one end. 'I think this bit comes off,' he said as he prised off a piece. A short length of string was revealed. 'Aha, whatever it is meant to be removed by pulling this string. Now we're getting somewhere.'

'Wait.' Ant's anxiety levels rose. Tyrant ignored him and yanked hard on the string.

A terrible bang deafened him as something shot out of the tube. Tyrant was sent sprawling on the ground with his hair on fire. The thing flew into the air, bursting with intense red light. It was as if a new star had been added to the firmament, one as bright as the sun. The star slowly descended, bathing the sea and the shore in a ghastly light before being extinguished on contact with the water.

There was a sulphurous stench in the air that was accentuated by the smell of singed hair. Tyrant was rubbing his head ruefully but seemed otherwise uninjured. 'What was that?' he gasped.

'I have no idea,' Ant replied. 'Perhaps a fire demon was imprisoned in the tube and you managed to release it.'

'If it was a demon, do you think it might come back and thank me?'

Ant laughed, glad that the crisis had passed without serious injury. He promised himself to keep the contents of the bag out of Tyrant's hands in future. 'That wouldn't be like any demon I've encountered if it did. Whatever it is, I think it's gone and not coming back. Be glad that you weren't staring down the tube when you pulled the string. You would have lost your head.'

'I could have used one of those things to fight the Greys,' Tyrant said. 'I think it was a weapon of some sort. Are there any more?'

Ant shook his head. 'Even if there were, they shouldn't be touched. It's too dangerous.'

'Sometimes one danger has to be faced in order to avoid another,' Tyrant said.

Ant looked carefully at Tyrant's face; there was something different about the way he looked. Some of his hair had been burned off, but that wasn't it. After a few moments, it became obvious what was causing the comical expression. His eyebrows were missing, as well as most of his beard. Ant opened his mouth to pass on the news, but closed it again. They'd grow again, at least he presumed so. Anyway, there was nobody else around to comment on it, so he decided not to tell him. Tyrant was very precious about his facial hair, preferring as much of it as he could grow. Knowing that he'd lost an essential element of his hirsute appearance would only make him grumpy.

As the darkness quickly closed in, Ant sat tending the fire while Tyrant, still unaware of the transformation his appearance had undergone, scavenged for wood along the foreshore.

Little Ant appeared in a swirl of sand and sat beside him. 'Are you still mad at me?' he asked.

Ant examined the resentment he harboured regarding his effigy. 'I'm upset, that's all. Not with you; it's not your fault things didn't turn out the way I wanted.'

'That's ridiculous. How could you even think about us in that way? I'm you, you're me. There's no blame to ascribe. Neither can you justify being disappointed about the way things are. That kind of woolly thinking is exactly why you need me more than you might imagine. Next, you'll be sulking because you would prefer the sun to be green and stay fixed in the sky so that it always shines on you.'

'I may be stupid, but I'm not that stupid,' Ant said. 'Look, I'm sorry. I'll try to behave better in the future. Tell me what would make you happy and I'll do it. I can't say fairer than that.'

'I doubt that happiness is a state we can achieve on a regular basis. What would help me, though, is for you to explore the possibilities of our relationship. See what we can achieve as a team. Seek my advice and take note of what I say. Treat me as a valued friend instead of a puppet. Let go of my strings.'

Ant reached out his hand towards his avatar. 'Well said, Little Ant. I understand what you're telling me, though I might need a reminder of it from time to time. Let's be friends and see where that takes us.'

32

Bee pushed Cassie hard in the chest, propelling her backwards into the arms of Gil, who had emerged from below decks. 'That's not fair!' she screamed. 'Tell her, Gil, tell her she's being a selfish bitch.'

The big man laughed. 'I think she's got the message. What are you two fighting about now?'

'It's her,' Cassie said, grabbing hold of Bee's hair and yanking it hard.

'Ow.' Bee lashed out, but Cassie evaded her swinging fist. 'She says she's going to be Queen of where we're going and she doesn't care about Cuthbert and she doesn't want to go back to Gort.'

'Well, well.' Gil's teeth gleamed in the sun. 'What's brought on this change in heart?'

'It's Cuthbert,' Cassie said. 'He's not the Cuthbert I first met. He's different now he's King.'

'But that's not my problem,' Bee shouted. 'You've had your go at being Queen, now it's my turn. It's me who should get to marry the King of whereveritis.'

'Kish,' Gil said. 'But I wouldn't be in too much of a hurry to marry that old fool.'

'Why not?' Cassie asked.

'For one thing, he already has several consorts. For another, I'm going to kill him and take over as ruler.'

'Good,' Bee said. 'I'd much rather marry you in that case. You'll need a queen, won't you?'

'Don't make me laugh. Even if I did need a queen, why would I take a little girl like you?'

'I'm not a little girl. I'm a fully grown woman, I'll have you know. And I'd make a good queen, after all, I'm already a princess and that's makes me illegible. Another thing, imagine how angry Cuthbert will get when he knows. You want him to attack you and that's going to make sure that he does.'

'But I'm the Queen already. If Gil marries me, he'll make Cuthbert even more angry.'

'But he can't. You're already married. It would only get confusing. Cuthbert would still have you as Queen, whatever you did. All he'd say is that you'd been unfaithful and therefore have you hanged.' Bee prodded her sister with her finger several times to emphasise her point.

'My spies tell me that your King has already sent a ship to intercept ours. Problem is that it should have been here days ago. I'm not sure how long I'm prepared to wait for it to show up. Maybe we should send a message back telling him of your defection. That might make him come to find you on Kish. I'm beginning to get bored of sitting on this boat.'

'Maybe they got lost,' Cassie said.

'They most certainly got lost,' Gil answered. 'Problem is how to find them. It's a big ocean out there. Unless we get very lucky, we might as well accept that the chances were always slim.'

'So, is it agreed?' Bee said.

'Is what agreed?' Gil replied.

'You're going to marry me and make me Queen. You are a king, aren't you?'

'I certainly am. The most powerful King in the world. I've ruled over my city for thousands of years.'

'You don't look old enough,' Cassie said.

'That's because I have special magic to stop my body from deteriorating.'

'Cuthbert could do with a bit of that,' Bee sniggered.

'Your King is different. He doesn't need to bother keeping a single body in good condition.'

'Why not?' Cassis asked.

'Because, if you hadn't already realised, Cuthbert is the same King as the one whose body I killed in the desert. When Cuthbert dies, the King will choose another host.'

'Is he a demon, then?' Bee asked.

'No, demons are something very different. Your King is a god. A very minor god, I should explain, but a god nonetheless. Gods are immortal. That's what makes them different from humans and demons. They can't die.'

'But you said you were going to kill him and take over as King. Are you a god? Can gods kill other gods?'

'I'm better than a god. I'm half human. My father was the most powerful of all gods and he intended me to inherit the whole world.'

'So, you can die, but Cuthbert can't?' Bee asked, her heart fluttering.

'I can be killed. But only by something as powerful as myself. No god or king or human exists that could do that. As for Cuthbert, I'll make sure his essence is banished beyond this earthly realm and will be unable to return.'

'Sounds good to me,' Bee said. 'Can I have a big wedding with lots of guests, please?'

Gil chuckled, but his laughter sounded less derisive than normal. Bee felt that him telling them all this stuff about gods was a good sign. Maybe he was softening a little. Perhaps she could get close enough to find a way to kill him.

Even though it was bright daylight, a red star suddenly appeared in the distant sky to the east. The gasps of amazement from the crew caused Gil to turn around and see what they were looking at. His smile broadened. 'It's them,' he said. 'Now we know where they are. Ready the cannon.'

33

Without Tyrant blundering a way in front, Malachi discovered that progress through the jungle was hard-fought and horribly slow. Every whisper of wind raised the hairs on his neck as he anticipated a sudden attack from the Greys. The short knife in his left hand provided little comfort. The small package in his right might give him a little more security, provided he was quick enough to deploy it.

The constant vigilance was as tiring as having to push his way through the undergrowth. At the back of his mind was always the feeling that his journey would be futile, even if he did know where he was heading, which he didn't.

A rat the size of a dog bared its twin incisors at him from the cover of the bush ahead. Malachi gave it a hard stare, and it thought better of the confrontation and withdrew. His anger gave way to disappointment that the creature had retreated without giving him the excuse to crush it. He resolved that the next thing that took his eye would get the full treatment whether or not it constituted a real threat.

Every step brought the opportunity to turn back to the vedhana and whisk himself away from this uncomfortable and dangerous place. It was as if his legs were getting more reluctant to function the further he went. It was a massive effort of will to force his body to act against every instinct of self-preservation. If Lone were here, she would be laughing at him, telling him he'd become soft and sentimental. Was that true? Was he using the precious cargo in the bag as an excuse to save his beloved Ant? That's what Lone would be saying. She'd also be pointing out that he was making a futile gesture that would almost certainly result in his demise. That he'd lost the ability to control his emotions and the capacity to prioritise.

Did saving Ant really matter? The boy was morose and unhelpful most of the time. The thing he'd hoped to learn from him seemed beyond his powers to teach, and so the transaction had become almost exclusively one way and in Ant's direction. Why did it matter to him what became of the boy?

Malachi remembered a fragment of teaching from his master. *Accept what is and don't look for reasons.* There was a time when enquiry became futile and obstructive to growth. *Why me? Why this? Why that? Why can't it be better? What have I done to make the world the way it is?* He stopped in his tracks, took a long breath, and cleared his mind of turmoil. Acceptance seeped through his being in its place. Attachment was a human necessity, despite the sorrow it brought. Pretending that he could remain aloof and uncaring was the worst exercise in self-deception.

There was a freedom in this knowledge that lightened his step. This was how things were and it didn't matter how he'd arrived at this moment or what lay beyond it. His head cleared, his resolve loosened, and he followed the urgings of his heart to protect his friends. Even Tyrant seemed worth saving in his newfound clarity.

Another rat poked its head out inquisitively, and Malachi crushed its windpipe without a second thought. It fell on its side and waved its legs in a death spasm. He kicked the dying rodent aside and carried on ploughing his way through the undergrowth. A tiny trickle of satisfaction lifted his spirits. He'd never liked rats. Never seen a point to them unless it was to make him squirm whenever one showed up.

High above his head, a new bright red star appeared visible even through the thick canopy. Malachi stopped and watched as it slowly sank out of sight. His heart raced as he considered the implications.

As far as he was aware, the only artefacts in the whole world capable of creating such a phenomenon were in the bag he'd brought with him from the ship. Someone had found one and managed to work out how to use it. There were only three possibilities; four if he included Tyrant, but he didn't. It could be a signal from Ant that he was alive, had the bag, and was looking for Malachi. The Greys could have plundered the bag and used the device. Or a third, unknown entity was involved.

Only Ant had the intelligence and training to work the device. Only Ant would understand the significance of its use. It could only be Ant that was trying to attract his attention. Ant would know that, if Malachi was anywhere in the vicinity, he would see the star and know what it meant. The other options were easily dismissed.

Malachi changed course and resumed his passage with renewed vigour. The bag and Ant couldn't be far away. Once he found them, he would take them back to Gort by way of the vedhana. There was nothing at all to be gained by lingering in this barbaric region a moment longer than was absolutely necessary.

34

Tyrant's forehead felt as if it was still on fire. His ears were singing as if his head was inside a metal pot being beaten with a ladle. He brushed his hand carefully over the top of his head, feeling for wounds and blood but finding none. Breathing a sigh of relief, he considered for a moment what had happened when he tugged on the string attached to the device. All he could remember was a bang and a flash before being deposited flat on his backside in the sand. Powerful magic had obviously been involved. He'd released an imprisoned demon who had been eager for freedom and who, hopefully, was long gone.

You couldn't trust demons; everyone knew that. Even doing one a good turn was no guarantee of getting one back. Mind you, humans behaved exactly the same. Ant was sitting on the beach talking privately to his little avatar. That seemed to be a good sign; those two needed to get along. He decided to take a stroll along the shoreline to give them a little space. There were interesting things to be found that the sea had washed up. Twisted pieces of ancient wood, the corpses of sea creatures and, occasionally, a nicely polished pebble that Petra might find attractive.

When he had been beachcombing for half the morning, something made him look up and out to sea. There was a speck on the horizon that hadn't been there the last time he'd looked. The curve of the shore had taken him out of sight of Ant, which had been his intention. Now, though, his discovery was something to be shared, and he made haste back to where he'd left the boy.

Seeing Ant still sitting comfortably in conversation was a relief. There was something about the speck that had alarmed him. 'Look out there,' he shouted, 'something's heading our way.' The speck had resolved itself into the silhouette of a ship by now.

Ant got to his feet. 'Our ship was lost, so it must be another one.'

'Maybe someone found our ship and is bringing it back to us,' Tyrant said.

'The only person who could possibly do that is Lone,' Ant replied.

'What about Malachi? We left him with the small boat. It's possible he rowed out to sea, found our ship, and here he is.'

'Either way, a ship is a welcome sight. We might enlist its aid to find the girls,' Ant said.

Ant's words were encouraging and Tyrant's heart felt lighter. This could be the first piece of good fortune they'd encountered on the journey. Without a ship of their own, the hunt for Cassie and Bee wasn't possible. Now, there was at least a chance they might find the girls before it was too late. He stood at the water's edge and waved his arms above his head.

As the vessel drew nearer, Tyrant could detect that the ship was very similar to the one they'd lost, if not identical. His money would be on Lone bringing it back. She was the one with the guts and the power to do such a thing. That's if she could summon the motivation. He doubted Malachi would have the fortitude to do such a thing by himself, though he fully expected the two of them to turn up once again like a bad smell released in company that followed you around, however vigorously you might fan your arse.

'Hold on.' Ant stood close beside him. 'I'm getting a bad feeling about this.'

'I can't see why. It's a ship. We need a ship.'

'But why is it heading our way? How did it know we were here?' Ant asked.

Tyrant considered for a moment. 'It has to be the demon that flew out of the tube. That's what told them about us.'

'More likely they saw it,' Ant said, 'and came to investigate its source.'

'That thing was Malachi's, wasn't it?' Tyrant said. 'In which case, he would have recognised it and known it was us. That has to be Malachi bringing the ship to us and if it is, Lone has to be with him. Stop worrying. It's a really good stroke of luck the way things have turned out.'

'I'm not so sure,' Ant said. 'Can you make out some of the crew standing looking at us?'

Tyrant squinted as hard as he could and was rewarded with the sight of several figures crowding the bow of the ship. He waved even more vigorously. They responded by putting their hands over their ears.

35

Malachi broke out of the jungle and reached the edge of the sea. A ship was in sight, so close to the shore that he could make out the individual sailors on its deck. A hundred or so paces to his left, Tyrant was jumping up and down and yelling at the top of his voice.

'Ant!' Malachi called out, and the boy turned towards him. Tyrant stopped gesticulating wildly and began to point at the ship. Ant picked up the bag and began to half drag, half carry it towards him. He ran towards his protégé as fast as he could, propelled by the bad feeling that the ship's presence had brought. His mind raced through possibilities and settled on one. The ship had responded to the signal exactly as he had. This might mean that its significance was understood. If it was, that would display a knowledge of ancient artefacts. One thing was certain: he wouldn't welcome an encounter with anyone with that sort of information. Ant's father and the King were the only two he knew of, but neither of them could be on the ship.

He reached Ant and grabbed the bag from him. 'Quickly,' he said, 'into the forest. We have to hide.'

Ant's eyes widened with surprise, but he made no protest and ran into the jungle with Malachi in close pursuit. As they reached the relative sanctuary of the trees, Malachi heard a succession of loud bangs. The trees around him splintered and shredded. Leaves and branches flew into the air. The percussive noises deafened him. Splinters pierced his face and neck as he flung himself to the ground.

More bangs, this time the tree right above his head came crashing down, pinning him to the ground by his legs. The undergrowth between him and the shore had been blasted asunder, and he could see the ship clearly from where he lay. Reaching inside his cloak, he pulled out the vial he'd prepared in readiness for a wasp attack or the return of the Greys. The dense white vapour poured into the air, creating a thick fog. Two more bangs shattered trees to his left, thankfully a safe distance from where he lay.

The respite caused by a sudden silence brought the pain in his legs into focus. The tiny bit of movement they could manage was accompanied by unbearable agony. Even when he kept perfectly still, they hurt terribly. He feared that his legs had been permanently shattered and that he'd never recover enough to get out of this jungle alive. The only one who might have helped him was gone. She could have saved him if she'd been here.

Ant began pulling at him and he screamed at him to stop. 'Get out of here; the smoke will soon clear and then we'll both be killed. They have a fiendish device on that ship that you have to get away from. Save yourself, Ant. Go.'

Ant's hands began to scrabble in the soft earth beneath him. The mist was clearing, being swept away by the breeze coming in from the sea. The ghostly sight of the ship was becoming clearer by the second, which meant they were easy prey for the infernal device being employed against them.

The tree was too heavy for half a dozen men to lift, so Ant was trying to dig him out as the only alternative. The stubborn lad was ignoring every word of command he could utter, steadfastly delving beneath his legs to loosen the soil. Malachi winced in anticipation of the next explosion and feared that it would be the last thing either of them heard.

When it came, it was ten times louder than previously. There was no corresponding effect on the jungle around them. Everything remained calm and undisturbed. Malachi strained his neck to view the ship and was rewarded with a very satisfying plume of smoke rising from the bow. He couldn't be certain, but there might even be a lick of flames becoming visible.

Ant's scrabbling became less frantic, and they were joined by Tyrant, who thought the solution to his predicament might be to drag the top half of his body away from the rest and leave his legs beneath the tree. A series of loud screams and curses were needed to persuade him to desist and help Ant with his burrowing instead.

Malachi's legs were becoming mercifully numb. The pain was confined to the lower part of his abdomen now and his head was filling with confusion. An icy realisation shivered up his damaged spine and dribbled its way into his sliding consciousness. His body was telling his mind that the damage was too severe. That there was no recovery. That this would be its final resting place.

His bodily damage and the suffering it was causing paled into insignificance in the face of the much worse mental anguish. There was so much more for him to learn, enormous opportunities that could no longer be grasped. Pinpricks of doubt became savage slices through his self-esteem. His whole life had amounted to exactly nothing. All the striving, all the work, all the cajoling and sycophancy, every bit of cruelty he'd inflicted, came down in the end to this. Lying in a jungle with his body crushed beyond repair. And for what? Some vague expectation of greater recognition by a wayward King who obviously loathed the sight of him? An attempt to extract a welcome hint of appreciation from his wife? Here he was, the master of coercing others to do things they would rather not, suffering the consequences of allowing himself to be manipulated in exactly the same way. The biter well and truly bit. The master becoming the victim of his own chicanery.

As for Lone, she'd barely notice his absence. No matter, in that case, it was better that he died first and be saved from the anguish that being without her would have brought. It might not qualify as conventional love, but he'd been devoted to her surly ways and single-minded ambitions.

At least Ant was by his side now, still struggling to extract him from beneath the bone-crushing trunk. There had never been any question of him having a son, but Ant had provided the nearest alternative. He suspected that Ant's suitability as his pupil far exceeded anything he could have expected from a natural heir.

Breaths were coming less frequent and harder to draw. A strange thing, breathing. All his life he'd been barely conscious of it, but now, at the very end, he was being forced to marvel at this miracle and savour every intake as if it were sweet wine never to be tasted again.

He needed to tell Ant what to do. Instruct him in the artefacts contained in the bag. Give him wise counsel regarding his future. Warn him of the pitfalls that lay ahead. Malachi opened his mouth, but his lips refused to form words from the limited air they were given.

It didn't matter. Telling him wouldn't make any difference. Information was useful, but the real power lay in experience. The darkness gently seeped into his vision until there was nothing left to see. Nothing left to say. Nothing left to think. Nothing left. Nothing.

36

The arrival of the ship was a wonderful stroke of good fortune. Either it was the one carrying Cassie and Bee, in which case their quest had been successful, or it was a replacement for the one they had lost and could be used to carry on the search.

Tyrant was cavorting in the sand as if he'd come to the same conclusion. Could this be the culmination of all their efforts? If it were the girls on board, all they had to do was bring them ashore and into the waiting portal. Things couldn't be better.

Or could they? Malachi's words jarred uncomfortably. *If it's too good to be true, then it isn't likely to be either.* 'Hold on,' he said.

The uncertainty held them both transfixed as the ship slowly headed towards them. None of the crew appeared to be waving back. His ominous feeling grew even stronger.

Malachi emerged from the jungle and called him. Grabbing the bag, he set off towards his master, who ordered him to hide in the forest with such power and certainty that he dashed headlong into the undergrowth to get out of sight of the ship.

The justification for flight came almost immediately and in the most terrible form. Whatever was launched from the ship flew over his head and blasted the trees all around him. Thick trunks were smashed to matchwood and brought the forest crashing down about him. There were more reports from the ship and even worse destruction followed. A foul-smelling fog enveloped him as he shook off the foliage that pinned him down and crawled his way to the place he'd seen Malachi fall.

His master looked to be in a very bad way. His face was ashen, and he was barely able to speak. Despite the instructions he received from the wizard, Ant couldn't leave him lying in full view of whatever devilish contraption had caused the devastation. One more bang made him cower but, thankfully, nothing flew close to them.

Malachi was stuck fast under a tree that ten men would have struggled to lift. Ant winced at the thought of the damage Malachi must have suffered when the tree fell on him. When Tyrant arrived and tried to pull him clear, Malachi screamed his protests, then went ominously quiet.

The smoke cleared and the ship became plainly visible. Smoke billowed from the bow as if something had caught fire. Ant hoped it might be the device that had burned, but was concerned that the flames could be part of regenerating whatever power it needed to continue with the destruction. Either way, Malachi had to be moved or he'd be at the mercy of the terrible weapon.

Digging beneath Malachi's pinned legs was frustratingly slow. His fingernails felt as if they were being torn off his hands as he scrabbled amongst the roots and tried to shift the dirt. Tyrant worked like a man possessed, either in fear of the next attack or out of concern for the stricken wizard. Ant felt confident he knew the answer to that question.

They succeeded in hollowing out enough space to gently extract the injured wizard who had lapsed into unconsciousness. Tyrant picked up the lifeless body and put it over his shoulder. 'Take him to the vedhana as fast as you can,' Ant said. 'Then try to transport yourselves to the monastery. They might be able to help him.'

'Only if you come too,' Tyrant said. 'Otherwise, I'm staying here with you.'

'We can't leave Malachi here to die.'

'Why not?' Tyrant replied. 'He left me to die without a second thought.'

'All the more reason to demonstrate that you're not like him. You have to take him, Tyrant. I'm going to find Cassie and Bee for you in return. Don't worry about me. If I hit any more trouble, I'll use a vedhana to escape and find you wherever you are. In the meantime, get out while you still can, take Malachi, and look after him for me.'

Tyrant gave him one of the ponderous looks he was so good at. It questioned everything he'd said without having to utter another word. If Ant harboured any doubts or reservations at all, he'd have changed his mind. The look was that powerful.

Tyrant lumbered towards the vedhana. Ant shouldered the heavy bag and emerged from the relative shelter of the forest, anticipating instant death at any moment, but being rewarded by faint sounds of anguish from the distant ship. Placing the bag into the small boat, he tried to push it off the sand and into the sea. It wouldn't move. No matter how hard he strained, it remained stuck. Tyrant was hesitating next to the vedhana, watching him. Ant waved him onwards. 'I'm fine,' he shouted. 'Just getting my breath back. Off you go.'

Tyrant shrugged, the body over his shoulders heaving in unison, then he stepped into the whirling lights and disappeared.

Ant dug sand from under the front and sides of the boat and tried again. This time, he was rewarded with some slight movement. Repeating the process, he manoeuvred the craft over the slight rise and it slid satisfyingly smoothly into the sea.

When he rowed out to the ship, the noises resolved into the screams of injured men. Nobody appeared to be aware of his proximity. There were no shouts of challenge or arrows fired. The ship seemed in turmoil.

He attached his boat to the stern where a rope ladder beckoned him upwards on to the deck. It was an awkward climb. He kept being battered against the hull by the motion of the sea and the flexibility of the ladder, but he managed to clamber on board without falling into the sea or dropping the bag.

The sight that greeted him was one of terrible carnage. There were dead and dying scattered around the bow area. One man had a huge wound in his belly that had released his guts onto the deck, yet was still whimpering. Another lay prone as the last dribbles of blood leaked from the stump of his severed leg. Three other sailors lay shattered and lifeless.

Ant was beginning to wonder if everyone on board was either dead or dying when a figure emerged from a hatchway. It was a man carrying a thin sword in his right hand. Most of his left arm was missing. What was left of it was swathed in bandages whose ragged edges dribbled a constant stream of blood that pattered onto the deck.

37

The crewman's name was Rog, and he'd been assigned to make sure that the girls stayed below in their quarters. Bee knew that he was a particular friend of the unfortunate Finn. Either this was an unhappy coincidence, or Gil had made his choice out of cruelty.

The sounds of activity above had quietened. Boots had stopped stomping about and the crashes as men jumped from the rigging onto the deck had ceased. The eerie silence below decks now spread above. Bee imagined the ship gliding towards the shore and wondered who it was seeking. Gil seemed very certain that the quarry he sought would be waiting for him. She hoped with all her heart that Tyrant wasn't standing on the beach in ignorance of who was coming to get him and the power of his cannon device.

'What do you think's going on up there?' Bee spoke to Rog in hushed tones. She didn't want Gil to hear the attempted conversation, though she was sure that he had more important things to occupy him.

Rog shook his head and put his finger to his lips.

'It's only you that's forbidden to speak, not us. We can say anything we want, can't we, Cassie?'

'Rog can speak if he wants. He's just not allowed to tell us anything we don't know or shag you.'

Bee laughed at the idea. Rog was fat and repulsive and balding. How he managed to be a sailor with a body like his, she couldn't begin to imagine. If he tried to climb up the rigging, she reckoned the mast would break. 'That's not a problem,' she answered, ''cos we know everything already, so there's no danger that Rog will get into trouble.'

'We know we're going to Kish,' Cassie said, 'and we know that Gil is going to kill the King of Kish as soon as we get there. He'll become King himself and make life terrible for the whole population. We've seen what he can do, and it's not nice at all.'

Rog's face was turning redder by the minute, but he kept quiet.

'All the women will have to give themselves to Gil so he can do unspeakable things with them. Not just sex, but horrible torture and abuse. He chops women up for fun; making people suffer and die is the only thing that amuses him. Just you wait and see, Rog. He'll butcher your mother and rape your sisters.'

'You can't possibly know what he'll do. Anyway, he's a friend and ally of our King. You're trying to upset me,' Rog hissed.

'Oh, we know him, don't we?' Cassie said.

'Only too well,' Bee answered. 'Our friend Tyrant is the only one who can stand up to him. They fought a mighty battle and Tyrant won. Everybody thought Gil had been killed and buried deep in the earth, but he must have dug his way out.'

'Tyrant has come to finish the job off,' Cassie said. 'If you help him, you'll be saving your people from oppression.'

'If he's so mighty, why does he need anybody's help?' Rog said.

'I'm thinking of you,' Bee said. 'If you help Gil, you'll make an enemy of Tyrant and that wouldn't be wise.'

'No,' Cassie said, 'and Tyrant will do what we tell him to because he's our special friend.'

'He's like a father to us but better 'cos he's chosen us to look after us, whereas fathers have to put up with whatever they happen to get,' Bee added.

'I can't believe that your King is so stupid as to assist Gil by giving him this ship. He deserves everything he's going to get if you ask me,' Cassie said.

'He's not stupid,' Rog said, his voice breaking out of a whisper into normal tones. 'Our King is very wise. Gil will protect us against the attack from the North that is coming.'

'They're only going to attack because Gil has kidnapped us,' Bee said. 'Otherwise, our King couldn't care less about a poxy island in the middle of nowhere. Are you going to fight and die to further the ambitions of someone who will bring only despair and destruction to your home?'

'It's not like that. You're telling lies just so I'll help you escape.'

Bee laughed her best false laugh, the one she used when Cuthbert said something he thought was funny and gave her that obnoxious look. 'We don't need your help. Tyrant is coming. It's you that needs help.' Three bangs shook the ship, and the vibrations thudded into her body. Gil was shooting his cannon now. She felt sure it was Tyrant he was killing.

143

Who else would be bothered to come to her aid except the big man whose devotion was plain for all to see? Two more reports slammed through her head. Gil was making absolutely sure that Tyrant and anyone who accompanied him was well and truly dead. Had he brought Petra? Tears welled up at the thought. She'd not be left behind under any circumstances, Bee was certain of that. Then there was her father. Had he brought soldiers with him to fight for her freedom? Whoever it was, they had to be dead by now. All she'd have left was Cassie. Keeping a brave face in front of Rog was impossible, and she gave in to her grief.

The next bang seemed different. Louder. Nearer. It was followed by screams up on deck. Bee stopped sobbing to listen. Groans of pain. Cries of anguish. Something bad had happened on the ship. Had the people on the shore managed to fight back? Did they too have a cannon?

The sounds died. An awful silence descended, broken only by an occasional whimper. Her sister stared wide-eyed and open-mouthed at her but she could find no words in response. Rog had the face of a startled rabbit that turned this way and that as if wanting to run somewhere but not knowing where. 'Stay here,' Bee said. 'That's what he told you to do. If you go up there, he'll kill you.' *If he's still alive,* she thought, and her spirits lifted at the possibility that Gil had been killed by his own device. That would serve him right.

38

Half of the man's face was missing, leaving a jagged mass of blood and bone. The rest was intact, an expressionless mask of white contrasting with the dark red mess. Even with his awful injuries, Ant recognised him as Gilgamesh, the cruel demi-god he'd buried in the ruins of his palace using the golem his father had conjured.

The tip of the impossibly thin sword danced a mere finger's width from his left eye. Drawing back his head made no difference; the blade remained implacably threatening to his eyesight. He froze, transfixed by the weapon's deadly proximity. 'You're that boy, aren't you?' Gilgamesh said. 'The wizard's assistant. I thought that was Malachi I saw on the shore. Please tell me he's dead.'

Ant nodded carefully, trying to keep away from the sword.

'And the big lump was Tyrant then? How satisfying if I got them both together.'

'It was Tyrant,' Ant said.

'And is he dead as well?'

'He's gone,' Ant said.

'Then all this pain and suffering might not be so bad after all. Don't be concerned about me. I can mend this face of mine so that it will be even more handsome than ever. As for the arm, well, that might need a bit more work.'

'What happened?' Ant asked.

'To me?'

'Yes.'

'It wasn't the result of some mighty piece of magic produced by your master, if that's your thinking. The device I was using to kill you all was old. Very old. It seems I made too much use of it and it broke. In a most violent and unfortunate manner. Such is the way of ancient things. Best not to rely too much on their efficacy, though I have to tell you that it was fun while it lasted. There are more like it buried deep below the ruins of my palace, so all is not lost as far as that source of amusement. But tell me, boy, what made you crawl aboard this ship instead of fleeing as any sane person would do?'

The sword tip waggled slightly, and he wondered when the final thrust would come. His hand gently brushed the pouch on his belt in an attempt to rouse his avatar to perhaps provide enough of a distraction to allow him to get away from the madman. It hung slack and empty. Either he was still on the shore or was readying himself to help. Ant knew his life depended on it being the latter. While he was waiting for him to appear, it was necessary to keep the man talking. 'I was wondering if I could be your assistant. Malachi was interesting at first, but he was weak and powerless compared to you. All he could manage was a bit of coercion and a few potions. To ordinary men, he must have seemed something special, but I've seen what you can do. I can help you. I can learn to use the devices on your behalf. Protect you from the danger of them breaking and injuring you.'

Gilgamesh's face was grotesque. Half his lips were gone so that his teeth were already bared on one side of his face in a lopsided grin. When the rest of his teeth were visible, he looked even less human. It was as if a skull had been roughly covered in fabric and a large ragged hole cut to reveal its mouth. Ant suppressed a shudder of revulsion. Gilgamesh was rotten. His mind had rotted away in a body that should have been consumed by maggots many lifetimes ago. The only thing that animated him was his hatred.

'Tell me what you learned from Malachi.'

'Mostly awareness. Learning to be present, that sort of thing. He taught me to observe people.'

'What about tricks? You know, spells and the like. There must have been more than that.'

'I was more of a servant than anything else. Malachi kept all his magical secrets to himself.' *He taught me to use your arrogance and your cruelty. To know that the stronger you think you are, the more weaknesses you betray. I buried you once and I'll do it again and make sure that there's no way out this time.*

'Then you're no more use to me than the fools that litter these decks.'

'Leave him alone, you big bully. Oh. What happened to you, Gil? You look a bit worse for wear if you ask me.' It was Bee, emerging from below decks followed closely by her sister, who stood staring at the carnage, her face contorted with pain.

Gilgamesh turned to the girl, but the sword remained unwavering in position. 'It's not as bad as it looks,' he said.

'It looks awful to me. Are you going to die 'cos of it?'

'Sorry to disappoint you, but I'll be back to my wonderful best in no time at all. In the meantime, though, I have this intruder to teach a lesson to. Which eye do you think I should stab him in first?'

'If you want my opinion,' Bee's voice was surprisingly strong under the testing circumstances, 'I think you need all the hired help you can get. Look what you've done to the crew. Who's going to sail the ship? Me and Cassie can't possibly do it, we're only girls. You don't look as if you're going to be scampering up the rigging any time soon.'

Ant noticed his out breath for the first time as the sword lowered. 'He's harmless anyway,' Gilgamesh said. 'Do you two know who he is?'

'Yes,' Cassie said.

'No, we've never seen him before in our lives,' Bee said at almost the same time.

Ant found that place inside him that wanted to fight. Wanted revenge for Malachi. The part of him that couldn't be held back from lashing out. The wounded child who knew that it was all his fault that the world was such a cruel place. He cradled himself, soothed his anger, absorbed his pain. In its place, he became a quiet, scared Ant who only wanted to please. Unimportant Ant, ignorant Ant. An insignificant boy who knew little and understood even less. His energy settled and his body relaxed. Gilgamesh might have registered the change because his stare became sharper for an instant and the sword quivered slightly in his hand.

A large sailor struggled up through the hatchway, looked all around, and began to vomit loudly onto the deck at his feet. 'What happened to them?' he asked between retches.

'Curiosity.' Gilgamesh laughed. 'They all wanted to see what destruction the magical device was causing. When it went wrong, they became part of the carnage themselves. Get this mess cleaned up. Throw the dead and dying to the crocodiles and tend to the injured. This boy will help. If he gives you any trouble, throw him into the sea.'

Gilgamesh turned away. 'I'll be starting my own healing process down below. As soon as you are able, set sail for Kish. You girls get back to your quarters and stay there if you don't want to be scooping blood and guts from the decks with your delicate hands.'

It may have been a result of his mind turning to the bag or some unconscious movement towards it that Gilgamesh suddenly became aware of it and turned back to face him. 'What's in the bag you're so carefully guarding?'

'I'll show you.' Ant picked it up. 'I thought you might be hungry, so I collected some fruit.' He opened the bag and put his hand inside, feeling around for another of those star launchers. If he could shoot it at his head, it might do enough damage to finish him off.

'Eat it yourself; I've better things to do.' Gilgamesh turned away again and disappeared down the hatch. Ant gave a long sigh and his legs almost gave way underneath him.

'You heard what the man said,' the sailor said and breathed a sickly stink in his direction.

Ant tended a man with head wounds lying at the front of the device. It appeared that the greatest destruction had been concentrated towards its rear, but this unfortunate sailor had received a severe blow to the temple. At first sight, Ant thought the crewman was dead, but there was a trickle of blood from the wound that pulsed gently. He took this to indicate a continuation of life and hope, so he fastened a makeshift bandage made from strips of the man's shirt around his head. Ant's head was close to the end of the tube that projected from the cannon. This end seemed undamaged in contrast to the rear, which had been blasted open so that shards of metal formed a macabre claw. Something was leaking from the tube. It was a grey powder that Ant instantly recognised. It trickled onto the deck and formed a conical pile. Ant swept it up with his hands and poured it into the pouch on his belt. The other sailor's attention was engaged with a surviving crew member who was sitting up next to the mast and rubbing his head.

Ant's ministrations were rewarded by groans from his bandaged patient. He filled a bucket of fresh water from an intact barrel lashed to the gunwales, then managed to get the man to drink some. The rest of the crew, six of them, were all dead. Unless there were more below decks, that meant there would be three to sail the ship, not counting himself. That might be enough. He hoped it would be.

Despite his protestations, Rog, the one uninjured member of the crew, made him take the wheel and pilot the ship unsupervised through the long night. It was a recipe for disaster, but his account of what had happened to the last ship he'd had to steer was unheeded. The ship heaved and rolled its way, Ant keeping course for the cluster of stars he'd been shown. Each course correction brought with it the prospect of a sudden wave and being washed overboard again. The prospect of another night in the sea made him terribly afraid.

The elements were kind, though. The ship negotiated the swell without any problems, and the wind seemed to be in the right direction. Overcome with fatigue, but determined to keep himself alive by proving his utility, he managed to stay conscious until he was relieved at the helm by Jed, the man whose head wound he'd bandaged and who seemed to be making a good recovery. As he lay down in a sheltered place in the bow, he cradled the pouch in his hands and felt into its contents. They remained distressingly inert. There had been no movement or other signs of life since he'd scooped it from the deck. It was as if his avatar's final effort had been to exit the tube and that had robbed it of all function. There was the disappointing likelihood that this had been his final act.

As sleep rolled over his thoughts, Ant wondered what had happened. How had Little Ant found his way into the tube, and why? In the face of that awful bombardment, the avatar's exit had not registered. Could he have flown all the way out to the ship and purposefully blocked the weapon, thereby destroying it? Were Gilgamesh's injuries caused by his avatar? He very much hoped so. That might be small consolation for the loss of Malachi, but it was something to give him hope. The demi-god might not be completely indestructible.

He had his avatar and the contents of Malachi's bag, on which he rested his head. The Queen and Princess had been located and seemed safe for the moment. Gilgamesh appeared to be prepared to dismiss him as a stupid boy who presented no threat. These were all positives that his aching mind and body could use as sustenance. If he could get to shore and create a vedhana, he could spirit the girls away to safety.

He needed to stay alive, but that was dependent on the whim of a cruel madman.

39

Jed spent all his waking time at the wheel issuing gentle instructions that Rog translated into shouted commands. Ant was mildly amused by the unthreatening nature of the man's belligerence. There had been no sign of Gilgamesh for three days now. The hope that he'd succumbed to his wounds, as had the fourth crew member to survive the destruction of the device, was an enticing one, but not something Ant dared to rely on.

The girls made the occasional brief appearance on deck and were obviously desperate to talk to him. Rog made a point of preventing this, and Ant didn't want him running off to tell Gilgamesh that his orders were being flouted. All he could manage were what he hoped were reassuring smiles.

Each night he'd slept with his inert avatar cradled in his arms and awoke with fresh hope for signs of recovery. There had been no discernible change to the contents of the pouch. He was becoming increasingly convinced that he'd seen the last of Little Ant. The sorrow of missed opportunities and unrealised potential was, at times, unbearable. In contrast, when he thought of Malachi, his sadness was tempered by the knowledge that he'd lived fully on his terms and left little, if anything, undone. It was possible for him to recognise that Malachi had imparted everything he could to Ant and that their relationship had not been close for some years. Still, he'd miss the old man despite his penchant for overblown theatrics.

After six days of sailing, the unremitting seascape yielded a smudge of contrast that slowly resolved to a long coastline backed by towering mountains. Rog was jubilant. So happy that he took it on himself to clatter below and bring Gilgamesh on deck for the first time since the night Ant had clambered aboard. During the voyage, Ant had stayed safely on deck, preferring the inadequate shelter of spare sails and rigging to the obvious dangers of confronting the demi-god below. He busied himself coiling and folding as far from the bow as possible. Despite his heightened anxiety, Gilgamesh didn't confront him or even give him a second glance before disappearing once again. Ant considered his appearance and concluded that it was sufficiently dishevelled to make him easily mistaken for part of the original crew.

His relief at not being targeted by Gilgamesh was tempered by a twinge of disappointment at the sight of him still obviously alive. At least his arm hadn't grown back. That would have been a very worrying turn of events, but one he had considered possible given his superhuman powers. Now, getting off this ship alive was tantalisingly close. However, there was the distinct possibility that he'd only been given a temporary reprieve until such time that he was no longer of use. Something drastic might have to be done to escape. Relying on Gilgamesh forgetting about him wasn't a safe enough option. One flick of that sword would be all it would take to kill him and make any plans he might have irrelevant.

He peered over the bow at the two small boats that bobbed obligingly in the ship's wake. His best judgement was that they'd not make landfall before dusk and that might give him the opportunity to slip away. He had to hope that they left him alone at the helm for the last leg of the journey, and both Rog and Jed spent the last night below. Otherwise, he'd be prevented from leaving and Gilgamesh would be roused. In that case, it would certainly be the end of him.

As the sun sank and the long shadows disappeared into darkness, Ant offered to take the wheel from Jed. 'Nearly there,' the sailor whispered in that quiet voice of his. 'Take a break and get ready for going ashore.' The wound over his eye had swollen so that he had a permanent wink, but otherwise, he'd made a good recovery from the injury. Ant wondered if he might persuade Jed to let him take a boat and escape. Perhaps there would be sufficient gratitude remaining from having his wounds tended. Anxiety threatened to drown him. Uncertainty gripped his guts. It would be a final cast of the dice. Could he rely on Jed being grateful? Or was he afraid of what Gilgamesh would do to him if Ant escaped?

The shore was fast approaching. Prickles of lamplight were sprouting from the darkness. It was now or never. Make a positive play or passively accept whatever fate Gilgamesh decided for him.

Cold fear told him the answer to his conundrum. If he left it to Gilgamesh, he'd be killed before he could set foot on shore. If he pleaded with Jed, the outcome would be the same. Either way, he was unlikely to survive.

Something about the thought jolted him into a realisation that it didn't matter what he did, as long as it was his conscious choice. His decision. Not what his father might require of him, nor what Malachi would expect. A miasma had been swirled by a wind of awareness and revealed a whole new beginning. He was Ant. He could act any way he wanted to. He didn't need to please Tyrant, nor curry favour with Lone. They weren't present and, even if they had been, his days of acquiescence were over. The basis of all his actions from here on would be based on what felt right for him. He allowed the realities of the present moment to sink in, felt the restrictions of a lifetime sliding from his shoulders like rain from his cloak, connected with the heart of himself, the one who knew him and loved him unconditionally. Then he knew what he had to do. It was simple, obvious and, more importantly, coming from the right part of him. The real part. The Ant part.

Jed wiped his brow with a bloodstained rag and stared back at him. 'Go below,' Ant repeated. 'You aren't needed until we have to dock. Rest your aching head. Gather your strength in readiness.'

Jed's head shook from side to side. 'I'll be fine,' he said. 'Not long to go now.'

'But your head aches so terribly. Lying down in a dark place will soothe it.'

A flicker of doubt creased his face. Ant deepened his voice. 'Go below,' he repeated, imbuing the words with energy. 'Leave this to me.'

As if waking from a dream, Jed let go of the wheel. 'You don't need me until we get beyond that promontory. See it? The dark area amid all the lights.'

Ant took the helm and watched him stomp across the deck and disappear down the hatch. As soon as his head was out of sight, Ant left the wheel, slung his bag over his shoulder, and ran to the stern. The rope ladder still dangled invitingly, and he lowered himself until he was perilously close to the swell that threatened to wet his boots with every wave. The knot that secured the small boat had been tightened by constant drenching and proved so obstinate he wished he'd brought a knife. Abandoning his precarious and futile attempts to unravel it one-handed, he felt for the boat with his foot, dragged it underneath him, and dropped the bag. There was a reassuring thud as the bag landed safely. Taking a precautionary breath, he let go of the ladder and jumped into the boat. It swayed and rolled alarmingly, but remained upright as he landed, tripped, fell backwards, and clung on until the motion became less violent. Then he crawled up to the bow and untied the rope securing it to the ship.

With the help of an oar, he pushed off and gained a satisfying distance away before placing the oars in the rowlocks and pulling hard. Rowing in the opposite direction to the ship's course would give him the maximum separation in the shortest time, even if it was taking him back out to sea. What he dreaded most was the ghastly sight of the half-faced Gilgamesh pointing some awful device in his direction, but this prospect faded into the darkness.

The ship quickly became invisible, so he altered course to take him parallel to the shore. His intention was to make landfall away from the lights and people who might prove to be unfriendly. The further he rowed, the lighter his heart became.

The lights were diminishing, and the shore seemed further away than ever, so he altered course to head directly for the land. No matter how hard he heaved at the oars, every time he turned to look, he was no closer. A strong current was dragging him out to sea, and his efforts were too feeble to resist it.

40

'It's not that easy.'

The words floated out of the vedhana, to be followed by a familiar but unwelcome sight. The long white face, spindly legs, and grossly misshapen body of that most peculiar horse she knew as Patch. This was the demon she'd held captive, but he was no longer in her thrall. Instead, he was a dangerous antagonist, and she was well aware there was no love lost between the two of them.

'Where do you think your portal will take you?' Patch asked.

'Anywhere I want,' Lone replied.

'Wrong.' Patch sniggered in a ridiculously horsy manner. 'It goes back to the burning fires and my minions, who won't be so reluctant to feast on your flesh as they were the first time they saw you.'

Lone was willing to believe she was being deceived, but felt disinclined to put it to the test. The terrible fate he described was well within his power to deliver, whether through the vedhana or otherwise. 'I'm happy to see you,' she said.

'Then you're more stupid than I thought. Do you think you can weave me into some ancient spell again without my consent? Are you trying to ensnare me even though you've had a taste of my power?'

'On the contrary, I've sought you out to offer you an opportunity that you would do well to consider carefully. I have something very special to offer you in return for a short period of cooperation.'

'There's nothing you have that I either want or need. Don't make me laugh. Now, how would you prefer to end your miserable life? Out here in the desert where you will slowly rot or back in my dominion where your death will be relatively quick but equally painful?'

'Before you condemn me, let me tell you what I want from you.' Lone's heart was stammering, and it was hard to keep her voice from betraying the panic welling up inside her chest. 'A few days where you help me with your power and majesty will be repaid by an eternity of worship and delicious good energy.'

'You promise to worship me? Is that all you have to offer?'

'Not me, but every female human in the kingdom. I intend to restore the rights of every woman to determine her own destiny. If you agree to support me in this mission, I will ensure that temples are set up in your name and that thousands of female acolytes will spend all their lives praising it. You will become a god to my people.'

'But I'm not a god, I'm a demon. Gods live forever, demons don't. Or has your grasp of ancient lore deserted you?'

'In human terms, your lifetime is so long it might as well be infinite. Terminology doesn't matter. What does is energy. Positive, delicious, nourishing energy that only devout humans can create. You received a taste of it at the monastery, and so did others of your kind. Think how it will be when you have access to as much of that as you want, with plenty left over to impress your friends and peers. Think of the bargaining power you'll hold. Remember, all of this will be entirely for your benefit. You will control the type of energy and the frequency. Your wishes will be paramount.'

The peculiar horse tipped its head slightly to one side before replying. 'You can say all these things, but I don't believe you can deliver any of it.'

Lone's heart quickened. He was taking the bait. She'd fastened the fattest, juiciest worm imaginable on the end of her hook, and now he was nibbling at it.

41

It was a fittingly dismal morning in Spelt. The early sun cast an eerie orange glow through the mist that illuminated the gathering, but failed to provide any cheer to the impending proceedings. The crowd consisted mainly of females who were obliged under threat of severe punishment to attend, with a scattering of men who were there for more prurient reasons. The atmosphere of resigned hopelessness deepened as the offender was dragged onto the raised platform and tied to the upright that supported the gibbet.

Little had changed since Lone had lived in this desperate place, narrowly escaping condemnation as a witch thanks to Malachi's intervention. The men who ruled were older but seemingly no wiser. The Elder addressed the crowd, who stood motionless in hushed silence, knowing well the penalty for paying other than rapt attention while a man was speaking.

'This is Miriam, wife of Horn, who has been found guilty of gross insubordination and aggravated assault. She is here to be punished and you are here to witness the consequences of disobedience to your husband's wishes. I will now let her speak her words of apology and hear her promises for better behaviour in the future. Then we will proceed with the flogging.'

Miriam was an imposing woman who stood tall and oozing defiance even before she spoke. Lone knew her as a generally gentle and compliant woman who had finally resisted one of her vicious husband's more vicious beatings by picking him up and throwing him into a latrine. His attempts at retaliation had been nipped in the bud by some solid punches to his head and a kick that propelled him back into the mire. Lone knew this because she'd been present during the altercation. If she were being truthful, she'd have to admit that she'd whispered a few words in each of the protagonists' ears in order to get things started. Patience was something she had been never been willing to embrace. Time was too precious to allow matters to take their own course.

Now Miriam's eyes blazed with anger as she replied to the Elder. 'Women,' she said, 'are not possessions. We are not animals. We are people. We have exactly the same rights and authority as men.' A murmur of astonishment greeted the words that Lone had taught her. 'My husband is a cruel and vicious man and I will continue to uphold my right to defend myself and my children from him. If he ever dares to lay a finger on me again, I will snap his miserable body like a twig and dance on his grave.'

Lone couldn't help smiling. Perfectly remembered, well delivered words that had wiped the smugness from the face of the Elder. 'Then you will be flogged until you admit your wrongdoing. Every day from now on, you will be brought here for punishment and the opportunity to repent. If you have not convinced us of your contrition by the fifth day, you will be hanged. This is what happens to a woman who will not accept the natural order of things.'

'This is not the natural order; this is the way of evil and weak men who are too afraid to treat women as the equals that they are,' Miriam replied in a strong voice that sent a ripple through the crowd.

'This is the way that the King has decreed and those that defy the King will surely be executed for treason.'

'The King is not my master.' Miriam was yelling now. 'I have prayed to the goddess Persephone for guidance and She has taught me the error of the King's ways. She is the supreme being and holds ascendance over the whole world. Even Kings must bow down before her. Praise to Persephone, protector of women and saviour of children.'

Lone could feel the assembly becoming more animated. Miriam was adding a few embellishments of her own to the script, but these were convincing and heartfelt words that were clearly having an effect.

'Strip her naked and begin the punishment,' the Elder shouted above the growing hubbub. A man stepped forward and grabbed Miriam's dress at the collar. Instead of ripping it from her back, he let go of it and retreated, his face wearing a look of confusion.

Lone breathed heavily. There was only so much she could do from here to protect Miriam. Help was needed and, to be honest, was becoming overdue to the extent that it was jeopardising the whole plan. If it didn't come very soon, she'd be forced into an overt intervention that would completely negate the positive message that Miriam was proclaiming.

She was winding herself up to kill the Elders and their entourage just so she could save Miriam when there was a gasp from the crowd and, to be fair to them, even the Elders adopted a look of amazement.

It was a shimmering, glowing figure dressed in dazzling white robes and wearing a light blue headscarf. She, for it was a woman of amazing beauty, glided above the heads of the crowd and hovered in front of Miriam. The ropes on her hands dropped to the ground, and she stepped forward to greet the apparition, then went down on her knees and touched her head to the ground in supplication.

Lone found herself impressed and jubilant. She'd had no way of knowing what Patch would come up with and had harboured a suspicion that his half-arsed horse might make an appearance and negate all the good work that Miriam was doing. In contrast, he really did look like a goddess. 'Rise, Miriam, and receive the sign of Persephone. Wear this ribbon as a mark of your devotion to me and my protection of you. No man shall ever survive the mistreatment of any woman who worships me. I grant you the powers of priestess and invite you to anoint whoever you find worthy. Anyone wearing the ribbon and worshipping me will receive my protection for ever and ever. All of you kneel in the presence of your god and pray for my protection and forgiveness.'

Patch was laying it on thick and in danger of losing his audience. The general feeling of awe was dissipating and Lone was concerned that the men would find their voices again and begin to undo all her good work. Her fears were realised when the Elder drew a knife and plunged it into Miriam's back.

42

Despite rowing as hard as he could, Ant was slowly being taken out to sea and away from land. The pricks of light were diminishing, fading, and disappearing, leaving him with only a vague recollection of where the land had been. At least the total darkness meant that it was becoming increasingly unlikely that Gilgamesh would be able to find him. He wondered if his absence had been discovered and whether the savage demi-god even cared that he was gone.

His arms and legs were tired, but rowing was the only thing he could do that might save him. Keeping as close to land as possible seemed the only way to save himself. Perhaps when morning came, he'd be able to find a solution to his problem. The current might even conveniently reverse. Did currents do that? Were they like winds or did they always flow the same way?

A shower of cold water drenched his head and shoulders. Something had leapt out of the sea and landed with a great splash. The water foamed silver where the creature had disappeared. Some sea monster had broken the surface to take a look at him. Was it interested? Would it return?

His answer came almost immediately. A black, smooth streamlined shape appeared so close to the boat that he could have reached out and touched it. This time it slid smoothly back into the depths, only to emerge again near the bow. Ant watched in trepidation. The creature seemed as large as the boat and capable of tipping him into the sea where he would be easy prey. The boat shuddered as it was nudged sideways. The creature was pushing the bow with its nose, forcing it to face out to sea instead of in the direction he thought the land was. There was nothing he could do to change matters. The creature was guiding the boat, and it was small consolation that it hadn't decided to sink him.

As it turned, the current seemed to catch the boat, and he felt his speed quickening. The creature swam alongside now, its triangular fin cutting through the gentle swell. Ant shipped his oars and hung on to the sides of the boat. He couldn't row for fear of hitting the creature and perhaps enraging it.

With acceptance came relaxation, and tiredness descended quickly. He awoke lying in the boat with the sun coming up to his right. Before he could begin to work out if this was a good sign, he sat up and saw the shore. It was a sandy beach, not unlike the one he had walked with Tyrant. It couldn't be the same one, though; it had to be Kish. The waves were breaking around him and swilling him forward in bursts of foamy motion. The bottom of the boat bit on the sand and he came to a sudden stop. Clambering out, he stood in the surf and used the intermittent waves to help propel the boat onto the sand. If this was Kish, he doubted he'd ever need the boat again, but he was reluctant to abandon it to the sea.

Unlike the jungle he'd traversed with Tyrant, the shore gave way to dunes with sparse fringes of sharp grass and then to open land that stretched as far as he could see. Smudges of higher ground were visible at a distance in the hazy morning light. The air was warm and fragrant. The land felt soft and comfortable and unthreatening. It was only when he realised this that Ant could feel the extreme tension he was holding. For as long as he could remember, every moment had held the threat of sudden death. He was alone, unscathed, and in what seemed a friendly and hospitable place.

He was hungry, thirsty, and undecided on what to do next, yet it was as if a heavy weight had lifted from his spirit. He was here, and it seemed for the first time in his life that this was where he was meant to be. Even the sadness he felt about losing Malachi was sharp and wholesome in contrast to the self-sorry gloom with which he'd previously been afflicted. All the work he'd done with Malachi was making sense in a way it hadn't while his teacher was still alive to tell him what to think.

Luxuriating in the wellbeing arising from being calm and unthreatened, the options were clear. Making a vedhana here would be simple and he could use it to travel back to Gort, tell the King what had transpired, and where his Queen had been taken. If he did, he had no doubt that Cuthbert would despatch soldiers through the device. History told him that, no matter how many were sent, it was unlikely that they would prevail over Gilgamesh, who had laid waste to a whole army during their previous encounter in the desert. The alternative was to adopt a more subtle approach. Find where the girls were being held, wait for an opportunity, and then spirit them away. Direct action was going to get everyone killed, whereas this option involved no bloodshed and a better chance of success. Unfortunately, it was the choice that would put him in danger.

He busied himself making a vedhana. Whichever option he chose, he'd need a way to get the girls back to Gort. The familiar process comforted him. When it was completed and the cold flickering flames began to rise, he sat beside them and allowed his mind to clear. Gnawing hunger deserted him, his raging thirst receded, peace descended, and with it came certainty.

Taking the pouch from his belt, he tipped the contents onto the leaf-strewn earth next to the vedhana. Cupping his hands, he reflected the energies towards the pile of dirt and watched the coruscations play gently around it, as if they were caressing a wounded animal. The intensity of the emanations increased very gradually, more of the energy was being sucked from the vedhana, and striations started to run through one side of the heap and out the other.

Ant closed his eyes and waited. His conviction grew in strength as he relaxed into a meditative state. The way forward was clear. Going back for help, even trying to find Tyrant, didn't feel right. This was his task now. The realisation brought him strength by banishing disturbing and energy-sapping uncertainty. How he proceeded didn't matter, nor did he worry that he might not survive. His decision came from his heart and whatever the outcome, it was the right one. This wasn't the scared Little Ant running away from trouble, nor was he the anxious to please Ant trying to gain approval. Real Ant was in command and knew what he wanted to do.

Little Ant's voice made him open his eyes to see the small shimmering representation standing shoulder high to his seated position. 'Whew,' the avatar said, 'that was unpleasant, to say the least.'

'What happened to you?'

'The last thing I remember, I'd decided to fill up that tube thing that was being used as a weapon against you. There was fire coming out of the end and I could see that this was going to kill you unless I did something. So, I sort of crawled inside and packed myself tight, hoping to stop whatever it was hurting you.'

'Then you did the right thing. The device was destroyed, together with most of the crew. Gilgamesh himself was badly injured, but not enough that he won't recover. Without your intervention, Tyrant and I would be dead.'

The effigy sparkled and its suspended grains shifted into a slightly larger version. 'What now? Are we going after him to finish the job?'

'Something like that, though the job, as far as I'm concerned, is to rescue the Queen and Princess and bring them home safely.'

'You do realise that to do that, you'll most likely have to kill Gilgamesh, don't you?'

'We'll deal with that possibility when we encounter it.'

'Are you capable of killing someone who has resisted death for many lifetimes?'

'Who knows? I managed to put him out of action for a long time on the first occasion our paths crossed.'

'But then you had Tyrant and Malachi and Lone all by your side. All fighting and supporting you.'

'True. But now I'm older, wiser, and infinitely more capable.'

Little Ant laughed. It was a gentle, whispering expression of merriment that lifted Ant's spirits and made him glad to be alive. How had he ever doubted that this avatar of his was anything other than a wonderful and supportive companion? The tiny figure represented everything good about his world.

'I need water and food,' Ant said. 'Otherwise, I fear that I'm going to collapse and then you'll have to carry me for a change.'

'What about the bag?'

'What about it?' Ant recognised he was talking to himself. That Little Ant was already well aware of everything he knew, and vice versa. Even so, the discourse was helpful. They were expressing his thoughts out loud in a very useful way.

'It's heavy. Shouldn't you leave it here if you're too tired to carry it? Or is there anything inside that might be useful?'

Ant opened the bag, pulled out the items inside, and laid them out on the ground. The long package bound in leather held another tube like the one Tyrant had discharged into the night sky. 'I don't think we'll need this,' Ant said. 'It's what betrayed our whereabouts to Gilgamesh and caused Malachi's death.'

'Isn't that why Malachi brought it? How else would he attract the attention of the ship carrying the girls?' Little Ant said.

'True, but there's no reason to do it again.' He unwrapped a small package that felt too heavy for its size. Inside was revealed a small box containing metal tubes the size of his thumb. The blunt ends were a light golden colour in contrast to the shiny silver casings that housed them. 'Any ideas?' Little Ant shook his head.

The largest item revealed a shocking secret. Inside a stout wooden box, nestling on soft fabric, sat a metal object that exuded menace. Ant picked it up carefully. It weighed heavy in his hand. There was a polished white grip that fitted his hand naturally, allowing his index finger to rest on the trigger guard, an item he recognised from its incorporation in the construction of sophisticated and expensive crossbows. This, however, was infinitely better than anything he'd previously seen. A fat cylinder was situated above the trigger and a tube the diameter of his finger protruded forwards. 'It's a miniature cannon,' Ant gasped. 'The things in the little box are tiny versions of the projectiles that Gilgamesh fed to his device.'

'Scary,' Little Ant said. 'Where did Malachi get such a thing?'

'Only one place he could have. We gathered lots of artefacts from Gilgamesh's palace before the golem buried it. These things must have been among them.'

'How does it work?' Little Ant asked.

Ant inserted small cylinders into the six holes available, then he pointed the device at the nearest tree and pulled the trigger. The silence was shattered by a loud bang that seemed to hang in the air. Ant's nerves were sent jangling. His body felt as if it had been battered by a sudden gale and struck by a lightning bolt. The tree was scarred and splintered. When he caught his breath, he considered what he'd seen. 'These little tubes must contain fire demons. Very angry ones at being imprisoned in such a tight space. This device gives them a kick in their rear that provokes them to burst out of captivity and wreak havoc on whatever they find.'

'Then we have a thing that will kill Gilgamesh. Isn't that what we've been looking for?'

'I'm not so sure,' Ant said, putting the weapon back in its box. 'You saw what the one he had on the ship was capable of. Gilgamesh had one with even bigger and angrier demons and he may have more. If this thing fell into the wrong hands, many innocent people could die.'

'All the more reason for us to have it. It will protect us. We can destroy anyone who stands in our way.'

'No.' Ant closed the box and fastened it. 'It's evil and dangerous. Whoever wields it will be corrupted by its power. I'm not going to take that chance.'

'What if it's our best possibility of rescuing the girls?'

'I'd rather fail than use this horrible thing. Don't you see? It would make me as bad as him. Worse, even, because I've made a conscious choice that he's not capable of.' Ant bundled the items back into the bag. 'We'll bury it where no one will find it.'

'What about the last package? What's in that?'

Ant unwrapped the greased parchment and discovered another box the size of his hand and, again, remarkably heavy. It opened to reveal gold coins neatly stacked and held in place with wax.

'There's enough gold in here to buy Gort,' Ant said with a gasp.

'Enough to buy the whole kingdom,' Little Ant said. 'Why would Malachi insist on dragging such enormous wealth with him on such a dangerous quest?'

'Maybe he hoped to buy the Queen's freedom,' Little Ant said.

'Or there was nowhere he felt he could safely leave his gold,' Ant replied.

'Either way, we've got it now.' Little Ant started jumping around and Ant realised he was dancing.

'Pity you can't eat gold,' Ant said. 'I'm starving.'

'You can buy all the food you need for the whole of your life with just one of these coins. You're the wealthiest man in the world. You can have anything you want.'

43

The frisson of shock and disappointment that coursed through Lone's body was suddenly checked and turned to amusement as she realised what was happening. An uncalled-for burst of admiration for the demon made her cheeks hot and her heart pound.

Persephone reached forward, plucked the knife from between Miriam's shoulders, and pulled her back to her feet with her hand. The ribbon on her breast shone brightly in the eerie half-light. Miriam's eyes shone, her face was radiant, and her invigoration was plain for all to see.

The Elder stepped back, face contorted as if expecting terrible retribution. Lone felt the crowd's intake of breath as it anticipated bloody retaliation. Persephone confronted the Elder and dangled the knife in front of his face. 'Try again,' she said in a voice that reverberated in the houses and trees surrounding the square.

The Elder took the knife with obvious reluctance and trepidation. Then his teeth were bared by tightened lips and a look of madness swept over his face. He raised the knife and brought it down with considerable force, burying it deep in his own abdomen. His cries began with astonishment, then changed to agony. He collapsed to the floor in an ever-spreading bloody pool.

'Come on,' Persephone shouted above the roars of the crowd, 'let anyone who doubts come forward and try to harm my priestess!'

Nobody moved a muscle. Not the men on the platform or those in the crowd. They stood, heads bowed, as if hoping to make themselves invisible. The Elder's self-inflicted suffering was the only source of sound.

One member of the audience broke ranks. It was a young woman dressed in pitiful rags whose male companion raised his arms to prevent her stepping forward, but quickly put them down again as he came under Persephone's gaze. The woman knelt in front of the demon, who fastened a glowing ribbon to her chest. Immediately, her drab clothes were transformed into a bright white flowing dress.

Two women came forward, then several more, until the whole female attendance formed a line. Persephone pinned every one of them with a ribbon, and as they received it, a visible transformation took place. The women of Spelt had been liberated.

Lone was still smiling long after Persephone had dramatically vanished in a shower of colourful sparks and the crowd had dispersed. Patch, in his now familiar and amusing horse manifestation, limped slowly from behind a tree. 'Well?' he asked.

'Oh, great one, please pin a ribbon on me, your humble and worshipful servant,' Lone said.

The horse snorted and dribbles of snot sprayed towards Lone. What would previously have driven her mad with anger, she now found amusing. If only she'd realised this from the outset she might have used his powers to start her female emancipation movement years ago when she had him ensnared by ancient magic. Now, however, was no time for regrets. She'd gambled her life, her soul, and her sanity for this chance. Now was time to enjoy the result.

'Very good,' Patch said. 'Do you think it went well?'

'Perfectly,' Lone answered. 'I have to admit, I've never seen anyone handle a crowd like that before. When you allowed Miriam to be stabbed, I thought you'd lost it, but it turned out to be a work of genius.'

The horse cocked his head to one side. 'Best to hammer home the point with humans. They tend to be very slow in appreciating what I'm capable of. As you probably realise, the knife I gave him to stab the woman wasn't real, though the one I returned to him was. A simple trick that needed only sleight of hand. You could have done it.'

'Performing it was one thing. The most impressive aspect was thinking of it in the first place. We only discussed you providing a suitable manifestation and leaving the rest to the superstitious nature of the audience. That alone might have been sufficient, but the stabbing was genius. Then tidying up their clothes when you gave them the ribbon was the snow on top of the mountain.'

'It's good to have your full approval,' Patch said with more than a hint of sarcasm. 'Now we need to see if you can fulfil your side of the bargain. Remember the penalties we discussed in the event of failure. I have better things to do with my time than manipulate humans.'

'It will be glorious, don't you worry,' Lone replied. 'Today was merely a start. There's much more work to be done before you get your temples. All you have to do is more of the same and be patient.'

She looked into the horse's eyes, and beneath the sardonic humour was a dark residue of malevolence.

44

Ant felt better after he'd drunk his fill from a stream that wandered gently down through the woods towards the sea. Now he was ravenous, but no longer in a state of collapse.

He'd taken a handful of gold and put it in the pouch that had housed Little Ant, who now skipped joyfully at his heels in the shape of a small dog. The rest he had buried close to the vedhana with the weapon and the signalling device.

The enormous wooden building was a welcome sight as he made his way through fields of gentle cows and frisky horses towards it. As they approached the house, the comfortable feelings turned to shocked fear as a huge dog, fangs bristling, came running from behind an outbuilding.

Little Ant, whose version of a dog involved a bulbous white body and spindly legs, yapped away in his high-pitched voice and stood between him and the beast. The slavering jaws opened to reveal yellow teeth and a slippery brown tongue. The animal was the size of a goat with the musculature of a bull. Tufts of darker hair stood erect in a ridge along its backbone.

It happened so quickly and Ant was so shocked by the dog's sudden appearance and vicious nature that he struggled to ground himself so that he could attempt a defensive move. Malachi would have throttled the thing just by looking at it, but Ant's grasp of the remote chokehold was rudimentary and required preparation time. Before he could let out a single calming breath, the attack dog snapped its jaws around Little Ant's body.

Little Ant stood his ground, seemingly unaffected by the savage bite. The dog began to whimper and paw at its snout. Head bowed, sneezing, and in obvious distress, it staggered away, tail curled under its backside. 'I think you got up its nose,' Ant said, mightily relieved.

The farmhouse was even more imposing close up. The man who stood in the entrance was old, his back bent so that he looked as if he was stuck in a permanent bow. In his hands he carried a cudgel of black polished wood. 'Be off with yer,' he shouted. 'Me boys will be back soon and then you'll be fer it. They'll skin you, so they will.'

'I only want some food,' Ant said. 'I mean you no harm.'

'Snarler!' the old man shouted. 'Snarler, where are yer? I'll set the dog on yer. Now beggar off.'

'I already met your dog,' Ant said. 'He took one sniff and decided not to bother me. I can pay for anything you give me.' Ant fished a gold coin from his pouch and held it up.

'Whassat? Issat gold? Show me. Bring it here.'

Ant approached, coin in his outstretched palm. The old man lowered the cudgel and reached out his hand. 'Gimme,' he said, 'so I can see it's real.' He grabbed it and bit hard on the edge of the gold piece. 'Has you got more I'm wondering?'

Before he could weigh up an appropriate response, a woman came out of the door. 'What are you blathering on about?' she demanded, taking the coin from the old man's grasp and returning it to Ant. Her hands were covered in flour, and her wild shock of frizzy hair was either greying prematurely or covered with the same substance as her hands. 'Where's your manners? You grumpy old fool, get out of the young master's way.'

She led Ant inside, where three girls were busily chopping and throwing meat and vegetables into an enormous black pot that was bubbling away in the heat of the fire. The cooking smells almost made Ant faint with longing. A tiny girl, about half Ant's height, staggered in through the back door carrying a wooden pail. The matriarch took it from her tiny hands, filled a tankard with the frothy white liquid it contained, and handed it to Ant. He gulped down the warm creamy milk, feeling it spreading its nutrition throughout his starving body. He was rewarded with a refill, then sat down at the table and served with a hunk of bread liberally covered in honey.

By the time he'd finished his milk and his bread, Ant was feeling much better. The food onboard the ship had been sparse and dull. The fruit he'd managed to forage in the jungle had been better, but hard to find and not at all plentiful. Now he felt replete for the first time in a very long time and his body relaxed in appreciation.

'I'm happy to pay for this wonderful food.' He proffered the coin to the woman who had delivered him from starvation.

'Nonsense.' She pushed his hand away. 'It's the least we can do. Now we need to clean you up and find you some clothes. I don't think you realise how awful you look.'

She led him outside to the rear of the great house where chickens and pigs were competing for scraps. A fire crackled underneath a metal tub containing water that was gently steaming. 'In you get,' she said. 'Wash off all that grime and let's see what you really look like.' Her face wore a broad smile that reminded Ant of the way Mona used to look at him. 'Don't be shy, I promise not to look, though I doubt you've got anything I haven't seen many times before. Leave your clothes on the ground; I'll find you some clean ones.'

The water was almost too hot to bear at first, but when he got used to it, the heat permeated his bones, driving out the chill that his long ordeal and near death had implanted. As he rubbed away the salty grime, he imagined minute creatures leaping off his flesh and swimming for their lives. Closing his eyes, he sank under the surface and gave his scalp time to cleanse itself.

By the time he clambered out of the tub, his hands were soft and wrinkled. His tattered, filthy garb had been taken away and clean, wholesome clothing left in its place. Only his boots remained together with the pouch that contained his gold. The delicious cooking aroma wafting from the house ignited his hunger despite having already consumed more nutrition today than he'd had in the previous week. The deep smell of the stew reminded him that he'd not had cooked meat since he'd embarked on the voyage to save the girls.

Quickly restoring his modesty in case there were prying eyes, he pulled on the clothes and found them a reasonable fit. The trousers were a little baggy around the waist, but he reckoned a few weeks of decent and plentiful food would sort that out. Having room to grow was something he could enjoy making use of.

The kitchen had become crowded. He counted seven men sitting at the big wooden table and another four standing up and talking to the old man that had threatened him with a cudgel. All faces turned to watch him enter, their expressions a mixture of fear and suspicion. All talking ceased and an uncomfortable silence closed in. Ant felt very awkward and exposed. His nervousness increased when the old man hissed at him. 'We doesn't want the likes of you here. Go while you're still able to walk.'

The cook turned from stirring her pot and wafted away the mist that was obscuring her head. 'You'll keep a civil tongue with our guest.' She narrowed her eyes and allowed her gaze to travel slowly around the room. 'And that goes fer the lot of you. One more word out of place and you'll be getting the ladle across your heads and no stew to follow.' Two men shuffled uncomfortably along a bench to allow room for Ant to sit at the table. A large wooden bowl of steaming stew was plonked down in front of him, to the obvious jealousy of everyone else. It scalded his tongue and his throat as he wolfed it down.

The general mood improved as the others received their portions. The bearded man next to Ant even addressed him in reasonably polite tones. 'Where you be from?' he asked.

'The north,' Ant replied quickly, then wondered if he'd said the right thing. 'I was on a ship headed here but fell overboard.'

'Which ship were that, then? Who wus the captain?'

Ant thought hard. These were seafaring folk, islanders who depended on ships for their livelihoods. He had to be careful. 'I don't know. I was a passenger in the company of two noble ladies who wished to visit Kish for the first time. We didn't mix with the crew, though from what I saw of them, they were all stout fellows.'

'Then they weren't from round here,' he replied to a murmur of approval. 'Folks from round here'll skin yer and eat yer soon as look at yer.' There was general laughter at this remark, which Ant found difficult to interpret. Either the man was making a joke or, worryingly, he was stating the truth. A sudden burst of humour seemed out of character for the gathering, which left Ant unhappy and defensive.

'I'm happy to pay for your hospitality,' Ant said. 'I mean you no harm.'

'Mean it or not, makes no odds with us.' The bearded man caught a glance from the cook and fell silent.

Ant felt the stares from the men round the table press down on his abdomen, threatening to squeeze the air and the energy from his body. The need to get out of here rose to prominence now that his belly had been filled to overflowing. 'I'll be on my way,' he said, rising to his feet and addressing the cook. 'That was the most delicious stew I've ever tasted and I thank you most sincerely for the bath and clean clothes. Let me pay you for your trouble, please.'

The cook shook her head vigorously. 'No need for that,' she said and drew laughter from the men.

A cold feeling enveloped Ant, and he shivered despite the cloying heat of the kitchen. He reached down to his pouch and weighed it in his hand. It was heavy enough, but didn't feel right.

45

By the time they arrived in Gort, Persephone had gathered a large following. Miriam headed a vanguard of fifty or so determined women of all ages and descriptions. The female inhabitants of all villages they visited had been receptive to their message once the menfolk had learned that it was inadvisable to interfere. The glowing ribbons announced their new power and invulnerability and the few males who attempted to restore the old order came to a spectacular and over-sticky end. It was the widows of these relationships that made the bulk of the travelling horde.

News of their coming had travelled ahead and the gate to the city had been blocked by soldiers. Nervous hands pointed arrows, over-zealous officers barked orders, and another bloody confrontation seemed inevitable.

Lone kept well away, preferring to join a surrounding mob of jeering men who were threatening the women from a safe distance. Patch, whether in horse form or any other guise, was nowhere to be seen. It was Miriam, protected only with dazzling white clothing that had remained miraculously spotless considering the long and dusty road she had trodden, who demanded that the soldiers step aside.

An officer stood in her path, hand on sword pommel. 'The King orders you to return to from where you came and resume your duties as wives and mothers. If you disperse immediately, you will be saved. Those of you who do not will be arrested and hanged.'

Lone was suddenly nervous. This was a critical moment. What happened next would determine the success or failure of her mission and, worryingly, might cast her into an abyss where she would languish in agony while Patch watched with amusement. She retained no illusions about the demon despite the rapport they had developed over the previous few weeks. In his Persephone guise, he had been wonderfully restrained in wooing the women and cowing the men. The few casualties that had been occasioned had been confined to the old and the madly belligerent. He had demonstrated an understanding of humans that was disturbingly perceptive. Each man had a mother and many had a wife who they held in great affection. It took a gentle nudge to deflect this vast majority towards a more equal relationship with them. To Lone's astonishment, Patch had pointed out that young men in the first flush of a relationship knew instinctively how a woman ought to be treated, and the job was to remind them of how it felt. The older, more set in their ways, needed a bigger jolt, but there was still that residual respect for their mother in their hearts, regardless of age and indoctrination.

She had always believed that men would have to be coerced to give up their misogyny. Patch had shown her another much more lasting and effective way. The thought made her shiver.

Gort was the prize. Without it, there would be no resolution and her fate would be a sorry one. No matter how many villagers they converted, unless the women of Gort embraced Persephone and all she represented, the result would be failure. Now that soldiers stood in front of them in place of a few weak and old men used to getting their own way without question, one wrong move would cause widespread bloodshed and, with it, disaster. Killing soldiers meant killing sons and husbands. A war might be won using the awesome destructive power of the demon, but the aftermath would yield nothing she wanted. A deep breath steadied her fast-beating heart as she stood powerless to do anything but watch the unfolding drama. She had to trust Patch to get the balance right. *Never trust a demon.* Malachi's wise words popped into her head and she wondered where her husband was now and how he'd react to the events she'd set in motion.

Miriam approached the officer, arms outstretched. 'We have no quarrel with the King or his representatives. The worshippers of Persephone carry no weapon other than the goodness in their hearts. Take us all to our King where we will submit to whatever fate he decrees.'

The officer's posture relaxed slightly, but there was a puzzled look on his face. 'If I do that, the most likely outcome is that you will all be hanged. The King has no tolerance for insurrection. Please turn around, disperse back to your villages and hope that he forgets about you.'

'It seems that we have more faith in the wisdom of our King than you,' Miriam said. 'We are all ready and willing to abide by whatever decision he makes. Now do your duty and escort us to the palace.'

Shrugging his shoulders, the officer signalled for the gate to be opened and allowed Miriam and her followers to walk calmly into the city. As they headed for the inner gate that would give them access to the palace, hundreds of soldiers hurried ahead to take up defensive positions.

Lone and the gaggle of onlookers straggled along in their wake. When they all reached the palace, Miriam waited patiently for admittance, and this was eventually granted, presumably after some general had evaluated the strategic threat of a group of unarmed females against a garrison of war-hardened troops bristling with weapons. Lone was prevented from following, so she accosted the young officer who had presided at the outer gate. 'Let me in. I am Lone, emissary of the King. I have returned from the mission he personally gave me and now I am here to report back.'

'Nobody's allowed in,' he replied. 'That's my orders.'

'I am.' Lone planted fear in the man's heart. 'Preventing my entry will get you hanged.' She constricted his gullet gently as she planted the image in his mind and was rewarded by a look of pure horror and a wave of his hand.

'Go on through,' he said, hand massaging his throat.

The soldiers stood aside, and she strode confidently across the stone slabs, overtaking the women who were being escorted by a greater number of soldiers with weapons at the ready as if expecting a sudden attack. Lone shook her head in disbelief. Men were so stupid. What possible threat was there from unarmed and compliant women such as these? In contrast, they allowed her to wander freely.

She arrived at the King's chambers without any further challenge. 'He's expecting me,' she told the ceremonially clad captain of the guard.

'Lone.' The King looked up from the map spread out on the table in front of him. 'What an unpleasant surprise.' The fact that Cuthbert hadn't confirmed her statement didn't appear to concern his bodyguards. They were presumably poised, ready to kill on command, and until that order came, they remained passive. Lone wondered if what she had to say might provoke him enough to give the signal they were waiting for.

46

His probing fingers told Ant the story he didn't want to know. Whatever was in his pouch, it wasn't gold. Thin metal in rough discs was a poor substitute for the perfectly round and heavily fat coins he'd previously held. Indignation rose in his craw. The instant angry response flashed through his system like the ripple of cold he'd experienced when falling into the sea.

Ant let his emotions course through his body, but remained seated at the table with a clear mind. Of course he'd been robbed. That's what people do when given the chance for riches beyond previous hope. If he'd been cudgelled to the ground and the purse ripped from his lifeless body, that would have been easier to bear than the betrayal involved here. But he'd been robbed by the woman who'd reminded him of his Mona. The one oasis of kindness he'd encountered in this strange land. His hope for salvation and succour. Perhaps even assistance in recovering the Queen and Princess. Instead, all his hopes had disappeared with the gold. He was dreadfully vulnerable now, at the mercy of this horde of dullards who sat slurping and dribbling around the same table.

Despair crept up on him. Self-belief surrendered to doubt. His wounded child surfaced, looking for reassurance and found only fear. It was almost too much to bear without screaming in pain and shouting in anger. His newfound perspective conquered his primal instincts and his anchor held, grounding him in the here and now. Reining in his regret at what had been and suppressing any speculation about what might come. He was fit and well. His belly was full. His mind was fresh. The air he breathed held a delightful aroma of stew and a less delightful stink of sweaty bodies. Muttered conversations provided a deep undertone to the higher pitched voices of the females. Things could be a lot worse. In fact, this was the best he'd felt for a very long time. There were plenty more gold coins buried a couple of hours' walk away. Once the indignation had been overcome, his loss was of little consequence.

Composing a gentle smile on his lips, he nodded politely in the direction of the cooking staff and walked out of the house. Barring his way were two of the many men he had begun to think of as brothers

177

because of their physical similarities and a revitalised and fully bristling Snarler behaving exactly as his name required.

Little Ant had disappeared when he'd first entered the house, but he suspected that whatever form he was currently taking wouldn't be far away. What he needed now was the sight of his little dog avatar turning up and seeing off his counterpart once again.

'Excuse me, I have to get going,' Ant said.

'Mama says you're to stay,' one of the brothers said. The other nodded his head and Snarler kept up his earthquake growl.

'Give Mama my thanks and tell her I'll visit next time I'm passing. Right now, I have some friends I need to meet.'

'Tell her yourself.' The men picked up Ant by the shoulders and marched him back into the house. The one on his right stumbled, coughed, and let go as Ant experimented with a remote chokehold. Before he could repeat the process, he was surrounded by the others. There were too many to fight.

He allowed himself to be manhandled up a flight of substantial wooden stairs and deposited in a room with one large bed, two small ones, and a view of the tub in the garden below. As soon as his captors departed, Mama, the cook, arrived with three young girls in tow. 'I want you to stay with us,' she said. 'This is Dot. She'll keep you company.' The girl smiled dutifully, as if she was doing what was expected without any enthusiasm.

'I would love to,' Ant replied, 'but I can't. Sorry. Maybe another time.'

'I may not have made myself clear,' Mama said, frowning. 'I hope you're not a stupid boy. That would be a disappointment.'

'I understood what you said perfectly well. Perhaps under the circumstances, I could stay for a short time to show my appreciation of your hospitality. I wouldn't want to be thought of as rude.'

'There you go again. Misunderstanding a perfectly obvious statement. I want you to stay. What Mama says goes in this house, so you might as well get used to it. Stay, in case you're in any doubt, means stay.'

The words were, at first, a little bewildering, then he absorbed the energy of them and the true meaning became distressingly clear. 'I have to find my friends and then go home. I can't stay here,' he said as gently as he was able.

'This is your home now. We are your family. This is your lovely bride. Don't you think she's beautiful? She can cook wonderfully well because she's been taught by myself. As for other wifely duties, she's completely inexperienced, but I'm sure that she'll prove more than satisfactory.'

Ant chose his response carefully. Pointing out that he didn't want to stay and wasn't interested in marrying the girl wouldn't get him anywhere with the implacable Mama. All he could do was to acquiesce and bide his time. 'I'm tired,' he said. 'Would you be kind enough to let me rest while I adjust to my new circumstances?'

Mama smiled. 'Of course. I'll leave you two lovebirds to get to know each other.'

Left with only Dot as company, Ant sat on the big bed and considered his position. It would have been better if he could have ejected them both and had the opportunity to discuss matters with his avatar. Knowing Little Ant, he wouldn't be far away. Mama's disposition was all too clear, though, and getting rid of Dot wasn't going to please her at all.

'What do you want me to do?' Dot said. Ant looked at her properly for the first time. She looked about twenty or even twenty-five, with long red hair, and a face full of freckles. Her manner was deferential and gentle in contrast to Mama.

'Nothing,' Ant replied.

'But Mama expects us to, you know, be married properly.'

'Why is she so keen for us to get together?' Ant asked.

'Because you're a fresh man and will make good babies.'

'Aren't there enough men around here for you to do that with?'

'There's loads of them, but their babies might not turn out right, Mama says.' The situation was beginning to make sense to him. The way Mama welcomed him, bathed him, and fed him was in stark contrast to the obvious resentment and hostility he'd received from the menfolk. They knew how much he was valued and their jealousy was understandable. Was it only this small community that thought this way or was it true of the whole island of Kish? 'Can't you get fresh men from another part of the island?'

'Everyone's the same. They all look out for fresh men; some even make long voyages in search of partners for their children. We're so far away from everywhere, so it's not often we get visitors.'

'I'm sorry, Dot. I'm not ready for marriage and children. I think you're lovely, and if I were looking for a wife, I'd be honoured if I could interest someone as special as you are.' A vision of Lone speared into his consciousness and threw his mind into turmoil. Was she really attainable? Of course she wasn't. Not for him or anyone else, he suspected. She was single-minded and ruthless. He'd been used to show her how to build a vedhana, then abandoned. Yet there was a frisson of excitement whenever he thought of her that couldn't be denied or controlled. Like it or not, she had him in her power and until that situation changed, he was tied to her as surely as if they were man and wife. 'I'm promised to someone else.'

'So am I,' she replied, her eyes lighting up. 'Me and Dug love each other, but Mama says we can't. It makes me sad.'

'Then we can work together. Make Mama think we're doing what she wants, but stay true to our loved ones. What do you think?'

Her face relaxed. 'I'll pretend if you do. Let's mess up the bed for a start.' She began to ruffle the bedclothes, then began to bounce up and down, making the frame of the bed bang against the wall. Ant suspected that, whatever Mama might have decreed, Dot and Dug had been practising. His heart lightened at the thought. Far from being distressed by his rejection, she was obviously relieved.

When she'd finished cavorting around, she messed up her hair with her hands and stripped naked. 'See what you're missing?' She laughed and pulled her dress back over her head, this time back to front. Ant was impressed with her capacity for deception. It did, however, bear testimony to the fact that deceiving Mama was a frequent necessity. If she succeeded in tricking the matriarch, it would be testament to her brightness and give him hope that he could do the same.

47

'Dug says he's gonna kill yer.'

Ant stopped chewing the food she'd brought him. Because they were newlyweds, they were excused the glowering animosity of the big table at mealtimes and permitted to eat together in the privacy of the bedroom. No doubt Mama thought this conducive to the production of offspring, but it had increased the resentment he felt from the men even further. Given the chance, and Mama's permission, of course, any one of them would take pleasure in ending his life. Maybe once he'd completed his procreational duties, she'd have no more use for him and that would mean the end.

'Haven't you explained our arrangement?'

'Naw, that would be telling. One look at his face and Mama would know what we're up to. Or that we're not up to anything at all.' She let out a gentle snigger from beneath a warm smile that had Ant wondering if he was doing the right thing in risking Mama's wrath. It was a thought that visited him often during the night when he felt her warm back pressed against his and he wondered what it would be like to really act like they were man and wife.

It was another example of the instinctual side of him pushing its way into his consciousness. His heart and mind were united in their certainty about the appropriate way of acting in the circumstances. She was in love with another man, he with Lone. He was intent on escaping from this homestead and never returning. She was resigned to living out her life under Mama's watchful eye. Still, though, the urges surfaced on an increasingly regular basis.

For her part, she showed no interest in him beyond a curiosity about his origins. At least this made his conscious decision a little easier to hold on to.

Little Ant was sitting in his customary place, perched on the window ledge in the shape of an owl. It wasn't the most convincing representation, but Dot hadn't seemed to notice. The little dog shape had been abandoned for practical reasons. Dogs weren't allowed in the house and Snarler took exception to him being anywhere else. An owl was able to perch, watch, and listen, because that's what owls do. When Dot was downstairs performing her domestic chores, the owl brought him news of the outside and they discussed escape plans. Two nights into the new arrangement and they hadn't formulated anything they thought might work.

Running for it was out of the question. Little Ant had scouted the homestead, and it was vast. There were many more dwellings scattered over a wide area, and these were all under the control of Mama. He could walk for days and still be in danger of recapture.

'Shouldn't you tell him, though? Otherwise he might do it and then where would we be?'

'You'd be dead, and he'd be shouted at, I suppose. At least there'd be no need to continue this charade.' She gave him a thin smile that projected little comfort. Dug was her obvious priority, and Mama's momentary displeasure might be a reasonable price to pay. Ant considered her position more carefully and began to realise that she'd be better off if Dug did kill him. Whether she had worked this out or not, it was something he had to be wary of. Not only would Dug get her back, but he could make her pregnant without incurring Mama's wrath, providing she believed it had been Ant's doing. Another compelling reason for him to leave without delay. The question was: how?

48

The monk, resplendent in his deep red robes, turned toward Tyrant with an expression of resignation. It was remarkable how the menace associated with Malachi had evaporated, leaving a frail body with parchment skin and pallor of death.

'Can you make him better?' Tyrant asked.

The monk slowly shook his shiny, shaved head. 'We can make his final hours a little more comfortable, but that's all we can do. His spirit is preparing to leave his body. The transition cannot be long in coming. Until then, we will keep his suffering to a minimum.'

Tyrant had never liked the wizard and the way he'd exuded menace every time he so much as looked his way. Now that he was out of the jungle, all he could think of was a swift journey back to Petra and a life-giving swig of licker. Malachi was on his last legs; there was nothing more he could do except leave him in the care of the monks until he finally died. Which, judging by the look of him, could be at any moment.

He could leave with his conscience clear. Ant had told him where to take his teacher and he'd done what he'd been told. The fact that they could do nothing for him here wasn't Tyrant's fault. The wizard's demise would leave the boy devastated, though. Malachi had been his closest friend for the last few years. He'd presided over the boy's maturation as if he was his father. Ant considered him more than just a teacher, and his loss would be greater than if he lost his real father.

Excuses played around Tyrant's head as he imagined the questions he'd be asked. *Did he say anything before he died? How were his last moments? Wasn't there anything you could do to save him?*

At the moment, the only answer he could give, whether it was Ant or Petra asking, was *I don't know* to all three questions if he left now. The final question was the one jiggling about in his head and stopping him from jumping back into the vedhana. 'Then who can?' he addressed the monk again. 'There must be some who can deal with this kind of injury.'

'Nobody here has the knowledge or experience to mend a badly broken body. There may be a physician somewhere with the special skills needed, but I fear it's too late in any case. Moving him will only hasten his death.'

'Then I'll bring them here. Tell me where to go.'

'I can only suggest that you travel to Gort and seek a doctor there. But hurry. Even if you do find one willing to come here and help, your friend's life has almost come to an end and it may not be possible to reverse the process.'

The idea came of making a tour of taverns in the city while he sought the information that might save Malachi. His heart leapt at the prospect. The more he thought about it, the better his plan appeared. Taverns were where a great many knowledgeable men gathered and drank themselves into a state where they were happy to share that knowledge, whether you wanted it or not. It was an opportunity for him to relax a little after a hard journey and let the solution to Malachi's problem come to him.

The vedhana at Malachi's home on the outskirts of the city seemed the sensible point to aim for. It would be a short walk into the city where he could begin his quest for medical assistance. Surely even Petra would understand him delaying his return for such sound humanitarian reasons. 'I'll get on my way,' he told the monk. 'Keep him alive until I get back.'

***

Malachi's house was like the man himself, cold and lifeless. The vedhana spat him onto an icy stone floor, where he briefly contemplated the advisability of keeping his thoughts on his footing rather than the best tavern to try first. The best chance of success surely lay in the most popular, and what made a tavern popular was the quality of its offering. His mouth watered in anticipation. His body longed for him to begin his quest. His mind still struggled to reconcile these feelings with the probability that his motive for choosing this option would be misunderstood. Even if he succeeded.

Astonished at his perseverance, despite the criticism that would inevitably come his way, he managed to visit five taverns before sunset. By limiting himself to two drinks in each, he combined patience with urgency in his quest to find a doctor for Malachi. Despite his best endeavours, the only medical advice he received was to avoid drinking the licker at the Four Candles Inn.

His fifth choice looked a little more promising, though. There had been a bit of a kerfuffle and several patrons were bleeding copiously. Tyrant sipped his drink and waited to see who, if anyone, attended to their wounds. If someone did, he was poised to accost them and explain his urgent need for expertise. Instead, all that came through the door was the obligatory handful of soldiers that always turned up too late to prevent bloodshed, but in good time to break some more heads while establishing that the culprits were long gone.

Jingling their mail and ironmongery, they marched right over to him and stood in what he assumed was their best attempt at menace. 'You,' the tallest one said, drawing his sword and pointing it at Tyrant's nose. 'Come with us. Any trouble and we'll chop you to pieces.'

'None of this was my doing,' Tyrant replied. 'Ask anyone. I only just got here. See this,' he indicated his drink, 'my ale still has scum on the top. Proves it.'

'Not interested in anything you have to say. Our orders are to find you and bring you in.'

'Whose orders?' Tyrant asked.

'By the order of the King,' came the cocksure reply.

'Obviously the King,' Tyrant said. 'All your orders are ultimately derived from the monarch. What I need to know is where are you inviting me to accompany you and who is it that wants my company?'

'Like I said, the King is who, and the palace is where. Now come along before we have to resort to violence.'

As he was ushered none too gently into the King's presence, Tyrant's brain was in a turmoil trying to think up an excuse for being in a tavern rather than faithfully carrying out the King's orders and pursuing the kidnappers of his Queen. Try as he did, nothing even remotely plausible came to mind, and he realised how much trouble he'd be in when he tried to explain things to Petra.

'Your majesty.' He bowed as low as he could until the dizziness threatened to tip him over. It had to be faced; he was out of practice when it came to drinking and the amount he'd consumed was getting the better of him just when he needed his wits to stay alive. The way he felt, staying awake was going to be a problem.

'Before you tell me why you abandoned the quest I gave you and I sentence you to be hanged, pray tell me what you know.' The King's voice lacked humour. This wasn't a surprise but it came as a bit of a disappointment. Seeing the funny side of the situation was a forlorn hope, but his best one.

'I came back under orders carrying the lifeless body of a comrade, your majesty.'

'And you didn't think to report to your King?'

'I was about to when your men arrived to give me safe passage to your glorious presence.' It was only a fat version of the boy Cuthbert sitting in judgement, but Tyrant reckoned a little buttering couldn't go amiss. The boy had changed almost beyond recognition since he'd assumed the throne. It had to be something to do with all the toadying and deference. It addled the brain and gave rise to illusions of grandeur.

'What do you know about the rumours I've been hearing? That my Queen has been abducted to a remote island in the southern sea they call Kish.'

'It could be true,' Tyrant said, desperately trying to remember where he'd heard the name before. 'We met a ship that could have carried your Queen, but it unleashed a terrible device that almost killed us all.'

'What manner of device and who was wielding it?'

'I don't know. It made loud bangs and sent things that destroyed everything. Malachi was fatally injured, and I brought him back to see if he could be revived. I took him to the monks but they couldn't save him. So, I came to Gort seeking medical help.'

'And you were looking for this specialist in a tavern?' The King's eyes rolled upwards in an exaggerated gesture that reminded him of Petra.

'That was my plan. I was also in considerable shock from the terrible things I'd experienced. We were beset by killer wasps and then captured by giant grey apes. After we escaped, along came this ship and began to smash everything to pieces. Anyone would need a drink to steady their nerves after such an ordeal.'

'If Malachi's dead or dying, what happened to the others?'

'Ant took a small boat and went to attack the ship. As for Lone, I've no idea what happened to her.'

'Then you should have an opportunity to ask her yourself.' The King waved his fat hand at the assembled soldiers. 'Bring her in.'

49

Seeing Tyrant was a surprise that Lone quickly recovered from. He'd presumably used her vedhana to return to Gort and, judging by the stench of licker that surrounded him, had lost no time in returning to old haunts and habits.

'Lone,' Tyrant gasped. 'I'm sorry.'

'What about?'

'Malachi,' he replied.

A cold feeling enveloped her. 'He's dead, isn't he?'

'He's with the monks, but there's nothing they could do for him.'

This wasn't something she'd anticipated. Malachi had been more than capable of looking after himself, even if he could be lax about extending that care to others. The prospect of life without him made her feel as if she'd been cast adrift. The emotions that welled up were a surprise. She'd always felt more than capable of managing without his constant over-protection. That's why she'd chosen to live her life deep in the southern desert, though he had a propensity to pop up there without warning to impart some cautionary wisdom. 'He's not dead, though?'

'He may be now.' Tyrant hung his head. 'They said it was a matter of a few hours at most.'

A forced laugh bellowed out of the King's mouth. 'Neither of you seem capable of telling me what I need to know. Fetch Malachi here. Dead or alive. If he's any breath left, I want him to expel it in my direction, explaining the nature and operation of the device that felled him. Not that I trust either of you, or him for that matter. It's just as likely that he's holed up somewhere comfortable and uninjured plotting against me.'

'The monks said that he'd die if he's moved,' Tyrant said.

'Then let's see if they're right.'

'I'll go,' Lone said.

'I think not,' the King replied. 'I've not finished with you by any means. Tyrant can go with the assurance that if he doesn't come back quickly, that tiny licker-brewing girlfriend of his will be strung up in his stead.'

Tyrant's shade of purple deepened as he was bundled out of the room. Lone felt the King's stare burning on her face. 'You told me Gilgamesh was dead,' the King said.

'We all saw him die. First, he was crushed by a collapsing building, then buried under a mountain of earth. No man could have survived.'

'He's no ordinary man,' the King said. 'Tyrant's account seems to confirm the rumours that he took Cassie and Bee and is holding them on this island. Only he has access to the destructive devices that Tyrant described. This map my men found shows the island's location. Gilgamesh no doubt provided it to make sure that I know where to find him. He wants me to go after him. That's what this is all about.'

'And will you?' Lone asked.

'Not a chance.' The King smirked. 'I'm stopping here where he can't get me. If he thinks he can goad me into precipitate action then he's overestimating the value I put on my wife and underestimating my will to survive.'

'Then he'll surely find another way to get you,' Lone replied. 'If it really is him, he's not going to give up if his first plan goes awry. This map and the information about him you've received can only mean one thing. That he already has a network of spies here in Gort. The abduction was carried out by people who had access to the palace. People who remain close to you.' She looked around the room. 'Possibly even members of your personal guard.'

Cuthbert looked suitably nervous. 'Then who can I trust?'

'Apart from me, very few,' Lone said.

'You? Don't make me laugh. You're beginning to sound more like your husband than ever.'

'I know Gilgamesh better than anyone else alive,' Lone said. 'I also know that everything I hold dear would be destroyed if he had his way. There's a deep hatred between us and if he's alive, he's going to be looking for revenge against me just as much as trying to usurp you. So we have common purpose.'

'Even if I trusted you, which I don't, what can you possibly do to help? It's my ancient devices against his. Nothing can challenge the power of old magic, not even you.'

'Then let me create old magic so powerful that it will sweep Gilgamesh aside. Free the priestess and her acolytes. Rebuild the temple so that they can worship their goddess.'

'What good would that do?'

'Persephone would be bound to intervene if her temple were threatened. She would make a valuable and decisive ally.'

The King's face developed several new fatty folds. 'Persephone is long departed from this world. Your friends are whistling into the wind. Whatever they worship is merely an illusion brought about by witchcraft. Why don't you admit that it's all your doing?'

'I'd admit it if it was true, but I'm merely an observer of the miraculous events associated with her worship. Whether or not you believe that this is Persephone's doing or not, powerful forces have been unleashed. It's your choice whether they are allied to your cause or brought to bear against you. Can you afford to make another formidable foe, in addition to Gilgamesh?'

'From what I'm told, the priestess and her friends gave themselves up meekly enough. I'm inclined to hang them to dissuade others from adopting a similarly disruptive stance. All this clamour about female rights is disturbing to a population used to the old ways. The last thing I need is civil unrest.'

'The old ways, your majesty? Your knowledge of the ancient is unrivalled. You know that trying to keep women downtrodden and treat them as sub-human commodities cannot sustain. The society you preside over has adopted these mistakes very recently and as a result of ill-founded fears. These are not the old ways. They are the ways of frightened men who keep the terrors of their inadequacy at bay by mistreating the gender who can make them whole.' Lone felt the words spit out of her like sparks from fresh pine wood thrown onto a fire. Was it too much? Probably. The King wouldn't take kindly to being argued with, especially by a woman. His face had become suffused to the extent that she feared he'd boil over. The knife in her stomach stabbed a painful response to her outburst, the ache in her heart wished she'd been able to hold her counsel.

'Is this some sort of threat?' The King's eyes glared, and his hands bunched into chubby fists.

'On the contrary, your majesty, it's the very opposite of a threat. Making women's lives more bearable will stabilise your kingdom, make you a popular king and rally your entire population behind you.'

'Fear is the only way to rule. Hanging the ones who criticise or oppose is the best remedy for insurrection. That's what works.'

Lone exhaled a breath of release. This wasn't the belligerent response she'd feared. It was important to tread carefully from now on, though, or she'd been sent down to join the priestess without further opportunity for negotiation. If only Malachi were here. His words always held power, appeared wise and considered, and were tailored to the instant mood of his listener. She had little of his expertise and none of his patience. Both were needed if she was to get what she wanted. 'Hanging can be a sign of weakness. Reducing the need for this ultimate sanction demonstrates how well your society is performing. It reflects the willingness of your people to accept your leadership. You are far better off with enthusiasm and appreciation than you are with fear.'

'But a little bit of fear can't do anything but help?' The King cracked a thin smile that created bolts of fire in Lone's body.

She returned the smile. 'Absolutely. Your perception is admirable. It's a matter of balance.'

His face grew stern again. 'Are you suggesting that I have the balance wrong?'

'You are powerful enough to tip the balance in any direction you wish. However, that takes energy and attention. Circumstances have changed dramatically. The reappearance of Gilgamesh threatens to upset the equilibrium you have maintained. There's a chance that leaning too far towards that threat might cause you to topple. I'm offering more stability. A strong platform from which you can defend yourself.'

'This will all be achieved by encouraging men to treat women more equitably, will it?'

'In many ways, yes. By allowing the temple to be reopened, you will be giving a clear signal to your population that women do matter and should be valued as equals. In return, you will receive the voluntary support of half the population and the cooperation of their god. Not only will you have less work to do in keeping order, but you will also receive valuable supernatural assistance in repulsing Gilgamesh.'

191

An uneasy silence descended. Lone had difficulty resisting the urge to fill it with words that could only weaken her argument. Everything had been said. What was needed now was for the King to absorb her words and weigh the advantages of the new order she was desperate to introduce. 'You sound more like your husband than ever, though I doubt his pleas would have been so impassioned. He likes to gnaw away at my mind like a hungry worm, while your manner feels more like being beaten around the head with a cudgel wrapped in a blanket. Let's be honest with each other. It's you, isn't it? All this talk of Persephone and worship is hiding some serious witchcraft on your part. Don't look so aggrieved. It's been blindingly obvious all along that you're a witch, and a formidable one at that. Come on, admit it.'

'First of all, Persephone isn't me. She's real and very powerful. Second, this accusation of witchcraft is one that any intelligent and resourceful woman has to endure in this society. That's what I want to change. Let women show their talents and use them for your greater glory and protection without being dragged into the centre of their villages and hanged.'

'So you're saying that you don't have magic powers?' The King didn't seem upset by her reply.

'No more than you do,' she replied, trying to keep the discussion as light as possible. These were murky areas and talking about them to the King was a dangerous business. She was rewarded with a snigger.

Cuthbert's demeanour changed. His hands began to fidget and his eyes swept around the room. 'This is all nonsense,' he blurted. 'I don't believe you, nor do I accept anything you say. You're a liar and a witch and I know exactly what to do to you.' He waved his arm at the nearest soldier. 'Fetch me General Oliver at once. Meanwhile, not another word from you, woman, or I'll have you killed where you stand.'

50

The intensity of the King's energy had changed abruptly. One instant she had been bandying words with him in a very positive mood, the next he had turned on her, spittle spraying from his raging mouth. Even the bodyguards were shifting feet nervously and looking uncertainly at one another.

The atmosphere crackled with tension. The King rose to his feet and stood menacingly now that his customary reclining posture had been abandoned. The soft, fat effigy now exuded power and menace that alarmed her. Her whole body was a jangling mass of nervous uncertainty. She could detect his scrutiny as a wave of energy that picked at her frayed defences. With a great effort, she allowed his probing to pass through them, resisting the urge to fight. He was testing her, looking for her identity, and challenging her capabilities.

The process was interrupted when the soldier returned with the man she recognised as the father of the Queen and Princess. 'The rest of you can leave. Get out. Guard the door if you want. I need some private time with these two.'

The soldiers shuffled out, exhibiting a strange reluctance to escape from such a difficult situation. When the door was shut behind them, the King turned to Lone. 'So, who can I trust? Are you suggesting that even my guards are in league with the enemy?'

'You can trust me, sire,' Oliver said.

'Of course I can; you're my father-in-law. That's why you're here and not sat on your arse fishing. The question is, can I trust this witch?' To Lone's relief, the King's demeanour had softened now that the other soldiers had left.

Lone replied, 'In so far that we have common purpose and a common enemy, then surely you can. I deny that I am a witch, though. Calling me that concerns me. It's as if you were already condemning me and makes me wonder if we can ever be true allies.'

'If you're not a witch, then what do you bring to the table? I need powerful allies to defeat Gilgamesh. You talk a good talk like your husband, but when it comes down to it, talk isn't going to get the job done. Black arts will be needed.'

'Are you telling me that witchcraft is now acceptable and not subject to the ultimate sanction?' she replied.

The King laughed. 'See what I mean, Oliver, about her tongue being as slippery as Malachi's? What I'm saying is that circumstances change. It's a matter of perception, after all. Terminology, if you prefer.'

'Then let's agree that I'm not a witch, your majesty, but that I may be able to use my knowledge of human nature and ancient history to your advantage.'

'May?'

'If I'm hanged, or imprisoned for that matter, my usefulness would be compromised.'

'I see. You want me to pardon you for being a witch. Very well, I pardon you. Be as witchy as you can as long as you're working for me. But if you ever turn against me, being a witch will make no difference to your fate.'

Lone relaxed, allowing her awareness to flood the room and its immediate environs. She felt no response from the King, whose attitude had ceased being threatening. Something on the periphery bothered her like a false note played on a lute. It was as if there was someone else in the room besides Oliver and the King. Her eyes cast about for signs of physical presence while her essence tried to detect non-human manifestation. Was Patch hovering around keeping an eye on things? She dismissed the notion. She knew what he felt like, and this wasn't him.

'Wait.' She held up her hand, then pulled aside a tapestry hanging next to the throne. Nothing was revealed but a bare stone wall. Feeling the wall with the palm of her hand, she closed her eyes and concentrated. She connected with the unmistakable aura of a man who was trying desperately to keep his presence from her. 'What's beyond this wall?' she asked.

'There's a storeroom between here and my bedrooms,' the King replied.

'Is there a door?'

'Of course there is, can't you see it?' The King waddled over to stand beside her and pressed hard on one of the stones that jutted out at waist height. A section of the wall moved backwards to reveal a crouching figure.

As soon as he saw the man, the King retreated at a speed that took Lone by surprise. The eavesdropper got to his feet and slid his sword out of its scabbard. Lone held him fast in her ghastly grip. His eyes stared uncomprehendingly as he found himself unable to move. A sword flashed past her and plunged into the man's throat. Bleeding copiously, he slumped to the floor.

Lone turned to Oliver. 'There was no need to kill him,' she said. 'We might have learned some valuable information. Like who he's working for and how he reports what he hears.'

'The King was in danger,' Oliver said. 'My first duty is to protect my King.'

'Quite right,' the King said. 'That has to be the first priority, whatever the circumstances. Lone was in more danger than me, though, and it should be her thanks that you're receiving rather than criticism.'

The gurgling and frothing ceased abruptly, and the man lay untidily still. 'I can look after myself,' Lone said.

'We know who he's working for and we can also be sure that there's more like him in the palace,' the King said. 'For that reason, I'm putting Oliver in command. Bring in only the men you know and trust. If in doubt, Lone will help you to question them. Any signs of treason should be summarily dealt with.'

'I'd rather you held any suspects for me to talk to,' Lone said.

'Agreed,' the King said. 'Then hang them after you've had a chat.'

51

Lone supervised the reassembly of the bed that had been dismantled so that it could be carried up the narrow confines of the spiral staircase that gave access to the high tower. She'd had it placed as close to the vedhana as possible and awaited Tyrant's return with her husband.

As soon as the familiar figure appeared, she dismissed the remaining staff. He stepped out of the device, carrying Malachi as if he were a sleeping child. His black cloak was draped over one arm. 'Is he alive?' Lone asked.

'I don't know,' Tyrant replied as he gently lowered the frail figure onto the mattress and draped his cloak over him.

Outside, stars twinkled in a majestic display that the red and yellow fires below failed to compete with. It was a chilly night. A cruel wind swept over the tower walls and forced Lone into the refuge of a blanket. 'Leave us,' she said.

Tyrant moved towards the vedhana. 'Where do you think you're going?'

He paused and looked around. 'Home,' he said. 'To see Petra. I'm long overdue and she'll be worried. It's about time I got back to doing something normal for a change.'

'I don't think so,' Lone said. 'Send word to her by all means, but you need to stay here. The King expects it. There's a war already begun and very few that he can trust. For all your failings, he considers you one of them. Your place is with the King now, Tyrant.'

'Since when did I become a babysitter for Cuthbert?' Tyrant replied.

'Ever since you dug him out of the rockfall on the North Road, as far as my information goes. He might not be the best king, but he's your King and an alternative could be far worse. Go down the stairs, get yourself some food and await orders. Your friend General Oliver is in charge now, if that makes you feel any better.'

Dragging his feet so that dust clouds were released to hang in the air around his feet, Tyrant plodded with obvious reluctance to the archway that led to the staircase. As soon as he'd disappeared from view, Lone summoned Patch.

'What?'

'Show yourself,' she asked.

The peculiar horse materialised next to Malachi's bed, its hooves making a ghostly clopping noise on the stone floor.

'Can't you become something more suitable than that horrible excuse for a horse?'

Persephone appeared, all blurry and white. 'Better?'

'Not much,' Lone said. 'If someone comes up here, they'll wonder what's going on.'

'What is going on?'

'Malachi needs to be revived. I want you to do it.'

'Why?'

'Because he's my husband. And we'll need him in the battle against Gilgamesh.'

'Gilgamesh?'

'I thought you'd know. He's kidnapped the Queen and is coming here to kill the King. At least that's what we think. Do you know any different?'

'All I know is that Gilgamesh is big trouble. Best avoided. If he really is coming here, then our arrangement, fun though it is, cannot continue. I, as they say where I mostly reside, am already gone.'

'You can't. I promised the King that we'd help him get rid of Gilgamesh.'

'My information is that he's not getriddable. Gods, powerful ones, have tried and failed. Why do you think they aren't present in your world anymore? Gods don't die, that's what makes them gods, but hanging around here with Gilgamesh loose was too much aggravation.'

'We got rid of him. He was buried under the ruins of his palace. We thought he was dead,' Lone said.

'And we being?' Patch shimmered a little brighter, making Lone wonder if the misshapen horse might have been preferable after all.

'Malachi, Tyrant, and me. Oh, then Ant managed to have the golem deposit a mountain of earth on top of the palace. I've been growing grapes on that hill ever since.'

'Remarkable. By all accounts, anything that aggravates Gilgamesh comes to an immediate and sticky end,' Patch said.

197

'If we have your help, we can finish the job. I'm certain of it. But we do need Malachi. You have to bring him back to life.'

'I don't think you realise what you're dealing with. Gilgamesh is a mistake and a big one. Even the gods who created him realised that when he turned against them.'

Lone sighed at the memory of her encounter with Gilgamesh. 'He's an arrogant man who had me thrown to the river monsters because I refused his advances. His arrogance will be his downfall if we combine our forces.'

'The bits of ancient lore that I remember would suggest that you're hopelessly wrong. Gilgamesh is an unholy fusion of all the worst attributes of god and human. The story is that the most powerful gods were fighting each other, using humans and exotic beasts to wage the war. Two of them decided to create something so powerful that they would be bound to prevail. That something was Gilgamesh, and they were successful. They won the war, got their way, and became supreme rulers of your world.

'Then they found that their supremacy was challenged by the very being that they had used to obtain it. In an effort to appease Gilgamesh, they yielded up their greatest city and gave him rights to extensive areas of land and much of the population. At first, this tactic worked, but after a while, his ambition grew and, despite being gods, his former masters were forced to flee, leaving him with dominion over the whole world. As far as I'm aware, they haven't been back since. Because Gilgamesh is part human, he has to take care of his physical body by living in a dimension where time moves slowly, if at all. At least that's what I've heard.'

'So how do we defeat him?' Lone asked.

'You weren't listening, were you? First of all, when it comes to Gilgamesh, there's no 'we' as in you and me. Count me out. Second, gods have tried and failed, so even if Malachi were still able to help you wouldn't survive an instant if Gilgamesh wanted you dead.'

'Tyrant survived him, so did Ant. We all survived our first encounter. He's not as strong as you've been led to believe. What about these gods? Can you find them and enlist their aid?'

'Gods are entities that I keep well clear of. Humans are better at that form of supplication.'

'Then I'll do it. Which god would it be best for me to petition?'

'None of them. Certainly not the one who hates him most. The god who was made to look weak and pathetic by him. The god who would destroy this whole world if she thought it would avenge herself against Gilgamesh.'

'Which god is that?' Lone asked.

Patch let out a snort more suited to his horsy manifestation than the delicate, flimsy apparition that hung in the air in front of her. 'The deity that personifies the divine feminine. The god of love, beauty, sex, desire, fertility, oh, and war. Gilgamesh would know her as Ishtar, but she has been called many other names by humans down the ages. Take my advice, have nothing at all to do with her. Don't so much as breathe a word of summoning in case she has her interest piqued. As far as humans are concerned, Gilgamesh, even with all his drawbacks, is a far better prospect for your kind.'

Lone's heart raced as she considered the opportunity that contact with such a powerful goddess might yield. Was she the one needed to achieve the changes she sought, or was Patch telling the truth when he warned her off? *Never trust a demon.* Malachi's words. She shuddered at the sight of the lifeless figure on the bed. 'Before we do anything, Malachi has to be revived. Can't you do anything?'

'I can do something, but I'm not sure that you'll like it,' Patch replied.

'Will I get Malachi back?' Lone asked.

'In a way. But not necessarily in the way you might like.'

'The only alternative would be to leave him dead, wouldn't it?' Lone said, trying to resist sliding into an abyss of black despair.

'That might be the better option, but I'm not the one to judge these things.'

'Then do it. Bring him back. I need him beside me if I'm to achieve the things I want.'

'Are you sure?' Patch injected a ridiculous whine into his voice that irritated her to the core.

'How many times do I have to ask you? Please, do the best you can.'

'Don't say I didn't warn you,' Patch said and disappeared.

The cold intensified and bit into her body despite the blanket draped over her shoulders. The vedhana cast a ghastly glow that began to flicker and become more intense. There was a sudden bright flash of silver light, then the familiar yellowish flames returned. A figure appeared in the device. Even with the distortion of the coruscating lights, the figure was unmistakably Malachi.

As he stepped out of the vedhana, seemingly unaffected by his terrible injuries, Malachi looked puzzled. Lone saw to her relief that the bed had been vacated and all that remained was the black cloak that Tyrant had brought with him.

'Ah, there it is,' Malachi said. He picked up the cloak and wrapped it around his shoulders. 'This isn't where I expected to be.' He let out a deep breath. 'What are you doing here in the King's high tower? If he discovers you, I fear it will be beyond my powers of persuasion to save you from the noose.'

'Don't worry, the King is comfortable with my presence. It's good to see you; I was worried that we might never talk again. Now we have many things to discuss and lots to catch up on.'

'I've lost my bag. The one containing the gold and some powerful devices. The grey monsters took it when they killed Tyrant and Ant. We have to get it back.'

52

The work at the temple was progressing well. Lone watched Malachi encouraging the labourers with strong words and a threatening look. The main building had been left intact, and all that needed to be done to bring the building back into use was to clear away the demolished portico. Most of the debris had been cleared to the side in order to allow access to Miriam and her acolytes who were busy sweeping, washing, polishing, and cleaning inside.

Tyrant stood beside her watching the sweating and heaving being lavished on the large pieces of stone that lay strewn untidily by the entrance. 'What's up with him?' He pointed at Malachi.

'He insists that you and Ant are dead. I'm sure that every sight of you makes him doubt his sanity. What exactly did happen with the grey apes?'

'They took me unawares, clobbered me over the head. Next thing I knew, Ant and I were in a cage and they were getting ready to eat us. If it wasn't for...' Tyrant's face contorted as if he'd said something he regretted.

'If it wasn't for what?' Lone asked.

'Oh, yes,' Tyrant's face relaxed. 'If it weren't for my strength and opportunism, we'd both be dead. I charged the biggest of them, flattened him, and then managed to retrieve my sword. That did the trick. A few swipes and they'd had enough and fled.'

'What happened to Malachi's bag?'

'Oh, that thing. I told Ant to leave it, but he insisted on dragging it along. After Malachi was injured, Ant took it with him when he rowed out to the ship.'

'If Gilgamesh was on board that vessel, I doubt Ant will have survived the encounter,' Lone said.

'There's more to the boy than you might think,' Tyrant said.

'Really? I don't believe anyone knows Ant better than I do. He's no match for Gilgamesh; none of us are.'

'Then why bother with all this?' Tyrant asked. 'If, as you say, he's coming our way, hadn't we best make ourselves scarce?'

'I promised the King that we'd help him,' Lone said.

'But what's all this clearing up the old temple about? Why are you bothering with that?'

'This is my price for supporting the King. This temple will help to liberate women from the yoke of oppression. It will change the whole dynamic of our society and women will get the respect they deserve at long last.' The words she uttered sounded more hollow than ever amongst the immense stone edifice that had once paid homage to a genuine god. Would her pretence hold up long enough to have the desired effect? Only if Patch kept his end of the bargain, and he'd been keeping well clear ever since he'd mended Malachi. His reaction to the revelation that Gilgamesh was involved had been disappointing, to say the least. She had the gnawing impression that he'd decided to get out while he still could and leave her to the consequences. If she survived, she had no doubt that he'd be back to deliver his promised punishment in the event of failure.

'How did you manage to restore Malachi to life and mend his shattered body?' Tyrant asked.

Lone looked him in the eye. 'Witchcraft,' she whispered. He nodded briefly, then walked away towards the bustling market down below. She went inside and was rewarded by a sight that lifted her mood. Dust motes made flashes of fire in the shafts of sunlight that pierced the gloom. White-clad women bent and scurried, scrubbed and swept, as if performing an act of devotion. The stone altar had already been polished to a dazzling shine. The serried rows of stone benches were being readied for a congregation of thousands. She fervently hoped that they would be able to fill that many seats when the time came. If the crowd was disappointingly sparse, she'd have lost even if Patch did decide to turn up.

53

'So you left poor Ant all by himself, then?' Petra asked. Tyrant had hoped that the opulence of his new quarters inside the palace would have had a more lasting effect on her mood.

She'd jumped for joy when she'd seen him for the first time, but the novelty of his reappearance had worn off quickly and she was hell-bent on finding out what had kept him away for so long. It seemed he was being asked to account for every moment, and then she was questioning what he had to say in a manner that suggested she didn't entirely trust his account. 'He told me to take Malachi to safety.'

'Oh, right. I understand what you're telling me. Your urge to get out of that dangerous situation was so great that you took the first opportunity you got. Even if that meant accepting orders from a young boy? Don't you think you should have taken charge? After all, you were the senior person there. What could Ant do on his own apart from getting himself killed? Didn't you consider that? Shouldn't you have brought him with you at least? What were you thinking?'

Petra was asking so many questions at once, Tyrant felt his head spinning. She was right, though. He should have made Ant come with him. But he hadn't known that it was Gilgamesh on the ship and it could have held the girls. Malachi needed urgent attention. Everything happened so quickly and now it was too late to change anything. 'He's not alone. He has,' Tyrant lowered his voice to a whisper, 'a sort of magical friend who looks after him. But nobody knows about him. It's a secret.'

'What about Lone and Malachi? Do they know about this?' Petra asked.

'Certainly not. And it's important that they don't find out.'

'Why?'

Tyrant thought for a moment or two. 'I don't know. It just is. That's what Ant wants and he will have his reasons.'

'Is it a demon?' Petra asked. 'He used to have one that told him what to do and where to go. Has he got himself a more powerful one now?'

'Not a demon. Better. More reliable.'

'Then what?' Petra pressed her face uncomfortably close to his.

'He calls it an avatar. I call it Little Ant. It's pretty amazing. It saved me from being killed by giant wasps and then from being bitten by a snake. Then it took the form of a giant and frightened off the grey monsters that were going to eat us. With Little Ant by his side, there's not much out there that could harm him.'

'I hope you're right. If anything happens to that boy, I'll never forgive you.' Petra's face convinced Tyrant that she meant every word.

'I had to bring Malachi back,' he answered without conviction. The sight and feel of him at the time had convinced him that Malachi had been injured beyond recovery. Yet he still took the chance to save his own skin and get off that beach before the destruction recommenced. Petra was right. Looking after Ant should have been his priority, whatever the boy said. It was Ant's kind nature that had caused him to want his mentor taken care of rather than himself. Tyrant knew he should have put up more resistance. Insisted on bringing the boy back with him or, failing that, stayed with him. Now, for the first time, Petra had exposed his fear that Ant had been lost. There was no reasonable alternative explanation. If he'd survived, whether or not the girls had been on board the ship, he'd have rowed back to the shore and returned via the vedhana to be with his injured master. The realisation dragged his spirits down into his boots. The world would be a much poorer place without Ant in it.

As if sensing his capitulation, Petra held his gaze and said nothing. 'I'm sorry,' was all Tyrant could manage before tears overwhelmed him.

54

Lone sat on the cool stone bench at the side of the altar watching proceedings. The numbers visiting the temple had been increasing every day and there was a decent-sized crowd of a hundred or more gathering to hear Miriam speak.

Despite frequent attempts to summon him, there had been no sign of Patch since he'd revived Malachi and told her that he wasn't prepared to stick around in the face of Gilgamesh's imminent arrival. His shimmering ghostly manifestation had been substituted by a spectacular statue of pure white polished stone that had been found in the recesses of the temple and erected in the centre of the raised altar. The statue depicted a naked female figure whose voluptuous form had been crafted down to the most intimate detail. Her shaven head had inspired Miriam and her closest acolytes to remove their own hair, giving them a powerfully distinctive appearance that meant they were recognised instantly everywhere they went.

The congregation was deep in prayer, creating a soft positive energy to the place that she wished Patch was here to appreciate. This is what she'd promised. It was a pity that he wasn't prepared to fulfil his side of the bargain in return.

The gentle silence was savagely punctuated by the arrival of an unruly mob. A dozen or so men, shouting the odds and no doubt fortified by copious amounts of drink, approached the altar. They made their way through the supine supplicants, making lewd remarks and grabbing at their bodies. The leader, a large red-headed man, confronted Miriam and put his hands on her breasts. 'Come on, baldy,' he said, 'what you need is the services of a real man.' He looked suggestively over his shoulder. 'You might even get lucky and we'll all have a go on you.'

The men following him bellowed with enthusiastic laughter. Lone allowed her rage to channel into strong energy that ran through the stone beneath her feet and sought out the man accosting her priestess. She prepared to squeeze his heart until it burst and then repeat the process on his friends.

Before she managed to make the connection, Miriam put one hand on the man's head and removed his hands from her chest. Lone watched with fascination as his aggression disappeared like a puff of smoke in a gale. He went down on one knee, head bent in supplication, and stayed perfectly still. Lone could almost hear the crackle of energy that was coming from the congregation and being channelled through the priestess as she took his head in both hands and held it to her stomach. Even from where she was sitting, Lone could see the convulsions of the weeping man and the tears streaking his face. His friends sank to their knees and put their heads to the cold stone of the temple floor.

Everyone seemed frozen in position. The disturbed air settled back to tranquillity and the silent devotions resumed. Eventually, Miriam released the red-haired man and walked back onto the dais to stand by the altar. 'Ours is the way of love.' She spoke in a strong voice that echoed around the temple. 'Our mistreatment is not an excuse for visiting cruelty and harm on our menfolk. They know no better. They are the product of their upbringing and their misguided society. We should show them how much we love them. We should care for them as if they were the children that their actions suggest. We should remind them that they are sons and husbands and fathers, privileges that require them to act with gentleness and compassion. Let us show them how. If, however, they refuse to respond and continue to abuse us, if they threaten our bodies with their violence, if they adhere to the old ways and deny us our right to live as equals, then they will feel the awesome wrath of Persephone. Only then. In the meantime, return to your homes, be kind to your husbands, nurture your children, and honour yourselves as embodiments of the divine feminine.'

Lone experience an outpouring of joy that swept her to her feet. Everyone was smiling and wide-eyed with joy. Even the red-haired man was hugging his friends as if they'd been lost and he'd only just found them. Something special had happened here, even without demonic intervention. The fabric of the immense building hummed softly to her and the stone appeared to be responding to the gentle humanity that rested on it. There was unimagined power in this place and she suspected that this was only a small taste. Her body shuddered with awe and excitement. If she was right, she may have unleashed a force that even kings and demons ought to fear. It could even be the real reason why Patch was nowhere to be found. Whatever the reason, she was no longer in control, and that made her feel vulnerable.

55

The King's response to his suggestion that he should leave Gort and bravely seek out Gilgamesh was underwhelming. Tyrant had expected to be firmly told that his place was at the side of his monarch and that he shouldn't put himself at risk. Instead, the King nodded and urged him to 'get on with it'.

Petra's insistence that she accompany him was easier to accept. She could witness his brave but futile attempts to find Ant, then let the matter rest once and for all.

The sand was warm, the sea gently lapping over the sand, and the heady smell of lushness greeted him as they stepped out of the vedhana. The feeling of the place was reminiscent of the desert where the two of them had spent such a glorious time and he'd become inextricably connected to his small female companion.

She smiled at him as if their thoughts had coincided and a warmth bloomed in his body that owed nothing to the bright sunlight. It all seemed so obvious. Why had it taken until now to realise what was going on between them? The understanding that everything Petra did, everything she said, every look she gave him, and every touch was evidence of her loving kindness towards him swept over him. The experience was almost too much to bear without bursting into tears.

Making him seek out Ant before it was too late was a supreme example of how she knew him better than he knew himself. Leaving the boy had been nagging at him more than he'd realised. If anything bad had happened to him, he'd never forgive himself for not at least trying to prevent it. Petra knew all this and was desperately trying to spare him the anguish he'd carry for the rest of his life.

It all suddenly made sense. When she scolded him about drinking too much licker, she wasn't doing it to deprive him. When she reminded him of his past foolishness, she was telling him that, despite everything, she forgave him. Every word, every look, every shrug of her shoulders was saying that she loved him. And he'd never understood any of it until stepping out onto this beach.

She was looking at him as if expecting him to say something. His mouth opened to form the words that explained his revelation, but he closed it again because his knowing was enough. Saying that he knew was pointless; he had to remember what he now knew and live accordingly. Then she'd understand that he had woken up at long last to the knowledge of how inexpressibly precious Petra had become.

'Well?' she said.

'It's no good. The ship has gone and there's no sign of the little boat that Ant took.'

'He might have landed further away. I suggest we take a walk along this nice beach and see what we can find,' Petra said.

'I'm not sure that's a good idea,' Tyrant replied. 'There are lots of nasty things in that jungle. We need to stay close to the vedhana in case we have to make a quick getaway.'

'You've got your sword, haven't you? And you're nowhere near as fat and useless as you used to be.'

Tyrant's newly formed awareness translated her words to *I'm not afraid with you by my side* and *you're stronger, leaner, and fitter now than you've been for a long time.* It was true. His belly had shrunk with exercise and meagre diet while his sword arm had grown powerful musculature from hacking his way through the undergrowth day after day. Petra was right. She had nothing to fear while he was by her side. 'I'll show you where Malachi fell and we dug him out from under a tree,' he said.

The splintered branches and shattered trunks lay testimony to the might that had been unleashed against them from the ship. Revisiting the site brought realisation of the awesome destructive power of the weapon and strengthened his belief that this could only have been the work of Gilgamesh. That being the case, he would have to find him and kill him all over again. It wasn't only a matter of reputation. There was the ultimate score to settle between them: the murders of his mother and little brother.

'How did you manage to survive?' Petra stood amongst the devastation, face set with concern.

'It stopped before I could run to assist them,' he replied.

'But you did run towards the danger, didn't you?' Petra asked.

'I mustn't have been thinking straight,' he said, and was rewarded with a smile.

'Come on.' She walked back towards the sea. 'Let's see if there's any signs of either the ship or the boat further up the shoreline.' He padded after her dutifully, enjoying the heat of the sun on his back and the warmth in his heart.

Bristling hairs on the back of his neck made him turn around and look back towards the vedhana. What he saw made all the heat leave his body to be replaced by cold panic. A dozen enormous grey apes had emerged from the jungle between him and the safety of the vedhana.

56

'I'm not sure I like the idea of leaving you behind,' Ant said.

His avatar cocked his owl head to one side. 'If you've got a better plan, then come on. Let's have it.'

'You know very well I don't or you'd know it already.'

'Look,' Little Ant said, transforming into a passable likeness. 'They'll think you're still here. Nobody will be looking for you. All you have to do is walk back to the vedhana and wait for me. When I think I've bought you enough time to do that, I'll turn into a bird and fly to join you.'

Ant poked his finger at his representation. It encountered no resistance. His image was insubstantial, made from suspended motes of dust. 'You look fine from a distance, but if anyone touches you, that will give the game away.'

'Then I'll keep my distance.'

'What about Dot? You'll have to share a bed with her. It will be obvious that you're not real.'

'I'll think of something. You better get going. It will soon be dawn and you could do with being well away from the house by then.'

Filled with fear and misgivings, Ant tiptoed down the staircase and past the sleeping bodies scattered around the hearth. The door creaked alarmingly when he eased it open to reveal torrential rain clattering into the boards and, beyond them, absolute darkness.

Taking the smallest garment hanging in the entrance, he slipped the waxed fabric cape over his head and pulled on the hood. His boots splashed in the mud being churned up by the thunderstorm, and he walked cautiously away from the house, guided by memory and the occasional revealing flash of lightning.

A few smacks across the face from trailing branches taught him to keep his head down. He tumbled into water-filled ditches three times before the early light allowed him to pick his way more surely, but the weather had at least given him the advantage of concealment long enough to be well out of sight of the house. As the light allowed, he hurried his step. Dot would be sneaking back into his room after a clandestine assignation with Dug by now, and he hoped that Little Ant would be able to fool her a little longer.

The first people he encountered were out in the fields, cajoling cattle towards milking sheds. He adopted the slump-shouldered, dangling arms posture common to the farm inhabitants as he skirted the edge of the field and was rewarded with a waved 'hello' and nothing more. Again, the inclement weather was a boon for giving him an excuse to hide within the cloak. On a dry sunny morning, he'd have stood out like a wart on a nose.

The further he walked, the better he felt. It was as if Mama's influence waned with every step. Even when he encountered an occasional farm worker, they seemed unthreatening and lacked the long-armed, short-legged appearance that characterised the men from the big house. Though his spirits were lifted by a new sense of freedom, there was a nagging thought that he should have reached the sea after two days tramping across fields. His plan, to find the shore then make his way to the vedhana by following the coastline was, for some reason that he couldn't quite fathom, not working. It was as if he'd been blindfolded and turned around and around and was now staggering around, disorientated and dizzy.

As a consolation, there was plenty for him to eat. Not the luscious sweet fruit he'd foraged in the jungle, though. He scavenged fat fibrous tubers that squatted under the earth and tasted of nothing much at all. When he chewed on them, he tried to imagine he was back in Mama's kitchen enjoying the richness of her stew rather than eating animal fodder.

His first welcome sight of the sea came when he was close to giving up hope of ever finding his way. The winding path down to the shore was flanked by small houses made from mud with pebbles pressed into it. He joined the straggle of pedestrians that wandered seawards and came to a stone quay where fishing boats bobbed and scraped as they were being unloaded. Ant had never been partial to fish because of the bones. It seemed hardly worth the trouble of sorting out the flesh from the carcass. These fish were nothing like the tiny sprats that he'd had in Gort, though. These were huge, as long as his arm and as thick as his thigh. They continued to thrash about weakly as they were lobbed into baskets and hauled onto the shore. Ant couldn't help feeling sorry for the poor things being taken out of the water to gasp in vain as they died.

Fascinated by the sight of the fish and the sounds of negotiation, the hand on his shoulder took him by surprise. 'Hello, Ant,' a familiar voice said, 'what are you doing so far away from where you ought to be?'

57

'Run!' Tyrant screamed at Petra. 'Into the jungle. We have to get away.'

'You've got your sword. They're the ones who should be running away.' Petra stood firm, a knife in each hand.

'You don't know what they're like.' Tyrant winced at the memory of how he'd failed to uproot the Grey that he'd hit with all his weight and strength. 'There are too many of them. We need to get away while we still have the chance.' His alarm increased as the Greys began to move towards them and the opportunity to escape dwindled by the moment.

Petra wasn't going to tolerate the ignominy of him picking her up and attempting to whisk her to safety. Neither would she follow him if he made a run for it. So, he held tight to his sword and braced himself. The best plan he could devise was to kill the first Grey to get within range and hope that might deter the rest. His experience of these creatures didn't give him much hope of succeeding.

She had other ideas, though, and was already running down the sand screaming and waving her knives. He could do nothing except follow, shouting unenthusiastically and hoping that the Greys had a sense of humour.

Petra's charge seemed to put them into a state of uncertainty and disarray. Then, as one, they ran headlong into the sea and submerged completely. The way to the vedhana was clear, so he steered Petra towards it. She was still shouting, but there was more joy in her screams than menace now. As they got to within a dozen paces of the portal, Tyrant heard the buzzing. He picked Petra up, lengthened his stride, and dived into the vedhana as the wasps arrived.

As the tightness in his chest grew, all he could think of was Ant and whether he had managed to get away from this awful place. The buzzing receded, the vedhana did its magic, and he was deposited in woodland, Petra still clasped firmly under one arm as a shower of dead wasps pattered to the ground. When he released her as gently as he could, he was rewarded by a cold stare. 'It was the wasps,' he tried to explain. 'That's what spooked the Greys. They would have got us if we hadn't been quick.'

'Admit it,' she replied, 'you panicked. I chased those apes away and then you were so scared by a few insects that you transported us here without any thought or purpose. We hadn't finished looking for Ant.'

'Maybe this is where Ant is,' Tyrant said.

'Well, I can't see him or any sign of him.'

'Let's look around carefully. Who else could have made this vedhana? Maybe there's something he left to guide us.'

Tyrant knew it was a long shot. He'd brought them to a random place that he didn't recognise. If there wasn't any indication that Ant had been here, she'd insist on going back to the wasps and the Greys.

He poked around in the bushes with little hope and even less success. His options all appeared bad. Going back to the beach would get them both killed, especially as Petra had chosen not to believe his account of how dangerous the Greys and the wasps were. It was unfortunate that events had convinced her that he was exaggerating, something that he had to admit to having been guilty of on occasions. Back to Gort and the King was almost as bad. Cuthbert saw him as expendable fodder for the ensuing conflict. He'd rather fight Gilgamesh on his own terms and with some trustworthy allies by his side.

They could sneak home. Carry on brewing licker. But they'd be discovered sooner rather than later and then he'd be in real trouble with the King. Things were looking as bleak as they had done for a long time. In fact, he struggled to remember being so lost for positive options.

'Over here.' Petra's voice roused him from his melancholy musings. 'The ground has been disturbed. Look, the grass has been cut away and then put back.' She lifted a sod to reveal recently dug ground.

His hands bit into the soft earth and retrieved a bag. The bag. Malachi's bag. The bag that Ant had carried with him when he boarded the boat. Exultation filled his whole body, and he began to dance and shout with joy. 'Ant's alive,' he said. 'He's here. All we have to do is find him.'

Petra's smile was broad and warm. 'Well done,' she said. Then she left a long pause before adding, 'For once.'

Tyrant slung the heavy bag over his shoulder and it settled into the groove it had carved during his expedition with Malachi into the jungle. He imagined the look on Malachi's face when he brought back his precious item and decided that he'd rather throw it into the sea than give him the satisfaction.

They soon found a wide track that led up to a large house. 'We'll call at the house and ask if they've seen him,' he said. Petra nodded; her step had been jaunty since they'd found the bag. She was enjoying the adventure, and he was glad to have her along.

The dog that faced them was bigger and nastier than any he'd seen before. It bristled and snarled and slavered and barked, blocking their progress and threatening to leap at them and tear out their throats. Tyrant kicked it hard in the ribs, raising it slightly off the ground before depositing it on its side. It lay in the dirt for a moment, then struggled to its feet. Its lips withdrew into a snarl as it stood unsteadily to challenge him. Tyrant reached over and patted the animal on the head. It stopped snarling and cowered. 'Sorry about the misunderstanding,' he said. 'No need for any more aggravation, eh?'

As they continued walking, the dog ambled by their side, completely devoid of menace.

An old man with a cudgel stepped off the porch to greet them. "Be off with yer,' he shouted. 'I'll have me boys come out and skin yer, so they will. We don't be doing with strangers around here.'

Four younger, larger men appeared at his shoulder as if to back up his threat. 'We're looking for a friend,' Tyrant said. 'All we want to know is if you've seen him.'

'No,' said the old man, 'we've not seen nobody.'

'He's never been here,' one of the younger men said, drawing angry glances.

'Who's never been here?' Petra asked.

'Nobody,' the old man said.

'Absolutely nobody, especially not Ant,' the young man added.

'Shut up,' the rest of them chorused.

'What's going on?' A woman appeared at the top of the steps.

'They're looking fer Ant,' the old man said. 'Told 'em we'd not seen anyone by that description, eh, lads?'

'We never told you his name,' Petra said. 'Is he here?'

'Come inside,' the woman said.

Tyrant and Petra took seats at a large table that could have accommodated thirty diners at once. The men were ushered to the other side of the room where they muttered amongst themselves. The woman brought them plates of food. Tyrant tucked in without further invitation.

'We could do with a big, strong man like you,' she said. 'There's plenty nice young girls that would be glad to take you as their husband. It's a good life here. Plenty of everything. Your little friend could stay as well as long as they made themselves useful.'

'No thanks,' Petra said. 'He's already got a wife. All we want is to find Ant.'

Tyrant wished he'd been quicker to reply and not left it to Petra. 'That's right,' he added, putting his hand on Petra's arm. She gave him a gentle look that made him feel relieved.

'He's gone,' the woman said. 'We gave him everything, looked after him, he took a wife, then, without even a single goodbye, he upped and left. Disappeared completely and for no good reason. Ungrateful, that's what I call it.'

'Do you know where he went?' Tyrant asked.

'If we knew that, we'd have brought him back. As it is, we've looked high and low for him, but without success. He can't have gone far. It was only yesterday that he was seen in his room.'

'Where are we?' Petra asked.

'That's a strange question to be asking. Are you from the same ship as Ant? Were you washed ashore as well?'

'Yes,' Petra said. 'What do you call this land?'

'The island of Kish, you mean, or our homestead?'

'Kish? Our crew came from here. Stands to reason they would sail home,' Tyrant said.

As they walked unchallenged out of the house, they were met by a girl. 'He's looking for the girls from the North who were brought here on a ship. He'll be heading for the City on the Ocean where all the large ships have to dock.'

217

58

'Dot?' Ant gasped at the sight of his pretend wife. If she'd found him, the rest of Mama's tribe would be close by. Perhaps even Mama herself had joined in the hunt.

'No, it's me.' Little Ant lowered his voice and flashed his eyes. 'How did you expect me to appear? A talking dog or intelligent owl might have caused these good people to accuse us of witchcraft, don't you agree?'

'But you gave me a shock. I expected Mama to appear by your side and take me back to the big house.'

'Don't worry, they will have only just discovered you're missing. I made a big play of standing on the stairs and shouting for Dot last night. After she'd slipped away to meet Dug, I owl-shaped and flew as fast as I could to the vedhana. Unfortunately, you'd decided to come here instead. It's taken me half the day to find you.'

'I got lost,' Ant said. 'I ended up here by mistake. Sorry.'

'Only kidding. This means we're closer to the city, which is where we have to be. The main port is only a couple of hours' walk along the coast from this fishing harbour.'

Weariness wobbled his legs and drowned his resolve. Rescuing Cassie and Bee seemed as far away as ever. As if saving him the trouble of expressing how he felt, Little Ant chipped in, 'Come on, take this business one step at a time. Remember your studies and concentrate on the here and now. It's stopped raining and there's a shop over there where you can buy bread with the coins that Mama put in your purse. Eat first, then decide what to do.'

'You're right, of course you are, but I wish I had someone here to help.'

'You've got me.' Little Ant laughed.

'And I'm grateful for having you by my side. But we're the same. Your thoughts are my thoughts. We couldn't disagree if we wanted to.'

'Yes, we could.' Little Ant laughed again. 'It's Lone you're missing, isn't it?'

A tingle thrilled Ant's body as he imagined how it would feel to have Lone here. Safe. She'd look after him with that imperious power she had over men. He could relax and leave the decisions to her. His warm feeling evaporated as he realised he was relishing the prospect of becoming a helpless child again. That couldn't be healthy. If that's all he could be around Lone, then it was no wonder that she despised him. 'No, she'd take over completely and do whatever was best for her, regardless of anything else. I need to take responsibility myself if I'm to grow into a man.'

'That was well said, but I bet you'd change your mind if she were standing behind you.'

Ant twisted his head but only saw haggling traders and Little Ant's smiling Dot face. 'You got me there.' He laughed and the release made his body feel lighter. Anything was possible, all he had to do was let it happen and enjoy it when it did.

Mama's coins were worth more than they had looked when he'd first discovered their substitution for his gold. The baker snipped a quarter from the meanest and thinnest of them before endowing him with a fat loaf. Ant's optimism increased with every mouthful.

The sun was high in a cloudless sky when they reached the outskirts of the city. The sight of it took Ant by surprise. It was huge, sprawling, teeming with people. As he walked along the seafront, he passed hundreds of vessels of many sizes and designs. The sheer enormity of the port robbed him of breath. Finding the ship that had brought the girls here would be more difficult than he'd anticipated. At most, he'd imagined a handful of ships that size; instead, there were dozens scattered along the shore and anchored out in the bay.

Little Ant had resumed his role as a dog, so he sat down on a bollard away from the crowds and whispered softly to him. 'These ships all look the same to me. I don't know how we're going to find the right one, especially if it's out there in the sea.'

'It might even have sailed again while we were stuck in Mama's house. Maybe it's better if we ask around after the girls. Someone may have seen them disembark.'

'It's a bit vague, isn't it? What do I describe them as? A Queen and Princess looking considerably worse for wear?'

'Then you should ask about Gilgamesh. We know his name and you could hardly fail to notice a man with half a face and one arm missing.'

Little Ant's suggestion was obviously sensible, but it made him feel very uneasy. Meeting Gilgamesh again was something he was hoping to avoid. In his fondest imagination, he saw the girls being kept in a different place where they could be rescued by subtlety and without confrontation with the scarily powerful man who would kill him as soon as he recognised who he was. For all he knew, Gilgamesh was already on the lookout for him after being angered by his escape from the ship. How would he know who it was safe to ask? As soon as he opened his mouth, word could be sent back to that monster and then he'd be in deadly danger.

Sitting with his back to the sea, staring at the distant hills that overlooked the city, he gathered his resources by connecting into the earth and becoming present in the here and now. What would be, would be. If he had to face Gilgamesh, then he'd do it the best way he could. Several deep breaths and he was ready to begin his quest.

As he rose from his sedentary posture, a bright star rose above the city. His heart pounding, Ant recognised it at once. Following the smoky trail back to the ground enabled him to identify the place it had originated. There was a large expanse of grassland on the opposite side of the city that held a woodland in the shape of a heart. The trail led back to these trees.

'That's meant for us,' he said.

'I agree,' Little Ant replied. 'But who else but Gilgamesh could summon us in that way?'

'Could it be Malachi, I wonder?'

'Unlikely, especially as he's most likely dead.'

'Whoever it is, I can't ignore it. Change into a bird and fly ahead.'

Ant ran as fast as he could, feet pounding in time to his heart.

59

The whole city lay before them with the sparkling ocean beyond. 'It's enormous,' Tyrant said.

'We have to find Ant, even if it means searching every building,' Petra said.

'That could take years. I have a better idea. You stay here out of danger while I go down there and have a scout around. I'll see what intelligence I can gather by asking subtle questions in a friendly manner. I'll blend in, gain people's confidence. Avoid attracting suspicion. Leave it to me.'

'Exactly where are you intending to conduct your enquiries?' Petra's face had grown a stern look.

Tyrant felt his cheeks getting hot. 'I don't know; I'll decide when I get there. Go with my instinct.'

'What about trying a tavern or two? They surely have them a plenty in a city that size. Had you thought of that?'

Petra's suggestion took away his breath. It was as if she'd been reading his mind. Her suggestion tallied exactly with his intentions, and it was remarkable how closely attuned his companion had become. A tavern or two made complete sense, but he'd been reluctant to reveal his plan in fear of being misunderstood. 'Now you mention it, I already thought that would be the best plan.' His words turned her face to stone. 'What?' he asked.

'So you intend to leave me here while you go to some inn and drink yourself stupid?'

'No,' he replied. 'I just think you'll be safer here than coming with me.'

'Safer? Is that what you think? There's grey monsters and killer bees and all kinds of deadly things here and you want to abandon me in order to get yourself a crafty drink or two?'

'That's not what I said.' Tyrant had many words swirling around in his head, but none of them seemed appropriate to getting himself off this particular hook. 'I was only discussing ideas, that's all.'

'Then start discussing something a lot more practical. We haven't got the time to be plodding the streets hoping to get lucky. The girls could be anywhere and Ant may be long gone by the time we get any word. They might not be here at all. They could have stopped for a day and then sailed away again. Think hard. There must be something we can do.'

Tyrant sat down beside the bag, preparing to think as hard as he could about any plan that didn't involve a lot of walking and certainly no drinking. He imagined Ant down there in the city with a similar problem, asking in vain for news of the girls' whereabouts. The priority was to find Ant, let him know that he wasn't alone, and join forces to rescue the girls. 'I know what to do.' He leapt to his feet, then bent down and rummaged in the bag. 'This is a fire demon in a magic tube.' He waved the package in front of Petra's face. 'Only Ant of all the people in that city will recognise it because he's seen one before.'

Before Petra could reply, he unwrapped the device, removed the base, and tugged on the string. This time he was ready for the demon and kept it well clear of his face. As the red star rose gracefully into the clear afternoon sky, he felt a surge of accomplishment.

They watched the burning demon slowly sink back to earth in a heavily built-up area of the city. A small plume of grey smoke marked the place it had landed. The smoke grew thicker and blacker, then flames began to lick around the buildings. If he strained his ears, Tyrant imagined he could hear the shouts of consternation as people began fighting the fire.

Petra returned his look with one heavy with derision. 'If the plan was to burn the city to the ground, you made a good start,' she said.

'It's not my fault,' he replied. 'I can't help what the demon does after it's released.'

'You might have thought of that before you released it.' She shook her head. 'I can't imagine what you thought to achieve.'

'Ant will see it and come here,' Tyrant said. 'Mark my words. It will turn out brilliantly. You'll be thanking me when he turns up. Anyway, it's only a small fire by the looks of it. A couple of buildings, that's all. They've plenty more.'

'Remind me what happened the last time you let out such a demon,' Petra said.

'It attracted a ship,' Tyrant replied, shivering at the remembered shocks of the dreadful device that had been turned against them.

'If I remember rightly, you almost got Ant and Malachi killed. Don't you think there's a chance that might happen again?'

'That time, they reckon it was Gilgamesh himself wielding the weapon. That's not going to happen here. Anyway, we're well away from the ocean here. Don't worry. Ant will turn up and then everything will be fine. I promise.'

60

'Is that Ant on the horse?' Petra asked.

Tyrant squinted at the figure galloping towards him. Too tall. Left sleeve empty and billowing in the breeze. Face unfamiliar. Not Ant. Who then?

'Maybe it's someone with news of him,' he replied without much conviction.

The black horse snorted as it was brought to a sudden halt and its rider jumped deftly to the ground. Tyrant was drawn to the man's face. It had an unhealthy, bloodless pallor. A dark red welt ran its circumference from the base of the chin to the top of his forehead. Tyrant found it an unnerving sight that sent his guts rumbling and his nerves jangling.

'So, it's you,' the man sneered. 'I had hoped for something more challenging.'

It was only when the impossibly thin rapier was drawn and pointed at his face that Tyrant knew for sure he was facing Gilgamesh. 'Get away,' he urged Petra. 'Run for your life. I'll hold him off as long as I can.'

'Is this the limit of your King's ambition? A fat fool and a midget? Couldn't he find better? What about that wizard of his and his dreadful wife? Are they lurking behind you in those woods?'

'Nobody is lurking. There's no need to point that sword at me. We're looking for Ant. That's all. You needn't fear us. We don't care what you're up to. It's no concern of ours.'

'That boy fell off my ship and was drowned. He was of so little consequence I'm at a loss as to understand why you're bothering to look for him. Or is that just a ruse to put me off my guard while your army gathers itself for an attack?'

'I assure you that there is no army. You don't look well, Gilgamesh. You seem to have lost an arm since we last met. Your face looks terrible; what happened to it?'

'Your signal interrupted my healing process, that's all. A little time is all that's needed and I'll be back to normal. You have no appreciation of how much inconvenience you've caused. It took me a long time to find a face that I liked. It's a painstaking process to peel it from the donor, especially when he's writhing around and reluctant to part with it. I could take it more easily if I killed him first, but I prefer it to be as fresh as possible when I apply it to myself. I find it makes for a more successful and aesthetically pleasing result. As for the arm,' – the rapier blade quivered – 'yours would make an excellent replacement. At least that might compensate me for the trouble of having to ride all this way.'

Gilgamesh took a step forward and plunged the tip of his sword into Tyrant's shoulder. The move was too swift for him to react; there was no time to draw his sword and the stabbing pain caused his arm to drop lifelessly by his side. 'That evens things up. Wouldn't want you to have an unfair advantage.' Gilgamesh withdrew his blade and his face contorted into a rictus smile.

Tyrant tried to revive his ailing arm, but it persisted in hanging useless and hurting terribly. The rage inside him erupted and took over completely. The tiny voice telling him to run away was drowned out by a wave of noisy anger. He charged at Gilgamesh, wounded shoulder first. The sword came up instantly and pricked him again in almost the same place. But it didn't halt his progress. Tyrant had twisted to his left at the point of impact and grabbed the sword arm with his good hand and hung on grimly. The collision had been akin to hitting the grey ape and equally ineffective. Gilgamesh remained disappointingly rooted and upright. As they wrestled for the sword, Tyrant felt himself being slowly overcome by the stronger man. His hand was gradually losing its grip. Once released, the sword would inevitably deal him another debilitating wound. The vision of having his arm sawn off and being powerless to stop it kicked him into drastic action. He bit Gilgamesh's nose and kept his teeth firmly clenched. Gilgamesh broke his handhold and smacked him across the head with the sword pommel.

Tyrant let go of his arm and fell backwards onto the grass. What felt like a soggy rag flopped over his face, obscuring his vision, until he shook his head to remove it and found that he still had Gilgamesh's nose between his teeth. The man standing over him had no face. His eyes protruded horribly from a sea of red mush, his lipless mouth drawn into a permanent humourless smile. A tiny glimmer of satisfaction crept into

Tyrant's pain-wracked body. At least he'd gone out fighting and he could honestly say that his opponent looked worse than him.

The rapier blade scored his cheek. It quivered and danced before his eyes, mesmerising him into inaction. One more thrust and he'd be dead. There was nothing he could do but hope it would be a quick end to the pain that throbbed and burned in his shoulder.

Gilgamesh let out a sudden yell and sprang backwards, allowing Tyrant to half rise and view the cause of his discomfiture. Petra had slashed a deep bloody furrow in Gilgamesh's thigh that had set him hobbling and shouting. Tyrant winced as she moved in for another strike.

This time, Gilgamesh was ready for her. He kicked her legs from under her, deposited her writhing on her back. Another savage kick to her head left her prone and lifeless, spread-eagled on the ground. Gilgamesh looked at Tyrant, then put his sword to Petra's face.

Tyrant struggled to his feet and whipped out his sword. 'Drop it,' Gilgamesh ordered. 'Put down your sword or I'll end her pathetic existence right now.'

Tyrant froze in mid-attack. He released his grip on the sword and allowed it to drop. 'Let her go,' he said. 'She's no threat. She can't harm a warrior like you. It's only me you have to worry about. I'll not fight you any more if you walk away from her.'

'Have you seen what she's done? Ruined my trousers and caused me considerable pain. You don't know how close she was to hobbling me completely when you tell me she can do no harm. She's dangerous. But I will spare her long enough for her to watch you die. There, see how generous I have become even though you've ruined my new face?' Gilgamesh pulled back his sword, hesitated, then plunged it into Petra's eye socket. A gush of blood made a tiny lake that spilled over into a red river that coursed down her face.

Tyrant heard himself bellow. It was a guttural roar that came from somewhere deep inside. He bent down to retrieve his sword, but as his hand touched the pommel, he knew it was too late. Gilgamesh was already upon him and the rapier tip too close to defend against.

61

Ant's breath rasped in his throat. His lungs burned. His legs were weak with weariness. He forced himself uphill towards the copse of trees that had been the source of the signal. His journey had been more convoluted than he'd wanted. There had been too many obstacles. Structures, people, fences, streams, and tangles of brambles had slowed his progress and diverted his path. Little Ant had returned several times to tell him he was heading in the wrong direction, otherwise he'd have been hopelessly lost. Now, however, his destination was in sight.

He ran through the forest, legs tangled by vines, face whipped and slapped by low branches. The sight that greeted him as he emerged from beneath the gloomy canopy shocked him to the core. Gilgamesh, face ripped to shreds and set in a deadly parody of amusement, stood over a fallen Tyrant. Petra lay still and bleeding a few paces beyond.

A cloud of wasps zoomed overhead, their angry buzzing causing him to instinctively throw himself to the ground as they screamed past. Gilgamesh frantically waved his good arm as the insects swarmed over his face. He staggered backwards, clawing at his head with the back of his hand, trying to wipe the crawling, stinging things from his eyes. He let out a loud bellow, then lowered his hand that still gripped his thin sword. 'What's this sorcery?' he yelled. The tip of his sword encountered a flying wasp and, with a deft flick, reduced it to powder. 'Some form of dust devil, is it?'

Ant watched in horror as the wasps began to decompose and drop to the ground as a stream of lifeless particles that Gilgamesh began to grind into the earth with the heel of his boot.

Tyrant seemed reluctant to rise from his recumbent position, but managed to get slowly to his feet to face his adversary, sword in hand, but his other arm hanging loosely.

Ant's concern switched from the fate of Little Ant and his valiant wasp forms to Tyrant, who looked unsteady on his feet and unusually non-belligerent. When he lunged, Gilgamesh was able to easily avoid the thrust by stepping backwards, causing Tyrant to stagger and almost collapse back to the ground.

Gilgamesh stood over Petra, sword to her tiny heaving chest. 'So you value the life of this ugly little creature?' He addressed Tyrant, who stood paralysed, sword lowered as if he'd already given up.

'I'll get you for killing her,' Tyrant replied with more weariness in his voice than menace.

'Oh, she's not dead. I only gave her a scratch to see how you'd react. Seems to me that her death would cause you considerable suffering, and that's something I'm very keen to do. Give me your sword, or I'll stab her through her miserable heart right now. Do what I say and I might keep her alive for a while as a grotesque pet to amuse my followers.'

Tyrant stuck his sword into the ground and backed away from it. Ant still lay flat in the grass, his view of Gilgamesh partially obscured by Tyrant's bulky figure retreating towards him.

Gilgamesh stuck his rapier into his belt and picked up Tyrant's sword. As he held it aloft, it seemed to shine brighter and a faint aura like silver smoke began to form around it. 'I knew it!' Gilgamesh shouted. 'This is the sword that I lost countless years ago when I fought the Bull of Heaven, who I had to rip apart with my bare hands. Ishtar thought she'd seen the end of me then, but I prevailed, as I always do. With my old sword, I'll be more invincible than ever.'

'You don't look invincible,' Tyrant said.

'All this is merely cosmetic. Bodies can be regrown, mended, regenerated, and renewed. Back at my palace, I have a place where I can perform that special magic that has kept me vigorous since time began. Don't concern yourself about me. It's your condition you need to worry about. I rather think I should have that arm of yours. I've a feeling that it would make a good match for the rest of me. My only concern is that if I take it from you now, it may deteriorate beyond repair before I get the chance to use it.'

'Then take me with you,' Tyrant said. 'Leave Petra. Spare her life and I'll willingly cooperate. You can take my life and my arm whenever it suits you. I promise not to give you any trouble.'

'Your promise means nothing because there's nothing you could possibly do that might cause me even the slightest inconvenience now that I'm reunited with my sword. It makes me smile to think that you've been in possession of an object of limitless power and too stupid to recognise it. With this weapon, I have challenged the gods and prevailed. Ishtar herself had to resort to attempted seduction, and when she failed, she fled screaming from this realm. Now you have made me all-powerful by bringing me my sword. I suppose I ought to thank you, but I won't. Instead, I'll show you how little I value your cooperation by killing your tiny grotesque mate with the sword you so willingly handed over.'

Ant crawled through the long grass, desperately trying to formulate a strategy that might save Petra. Standing up and revealing himself might distract Gilgamesh for a few fleeting moments, but Tyrant was unarmed and appeared in no state to take advantage. Little Ant had disappeared into the earth, seemingly unable to fight on.

His hand touched a familiar object hidden in the grass. It was his bag. Or rather Malachi's bag that he'd buried near the vedhana. It gave him a chance to intervene, although he feared that it was already too late.

62

The wasps had disappeared as quickly as they'd arrived and there was no sign of them returning. Which was a pity because they were the only things left that might cause Gilgamesh enough distraction for Tyrant to get between him and Petra's prone figure. She looked dead from where he stood and Gilgamesh was the last person he'd trust, but there'd been no option other than giving up his sword. The wound in his shoulder hurt terribly, but even worse was the languid feeling that had taken over his whole body. He was so tired, he could hardly stand, let alone fight with a monster.

Gilgamesh held his sword aloft in exultation. A weird stream of light flickered and danced skywards from the blade. 'You've got what you wanted,' Tyrant said without conviction. 'Leave her alone.'

'I want her to see you suffer,' Gilgamesh replied. 'After that, no promises.'

'Get down.' A voice from behind made him turn around. Ant stood a few paces away, holding a metallic device unsteadily in his hands. Even in his depleted state, Tyrant knew immediately to flop to the ground in order to get out of the way from whatever demon Ant was about to release. As his face hit the grass, a tremendous bang shook the birds out of the trees and echoed back more faintly from the hills behind.

Gilgamesh fell backwards as if he'd been hit by a charging bull. The thing in Ant's hands emitted a wisp of blue smoke from the end of its tube. Tyrant scrambled to his feet. 'Nice work,' he shouted over his shoulder as he ran to Petra's side. Her little chest was still rising and falling gently as he wiped the blood from the deep cut that had been gouged just below her eye. Her eyelids flickered as she attempted to open them.

'Where is he?' she asked.

'Lying dead over there,' Tyrant said.

'Well done, so you got him, then. I knew you would.'

'Actually, it was Ant who finished him off.' Tyrant smiled as her customary vitality returned and she sat upright, holding one hand to her injured face. He couldn't help but add, 'I did most of the hard work, though.'

He helped her to her feet, and they stood over the prone Gilgamesh, who was oozing blood from a wound in his chest. Tyrant picked up his sword from beside the body. 'I think he's still alive,' he said.

'Chop off his head,' Petra said. 'Can't be too careful with men like him.'

He raised the sword and readied himself for one final mighty blow that would make sure that Gilgamesh never murdered anyone else. A blow that would avenge his mother and brother. Retribution that had been waiting a lifetime to come. 'Wait,' Ant called. 'Stop, don't do that.'

Tyrant kept the sword aloft. 'He may not be dead. We need to finish him off.'

'I don't think that's a good idea.' Ant walked over to stand next to him, keeping his device pointing towards the fallen monster.

'Why not?' Petra asked. 'It's what he would have done to us all if we'd given him the chance.'

'I've a bad feeling about killing him. It may be what he wants.'

'Really?' Tyrant lowered his sword because it was making his shoulder ache almost as badly as his injured one. 'Is that a reason to let him live and perhaps recover to kill more people? He's sure to come after us seeking revenge.'

'Look at him,' Ant said. 'I think he's damaged beyond repair. Even he can't expect to recover from those wounds. If you kill him, I fear that you'll only be putting an end to that particular body and all you'll be doing is releasing his nastiness so that he can find another one. Perhaps even one of ours. I don't know how these things work, but we have to bear in mind that Gilgamesh isn't human. He's been battling with gods and prevailed. Chopping off his head can't be the answer to him or else he'd not have survived all this time.'

'So we just leave him?' Petra said.

'Walk away. Let him live with that shattered body to contend with. Who knows, it might take him many of our lifetimes to become whole again. Killing him gives me a very bad feeling, that's all. If you think differently, then there's nothing to stop you from chopping him to pieces. I might be wrong,' Ant said.

231

Tyrant thought about it. He'd never been one for hitting a man when he was down, and even if this was a monster, it still didn't feel right. As for the risk that Gilgamesh would rise again and seek him out, that was something he was willing to leave to fate. Ant's words rang true. He was a man wise beyond his years and absolutely trustworthy.

'Let's go, then, we need to find the girls,' Tyrant said, removing the rapier from Gilgamesh's belt and sticking it in his own. 'No need to leave him his favourite sword, just in case he does make a miraculous recovery.' His wounded shoulder had begun to hurt once more now that living was again a real prospect. He watched Ant place the device carefully inside a wooden box and return it to the bag.

The three of them walked down the grassy slope towards the city and were approaching the edge of the large field when he heard the shouting from behind. He turned to see Gilgamesh on his feet and screaming.

63

From her vantage point in the palace tower high above the city, Lone could see swarms of women heading for the temple. Even at this distance, she could make out the gentle strains of happy singing that drifted up through the air.

The remarkable success of the temple was making her nervous as well as exuberant. Part of her wanted to join in the singing; the rest of her was fearful of the consequences of her project getting out of control. Thankfully, the King seemed oblivious to the huge crowds that gathered daily and she put this down to his preoccupation with an imminent visit from Gilgamesh.

Malachi was getting on her nerves. Since his miraculous recovery, he'd been even more morose than usual. 'Cuthbert won't be happy,' he said for the tenth time today.

'Cuthbert agreed to my reopening the temple and holding gatherings to worship Persephone. What makes you so certain he's going to be unhappy about it?'

'Worshipping a false god is one thing, but insurrection is another. Every time that madwoman opens her mouth, she comes up with some new nonsense that erodes the rule of law,' Malachi replied.

She knew he had a point, even though she resented it being constantly waved in front of her face. Most days, the temple was packed to overflowing. Women flocked there from every part of the kingdom to hear what Miriam had to tell them. 'If you consider encouraging women to become strong and independent as a sign of madness, then I'm the craziest of them all. Persephone appeals to women because they know in their hearts that they deserve equal consideration. Most men, if they were being honest, feel the same. I only wish you had the sense to be one of that majority.'

'I'm only telling you the truth,' Malachi said. 'Once this ridiculous Gilgamesh rumour fades away, Cuthbert will turn his attention to more pressing matters. Then he'll recognise how badly you've tricked him. Put a stop to all this nonsense before that happens or we will both be in serious jeopardy.'

'When Gilgamesh comes, even the King will be threatened. He knows that and relies on us to help him.'

'But he won't ever come. It's all a contrivance, admit it,' Malachi said.

'I don't see how you can say that. Gilgamesh almost killed you and he's on his way here to finish the job.'

'That's where you're wrong. I only have Tyrant's word about what happened, and he's the least reliable man in the world. Anyone could put the most fanciful notion to him, and he'd embrace it as the whole truth. I have no recollection of any ship, any device, and certainly no experience of being injured. I think you will agree that had I been crushed so badly that my life was in doubt, then I would at least have some memory of it.'

'So, you think it's all made up, and I created this charade to get my way?' Lone felt her irritation rising to levels she'd not experienced before. Malachi could be stubborn and awkward, but never stupid. She'd benefitted from his sharp insight for many years, but never before felt that he was being unwise. The serious nature of his injuries had undoubtedly affected his mind. His most dramatic and painful memories appeared to have been lost. Even so, she needed his cleverness to assist her decision-making. All he was contributing at the moment was negativity. Malachi was belittling everything she had accomplished and all that she stood for. She could forgive him for the moment because of his recent suffering, but patience was something she'd always kept in short supply.

'Of course you did. Don't get me wrong, I admire your strategy. It's the purpose of it that eludes me. You could be using your hard-won influence in more positive ways than enabling some pretend priestess to exhort young girls to reject their rightful place in society. We should be positioning ourselves right at the heart of government and making sure that our position is safeguarded, come what may. Instead, you're insisting on this temple business, which is only going to end in blood and tears. Your blood and my tears, most probably.' Malachi's eyes glowed red in the reflected rays of the morning sun.

A shiver ran through Lone's body as she looked into them. Patch's words were gnawing away at her brain. *I can do something, but I'm not sure that you'll like it.* Perhaps Malachi's unhelpfulness was a temporary matter. Maybe he'd regain his memory and become the Malachi she knew and could rely on. In the meantime, she constantly revisited Patch's final words before he disappeared and Malachi came back through the vedhana. *Don't say I didn't warn you.*

'Something is coming through the vedhana,' Malachi said.

She turned to see three ghostly shapes gradually take form.

64

Lone watched as the King displayed increasing signs of irritation. Malachi had insisted on telling the story on behalf of everyone because, as he had explained several times, it was vital to maintain the King's confidence in them. Certain aspects of the tale had displeased him mightily, and he had been particularly scathing when Ant had explained their decision not to chop Gilgamesh to bits when they had the chance. He'd called him a stupid boy who would never amount to anything. Ant had responded with a puzzled expression and whispered something to the little dog he'd brought back with him.

'Yes, yes,' the King said, 'Tyrant did this, Ant did that. But you weren't there, were you? I've heard everything about your experiences several times already. What I don't need is you telling me what you've no actual knowledge of. Let them tell their own stories, Malachi. Spare me the conjecture.'

'None of this is conjecture, your majesty, but the distillation of the pertinent facts based on the experiences of all present. It's my concern that allowing individual accounts would be long-winded, duplicitous, and a waste of your majesty's valuable time. Time that could be better used in discussing the import and significance of the information. Time that could be spent in responding to events in a manner that would—'

'Shut up, Malachi.' The King rose to his feet. 'I don't want to hear another word from you. In fact, you can go now. You're dismissed. Close the door quietly on your way out.'

Lone suppressed a smile as Malachi visibly bristled at the King's order. For a fleeting moment, he looked as if anger would get the better of him, but it subsided, leaving him pinch-faced and red in the cheeks. He rose slowly from his chair, performed an elaborate bow, then padded softly out of the King's chambers. The atmosphere inside the room lifted. The girls, who had been silent and deferential to this point, began jabbering excitedly to each other. Ant sat impassive, Petra kept hold of the girls' hands, and Tyrant's bored expression didn't alter.

'Cassie,' the King said. 'Pray tell me what you know.'

'We was captured and treated horribly,' Cassie said.

'He dangled her over the side of the boat,' Bee said. 'Threatened to feed her to the river monsters.'

'Gil wouldn't allow the crew to talk to us,' Cassie said.

'Except one of them did and was brutally murdered 'cos of it. He was called Finn and he was really nice,' Bee finished her sentence with a catch in her voice.

'Are you sure that your captor was Gilgamesh?' the King asked.

'That's what he called himself,' Cassie said.

'And it's a silly name, so he's not likely to be making it up,' Bee added.

'He said he was waiting for you to arrive with an army so he could destroy you. When you didn't come, he took us to Kish so you'd come after him there,' Cassie said.

'The food was terrible,' Bee said. 'Fish, fish, and more fish. All those people seemed to eat was smelly fish. The stink drove me mad. I was so happy when Tyrant found us and brought us home.'

Lone's mind was racing as the girls were speaking. It seemed obvious where the King was going with this. Malachi had been excluded once it was obvious that he'd played no active part in the defeat of Gilgamesh. Now the attention would transfer to her. She'd left them to it, after all. She'd disobeyed the King's command. Her actions might even be classed as desertion if he decided to look upon them unfavourably. In any event, the story was panning out to reflect negatively on her. Malachi had been doing his best to massage the facts into a more pliant and digestible form, but his normal powers of persuasion had deserted him and he had failed to convince the King. She decided to interject before it became too late.

'The mission became very difficult after the treachery of the crew and the subsequent loss of our ship, your majesty. It became obvious to me that the chances of confronting the kidnapper's vessel had receded badly and that another approach was required. I left Ant to gather the remainder of the party and rendezvous with me here at the palace so that we could report back and receive the wisdom of your advice.'

The King let out a snort. 'Yet you turned up here with only a gaggle of women and demands to reopen the temple. Hardly devotion to duty, I'd say.'

237

'On the contrary, your majesty. I have demonstrated complete loyalty to the most important issue, which has to be protecting you. With respect, I came here in a timely fashion and brought with me assistance that might yet prove decisive if Gilgamesh remains a threat.'

'And does he?' The King pointed his nose towards Tyrant. 'You're the one who claims to have bested this legendary and invincible monster. Tell me whether I need to have any qualms about his threats towards me.'

Tyrant shuffled from one foot to the other and looked down at his feet. 'I'm not sure what he can do with no face, one arm, and a big hole in his chest. If he were normal, he'd have been dead ten times over. As it is, we left him soundly defeated. Not only that, but I took his sword from him.'

The King sighed. 'I'm finding all this hard to swallow. Gilgamesh has a reputation for defeating whole armies whereas you, Tyrant, are renowned throughout Gort for idleness and intoxication. Hardly a fair match, if you ask me.'

'I had help.' Tyrant looked up, his chin jutting out.

'A boy and a woman of, shall we say, less than average stature. What did they do? A little dance to distract him?'

'Petra hobbled him with her knives while Ant...' Tyrant's voice faded away, then came back to say, 'there's more to Ant than you might think.'

'I would sincerely hope that there is. Though apart from the ability he shares with his father to make those infernal devices, I'm at a loss as to what more there is. I sent him with you in the hope that he would make a way for the girls to return, and that he's done. As for fighting, he hardly seems the type.' The King's eyes connected with Lone's and he waved his hands in the air. 'I've heard enough of this garbled tale for one day. Off you go. I need time to consider.'

The chamber doors were opened and a small gathering of servants was revealed. Most carried food on silver platters, obviously intended for the King's sole consumption. One portly woman with thick black hair burst from the crowd and flung herself at Cassie and Bee. Ant jumped as if he'd been stung by a hornet, then he ran to join the group hug. 'Mother,' he cried. The woman burst into tears and grabbed a tight hold of him.

65

'Not you,' the King ordered as Lone moved towards the door. 'I need to speak with you privately.'

When the doors were closed behind the sobbing reunions, the food had been placed on the table, and the servants dismissed, the King sat down, a chicken leg in one hand and a goblet of wine in the other. 'None of that makes any sense at all,' he said. 'I'm inclined to believe that you're all in cahoots with Gilgamesh and part of his plan to usurp me. That's if he actually exists.'

Lone took a breath and considered the tale that Malachi had concocted to make himself appear heroic and the architect of Gilgamesh's downfall. It had been over-indulgent even by Malachi's standards. 'Your majesty, Malachi attempted to weave together the testimony of all the participants into a coherent narrative. I'm sorry if that didn't explain the events as well as chronicle them.'

'Explain? Chronicle?' Bits of chicken flew out of his mouth. 'More like lies and deceit to my ears. I've seen Gilgamesh in action. He defeated an entire army single-handed. I watched as he strode unscathed through hundreds of attacks from well-trained men. I saw the awesome weaponry he commanded. He used fireballs that rained from the sky and burnt up entire battalions. But most impressive of all was his invulnerability. Nothing could hurt him.

'Now, you expect me to believe the greatest warrior ever known was defeated by a fat licker-swilling good for nothing like Tyrant?' The King threw down his chicken bone and wiped his hands on his shirt. 'I don't believe any of them even glimpsed Gilgamesh, let alone confronted him.'

'Surely you believe Cassie and Bee? Their account tallies with what we know about Gilgamesh.'

'Could be anyone calling himself that name.'

'But he survived having his face torn off and losing an arm. That's not something that a normal man could do.'

'Good point, I'll grant you that. However, what was Gilgamesh doing on that ship? If, as we surmise, his agents performed the kidnapping, they could have brought them to him anywhere he chose. There was no need for him to make that long journey.'

'He told the girls that he was waiting for pursuit. Hoping that you would come after him,' Lone replied. 'It was a ruse to get you out of Gort.'

The King sucked a finger and his dark eyes stared past Lone's shoulder. 'Remind me of your previous encounter with him in the City on the River. I was assured then that he was dead and that you had killed him. What really happened?'

'It's exactly as was originally described. Tyrant faced up to Gilgamesh and while they were fighting, the palace came down about their ears. I managed to extract Tyrant, but Gilgamesh was buried in the rubble. Then the golem came along and deposited a mountain of earth on top of where the palace had been. It wasn't unreasonable to assume that he was dead after all that, whatever his reputation.'

'Am I to believe that Tyrant is his nemesis?'

'Yes, I believe that to be the case,' Lone replied, wondering where all this discussion was going to end. The King was wily enough to have already thought of all these things and more. She had a bad feeling that he was playing with her, having already decided her fate.

'Tell me about Tyrant, then. Can he stride unscathed through armies of swordsmen? Is he so mighty that I should be in awe of him? Is he a threat to the throne?'

'Tyrant is what you see, a big man with limited abilities. I've seen him struck down and incapacitated by a single arrow. I don't believe he's any threat to anyone, despite the reputation he likes to maintain. Tyrant wants as easy a life as possible. He's no ambition beyond his next jar of licker.'

'Hardly a man to threaten the greatest warrior ever known?' The King sighed. 'How do you explain his remarkable, if not miraculous, success?'

'He did have help from Malachi and myself in the first encounter, then from Ant and Petra in the second,' Lone said.

The King shook his head. 'A boy and a half a woman hardly constitute what I would call useful assistance under the circumstances. What could they do?'

'Whatever they did, it worked. Gilgamesh was defeated again. I wasn't there to see the method, but I believe that's what happened.'

'Yet Tyrant said that he declined to kill Gilgamesh when he had the chance. That's hardly the action of a victor after a hard fight.'

'Maybe it's what marks Tyrant out as different,' Lone said. 'Compassion can be a powerful weapon. He says that Gilgamesh wanted to be killed so that he could take another body. That chopping him to bits would only have hastened his recovery. There are stories of immortal entities who have the ability to take on a new body when the old one is finished with. I'm sure you have heard of this?'

The King showed his teeth, but his eyes declined the invitation to show amusement. 'The stuff of myth and legend,' he replied.

'As is Gilgamesh himself,' Lone countered. The King's face snapped into a frown and she immediately regretted her attempt at verbal jousting.

'Unlike witchcraft, something real and punishable by death,' the King responded. 'A punishment that awaits you in the event of disloyalty. This is all very unsatisfactory. If Gilgamesh wants my throne, he'll be difficult to resist. His professed reluctance to face me in my own city may be providing some respite, but sooner or later, he'll decide differently. Before he does that, I need him to be stopped once and for all. Even if he can't be killed because of this transmigration business, I want him laid to rest for generations to come. I want his threat nullified and lifted. A wounded rat always returns to its burrow, and he's no different. Go back to the City by the River, Lone. Find a way into his palace and put an end to him if he's there. If not, wait for him to return and then deal with him. You do it. I'm holding you responsible for making it happen. Take Tyrant, Ant, Malachi, and Petra with you. They may provide some assistance. I do not expect any of them to survive whatever the outcome. Understood?'

'Yes, your majesty.' Lone's heart was banging in her head.

'Another thing, this temple business has gone too far. I want it stopped. Either you do it, or I will.'

Lone tried to formulate a protest that might have some effect, but the implacable look on his face stopped her from saying another word.

241

She obeyed the imperious wave of Cuthbert's hand and left the chambers. Ant's small dog, who had been sleeping in a corner, trotted out with her.

66

Ant's eyes were still blurry with tears. His heart felt as if it could burst at any moment. Mona, his mother and the object of his intense longing for much of his life, whose loss had caused the deepest of all wounds, was fussing around Cassie and Bee. It was a pure joy to see her busy figure again and to have the recent memory of her strong arms around him.

'You two look as if you've been thrown from a galloping horse into a midden,' she said. 'Off to the bathhouse with the pair of you and don't come back until you've scrubbed all that dirt off. As for you,' she said and turned towards Ant, 'you can stay here with me. I want to hear what you've been up to since I left your father's employ.'

Twinkling with merriment, the girls danced out of the room. Ant couldn't help bursting into tears yet again. 'I missed you so much,' he wailed. She clasped him to her warm bosom and patted his head. It was the most wonderful feeling. There had been so many long, lonely nights when he'd dreamed of her comforting embrace.

She sat him down, clasped his hands in hers, and stared at him with her kind eyes. 'My, how you've grown,' she cooed. 'I bet you have all the girls chasing after you now that you've turned into a handsome young man.'

Ant's breathing was becoming easier as his bouts of sobbing diminished in frequency and intensity. Her words grated on his nerves. Under the circumstances, her comment felt empty. Unnecessary. The kind of remark made by a distant relative with scant interest in him. He expected better from her. 'I can't believe you were living here all the time and never even visited me. You could have at least let me know you were alive,' he said.

'Your father found me work in the palace and warned me of the consequences if I ever saw you again. It was his decision, not mine. Of course I missed you. You had been my whole life for many years. But you have to understand that I'm not your mother, Ant. I was your father's servant. He paid me to look after you and while I found intense joy in that work, I had no voice in your household. Even though I knew you better than anyone, I couldn't protect you from him. Imagine my heartbreak at knowing what you needed but being unable to provide it. His indifference hurt you and that caused me such pain. I was mistreated as well, but that was nothing compared to the desperation of seeing you so disappointed.

'When he told me I was leaving, I was both sad and relieved. I hoped he'd adopt a more caring attitude towards you in my absence. In any event, as I say, it was none of my doing. I'm a servant. That's all.'

Her big brown eyes sucked him into her heart. All resentment at her abandoning him evaporated, leaving a residue of grim hatred for his father.

She must have seen this hatred clouding his soul, because she continued. 'Don't blame your father. He was doing the best he knew. Everything he did, good or bad, was done in love for you. By sending me away, he imagined that you'd grow up more independent and resourceful. More able to make your way in a hard and unforgiving world. My contribution was, in his eyes, making you too soft and he feared for the consequences when he was no longer able to protect you. Try to see it from his perspective, Ant.'

'I wanted to go after you, but he made it very clear what would happen if I ever tried to contact you,' Ant replied.

'And if he'd told you that I'd left you willingly, how would that have felt?'

'It would have broken my heart,' he said. 'No, that's not right. I wouldn't have believed him.' The awful truth began to sting him like a cloud of wasps. He'd seen her at the market, yet hadn't had the guts to disobey his father's command. Even after he became independent, all he'd managed was the occasional whimper of regret at the loss of her love and attention. He'd never made a proper and concerted effort to find her. Jeremiah, his companion demon, could surely have located her if he'd asked, but he'd been too caught up with his own plans for revenge against the King who had hanged him.

She was a warm and loving woman. It was wonderful to be back in her presence. She was right, though. She wasn't his mother, but even if she was, there had to be a time for any child to make their own way in life. His father, rightly or wrongly, had decided when and how this would happen. The only complaint he could have, was being unable to make that choice himself.

There was no doubt that he loved her more than anyone or anything he'd ever loved. He was also sure that he didn't need her to look after him. That she had a right to her own life away from his domineering father, making things difficult and painful. There would be a time when he had processed this situation sufficiently that he could feel peace about how it had all been for the best. That time wasn't now. It wasn't even close. He had to trust the time would come when he could forgive his father and himself.

Little Ant trotted into the room, his dog-form as ungainly and awkward as ever. Sitting at his feet, he looked up at him and whimpered. 'Not now,' Ant said. 'I'm talking to Mona.'

The pretend dog shook its head and pawed at his leg. Cassie and Bee burst through the door, flicking droplets of rain from their soaking wet hair and laughing. 'Come in, you two, we have to leave right away if we're to get to the temple in time for the service,' Mona said.

'Do we have to?' Cassie asked.

'Yes, you most certainly do. I want to present the pair of you to Miriam, the high priestess. You're the Queen, Cassie. It's important that you pay your respects,' Mona said.

'I'll come with you,' Ant said. 'I used to sit up there with Col and Pepper looking down at the marketplace for hours on end. In those days, it was all ruined; there were stones strewn about everywhere.'

'Not now,' Mona said, her eyes aglow. 'Everything has been rebuilt. It's magnificent, especially inside. You can come with us, but only as far as the entrance. Men aren't allowed to enter the temple.'

'That seems hardly fair,' Ant said. 'Depriving men of the opportunity to visit the temple and worship the gods makes no sense.'

'There's a lot of things that men stop women from doing that are much less fair, if you ask me.' Mona's eyes flashed. 'Men aren't allowed because they are too immature to appreciate our god; they get too easily distracted. They're disruptive. A bad influence. They disturb the peace inside our place of worship.'

'I promise to be quiet and respectful,' Ant said. 'I'll slip in quietly, don't worry. Nobody will know I'm there.'

'She will.' Mona shook her head.

'Who?' Ant asked. 'This high priestess you mentioned? I don't see how she can stop me.'

'Not Miriam,' Mona said. 'Our god has decreed that any men trying to invade the sanctity of her holy place will be struck down. It's a sanctuary, that's what it is. Women have somewhere they can go if they feel threatened.'

'And are they struck down?' Ant found himself laughing nervously.

'Always.' Mona smiled. 'Rendered to dust if they so much as set one foot inside the door.'

67

'Patch?' Lone gave an involuntary shudder at the sudden return of his gloomy voice inside her head.

Were you expecting someone else? You've been trying to attract my attention for several days now.

'So where have you been?' Lone regretted the automatic remark as soon as she thought it.

That's for me to know and no concern of yours.

'But I need your assistance. I've kept my side of the bargain and supplied you with an enormous quantity of positive energy for you to bask in. Now I need you to keep the temple safe while I complete one more task. I'm going to the City on the River to destroy the place where Gilgamesh rejuvenates himself. Without that, he'll wither and die like any other man.'

Eradicating Gilgamesh will not be easy.

'It's the price I have to pay to preserve the life I have. My vineyards sit atop his ruined palace. They'll not remain long when he returns, as he must. Tyrant left him in a sorry state and in need of urgent repairs.'

No matter how badly injured he might seem, Gilgamesh is too powerful, even for you.

'I know that. But Tyrant appears to have the means to resist him. Malachi and I will find a way to take advantage of that.'

Are you willing to sacrifice your husband and Tyrant just to secure some patch of farmland?

'No, of course not. The King requires us all to defeat Gilgamesh. Tyrant did it once already without my help.'

But the King also wants you to make sure that Tyrant doesn't return.

'You're well informed, as always. That's his plan, but not mine.'

Then your plan is a bad one. Even if you do prevail over Gilgamesh, you will still have to answer to the King. If you don't deliver exactly what he orders, you might as well have not bothered with any of it.

'Killing Gilgamesh will make me immensely powerful in the eyes of the King. He'll not want to pit himself against me.'

On the contrary, it will force his hand.

'Then I'll have to deal with that if and when it happens.'

Oh, believe me, it will happen. It's already happening.

'Are you suggesting that I should leave Gilgamesh and pit myself against the King? I'm not sure that I'm ready for that.'

I'm sure that you're not capable of overthrowing the King. You never will be, if you ask me.

'Maybe not alone, but with your assistance?'

Not even with my assistance. Remember, I'm perfectly capable of interfering with the breathing functions of humans. I can cast illusions that interfere with their senses. There are many minor acts of unkindness that I can perpetrate. The King is different. So is Gilgamesh. Neither is human, even though they appear that way.

'So, have you come back merely to taunt me?'

Not at all. This is by no means taunting. This is me imparting wise counsel. You would do well to heed it.

'Even so, you haven't come up with a better plan than my original intention. Kill Gilgamesh, then try to negotiate with the King. If I'm to leave Gort, I need you to safeguard the temple, that's all. The King may try to destroy everything we've created and I can't bear the thought of the hopes of all those women being dashed. It would have been kinder if I'd never given them hope in the first place.'

You've succeeded even more than you realise. The volume of sheer joy being generated in that temple is quite spectacular.

'So you're getting everything I promised and more besides. All the more reason for you to do as I ask.'

Unfortunately, our efforts have drawn unwelcome attention. We've been too successful. I tried to make myself scarce, but now find myself unable to escape. Things have gone too far. Don't say I didn't warn you.

'Is it too late to save the temple?'

Saving the temple isn't going to be the problem. Saving ourselves is the problem. I'm in this up to my neck the same as you are.

68

As she shielded her eyes from the desert sun, Lone felt the heat enveloping her body. Pinpricks of perspiration tickled her face and arms as she strode through the bustling City by the River. Ahead, she could see the hillside where her vines thrived above the catacombs of Gilgamesh's destroyed palace. Dozens of workers could be seen tending the vines and preparing them for the next season of growth. Her heart filled with joy at being able to return to the place she called home.

Her nostrils filled with the heady scent of cinnamon and cloves. This is what she'd missed most in the gloomy north. The smell of the place. There, damp grass and animal dung. Here, exquisite flavours to titillate her palate. There, brown mud that clung to her boots. Here, incandescent sand that warmed her toes. These were sensations worth fighting for. Her lip curled in determination as she contemplated the tough road ahead before she could settle back into blissful normality.

They were supposed to come here together as a team. That was the King's intention. Patch had prompted her to get out of Gort as soon as possible, though, promising some serious but unspecified trouble if she didn't. Tyrant needed more time to recover from his shoulder wound, and Petra was adamant that neither of them would budge until he was completely healed. Lone doubted that would ever be the case if Petra had her way.

Malachi had been very reluctant to leave Gort. Even when he was told in no uncertain terms that the King required him to help her eliminate Gilgamesh, he'd muttered an excuse about having to go back to his house to 'pack a bag' and not returned.

Only Ant seemed to have survived recent events in good spirits, due in no small part to his reunion with Mona. He exhibited a new lightness to replace the brooding intensity that she was used to. Whether he'd succumb to the pressure and leave her to fight Gilgamesh was uncertain.

Out here in the desert, the tribulations and responsibilities that had weighed her down in Gort left only a distant residue. Let the King sort out the rest of them. If they didn't arrive, she would be free to do as she saw fit. The problem the King had set her couldn't be resolved unless he persuaded them to accompany her. She couldn't be expected to eliminate them if they weren't here.

As for Gilgamesh, she'd deal with him if she had to, but in her eyes, there was the distinct possibility that he'd stay skulking in his lair long enough not to bother her or anyone else. That's if he'd managed to survive the difficult sea voyage from Kish.

As she walked through the vineyard, female faces turned from the vines to look at her, then quickly back again. Nobody spoke a word of greeting. There was no singing, something she'd always encouraged. These were the same women she'd left happy and contented reduced to sullen servitude. What had Ayesha been doing to cause this change?

'Where's Ayesha?' She addressed the familiar matronly figure of Sheba, a lady of previously sunny disposition.

'You can't come here, Lone. You'll get us all killed. They'll take it out on our families again if we so much as look at you. Please, go back to wherever you've been.'

'Where's Ayesha? I need to talk to her,' Lone replied.

'Gone,' Sheba hissed, keeping her face turned away. 'They took her away. Shot that big cat full of arrows when it tried to protect her.'

'Who?' Lone asked, her rage barely controllable as she thought about her beloved Cat being killed.

'Too late.' Sheba's eyes flicked sideways. 'They've seen you. Move away from me, please. They're coming and they'll kill me as well if they see us talking.'

Three men ambled towards her. Their approach was unhurried, casual almost. Their gait had an arrogant swagger that spoke of absolute confidence. Men who were used to having their way, unused to any sort of challenge. She decided to swallow her bile and wait until she could look them in the eye while she shredded their vital organs.

'Get back to work.' One of the men raised a whip as he spoke.

'This is my vineyard,' Lone said, feeling the ground beneath her feet. The earth was familiar and special. It was fertile northern soil that had been animated by Ant's father and sent on the long journey south.

Energy coursed up her legs, invigorating her body. She sent tendrils of power in return that connected with the three men that confronted her. The man dropped his whip and put his hands to his throat. His eyes

250

widened ever larger as his face went purple. Lone increased the gentle pressure on his windpipe, enjoying the consternation being shown by his colleagues as he sank to his knees, gasping helplessly for breath that would never come.

'Stop!' Sheba tugged at her sleeve. 'If you hurt them, they will make us all suffer.'

Lone relaxed her grip. Her momentary loss of concentration allowed the men to grab hold and throw her to the ground. One of them placed his boot across her throat. Lone fought hard against her instincts that were screaming at her to destroy her attackers in one blast of anger. Despite the sore provocation, she calmed her racing heart with concern for her workers. Compliance had to be her best strategy, no matter how difficult it would be.

She was still wrestling with the choice when a heavy boot slammed into her head and everything went black.

69

The pain in Lone's left ear served as a constant reminder of the vulnerability she shared with all women. The strongest and most ruthless prevailed in this harsh world. While she had the technique to defend herself, she realised that very few women possessed enough strength and determination to oppose a ruthless man.

Fighting, even if it were possible, wasn't the way to oppose tyranny. She had chosen not to destroy her attackers out of concern for the women in the vineyard, and received a savage kicking as reward for her restraint. If she'd killed the hired brutes, though, they would have been quickly replaced. She could have gone on killing until her energy failed her without exhausting the supply of thugs available to whoever was controlling this situation. Better to wait. Bide her time. Confront the 'big man' then show him and the women he was exploiting that he's not so big after all.

After three hot days and four cold nights of being confined in a tiny room with brown earth walls, her vow of patience was close to fracturing. The man who delivered her tepid sandy water and flyblown hunks of fruit wouldn't respond to her questions. Either he was deaf or obeying strict instructions.

Sitting on the sandy floor in the darkness gave her plenty of time to reflect, though.

The more she thought about it, the more she realised that she needed to repeat the spectacular success of her campaign in the north here in the south, where the traditions were even more prejudiced against females. Organising women was one thing, but they had to be imbued with a sense of worthiness for them to make their mark. To do this, the shackles of their upbringing had to be released. Physical strength would never be enough, regardless of gender.

She thought about Malachi, the most powerful man she'd ever encountered. He wasn't the largest physical specimen, but his self-belief and presence were enough to cow just about everyone he met. Admittedly, he did have a technique to deal with the doubters, but he needed to use it on very rare occasions.

She had to demonstrate that women were capable of resisting tyranny and that by working together, they would change the way the world treated them. Unfortunately, her patience was a commodity that had been in short supply; she'd quickly used it up and there was no source of replenishment. She decided the next time the door opened, she would kill whoever came in and find a less passive way to confront the man who had stolen the vineyard.

Her mind raced ahead. She'd kill the dumb guard and anyone who stood in her way. Then she'd bathe in the cooling waters of the river and woe betide any crocodile that dared challenge her right to swim. After that, she'd find a way of confronting her quarry in a public place. His demise would be the beginning of her campaign of emancipation.

Disappointment gnawed at her guts for wasting valuable time with what had to be a side issue. All that she'd gained in the north was at risk, unless she could deal with Gilgamesh. That had to be her priority. Yet she'd sat quiescent in this hovel, nursing her sore head for days when she should have been getting on with it. All she could do was to put her inaction down to the confusion caused by her head being kicked.

Instead of one man with food and water, two arrived, grabbed her by the arms and pulled her outside into the harsh sunlight. Lone decided not to resist and wait to see if her original plan came to fruition. She'd save her energy for tearing the ringleader to pieces in full view of as many people as possible.

Flanked by a dozen guards carrying drawn swords, she was led around the foothills of the vineyard to an enormous square flanked by white stone buildings. It was seething with people. A crowd that exceeded the entire population of Gort was packed into the area. Her wish for a public confrontation was being fulfilled in a spectacular manner.

Her captors jostled and shoved their way through the mass of humanity until she reached wide stone steps that took her onto a raised area overlooking the crowd. Behind it was a dark entrance that led into the hillside beneath the vineyard. A vast roof was supported by massive columns of dazzlingly white stone. It was as if the temple of Gort had been transposed into the desert, but at the same time expanded to twice its size. The majesty of the building took her breath away. Then she became even more awestruck when she realised that none of this had been here when she'd departed in the ship a few short months ago.

No matter, it would make a wonderful place of worship. All she had to do was to take it from its current occupier. A surge of excitement rippled through her as she anticipated her next move by grounding herself into the stone beneath her feet. She prepared herself for whatever and whoever might emerge from the darkness.

Her entourage sank to one knee as the man stepped forward and the sun caught his face. It was as white as the stone in the fabric of the building and just as impassive. He was also sickeningly familiar.

70

The inevitability of seeing Gilgamesh again did nothing to alleviate the shock. Lone didn't so much feel surprised at his appearance as foolish at not anticipating it. Now she came to think about it, without the haziness caused by her kicking, it should have been obvious from the beginning. Her vineyard was sitting on top of his palace. He'd emerged to hatch a plot to overthrow the King by kidnapping Cassie and Bee. Of course, he'd re-exert his local authority and her beautifully kept estate was an obvious start. Cat would have been able to see off any threat from normal men. The King of the South was an entirely different proposition, but one she should have anticipated.

As he walked out into full view of the multitude, a reverent hush fell on the crowd. Even the babes in arms stopped mewling. Lone took a deep breath, re-established her contact with the earth beneath her feet, and felt for the sinews of energy she needed. She pushed and probed with her mind until she came across a sweet river of pure power. It seethed through the stone, guided by her concentrated being until it connected with Gilgamesh. Up through his legs it flowed. She followed it into his abdomen, where she gained access to his heart. Her mind enveloped his most precious organ like a fist closing around a soft fruit. Slowly, she began to squeeze.

Gilgamesh looked exactly as Cassie and Bee had described him before his injury. His face was strangely unresponsive, yet she knew he was suffering. She had his heart and was about to squash it like the rotten piece of meat that it was. Her energy surged as she strove to complete the stranglehold and finish him off. Suddenly, she met resistance. It was as if a solid wall had been placed between her and her quarry. All contact with his internal organs ceased abruptly and instead she found herself being invaded in turn.

She had a horrible sensation of clammy tendrils creeping up her legs, flickering and probing. As if trying to catch hold of something inside her that might make her suffer. With an extraordinary effort, she countered. Expelled the evil energy from her system and felt it dissipate back into the stone. Exhausted, she watched a black-clad figure emerge from the gloom and stand shoulder to shoulder with Gilgamesh.

'Malachi?' She gasped.

'Remember, it was I who taught you that little trick. Oh, I grant that I may not have the vigour to resist you in a prolonged battle of wills, but I can quite effectively negate your attack on my master.'

'What are you doing? Helping this monster?' Lone said.

'Hardly any more monstrous than the King you serve, my dear. Sometimes you have to make a choice, and when that time comes, I like to choose the winning side. Gilgamesh was always going to prevail. Surely you knew that, didn't you? We were all being sent to our deaths. Let's face it, your King didn't expect any of us to survive the first encounter. Come on, Lone, wake up. You've been duped. You only have yourself to blame,' Malachi said.

'Do you expect me to join you in serving that half-dead abomination? If so, you're both going to be sadly disappointed. I would rather die,' Lone said.

'Then you'll get your wish,' Gilgamesh's voice rang shrill in the still air. 'Your execution will demonstrate to these people the futility of opposing my wishes.'

'Sorry, Lone,' Malachi said. 'You made your choice, and it was the wrong one. I can't help you this time.'

Three hefty men shoved a bloodstained wooden block to the edge of the steps, where it was in full view of the audience. A big man wearing a golden turban hefted a thick curved sword over his shoulders and stood poised as she was forced to kneel at his feet, staring out at the assembled onlookers. To the right of the crowd was a paddock teeming with horses and camels. One spindly mount stood out because of its glowing whiteness in a sea of light brown. Its big sad eyes looked directly at Lone as if apologising not only for its ungainly appearance but also for the plight she was in.

When she looked away from the horse and down at the crowd, she saw Ant looking up at her. He returned her gaze steadily, but his face remained set in a serious frown. Next to Ant was a tiny figure straining to see over the heads of those in front of her. By her side, wearing a gilded floppy hat with a feather sticking out of the side, was the bulky figure of Tyrant who, in contrast, appeared to be enjoying her discomfiture.

Strong hands grabbed her and forced her head onto the block. She saw the shadow of the curved sword on the white stone floor as it was raised overhead.

71

The look in Lone's eyes shocked Ant to his core. Her hope was gone. Her fire had been extinguished. She'd become an ordinary woman. A victim. His heart couldn't bear the sight of her in such a vulnerable state. Something was terribly wrong.

Ant's feet had trembled as he experienced the violent energy that Lone had directed towards Gilgamesh. At first, he'd been convinced that nobody, not even this all-powerful demi-god, could resist her. As her energy flowed into her quarry, he tracked it with his awareness, gathered his strength, and prepared to add his contribution if required.

Gilgamesh had been on the verge of collapse when the intervention came. Gilgamesh's resistance had been crushed and the sudden surge of countermeasures came as an awful surprise. One second she had been on the edge of victory, the next she was fighting for her life. The worst part was discovering that Malachi was involved.

The days after Lone had left for the south had been spent arguing between themselves. Little Ant's discovery that the King wanted them all dead hadn't improved anyone's mood. Tyrant was all for packing up and going home. He said he'd take his chances when the King decided to come after him and at least he'd be ready. As for Lone, Tyrant had no doubt that she was as much the villain in this piece as his monarch.

Petra had been more circumspect in her appraisal. She'd wondered if Lone was playing the King along and intended no harm to any of them. Ant had liked this notion more, but recognised the complexities it brought to the situation. If the King was the real enemy, why go off and fight Gilgamesh? If they won, and that was by no means certain, they'd still have the main problem to deal with.

Malachi had remained silent throughout the discussion. Since his recovery from injury, he'd barely spoken to Ant, and only then to be critical. Any concern for the plight of others seemed to have deserted him. It was little surprise that he'd vanished one evening and failed to reappear until now.

Gilgamesh and Malachi stood together like a pair of predatory birds. Malachi the hooded crow and Gilgamesh the white eagle. Their attention was on the executioner, resplendent in his gold finery, and the heavy sword he was brandishing over Lone's head.

Ant could bear it no longer. Lone appeared to be beyond protecting herself, and he had to intervene. 'Stop!' he shouted and ran up the steps towards the kneeling witch. The sword paused in mid-stroke. Malachi's eyes burned into Ant's mind, making him recoil at the spite and venom being directed towards him. This was Malachi – his teacher, his mentor, and his friend. No longer, it seemed. The wizard appeared intent on serving the interests of his newfound master without any regard for the past. Ant felt as if he had been thrown from a great height and was plunging to a bloody end. Attacked by the man he'd come to love as a father to replace the one who'd let him down so badly. This betrayal was even worse. It was unendurable.

Malachi was probing his system, latching on to internal organs, twisting and hurting him. Ant's legs threatened to give way under the onslaught. His mind was already in sullen retreat towards accepting the inevitable. Lone's pathetic plight gave him a little strength that he could use for resistance. He pushed back, trying to concentrate on the sensations beneath his feet, but distracted by the wavering sword about to be brought down to sever Lone's head from her body. Even so, he wrestled with Malachi's energy slowly, expelling his grisly presence from his body and tracking it back to its source.

As Ant arrived breathless at the top of the steps, he took the look of pain on Malachi's face as encouragement. The old wizard was struggling to contain him, and that gave him hope. Unfortunately, the contest was too evenly poised for him to transfer any attention onto the executioner without being completely overwhelmed by Malachi. Lone was on her own, as far as that was concerned. He only had to hope that she had sufficient reserves to prevent herself from being decapitated.

72

Tyrant watched as Ant ran screaming up the steps towards Lone. Her head was on the block and a fat man with a scimitar was preparing to chop it off. This wasn't what they'd discussed. It had been Ant's plan. They had all agreed to it. Now Ant seemed to have lost all control of his senses.

Malachi was up to his usual tricks, it seemed. After the initial shock of seeing him standing against them, Tyrant quickly recovered from his surprise. If he were Gilgamesh, he'd worry more about the wizard who was professing to be on his side than any of the others that had been gathered against him. Malachi was just as likely to stab him in the back as anything else. Either it was part of a bigger plan that he'd not been party to or Malachi had really abandoned them in pursuit of self-interest. Either way, there was nothing he could do to change things.

When they'd arrived at the City by the River, Lone's arrest and impending execution was on the lips of everyone they spoke to. That and the resurgence of Gilgamesh's interest in the affairs of the city. Ant had quickly persuaded Tyrant and Petra that their best opportunity lay in a public confrontation. Gilgamesh had decreed that attendance of the event was compulsory and Ant decided that this guaranteed that he would emerge from his underground lair.

Tyrant had to agree that anything was better than having to go into the tunnels and search for their quarry. Down there, Gilgamesh would have access to all manner of dreadful devices. Ant had also pointed out that it might not be possible to actually kill Gilgamesh and that public humiliation might be sufficient to send him into hiding for a very long time. Tyrant hadn't agreed with this. The man had to be killed, and he was the one to do it. That felt like his destiny, not because Gilgamesh had killed his mother and brother, but because this was the third time they would meet in battle and third time pays for all. Or so they say.

Now Ant had broken ranks and was threatening to ruin the whole situation. It was Tyrant who was supposed to walk calmly up the steps and issue a challenge. Ant would remain hidden in the crowd, ready to use his particular talents to hamper Gilgamesh and make him more vulnerable. Petra, of course, had been told to keep out of the fighting unless needed as a last resort. Tyrant doubted she'd manage to keep her cool and was determined to finish off the fight as quickly as possible in order to protect her the best way he could.

He looked down at Petra. Her eyes blazed with excitement. 'What are you waiting for?' she hissed.

'Stay here,' he replied, hitched up his trousers, drew his sword, and set off after Ant.

As he loped up the steps, Tyrant assessed the opposition. Three men holding the witch down on the chopping block. One holding the big sword above his head as if unsure what to do next. None of these could be any concern of his unless they got between him and Gilgamesh. He'd stick to the plan, even though he had no faith that it was a good one or that it hadn't been compromised by Malachi's unexpected intervention.

Malachi worried him, though. The wizard only had to do that choking thing to him, and it would be all over. In comparison, Gilgamesh, for all his prowess, was straightforward. Stab him and avoid being stabbed back was the way to get that job done. Simple. He'd done it before, but that had been more luck than judgement and had needed the timely assistance of a collapsing palace and a monstrous golem to finish the job. Tyrant's left shoulder flared with remembered agony as he arrived on the platform and stood at Ant's side.

The boy looked to be in some discomfort and was staring directly at Malachi. Probably a good sign, Tyrant thought.

Gilgamesh stepped forward, holding a long two-handed sword in front of him. This wasn't the usual unwieldy armour bashing implement, but a slender affair with a round pommel and a slightly curved blade. 'I see you've returned my favourite sword,' he said, making eye contact and holding it.

'I see your arm grew back,' Tyrant replied. 'That's quite a trick. Pity you couldn't do something with that hideous face, though.'

Gilgamesh charged. Tyrant was almost deceived by a swift feint followed by an attack to his head, but managed to get his sword up just in time to deflect the strike that would have cloven him in two. The weight of the blow staggered him, though, and he was forced down on one knee. As he struggled to rise and defend himself, something gripped

261

his throat and stopped him from breathing. A terrible dread froze him in a half-standing position. Gilgamesh smirked and drew back his sword, ready to strike.

73

The executioner was taking an age to strike. Lone felt the hands release her and the men stand back out of the way. She rolled to her left and off the edge of the block, ending up sitting on the floor staring at the man with the golden turban on his head, a heavy sword in his hands, and a puzzled look on his face. It was as if he was unsure what to do next. Which was ridiculous. His job consisted of one action. Lift up sword, bring it down on someone's neck. Job done. Collect pay.

There was no time to feel amused or even to wonder about the absurdity of the situation. Ant had run up the steps onto the platform, quickly joined by Tyrant and Petra. She was about to address the problem of the executioner when Gilgamesh attacked Tyrant. One blow was all it took to drop Tyrant to his knees from where he was, causing him difficulty in standing up again. Malachi's face distorted into a fixed grin. Ant screamed and held his head in his hands. Gilgamesh moved in for the kill.

She couldn't gather herself in time to intervene. Malachi was holding Ant and Tyrant fast so that they were at Gilgamesh's mercy. She wondered if such newly won loyalty was being appreciated or whether Malachi would suffer the same fate as everyone else when his new master took stock of the situation. The problem with betrayal was its universality. However much he might argue, Malachi wasn't going to convince a wily man like Gilgamesh that he wouldn't turn on him in due course.

In the meantime, though, her husband was the master of the situation and intent on demonstrating his value. Unless she did something to stop him, the fight would be over even before it had properly begun.

While she struggled to rally her depleted resources, the executioner came to life. As the giant blade swished through the air, she threw herself sideways and rolled away. She crashed into Tyrant's legs and fell into a sticky river of warm blood. As she rose to her feet, the executioner was standing between her and Gilgamesh, staring down at Malachi's decapitated body.

Gilgamesh screamed in frustration and felled the man with a single swipe of his sword.

Lone felt the suffocating pressure of Malachi's energy dissipate. She was able to get to her feet and pull Tyrant to his. Tyrant stood shakily with sword raised in feeble defence against Gilgamesh's all-consuming wrath. One parry was all he could muster. The next thrust went deep into his thigh, dropping him to the ground again, his blood mixing with the river flowing from Malachi's body.

She reached into the stone in a final attempt to gather enough strength to fight back, but the process was too slow. She needed time, and Gilgamesh was upon her in an instant. Ducking desperately, she evaded his swipe to her throat, but was thrown off balance by her need to move suddenly. It was impossible to squirm away completely from the follow-up thrust to her midriff and it speared her innards like a burning column of fire.

Gilgamesh's face was frozen in a contorted grimace as she sank to her knees, trying to stem the blood flow with her hands. The sword flashed the white brilliance of the reflected stone as it was brought down level with her face. She was helpless. Her energy had been spent. Her connection to the earth severed. Her life was ebbing away as her blood stained the ground. 'You can't defeat me.' Gilgamesh raised his voice to talk over her head at the assembled multitude. 'No one in this land or any other can overcome the mighty Gilgamesh. See how I deal with this pack of dogs sent by the usurper to my throne in the North? I'll cut off their heads and throw their bodies to the river monsters.'

The sword in front of her eyes was suddenly gone. Gilgamesh was staggering backwards, thrashing with his left hand at Petra, who had leapt onto his back and was slicing his throat with a knife. One of the blows was hard enough to dislodge her and Gilgamesh, streaming blood down his front, grabbed her with his left arm, shook the knife from her grasp, and held her squirming body like a shield.

Lone waited for the final blows that would despatch her and Tyrant, but Ant stepped between them. His face was set in a concentrated frown aimed at Gilgamesh. Whatever energy he was employing appeared to be having an effect. Gilgamesh stood still for a moment as if unsure of his next move, then turned away and began to walk back towards the darkness, still holding Petra under his arm.

74

Tyrant's left leg was incapable of supporting him. The slightest movement intensified the pain to unendurable levels. He was resigned to his fate. Gilgamesh was too strong, even for all of them combined.

He watched passively as Gilgamesh proclaimed his supremacy and winced at the prospect of seeing Lone being decapitated before it was his turn. He'd done his best. He'd always done his best. All he'd ever wanted was a quiet life. To be left free to wander wherever the fancy took him. Life wasn't like that, though. It was much more complicated than he'd ever imagined. Despite his best efforts, he'd made connections. Deep relationships that took precedence even over the life he'd prefer to lead. On the positive side, he was going to die alongside people he cared about. On the negative side, they were all going to die with him.

Petra, bless her, had other ideas. She did her usual trick of tackling a much bigger opponent by jumping on his back and slitting his throat. She was extremely adept at that. Unfortunately, Gilgamesh was unnaturally tough. What would certainly have finished a normal fight provided only a momentary distraction.

Tyrant tried to raise himself and managed to stand on one leg, using his sword as a support. Ant's timely intervention halted Gilgamesh in his tracks but failed to get him to release Petra, who was writhing about and screaming profanities. All he could hope for now was one final swipe at Gilgamesh, but instead of staying within range, he turned and carried Petra towards his underground palace.

Tyrant managed one short step in pursuit, but the pain almost had him back on the ground and he had to stop moving at all. The thought of what Gilgamesh would do to Petra in the black confines of his lair deeply disturbed him. Dying out here in the sunlight was bad enough. Being killed while fighting a despicable tyrant would have been some ways a good death. Lying helpless up here while Petra was subjected to untold tortures was too much for him to bear. Gilgamesh was retreating because he had been hurt, and it had been Petra who had hurt him. Her actions were compounded by the way that she'd done it in front of his subjects and immediately after he'd made his claim of invulnerability. Gilgamesh would be sorely troubled and horribly embarrassed.

The realisation swept over him that Gilgamesh couldn't retreat without lasting damage to his reputation. And reputation was everything, as Tyrant knew only too well. A fighting man's reputation was hard-won over years of conflict, but could be lost in an instant if he ever backed down. Gilgamesh had to end it here and now. If he was retreating, it would be a temporary state of affairs. He would be going back inside for a purpose, and that had to be to collect some magical device that would demonstrate his supremacy. Perhaps even one that Malachi had delivered. The very instrument that had defeated him in Kish.

'Stop him!' Tyrant shouted, urging his damaged hip forward, but being successful only in causing himself more agony. Suddenly, he saw himself emerging from the gloom. Sword glinting in the sun, face beaming in a smile, legs whole and operating very nicely, thank you. Tyrant realised that the shock he was experiencing could be nothing in comparison to Gilgamesh, who backed away from his nemesis.

Tyrant dragged himself closer. Gilgamesh slowly retreated towards him as if reluctant to face a fresh whole Tyrant. As if a switch had been pulled, Gilgamesh suddenly stopped moving. Still holding Petra under his left arm, he flashed his sword at the new Tyrant. 'Be gone devil of dust!' he screamed. Tyrant managed another half-step closer, still having to lean heavily on his sword to keep upright.

The other Tyrant dissolved into a haze of particles that scattered onto the ground. There was a bellow of satisfaction from Gilgamesh. Tyrant, balancing on his good leg, brought his sword up to bear on his opponent.

Two things might happen now. Gilgamesh could either walk back to the darkness, or he could turn around to face the real Tyrant. If he walked, he was out of reach. If he turned, Tyrant might have one chance to strike. There were two ways he could turn. If he was attacking, he'd turn to his right, sword arm first. If he was defensive, he'd turn to his left, holding Petra as a shield.

Tyrant decided to take a chance. If the sword came first, it would sweep down from on high and he'd be forced to parry upwards. If Petra were exposed, he'd have to go for the legs otherwise risk killing her.

Without waiting for an answer, Tyrant sliced sideways at knee height. Gilgamesh was in mid-turn, shield first, as the sword cut into him. His own sword was trailing too far behind for him to parry effectively. It all happened in a tiny fraction of an instant. Tyrant's anticipation had paid off. He'd guessed correctly. His blow had landed and, while not fatal, it was sufficient to take Gilgamesh's legs from under him and deposit him on his backside. Another public indignity that he'd struggle to recover from whatever the final outcome of this fight.

Unfortunately, Tyrant's injuries prevented him from following up his successful foray and finishing the job. Gilgamesh sat too far away to reach with his sword and was able to struggle back upright, balancing on his one good leg. His other leg, his right, was half-severed and hung down loosely from his thigh. Neither of them were going anywhere, Tyrant realised.

One more half-step from him, a hop closer from Gilgamesh. Then a halfhearted clash of swords as the two men measured the distance. Tyrant's sword was shorter, but was light and nimble in one hand. Gilgamesh had the longer blade, but it needed two hands to control it and deft footwork to make room for it to be used effectively. Tyrant forgot his pain. Put aside all concerns for Petra. Concentrated on one final task. Prayed for one more piece of good fortune. Another pre-emptive strike predicated on Gilgamesh's next move.

With only one leg, his left, Gilgamesh would be forced to stay planted on that foot. This meant that he'd most likely swing his sword from the right in a wide arc. Thrusting straight would be difficult and stepping back to defend, impossible. Tyrant decided to take the chance and chopped at the position he anticipated the sword arm would be after delivering the blow. If a thrust came or a cut from any other angle, he'd be unable to defend himself and that would be the end of him.

Another gamble paid off. It was as if Gilgamesh threw both his arms onto Tyrant's sword to purposely cut them off at the elbow. The sword clattered to the floor, still gripped by useless hands no longer part of their master.

Tyrant sank to one knee and gasped with pain. Gilgamesh, stumps dangling and leaking, collapsed in front of him. 'Kill me,' he panted. 'This time finish me off, or I'll come back stronger and make you rue the day you were born. I'll chop you up one tiny piece at a time. I'll make that midget of yours scream with agony as I drain her blood onto your face—'

Tyrant was remembering Ant's caution about killing Gilgamesh. He was begging for death again, exactly as he'd done before. The quandary was that it was perfectly clear now that whatever terrible injuries he sustained, if allowed to live, he'd be back wreaking havoc and revenge before very long. Defeating him again, especially if there were magical devices involved, might not be possible. This one had been achieved at a high cost. Malachi was dead and Lone looked unlikely to recover. He knew it had to be done, but he still held reservations. Killing him in the heat of battle was one thing, but despatching an unarmed man in every sense of the word made him feel queasy. The knowledge that Gilgamesh wouldn't hesitate to do it to him were the roles reversed offered no comfort.

Reluctantly, he raised his sword. Before he could plunge it into Gilgamesh's evil heart, Petra beat him to it. Her knife bit deep; Gilgamesh coughed once, then slumped forward. A long breath moaned from his lungs before he became as still as stone.

The crowd erupted from their silence. At first, there were cries of disbelief and anguish, then someone began cheering. It was taken up by more and more of them until the whole place was jumping and clapping with obvious delight.

75

Ant watched as the beetle crawled up the stem and began to gnaw its way through the bark. It feasted greedily on the green flesh beneath and he became agitated by the destruction it was causing to the vine he was tending. Ayesha was two dozen paces down the line, bending in graceful conversation with a muscular man who had, until recently, been one of Gilgamesh's troop of enforcers.

The instruction she was giving him seemed over long as well as undeserved. How she could forgive so easily was beyond him. Every last one of those thugs should have been driven out into the desert and abandoned as punishment for sustaining Gilgamesh's evil reign. Instead, Ayesha was gently teaching him and his kind the process of viniculture. Sweat poured off his brow in response to the heat generated by his thoughts. Even from this distance, and despite the man's size and obvious strength, Ant fancied his chances of choking him to death. Temptation tickled his mind for a few moments before being rejected as a bad idea. Ayesha would be angry with him.

The bug fed silently, slicing further into the slender branch. This had to be a bad thing. Something he ought to stop happening. The black and brown mottling on its back made the insect difficult to see in the light filtered through the vine stems. As Ant adjusted his focus, he saw with horror that the terrible thing had company. There were several more of its kind engaged in the same destruction. 'Ayesha!' he shouted and was rewarded by a dark-eyed look and the flash of a smile.

He couldn't decide if her smile was one of pleasure or a grimace of irritation at having her conversation with the big, strong man interrupted. Nervous anticipation gripped him as she bounded lightly to her feet and walked towards him. It was only a few beetles. Would she think him foolish to have called her over? Was he doing something wrong that had attracted the nasty things?

A sudden movement dragged his eyes away from the approaching young woman. As if surfacing from the depths, a dark yellow lizard appeared, shaking crumbs of earth from its back. It skittered towards him, legs splayed out sideways in a comical fashion. Stopping suddenly in the shade of the vine, it cocked its head sideways and looked him in the eye. A fat purple tongue flicked in and out of its mouth. Another jerking movement brought it level with the beetle gorging itself on Ayesha's precious plant. Faster than his eyes could follow, the insect disappeared into the lizard's mouth. There was a distinct crunching sound as it was chewed and swallowed. Then it picked off all the others one by one and devoured them just as greedily.

'What is it?' Ayesha squatted down beside him.

His nostrils filled with her delicious scent. A heady aroma of spices. Cinnamon, cloves, sandalwood with a deep undertone of something darkly alluring that grabbed at Ant's guts and sent them into a painful turmoil. Her hair was black, thick, and lustrous. Her skin was the colour of polished wood and it accentuated the whiteness of her smile as her dark eyes locked with his. 'Bugs,' Ant said, trying to find his breath.

'Weevils,' she replied. 'Horrible little things can ruin a whole vine. Pick them off and put them in a jar.'

'There was a lizard did it for me.' Ant continued to stare at her face, mapping every line and pore of her perfection with his greedy eyes.

'Aren't you the lucky one, then?' She laughed. 'Come with me; let's take a break.'

She took his hand and helped him to his feet. Her touch was comforting, and he found himself clinging to her longer than he should have. She led him to a shady awning where there were jugs of cool water. Much to his relief, everyone else continued working, and they had the nook to themselves.

'Why are you always so sad, Ant?'

Ant almost choked on his drink. 'Am I?'

'That's how you seem to me.'

'I don't mean to be miserable. I like it here,' he replied, then wished he'd been brave enough to add the words 'with you.'

'It's been hard for you, I know. Lone has told me a little of what you've experienced. Everyone is grateful for what you've done.'

The invigorating effect of Ayesha's presence dissipated and his spirits sank back into the familiar swamp of despair. 'I helped kill Malachi, and I'll never forgive myself for that.'

271

'Lone has told me that you two were very close,' Ayesha said. 'She also says that he died from the injuries he sustained after being crushed by a tree and you did everything you could to save him.'

'How can that be true?' Ant said. 'He stood at Gilgamesh's side and almost killed us all. I'll never forget the hatred I felt in his attack. How can a man change so much?'

'Ask Lone. All I know is that it wasn't your Malachi that fought you. He died long before.'

76

Ant found Lone sitting up in bed for the first time since the battle. She seemed to be recovering well from her dangerous stomach wound, no doubt assisted by the healing effect of her purring companion. Lone had been ecstatic when Cat had popped out of nowhere, completely unscathed.

Ant eyed the big animal suspiciously and received a warning look in return. Lone reached out and stroked the big head. The rumbling increased in volume and frequency, making the fabric of the building resonate.

When he looked at Lone now, he couldn't bring back the intensity of feeling that he'd harboured for so long. It was as if it had been a different Ant that had been so inflamed with desire. Lone was still an object of admiration from him, but he didn't go weak at the knees each time she looked his way. Instead, he had begun to understand what lay behind her single-mindedness. This wasn't born out of selfish desire, but rather an overwhelming need to bring about the changes necessary for women to receive the respect they merited. Her lust for power wasn't personal, but something she wanted to use for the good of others. Ant had resolved to help her, regardless of what sacrifices he'd have to make. Not out of his old compulsion to gain her approval, but rather because he was wholeheartedly supportive of her objectives.

'Tell me about Malachi,' he said.

'That wasn't Malachi who opposed us,' Lone said, hand held protectively touching her midriff.

Ant remembered the subtle differences he'd experienced since Malachi's recovery. The changes in his master's energetics, the lack of regard for his wellbeing, and his unwillingness to speak to him. The worse thing was feeling the hatred of his attack. 'Are you saying that his mind was damaged when the tree crushed him?' he asked, trying to quell the roiling sea of disquiet within him.

'No, it's more fundamental than that. Our Malachi died from his injuries. This Malachi took his place. They were not the same person, even though they had many characteristics in common. The new Malachi was different. He'd never been injured by Gilgamesh's device because he'd chosen to return to Gort through the vedhana when he saw you and Tyrant taken by the grey apes. The old Malachi made a different choice, to try to save you, and it was that choice that led to his death. So, Ant, mourn for the old Malachi. Your Malachi, who loved you in his own way, which was the best way he could. You were the son he could never have. Harming you was something he was incapable of.'

Ant drew a breath. Lone's words resonated with reassurance. His mind was finding it difficult to accept what she was saying, but his body already knew she was right. 'How could something like that happen?' he asked.

Lone leaned forward and took his hands in hers. 'I loved him too, Ant. I was desperate to save him and took the only chance there was to do it. It was Patch that conjured the new Malachi.'

'The demon? The one I rode on for all that time without realising he was such a powerful being? I thought that you and he were sworn enemies,' Ant said.

'I went to his realm to seek his help. That's why I needed to learn how to construct a vedhana, Ant. We've been working together on a matter of mutual interest.'

'Then all our suffering was for nothing?' Ant's heart leapt with sudden vigour. 'That demon could have turned into his dragon self and scorched Gilgamesh to cinders. Why didn't you employ him to help us? I don't understand.'

'He helped as much as he could,' Lone answered. 'It was Patch who caused the executioner to kill Malachi. He tells me that even that degree of interference could have been fatal to him. Gilgamesh was created to destroy demons like him, and there was nothing he could do directly against him without risking his own existence. Patch killed Malachi because he realised that he'd already interfered by bringing him here. His fear of being held to account if Gilgamesh was victorious because of his mistake overcame his reluctance to interfere. So, he removed Malachi, as he put it, *to even up the odds.*'

Ant's breathing had cleared and his mind was catching up with the implications of Lone's account. 'So Patch knew that we would defeat Gilgamesh, provided Malachi was out of the way?'

'If anyone was going to cause Gilgamesh's death, it was always going to be Tyrant,' Lone said. 'Tyrant is special and I think he knows why.'

77

Tyrant's damaged hip had healed very quickly, and he was witnessing the intricacies of winemaking at Petra's side. 'It's a bit more complicated than distilling licker,' he observed.

'It's not much different,' Petra said, 'and each bottle commands double the price of a jug of licker. It's the drink of kings and courtiers. People with wealth value the sophistication of wine and the subtleties of its flavours.'

'Personally, I don't see the point,' Tyrant said. 'Licker's a fair bit more potent and gets the job done sooner, if you ask me.'

'By that, you mean poisoning you so that you're incapable of movement or speech, do you? Licker is the last refuge of the stupid and the unfortunate, whereas wine is an essential ingredient of civilised society.'

'You're not suggesting that we start making wine instead when we go home?' Tyrant asked. 'I for one like licker. It does me good. It's medicinal.'

'I'm suggesting that we don't have to go home at all. Why not stay here and help Lone and Ayesha?'

'No chance,' Tyrant said. 'You know that we don't get on. I don't trust that woman at all. Don't forget she promised the King that she'd make sure that none of us returned to Gort. Malachi's dead and that's just the start, if you ask me. The sooner we get away from her, the happier I'll be.'

'You've been completely miserable ever since you defeated Gilgamesh,' Petra said.

'I'd rather not talk about him,' Tyrant said.

'I know that,' Petra replied. 'All I'm saying is that you've proven yourself a better man than he ever was. You bested him three times. I'm only concerned that you don't appear to be giving yourself any credit for what's the most significant victory ever achieved. He was supposed to be invincible. He'd been alive for countless generations. Everyone had tried to kill him and failed, including, I'm told, gods. He chased the gods away.

Yet along comes Tyrant and he's gone. Come on. You've got to be happy and proud about that.'

'It wasn't me that killed him,' Tyrant said.

'I might have finished him off, but it was you that defeated him,' Petra said. 'You should be happy. Instead, you're even more miserable than usual.'

'I'm scared.' Tyrant's voice was barely audible. 'Ant said he might come back and take me. You know, get inside my head and make me do things I don't like.'

Voicing his fear released a wave of discomfort of his own. He'd been numbed by the shock of the fight with Gilgamesh, and that had helped to keep his feelings in check. Now he found himself sobbing with despair.

Petra put an arm across his shoulder. 'It's not possible for Gilgamesh to do that, is it?'

'If he comes back as anyone, it has to be me,' Tyrant said. 'Ant thought he'd killed the man who had become closer to him than his natural father. I brought about the death of my real father. I know how evil he was, and that he had to be killed, but can't you see that because he's my father, then I've no choice but to be like him. It's in my blood. All this time I've been keeping it at bay, stopping myself from acting like the tyrant I'm named after, but now I'm scared that it will all burst through and I'll be a danger to everyone around me. Like father, like son. Isn't that what they say? I'm going to have to leave you and take myself to somewhere where I can do no harm.' Tyrant rose to his feet.

'Wait,' Petra grabbed Tyrant by the arm. 'Before you do anything stupid, let's see what Lone has to say about that.' Petra grabbed his other hand and pulled him down beside her. His body was pliant and soft, as if he was devoid of all hope.

78

Lone watched Tyrant and Petra shuffle into the room and sink down beside Ant. Cat made a brief noise of protest, then slunk away as if too many humans in one place had upset her.

The meeting was at Petra's insistence. She wanted her to reassure Tyrant about the prospect of Gilgamesh's return. It seemed that Tyrant was even more troubled about Gilgamesh than Ant had been about Malachi.

'How are you feeling?' Petra asked.

'Much better,' Lone replied.

'Well enough to have us all killed as you promised the King?' Tyrant asked.

'How did you find out about that?' Lone asked.

'That doesn't matter,' Ant said. 'We've known all along, yet we still came to save you. That must count for something, surely?'

'Believe me,' Lone said, 'it was never my intention to do his bidding. However, I felt I had no choice other than to find Gilgamesh and try to defeat him. I acknowledge that, without your timely assistance, he would have certainly have killed me. Ant will have explained to you what happened to Malachi and how I made a grave error in getting Patch to bring him back to life. All I can say in my defence was that I loved him and I knew that Ant would be terribly distressed if he died. I had no idea of the consequences.'

'Seems to me that you should have learned not to mess with demons by now,' Tyrant said. 'I can't believe you had the audacity to take up with the demon who swore vengeance after you trapped him and kept you marooned in the desert all that time.'

'But I did,' Lone said. 'Patch was the only means I had to make my mark on the world. I had to take that chance to improve the lives of women. There's another thing you should know about Patch, Tyrant. The price he exacted for letting me out of the desert was a binding commitment to you. I am obligated to protect you by a solemn oath. Even if I wanted to get rid of you, I couldn't. I'd be consigning myself to an eternity of torment.'

'Tell Tyrant what you told me about Gilgamesh,' Ant said.

'Very well,' Lone continued. 'I have been researching the ancient texts to find what I can about Gilgamesh. Patch, albeit reluctantly, has filled in some of the details that have been lost along the way. You need to hear the full story to understand it.

'There was a time when demons and gods dwelt in our world alongside people. They enjoyed our worship and, in return, would grant favours and benefits. In time, demons and gods fought for supremacy. The most powerful god created a powerful weapon to use in the battle. Part god, part human, this was the ultimate fighter. He was made invincible. This was Gilgamesh and he was the scourge of demons and banished them from the world. Then squabbling broke out amongst the gods as they contested the territories vacated by the flight of the demons. Gilgamesh proved so powerful that even gods couldn't withstand him. The god who made him claimed supremacy over the whole world.

'Gilgamesh, however, had other ideas. He was his own man and feared nothing and nobody. He took the best and most fertile land, with the greatest population as his own kingdom. He declared himself king of the world. He built himself a great palace and a huge city. That city is the one we know as the City by the River Oort which was named Uruk in the old language.

'There was one god who refused to flee before Gilgamesh's power. Her name was Ishtar, and she first tried to control Gilgamesh with her feminine wiles. She was, and still is, the god of fertility, love, and war. Much to her dismay, Gilgamesh resisted her charms and rejected her love for him. This made her very angry and even more determined to get rid of Gilgamesh.

'She decided to create a being that would be a match for Gilgamesh. Something that could defeat him. She enlisted the assistance of the most powerful gods and made Enkidu, a wild giant covered with hair who liked to live naked in the woods. She pitted the two of them against each other and they fought a terrible battle that went on for years without either of them being able to obtain a decisive advantage. In the end, Enkidu grew weary of conflict and offered Gilgamesh the hand of friendship, which he accepted.

279

'For many years, the two of them lived in harmony. Gilgamesh enjoyed his city and Enkidu his wilderness. The two of them were inseparable. When the gods sent another creation, a mighty bull, to destroy them, the two of them fought side by side to defeat it. The gods gave up and left the world to Gilgamesh, vowing to return only when they had an effective counter to his might. Some minor deities lingered on the fringes of the civilised world, but they kept well out of Gilgamesh's way. Ishtar, however, was so incensed that she arranged for Enkidu to be seduced and take a wife. Eventually, Ishtar managed to exploit his susceptibility to affection and inflict him with a wasting illness. She succeeded in killing Enkidu, but failed to destroy Gilgamesh.

'Gilgamesh was deeply troubled by the death of his friend and ally. Fearing death himself, he devoted his time and energy to exploring ways to prolong his own life. At the same time, he knew that one day another challenge would come, and he had to be able to resist it. Many generations later, it dawned on him that Enkidu's offspring might provide a threat to his existence, and he set about hunting down and killing anyone he thought might be related to him.

'Tyrant, that's why he killed your mother and brother, thinking they might be Enkidu's progeny,' Lone said.

'Are you saying that Gilgamesh wasn't my father?' Tyrant asked.

'Gilgamesh never had any children. He was incapable of becoming a father. Ishtar saw to that. But Enkidu was different altogether. He had many children. He was also a big hairy man who liked his own company and to wander about in the woods. I can't be certain that you're related to Enkidu, Tyrant, but I can assure you that you've not killed your father.'

'That sounds just like you,' Petra said. 'The nice, simple life is all you ever wanted. This Enkidu appears to have had the same notion. Why he even became friends with his assailant rather than fight on. That's exactly what you've always done. Avoid bloodshed whenever possible. Only fight when you have to. Leave everyone alone. You've no interest in conquest or possessions. I'd say for sure that you're more like Enkidu than that greedy killer, Gilgamesh.'

Lone watched the stress lift from Tyrant's face. The frown lines dissolved as if he had become a man of half his real age. His smile twinkled for the first time in a long time.

Out of the question.

Lone faced Patch's shimmering attempt at a goddess and felt her frustration rising. 'One more tiny bit of support, that's all I'm asking. Come with me back to Gort. Protect the temple while I try to deal with the King.'

You don't know what you're asking. Listen, I'm feeling reasonable for a change and am prepared to let bygones be bygones. I'm not going to cast you into a realm of fire and suffering, if that's what's bothering you. Think of this as my parting gift.

'I've kept my side of the bargain so there can't be any question of punishment.'

Oh, but there is. My intention all along was to make you suffer long and horribly, whatever the outcome. I still haven't forgotten the cramped feeling of being in your power. That's not something I can forgive. Trawling around and snaring me wasn't an act of kindness, or don't you realise that?

'I thought we'd agreed to put all that behind us and start afresh.'

You may have, but I certainly didn't. Let's leave it at that, shall we? Be happy that punitive measures have been put on hold.

'I don't understand. The temple in Gort is a wonderful success. You should be enjoying it with me instead of slinking off into the darkness.'

Then allow me to explain. Remember the monastery? All those undesirables clinging to the roof feeding off that devotional energy? Those nasty demons that caused so much death and destruction?

'How could I forget? But you cleared them out, didn't you? You can do that again.'

Think of the monastery as a light in a firmament of dark. A light that attracts all manner of beings. Usually bad ones because anything good has better things to do than hang around in places like that. Your temple is the same, but bigger. Much bigger. If the monastery is a candle in the forest, then the temple is a huge bonfire on the top of a mountain. Something that can't be missed. Something that will attract the most unwelcome attention. Something that I can no longer risk being associated with. I'm out of here, Lone. And if you have any sense, you'll make sure that we never cross paths again.

'Don't go.' Ant's plea was heartfelt. The prospect of Lone returning to Gort, where she would face the wrath of the King, was a disturbing one. He was convinced that if she went, she wouldn't return.

'I have to,' Lone said.

'We're safe here,' Ant said. 'The King is unwilling to use a vedhana and is unlikely to risk the arduous desert crossing. If he sends soldiers, we have more than enough of our own to resist any attack.'

'I have to get back to the temple and the women who rely on me to protect them,' Lone said.

'Then take me with you,' Ant replied.

'No, you stay here with Ayesha and help her with the vineyard.'

'She doesn't need my assistance. Anyway, she's got Tyrant if there's any trouble.'

'It's Tyrant you need to help with, Ant. His professed dislike for wine is fast changing into an enthusiastic appreciation. I rarely see him without a bottle in his hand these days.'

'He tells me he's doing a study. Trying to determine the best conditions for making the stuff by testing samples from every part of the vineyard and each year of production.'

Lone laughed. 'He could do that with one tiny sip of each. Instead, he drinks several bottles before making up his mind. Then he forgets what he's been drinking and has to repeat the exercise. At this rate, by the time he decides what's best, there will be nothing left of it to sell.'

'I'm afraid you'll have to enlist Petra if you want to limit the big man's consumption. She's the only one with any influence. I'll come to Gort and help you.'

'No, Ant, I don't need you. If things are as I hope, the King will have allowed the worship to continue at the temple. If not, I'll have to find a way to force him to make the changes I want. I know you mean well, but you're not Malachi. Your powers are limited, to say the least. I'd find myself worrying about your safety without you being of any assistance.'

'I think you're underestimating my capabilities,' Ant said. 'Remember how I boarded the ship and outwitted Gilgamesh? I made the vedhana that Tyrant used to join me. We defeated Gilgamesh together.'

Lone gently touched his shoulder with her hand. 'I don't doubt your bravery; I've seen it at first hand when you confronted the crew in order to protect me. But, as then, I'm able to look after myself.'

'But not defeat the King,' Ant said.

'Nobody can do that,' Lone said. 'I have to try to persuade him, though.'

'It would be foolish to rely on a demon for defence if you fail to sweet talk the King.'

'Patch has helped all he can. His final act was to manifest as Tyrant and force Gilgamesh back onto the real Tyrant's sword. I call that real assistance. It was the decisive act in the fight,' Lone said.

Ant couldn't let that go, despite his misgivings. Lone was dismissing him, and that hurt. But more importantly, she was rejecting assistance that she might sorely need. He couldn't allow her to choose to go alone without knowing what she was rejecting. 'I have a plan that might get rid of the King. One that only I can carry out.'

'He's a god, according to Patch. Neither of us is able to compete with that,' Lone replied.

'Why do you think he won't use a vedhana?' Ant asked.

'I don't know. Maybe he has no need to.'

'Cuthbert was the nearest person alive when Gilgamesh killed the old King. What if the King passed over into Cuthbert so he could carry on where he left off? I can't detect much difference between the old and the new, can you?'

'No, I can't. Cuthbert appears to remember things that only the old King had knowledge of.' Lone's face was furrowed and her breathing had become faster.

'So, we have a god who takes over a human body? That would make sense, wouldn't it? If we managed to kill the Cuthbert body, he'd take a new one,' Ant said.

'That makes him invincible. Even more dangerous than Gilgamesh. I don't see how your theory helps. If it's true, there's no possibility of ever changing the King. We're stuck with him forever.'

Ant felt excitement welling up inside him. 'Not if I'm right about the vedhanas. Tell me, could Cat use a vedhana?'

'Out of the question. Cat's different. I couldn't bring her on the voyage because I knew we'd have to return through a portal. That and the prospect of her killing the crew on the first day of sailing. She has her own way of flitting about.'

'Maybe the King has a similar problem. If we could get him into a vedhana we could find out. I have a feeling that might do the trick and get rid of him altogether.' Ant's excitement was growing. He could do this. He had the technique and a plan. He also had Little Ant.

81

It was a long shot, but Ant's plan was all she had. After what the King said to her at their last meeting, she knew that he had no tolerance for the temple. Added to his insistence that she find a way to kill Ant, Malachi, and Tyrant, the prospect of an amicable arrangement was well-nigh impossible.

Ant had to tag along. Even if she'd rejected his plan, she needed him to pilot her into the vedhana at Malachi's home. Arriving in the King's tower wouldn't have been wise. She'd be effectively giving herself up without a fight.

As they stepped out of the whirling lights into Malachi's abode, Ant seemed in surprisingly good spirits, considering that he'd had to leave Ayesha behind and was heading into deadly danger.

Ant's plan was simple. It consisted of somehow making the King enter the vedhana. Grabbing him, pushing him, any means possible, Ant had said. He'd look after that side of it. Her job was to entice him within range.

The more she thought about it, the less she liked it. Getting the King up all those stairs into the tower was going to be extremely difficult. The physical effort alone almost certainly ruled it out. Even if he agreed to be carried, there were the practical considerations of negotiating the narrow winding staircase with such a wide monarch.

The story they'd decided on involved a rare and powerful artefact that had been recovered from Gilgamesh. Ant was sure that this would have the King hooked, but Lone had her doubts. Malachi had always warned her about the extent of the King's knowledge and perception. *His appearance is designed to be deceptive. If you assume he's ignorant and stupid, you do so at your peril.* What if the King sniffed out the conspiracy? He was, without doubt, very cunning and might even have abilities that gave him access to the very information she was seeking to conceal. If that were so, she was doomed to failure.

'This artefact,' she said. 'What manner of item is it? I need to be able to describe it convincingly or the King will know I'm spinning him a tale.'

Ant patted the bag he carried. 'It's in this bag. The one Malachi insisted on keeping by him throughout our travels. It's a weapon. I used it on Gilgamesh when he confronted us on Kish.'

'Then perhaps it would be better if I took it to the King and showed it to him. Then he might make the arduous trip up the staircase if he were promised more of the same.'

Ant frowned. 'I would rather keep it in my possession. If necessary, I plan to use it on the King.'

'We agreed that killing him wouldn't work, even if that were possible.'

'I'd seek to incapacitate him, then carry him into the vedhana. From there, take him away and hope that the King part of him fails to make the journey,' Ant said.

Lone's guts heaved. Ant was wrong. None of this made any sense at all. The plan was so full of holes that even a blind king would see right through it. Although it was all she had, it wasn't nearly enough. Unfortunately, she couldn't for the life of her think up an alternative that would offer a better chance of success.

'Wait here until dusk, then transport yourself to the tower. I will try to have the King there to greet you.'

She emerged from the gloomy house into the hazy morning light. Before her were the gates to the city, beyond them the tower above the palace where she needed to be. First, though, she needed to check in with Miriam at the temple.

The marketplace was busy. Unwashed bodies pressed on every side; stallholders grabbed at her arms as she struggled through the throng. It was a relief to reach the entrance of the temple where it was still busy, but in a more subdued way. The stallholders that had set up close to the temple were all women selling various items of devotional significance. Tiny statues, white linen headdresses, counting beads, pictures of wispy women hovering majestically over a sea of kneeling supplicants.

This, she concluded, was a positive sign. The King couldn't have made good his promise to prevent further worship taking place. On the contrary, the building retained an air of calm sanctuary as she joined the trickle of supplicants passing beneath its portal.

Inside, the magnificence of the main altar had been embellished by a new central statue of huge proportions. It stretched high into the vaulted roof space and dominated the whole area. It was impossible for her to imagine how such a massive likeness had been constructed and installed by human hands. It was too big. Too magnificent. Too impressive. This had to be the work of potent magic. There was no other explanation for it. Had Patch achieved this before he abandoned both her and this project? She doubted it. The likeness was nothing she'd seen before. It wasn't the Persephone that Patch had created, but a more fearsome figure that glared down at her as if she'd done something wrong.

The feeling of unease intensified as she searched through the ranks of white-clad women in search of Miriam. Some of the priestesses looked familiar, but none of them so much as acknowledged her. There was nothing left of the joyful energy she'd come to expect and enjoy. Something had changed. This was no longer her scheme; it had developed far beyond the project she and Patch had initiated.

It was a relief to emerge into the bustle of the outside. Even the stink of the sweaty masses came as a welcome contrast to the cold purity inside. As she made her way to the palace, it was hard for her to decide if the prospect of having to face the King was more upsetting than her experience in the temple.

82

Lone was ushered into the King's empty chambers and was struck by the changes that had been made since she left for the South. The harsh tapestries depicting ancient battles had been replaced by soft fabrics in gentle colours. The couch that usually accommodated a semi-reclining monarch was gone, and in its place two sturdy upright chairs that stood side by side. The flowers festooning every corner lent a gentle fragrance to the air once replete with the stink of burnt chicken fat and discarded food.

The change was less alarming than the situation in the temple, but still disturbing enough for the hairs on her neck to stand on end. Gort was nothing like she had left it. Ant's plan seemed even more outlandish under the circumstances. She resolved to tread extremely carefully with the King, dance around the issue of the temple, and instead try to convince him that Gilgamesh's defeat was sufficient for him to keep things the way they are.

The King entered, flanked by the Royal Guard holding swords aloft in salute as he passed beneath them. He looked considerably diminished, both in size and spirit. While he wasn't as scrawny as Cuthbert had been prior to assuming the throne, he no longer had the fatty torpor she associated with the monarch. His dress was simpler, his hair short and neat. When he sat down, he waved for Lone to do the same.

'Your majesty,' Lone began.

'Wait,' Cuthbert ordered. 'We are not all assembled yet and I don't want to put you to the trouble of repeating what you have to tell us.'

Lone bit back the questions she longed to pose. The energy she was experiencing around Cuthbert was totally different from the feeling she had when previously in the company of the King. Something fundamental had changed. She wondered if Ant had ignored her order to wait and proceeded with the plan without her. Was this really the King or had Ant managed to strip Cuthbert away as he'd promised and banish the King to oblivion?

Cassie came in. She was dressed in white, her hair covered by a shawl, and accompanied by Miriam, who possessed even more of the brilliance that Patch had created. Lone caught her breath. Suddenly, she felt weak and useless. Her resolve had evaporated and with it, any question of trying to manipulate events.

'Hi, Lone,' Cassie said, sitting beside the King and briefly touching his right hand with her left.

'Your majesty.' Lone rose to her feet, bowed as gracefully as she could, then sat down again, grateful to take the weight off her wobbly legs.

'Do tell us all about what happened in the South,' Cassie said. 'We're dying to hear about your adventures, aren't we, dear?'

Cuthbert nodded in a dutiful manner that disturbed Lone even more.

'Gilgamesh was defeated and killed, your majesty,' Lone replied.

'Ooh, that sounds a bit nasty. I do hope that Tyrant and Ant are unscathed. Horrible thing fighting, but I suppose it has to be done from time to time.'

'They are both well, your majesty. Tyrant was injured but has recovered wonderfully.'

'He's a good healer,' Cassie said. 'I know that from experience. Why didn't you bring him with you? It would have been lovely to see him.'

'You'll have the pleasure of his company soon enough, I imagine.' Lone wrestled with the absurdity of the situation. Cuthbert sitting quietly and seemingly content to do so while his Queen enquired gently about people he'd ordered her to kill. Was this some form of test? Was the King playing with her before suddenly reverting to his true nature? 'Unfortunately, Malachi was killed in the battle,' she said.

Cassie wrinkled her nose. 'Poor you,' she said, without a hint of irony. 'Anyway, very well done about that nasty Gilgamesh. Bee will be ever so pleased that he's dead.'

'Everything seems different,' Lone said.

'And it is,' Cassie said. 'Different and better. Miriam has got my Cuthbert back from the horrible clutches of the old King. Tell her what you did, Miriam.'

Miriam looked at Lone with an intensity that made her wince. 'The old King was a parasite that had taken over poor Cuthbert's body. After the Queen was introduced to the temple and became one of us, I interceded with the goddess to right that wrong and she graciously granted my prayer. She swept all traces of his evil stench from this realm and forbade his return. Now we have a Queen and King who know the value of worship.'

'Have women also been granted more equal status?' Lone asked, her heart racing.

'That isn't something anyone can grant,' Cassie said. 'Women already have that right. All I'm doing, with Miriam's assistance, is making sure that everyone understands. Men are such stick-in-the-muds, aren't they? Sometimes they have to be reminded, but I leave that to the goddess and her infinite mercy.'

'And she can actually do this?' Lone asked.

'Now that she is back amongst us, we are all blessed,' Miriam said.

'Persephone?' Lone asked.

'Persephone was only a tiny aspect of the supreme being. She heralded the way for the great one to descend upon us once again and fill our lives with meaning and purpose,' Miriam said. 'We are all grateful servants of the most holy and gracious Ishtar the magnificent, personification of the divine feminine and goddess of fertility, love, and war.'

Ishtar. Patch had warned her that the temple was liable to attract unwelcome attention. Now that Gilgamesh was gone, she had returned. What was it that Patch had said? *Take my advice; have nothing at all to do with her. Gilgamesh, even with all his drawbacks, is a far better prospect for your kind.* Lone's heart threatened to burst from her chest. She'd achieved everything she'd ever dreamed of, but at what price?

83

The breeze from the lake felt cool and pleasant on Ant's face, which had grown accustomed to the harsh heat of the desert. It amused him to acknowledge that living in the South had made his skin darker as his heart had become lighter. He'd changed so much he wondered if his own father would recognise him.

Ambrose was sitting in his garden, staring at a heap of soil at his feet. He looked old and tired. Thin and unhealthy. His skin was mottled by dark dots beneath his eyes and on the backs of his hands. His house smelt of rotting vegetation.

'Hello, Father.' Ant spoke softly.

Ambrose's head jerked slightly; his eyes widened but remained focussed on the ground. There was a long silence during which Ant feared that the power of speech had deserted his father. That he'd left this conversation many years too late. That his father no longer possessed his faculty of reason. Regrets began to tear at his composure. It had taken too long for him to bury his burning resentment and become whole enough to face his father again. He should have been quicker. He should have been better. He should...

But that was the old Ant. The *might have been* man. The disappointment. The thoughts may resurface and curdle his mood, but he now recognised them as an old pattern that had no further relevance. The only thing that mattered was the here and now. In this tiny fragment of time, there was no room for past or future, for yearnings or regrets. He took his place at his father's side and felt the wind through his hair, listened to the rustling of the trees, smelt the almost imperceptibly subtle fragrance of the grass, and settled his energy into the ground beneath.

'You're back.' Ambrose's voice was a rusty croak, as if it hadn't been used for a very long time.

'I found Mona,' Ant said.

Ambrose's head jerked in response, then he turned slowly to look at his son. 'You look as if you've caught the sun,' he said.

Ant lit up inside with relief. 'I'm living in the desert now,' he said. 'I've come to tell you that you've become a grandfather. I'd have brought mother and daughter with me, but it's too early for them to travel.'

'And you found Mona, you say?'

'Working at the palace,' Ant said.

'I should explain,' Ambrose said.

'There's no need,' Ant replied. 'You were doing your best for me. That's what I need you to understand.'

'She's not who you think,' Ambrose said. 'She was trouble right from the start. I shouldn't have kept her as long as I did, but you loved her so terribly. I waited as long as I could.'

'I know she's not my mother,' Ant said. 'She was what I needed though, and I thank you for providing me with her. Sending her away was hard for me to forgive, but I've finally come to terms with the reality of the situation. She's been a great help, Father. I suspect that she hardly gave me a second thought after you sent her to work at the palace. All the resentment I've been harbouring about her has gone. Now all I want is to be the best father I can to my children, exactly as you have been to me.'

Ambrose's face remained stony still, apart from a tear that emerged from the corner of his right eye.

THE END

Printed in Great Britain
by Amazon